terminal café

books by ian mcdonald:

The Broken Land
Out on Blue Six
Scissors Cut Paper Wrap Stone

terminal café

ian mcdonald

01726 5585

BANTAM BOOKS
New York Toronto London Sydney Auckland

TERMINAL CAFÉ
A Bantam Spectra Book / November 1994

SPECTRA and the portrayal of a boxed "s" are trademarks of Bantam Books, a
division of Bantam Doubleday Dell Publishing Group, Inc.

Book design by Maria Carella

Library of Congress Cataloging-in-Publication Data

McDonald, Ian, 1960–
Terminal café / Ian McDonald.
p.   cm.
ISBN 0-553-37416-8
1. City and town life—California—Los Angeles—Fiction.   2. Los
Angeles (Calif.)—Fiction.   3. Immortalism—Fiction.   I. Title.
PR6063.C38T47   1994
823'.914—dc20   94-21958
                              CIP

Published simultaneously in the United States and Canada

Bantam Books are published by Bantam Books, a division of Bantam Doubleday Dell Publishing Group,
Inc. Its trademark, consisting of the words "Bantam Books" and the portrayal of a rooster, is Registered
in U.S. Patent and Trademark Office and in other countries. Marca Registrada. Bantam Books, 1540
Broadway, New York, New York 10036.

PRINTED IN THE UNITED STATES OF AMERICA
BVG   0 9 8 7 6 5 4 3 2 1

Watson's Postulate   Never mind turning trash into oil or aster-oids into heaps of Volkswagens, or hanging exact copies of VanGoghs in your living room, the first thing we get with nanotechnology is immortality.

Tesler's Corollary   The first thing we get with nanotechnology is the resurrection of the dead.

terminal café

morning and afternoon

november 1

In the morning there was a dead man melted into the street wall of Santiago's house.

Wakened by the first spasms of the skysign fifty kilometers above the city, the bodyglove spat Santiago out into crash, loathing and the dawn's early light. Virtuality dreams disconnected neuron by neuron. Tendrils of intimate tectoplastic uncoiled from his cochlea, his hemispheres, his eustachian tubes, slipped free from his optic nerves. The film circuitry of the bodyglove peeled back from his skull, his spine, his genitals, flowed across his skin like amniotic fluid, down his arms, to reform in a trembling sphere of semi-intelligent nanopolymer in his cupped hands. *Introibo ad altare*. The chemical fire that had burned through his bloodstream all night settled in flakes of narcotic ash in the bottom of his veins.

The skysign was a tortured writhe of crimson fire, an artificial aurora of microscopic light-emitting tectors hung across the tropopause and kindled by the touch of a sun still below the eastern mountains. Its light fell through the studio's transparent roof onto the bodies of his companions lying spread-eagled on the floor. Lurid little crucifixions. Toy Golgothas. Saints and martyrs.

Santiago collected saints and martyrs.

He replaced the dormant bodyglove in the carved wooden cinerary casket he had bought down in the teeming necrovilles of Viejo Mexico.

Glimpsed in the decorated mirrors that lined the walls, he was no longer an angel wreathed in silver filigree nanocircuitry, Lord of the Web. He was only Santiago Columbar, twenty-seven. Two meters and some. Big. Massive. Black hair scraped back into an economical queue, emphasizing the geomorphological solidity of his features. Neurochemical artist. *Virtualisto*. It had been enough once. No more. It did not do it anymore. He was Santiago Columbar: low. Cold. Naked. Disgusted. Alone. *Mortal*.

The balcony was one of the many architectural eccentricities Santiago had inherited from his *residencia*'s previous owner. Uniquely, it had survived the transformations of his suites by reconstructive tectors. West-facing, its creator had intended it for twilit parties with intimate friends viewing the sunset among the luxuriant hills of Copananga. Santiago used it to watch the coming of the army of the dead.

Batisto, his dead servant, brought Santiago *agua minerale*, lightly pétillant. He drank nothing stronger. Caffeine, alcohol, threw erratic variables into the precisely calculated curves of his drugs.

The veils of the dawn skysign throbbed overhead. Geneered monkeys gibbered and rattled the branches of Copananga's many trees. Curfew ended, the *seguridados* and their *mechadors*—defenders of the night—had withdrawn. The gates to the necrovilles were unsealed, the borders opened. Living and resurrected might cross into each other's demesnes. Between dawn and dusk skysigns the dead could move among the living—the meat—but never as equals. Life was life and death was death, nanotechnological resurrection notwithstanding. Thus spake the Barantes Ruling. Forty years since the dead walked and no one had succeeded in toppling that pillar of the new world order. History enshrined the precedent and discarded Barantes. When where who what had it been about, that epochal case? YoYo would know, clever little lawyer girl. He must remember to ask her. Tonight, at the Terminal Café. Money probably. An inheritance, like as not. Where there's a will, there's a wrangle. The pun worked only in English.

Heard before seen; the army of the dead channeled up Copananga Canyon, along its steep, twisting avenues and closes: houseboys, gardeners, cooks, maids, valets, chauffeurs, swimming pool attendants, butlers, sports coaches, personal trainers, tutors, governesses, baby-sitters, nannies, private secretaries, amanuenses, sculptors, painters, craftspersons, builders, masons, joiners, architects, designers, masseurs, spiritual guides, lovers, sex toys. The world of the living is upheld by the hands of the dead, the woman who called herself Miclantecutli—his spirit guide, lover, tormentor and muse—had once said. But Miclantecutli was five years gone, down with the dead in the Saint John necroville. Not for her the Death House contract, that second pillar of the world. Institutionalized indenture. The Miclantecutlis of the Tres Valles Metropolitan Area afforded *Immortalidad* policies to pay their ferryman's fee. Lump sum, with interest. By side gates and service entrances the morning migration was absorbed into Copananga's haciendas and *residencias* and split-level retro Frank Lloyd Wrights. Another working day in heaven. How many thousand journeys before the price of resurrection was paid back to the Death House and its monolithic one-eyed Baal, the Tesler-Thanos *corporada*?

Santiago swigged back his *gaseoso*. An eyebrow of light lifted above the hills of Old Hollywood.

"More water, séor?"

Three years of service had not accustomed Santiago to Batisto's unnerving talent for preempting his wishes. He accepted the second bottle of Tres Marias.

"Why not? After all, it is the Day of the Dead. ¡*Salud!* Batisto."

"¡*Salud!* séor."

The scream rent the deep, clean silence that filled Copananga's leaf-shady avenues. Desperate, terrible, and long long long, the scream of a woman, who has finally come face-to-face with everything she has ever dreaded.

One more scream on Estramadura Avenue would not have troubled Santiago, but that it came from outside his gate.

A few meters from his craftsperson-wrought iron gates, what remained of a man was fused with the lower part of the white perimeter wall that let onto the service alley. Séora Sifuentes, the neighbor Santiago notionally tolerated, stood staring, unable to tear her attention from the one thing she could least bear to see. Her Tuesday Thursday Saturday fitness regime had sent her jogging past the execution site.

Santiago squatted to study more closely the obscene thing.

Dead man dead. Death by tesler was unmistakable.

"MIST 27s," Santiago surmised aloud. Multiple Impact Self-targeting. A needle of intelligent tectoplastic accelerating from tesler muzzle at a constant twelve gees, seeking its target by biofield resonance. Thirty centimeters from impact, it reconfigured into a hail of submunitions, each the size of a coriander seed, each capable of fatally disrupting the tector systems of the resurrected dead. Sure kill. Big Death, that not even the Death House could reverse. The resurrected's only fear.

The tesler round had taken the dead dead man square in the body. *Tan Tien*, the center of being. And not-being. The lower half of his body was a fetid stew of blacktop and synthetic flesh. His hands reached out of the blistered wall in futile pleading. His upper torso leaned forward like some piece of extreme high-relief sculpture. The impression that the man had been walking through the wall when his unclean dead voodoo suddenly failed him was eerily insistent. His head inclined sadly to the left. The declination of Christ on the cross. Christ would have worn the same expression. Horror. Pain. Anger. Sorrow. Betrayal. *Eloi eloi lamach sabachthani*, cold-welded onto the backs of his eyes. An old, old belief, from the very dawn of the Information Age: that the retinas of a dead man's eyes shoot a snapshot of the last thing he ever sees.

Even in death, he was beautiful. The dead were a beautiful people. When flesh can be dismantled and reforged into any shape, beauty is easy, youth cheap. Ugliness too, and age, strange great monsters, elegantly disturbing deformities, the faces and forms of the famous moviedrome starlets.

Genetweak macaques in their coats of many colors had already been at work on the fingers, peeling tectoplasm from synthetic bones. One lay dead, a huddle of iridescent fur in the storm gutter. Others would follow, poisoned by the sweet, treacherous meat of the dead. Soon the birds would come for the eyes, the ears, the lips.

Santiago examined the dead dead man's hand. The palm was intact, entire.

"No deathsign?" Mrs. Sifuentes voiced their shared concerns.

The vee-slash in the palm of the hand—the descending stroke of entropy-bound meatlife, the ascending diagonal of resurrected, eternal life, the horizontal crossbar of mortality—was the ineradicable imprimatur of the Death House. Very rarely, spin-variables during reconfiguration might stamp it in the left hand rather than the right, but the Jesus tanks never missed. As impossible to be reborn unsigned as to be without hands, heart, head.

Mystery, here at the foot of the wall.

"Shouldn't someone, I don't know, like, take it away or put something over it?" Mrs. Sifuentes asked, revulsion finally overcoming curiosity. "I mean, before the staff see it or something."

"I'll call Copananga Securities," Santiago said. "In the meantime, I'm sure you've had a nasty shock, Séora Sifuentes; if you like, I can have my man make you a pot of tea or something."

Séora Sifuentes declined politely. Santiago had always been aware that he was something of a dragon in Copananga's sprinklered Eden. He watched the woman hurry up the road, Lycra-bound ass swinging, to the succor of her houseware trauma counseling service.

A shout from within the walls.

"With you in a minute, Batisto," Santiago called back. Crouching on sun-warmed Estramadura like one awaiting the image of Christ stamped on a wafer, Santiago took the dead dead man's head between his hands. He leaned forward and kissed the dead dead man on the mouth. The dead dead man's lips were soft and tasted of strange musks.

Batisto led Santiago through parts of his grounds long untended, lushly overgrown. When even your own home becomes an alien planet to you, it is time to re-examine your life-path.

In the shelter of a small stand of jacarandas heavily burdened with tropical epiphytes stood a dead *mechador*. The killing machine stood askew in a shallow furrow of soil. Its impellors must have failed suddenly, catastrophically. The beaked head studded with sensory systems was locked in a final snap of defiance. The tesler arm was still aimed at the coordinates of its last target. Santiago examined the weapon. Four rounds chambered, two fired. Over the manufacturer's ident and serial number, the Copananga Securities trifurcate yin-yang.

The robot's self-repair systems had been overwhelmed before it could transmit a distress call. The left side was gone, the left arm subsumed into the black cancerous slag that coated the wound. There were eyes in the black slag. Eyes, and mouths. Between the eyes and red-lipped mouths, centimeter-long fingers complete with black nails and prints, followed, pointing, the movements of his eyes. The center of the cratered mess had crazed into untidy hexagons. Oily black insects crept from the fissures and gathered in a hovering, droning cloud.

A dead dead man who never was, a destroying angel destroyed. Deep mystery here. More: signs and wonders. Spirit messengers, eldritch omens. The night before, after he had watched Mislav and Cheetah dissolve into the virtualizer, he had prayed as he pressed the hallucinogenic spider to his forehead: *give me a sign: whether it is meant to be or not to be.*

Are you answered, Santiago Columbar?

His parents, whom he had not seen in the ten years since they had adapted to join the Milapa Kelp Swimmers community, were lapsed New Revelation Buddhists; Santiago himself had no interest in orthodox religion except as a system of belief to be compared to similar systems, physics, mathematics, post-Mandelbrot economics.

Santiago believed in the junk esthetic. Drugs, to Santiago, were alternative programs for the meat computer. Coupled with virtual reality, they became tools for the exploration of the limits of the self. Understanding machines, subtle guillotines severing spirit from flesh and sending it out into darkness, into the void, and, beyond the void, primal light.

Until the day he woke up (he can finger the exact date, time, microclimate, world news, state of the Rim Dollar against a basket of competing currencies) and found that it did not do it anymore.

The doors of personal experience, through which he had attempted his years-long escape from himself, slammed one by one behind and before him. Had been slamming, almost unheard, far away down the immensely long corridor of being, all his life, until, that California winter morning almost a year ago, the final pair of doors closed and locked him within his Santiago-ness. Nowhere to go. Until one night the dark angel whispered into his numb dreams *there is a way, the better way, the braver way, there is a way that is higher, if you have the courage to take it. The highest game of all.*

For a year he had looked at it, contemplated it, planned and prepared it, and in the end he was still not brave enough to face it alone.

The polymorphous house unfolded its transparent carapace to admit Santiago. He had given years to its loving conversion into a shrine to those who had found it better to burn out than rust. The halls and landings of his shapeshifting hacienda were occupied by the monochrome likenesses of the brief and bright. James Dean. Buddy Holly. Jimi Hendrix. Mama Cass. Judy. A warped plastic cochlea, the Amadeus room—one of his earliest forays into the land of premature death— would automatically play selections of Mozartiana and sow the air with mood enhancers of Santiago's own design. His Vincent room immersed its visitors in shivering color and subharmonics tuned to the exact key of schizophrenia. Elsewhere, Isadora Duncan danced, scarf flapping behind her, while antique automobiles from the gasoline age shaved past, perilously close. Again, body-heat would trigger an antique Moviola and fill a discreet wall alcove with a hand-colored D. W. Griffiths crucifixion. Jim Morrison and John Belushi were the two thieves, Harry Chapin and Charlie the Bird Parker lifted a sponge soaked in vinegar to Christ's lips while a leering Keith Moon ran his spear between fifth and sixth ribs and let forth the water and the blood. Kneeling at the foot of the cross, Billie Holliday played Mother Mary with just the right touch of pain and pathos while Mary Magdalene, wearing a slightly louche smirk, was Jean Harlow. The old swimming pool had been floored with a mosaic of Andy Warhol's Marilyn Monroe icon. Santiago no longer swam there, though his guests loved to splash and submerge themselves in its blood-warm waters, but on nights when the heat in the house grew too great to bear he would lie prone atop his Marilyn, breathing through a skinsuit and listening to the unearthly throb of Robert "Crossroads" Johnson from the underwater speakers while monkeys leaped through the riotous trees, noisily decrying the sluggish, inexorable invasion of their territory by jewel-bright, feral tectosaurs.

In the hope that they had crept away, disgusted with themselves, while he was occupied in the grounds, Santiago peeped in on his night-guests. Candle smoke and spew.

Mislav's face was wracked in introverted agony. Neurological fire burned along the delicate silver feathering of his bodyglove circuitry. Cheetah lay curled fetally on the parquet floor, sensory skin peeled back from breasts, belly, loins. Her eyes were closed. Her lips moved silently. Her skin was spattered with vomit.

Niños, niños: learn: some day it will not do it for you anymore. Delphic wisdom from the heady heights of twenty-seven.

Santiago closed the door on their private heavens and hells. To his study, and business more important than teenage Hansel and Gretels who had dared each other into the candy-witch's lair.

Santiago's study was a place between, not quite house, not quite gardens, possessing the spirit of both. Mahogany shutters kept out the already stifling heat of the Copananga day: promise of storms to come in this monsoon humidity. Slats of light fell across the coir carpet, the antique wooden desk he had infected with information processing tectors. Wood and illusion. He summoned icons to the surface of the desk. 'Wares and familiars went howling out into the web and called Miclantecutli to the surface of his desk. *Visual hold*, blinked the icons. *Speech only*.

"Santiago." The voice seemed to speak from the air. Clever, expensive audio. The last time Santiago had seen the face behind the words the translucent lid of a Jesus tank had been closing over it. ODs left clean corpses.

"Miclantecutli."

"If you're going to play the game, call me Miclan. All God's chillun gotta have street names. Pack rules. I presume because we're having this conversation that you are insistent on following through this little Night of the Dead Trick or Treat?"

"A dead dead man and an assassin assassinated say I should, Miclan."

"You always were a too-smart *cabrón*, Santiago. I never could teach you a thing."

"You taught me everything I know."

"That's why you're selling it back to me in centavo bags. I'll be there with the pack at the allotted place, the appointed hour, never fear, Santiagito."

She returned to the depths of the desk.

Santiago could not remember the last time he had used the text manipulation program. His party invitations had always been by word of mouth, or courier-delivered gift boxes containing a single spider with custom hallucinogens pressed up tight against its belly. This conclave demanded the dignity of the written word. He toyed with Gothik deathsheads grim reapers crossbones hour glasses *danses macabres*. Hackneyed and worse. This was no *carnivalisto* dance-and-drugs party. He had spent a year preparing this trip to the bitter roots of the soul, a journey into the heart of darkness and beyond. Simplicity. Times New Roman.

Santiago Columbar invites . . . (the 'ware would mailshot the names) *to the Terminal Café District of Saint John to the annual celebration of the Festival of Our Lady of All the Dead.*

Paragraph. Center.

Nightfall. November 1.

Santiago addressed the cards to the faces he had summoned onto his desktop. His 'ware consigned them to the web.

Santiago smiled. His smiles were rarer than summer rains, and like them, signified deep, distant climatic change.

The heat. He found a bottle of *agua minerale* in the kitchen cooler. Santiago slopped the water over his forehead, the nape of his neck, his wrists. Pale, drawn, deader than any true dead Santiago had ever seen, Cheetah wandered into the kitchen.

"Food?" she whispered plaintively. Santiago indicated the open cooler door. Seized by a sudden spasm, Cheetah lunged for the drainer to be sick. Gobbets of melted bodyglove trailed across the terracotta floortiles, like morning slime behind an oleaginous tropical slug.

Santiago's tagalong chimed. *Fiel* Batisto, in the gardens.

"Séor, the *seguridados* are worried about the destroyed *mechador*. They suspect possible misreplication infestations." Boy-knights riding out against the legion of the undead in tectoplastic bodyarmor and head-zup helmets.

"So, what do they want to do about it?"

"Their expression is 'cauterize the infection,' séor."

"Well, they must do what they have to do."

Santiago awaited the sudden shocking hammer of sustained tesler fire.

Cauterizing the infection.

The bushland burned in the southern heat. The firezone was a horizon-hugging line of black smoke. Aerial reconnaissance reported the group of pachycephalosaurs eight kilometers southeast, relaxed, yet alert. Trinidad imagined blue-skullcapped heads raised, nostrils twitching, flaring. Smoke. Burning. *Brushfire.* Two silly thoughts: first, that the pachycephalosaurs were so ancient, they predated fire. Any fire she had ever known had been of human origin, so it seemed a product of human technology. Nothing was that pre-Promethean, that primeval. Second silly thought: that the pachys were not primeval at all.

Embossed on each gorgeous hide, just below the breastbone, were the words © *The Walt Disney Corporada.*

The *Second* Thing we get with nanotech, Disney's P.R. department had crowed on the heels of Watson's Postulate on the nature of the First Thing, is *dinosaurs.*

SEE the mighty diplodocus and brachiosaurus!

GASP as real pterosaurs swoop overhead!

WONDER at the incredible stegosaurus, the amazing anatosaurus, the astonishing ankylosaurus!

QUAKE WITH TERROR at the sound of the footstep of the Terrible Tyrannosaurus, the most fearsome predator ever to walk the earth! (All major currency cards accepted.)

The reality had been somewhat different.

WATCH from the comfort of your own living room a triceratops tear up your garden.

FLEE IN FEAR as an iguanadon smashes through your house at two o'clock in the morning.

CRASH AND BURN as twelve tons of anatosaurus come lumbering onto the Sherman Oaks feeder at peak time and piles them up twenty back along each lane.

The Peruvian Special Economic Zone Court that heard the compensation case maintained the Walt Disney *corporada*'s legal responsibility to provide a safe and secure product by ensuring against the very kind of tector misreplication and program mutation that had enabled their creations to exist independently of their controlled environments and reduplicate themselves. The accumulated costs and settlements to claimants, who numbered into the thousands, fatally harpooned Disney Co. Tinker Bell folded her wings and died. Nobody believed in fairies anymore. New wings beat in the air above the hulk of Disneyland and roosted on the GRP ledges and arrettes of the mock Matterhorn.

The big saurians, finding the climate of the coast and the armed hostility of its people not to their taste, migrated east along the line of Interstate 10 and thus south by southeast into the high chaparral of southern Arizona and northern Chihuahua. Those that remained were mostly small and brilliantly colored. Attracted to sunny spots in which to photosynthesize and with an idiosyncratic taste for trash polyethylene, they quickly established an ecological niche in coast culture. In time they came to be objects of public affection, bestowers of good luck and the favor of the saints, like storks in Europe.

Theme park attraction to public scourge to the Last Safari.

They had flown in from the hot, damp coast the previous day, Tomas and Benny and Pilar and Sevriano the hunt master, Edge and Albuquerque and Vaya and Bellisario and Trinidad, and their dead servants with them. The *estancia* was well used to hunting parties, its dead staff familiar with the excesses of the young and wealthy. Before dawn they had risen and driven out into the enclosing darkness that slowly yielded to reveal the true vastness of the empty land. Guided by *estancia* deads, the lifter craft had gone before them to set the burnline, the line of yellow fire that drew the hunters across the brightening plain to their quarry.

"Next thing you know, some conservation bastard will have slapped a protection order on them," said Bellisario, the man Trinidad pretended to love because he pretended to love her. "They allowed hunting only because the local landowners bitched about them tearing up the range and then realized they could make more money out of ranching dinosaurs than ranching beefheads." The smoke line writhed in the reflective curve of his glasses as he scanned the horizon.

Thirty-eight days and the affair was past its half-life. No especial record for brevity in that; she was surprised Bellisario had held her attention so long. The needle of it was that he was the one whose attentions were refocusing behind his scanshades. All the long long way to the woman propped attractively against the bushpuppy wheel. The one with the legs that went all the way up to *here*. And knew it. Cute eyes too; expensive. Pay what you like, but it's never going to put anything behind them.

Vaya Montez.

You want to fight me for him, Vaya Montez of the design shop thigh muscles? You would, you are of that type that fight for love because you think that is the only way to know it is real. I was That Type, once, and I am no wiser now, only more tired. So: Trinidad gives him to you, cute Vaya; José-Maria Bellisario is not worth mud in my hair, another coup scar on my arm. Have him, and I will light a candle for you in the shrine to Nuestra Madre Queen of Angels down under the mission oak that you might love him because I do not. I *something* him, but not love.

It was all she had been capable of since the lid of the Jesus tank closed over what remained of Peres: *something*. Desperate to lose herself in other people, she had rammed through the complex social and sexual geometries of her *cerristo* class only to find her relationships breaking like wasted bones because all she had to nourish them was *something*. She had fought, she had battled with all her strength and will, she had collected a score of pale V-shaped coup scars on the dark brown skin of her upper arms over men and women for whom she felt nothing to make *something* become love. *Something* is not worth any kind of scar.

The lifters thundered low overhead, bush-hopping, whipping dust from the skull-dry earth and ashes from the fire around which the dead servants sat, burning things.

"Want some?"

Vaya of the Beautiful Thighs squinted at the figure standing in her light, slow to recognize it as Trinidad.

"Mescal?" The flask was New Spanish silver, four hundred years old, beautifully patinated and sweet to the hand. You don't find craft like that anymore, was the standard saying. Except now the economics of a city of twenty-two million people, half of whom were dispossessed dead, had brought back the Age of the Craftsperson, renascent, reborn, like so many other buried things in this age of resurrection. "It's good. Spirit of the Jaguar God."

Vaya Montez uncapped the flask.

"How far are they?"

Trinidad pulled data from the circling aircraft onto her glasses.

"About six kays away from us, moving ahead of the fireline at about twenty kph. Sixteen of them."

"About fifteen, twenty minutes away." Beautiful Vaya shook out her hair and tilted back her head to swallow the hallucinogenic liquid. She wiped her mouth on the side of her hand, pouted at the red smear of lipgloss and rubbed her hand on the leg of her camouflage shorts. "Jesusjosémaria, I got to do something about this face."

Trinidad walked to the edge of the small encampment of bushpuppies and their dead crews and let the scanshades drop on the cord around her neck. The burnline drew a soft charcoal border across the high plain but the perspectives were still immense, rushing off around the curve of the planet in every direction. Low bluffs eroded by Paleozoic streams lay behind the camp, anchoring it in the sun-bleached landscape of scorched scrub waiting for the autumn monsoon; but for them the sense of isolation, of agoraphobia, would be overpowering. Like all her fellows, Trinidad had grown up under the canopies of tall trees in the moist heat of the coast, where there was no horizon, only trees and houses, falling water and the slow, cool figures of the dead. A landscape to be wrapped around you and pulled tight. You are not alone. This land stripped naked, flensed and tested souls against its immensity.

What would happen if you were abandoned here?

You would die. Without hope of resurrection. Clean picked bones, big grin, Big Death.

"Séora?" The dead woman seemed twenty-five: had she lived she would have been over ninety. A Generation Zero child, Trinidad did not fear the close proximity of the dead, as many of the pre-resurrection generation did.

"Sula?"

"A message. It came through the bushpuppy 'ware."

She had been expecting it. She had never been to one of the ghastly little Night of the Dead covens at the Terminal Café, intended never to go. The group was dead; those relationships could never be resurrected. She was not sure she wished them ever to be. Sula gave her the card.

Santiago Columbar invites Trinidad Malcopuelo . . .

The high plains wind tugged at her hair, flapped her open jacket, hummed over the strings of her scanshades.

Long before they met, Trinidad had heard of Santiago Columbar. Valley *noncontratisto* or hillside *cerristo*, you had not only heard of him, but some of his stuff had probably given you one of the greatest nights in your life. When Peres had told her The Santiago Columbar was a compadre in this queer circle of friends into which he was locked, the prospect of meeting with greeting with sleeping with the great *virtualisto* electrified her. It had been the Night of the Dead then, too, when they met. The dead had been swirling through the hot, dusty streets on their furious dark carnival.

They say you should never meet the author. Instantly, her mind had jumped from the moist pressure of his lips on the back of her hand to the imagined mass of his body pressing down on her, crushing the life out of her lungs, bending her ribs, snapping them, cracking her pelvis as he pumped blindly, her slim black legs straining to meet around his flanks and back. The legend was too solid, too mortal. Too fleshly. Santiago Columbar terrified her.

She had confessed her fear to YoYo as they sat by firelight, listening to the monsoon on the rooftiles and YoYo had whispered that Santiago was not hetero or homo or bisexual, but no kind of sexual at all.

"I don't know what gets him off," YoYo had said. "Except himself. Autosexual."

"Any reply, séora?"

Trinidad shook her head, suddenly, strangely, silenced by unexpected emotions.

YoYo and Camaguey and Toussaint and yes, Santiago: none of them understood. Trinidad did not go down to Necroville because she feared she would meet Peres. It was a paradoxical, two-edged fear. She feared him loving her still, beyond death, yet she simultaneously feared that love having died with him, that she was just a shadow on the far side of the translucent plastic carapace of the Jesus tank and that down in the projects and shanties and cabañas he had found other, stranger, loves.

The shockwave of lifters on one final pass shook her back into time, place and self. A line of dust, yellow against the smoke, was the pachycephalosaurs on the move. The hunting party was readying itself. The dead drivers stirred themselves. Bushpuppy engines fired up and settled into lean, mean idles. Kill markers and skinners hired from local towns made for the follow-trucks. Trash-poor *noncontratistos*, the new underclass disenfranchised by the labor economics of resurrection. Better off dead, they said, though none had ever put it to the test.

The hunters clipped magazines into gun housings and tested the swivel action. Safety harnesses snapped shut. Safety helmets were clicked on, interfacers jacked into targeting computers. Visors lit with test patterns.

"Yes, Trinidad!"

"Hey, Trinidad!"

"You going to get one, Trinidad?"

"Needle one for me, Trinidad!"

"Love you, Trinidad."

"We'll celebrate tonight, Trinidad!"

Tomas and Benny and Pilar and Sevriano and Edge and Albuquerque and Bellisario and Vaya were lined up, the drivers awaiting hunt master Sevriano's order to move out.

A twist of the wrist set her this-year's-model huntwear morphing from bolero colors to high plains dust and rust. Glitter of chains and metal. Clip: magazine. Snap: safety harness. Click: helmet on, systems *up*. The gun moved with silky precision on its magnetic mount. Sula eased into the driver's cockpit, set the engines growling and squabbling.

"Let's do it."

The bushpuppies moved out. Someone without one microgram of irony in his soul had kicked dirt over the fire. The huntline expanded to form an eight-kilometer killing front. Nine pairs of parallel tracks radiated out from the footprints and biodegradable maragarita-4-1 cartons. Trinidad held the southwestern extremity of the line. Vaya, her nearest neighbor, was half a kilometer to the north. Nine plumes of dust advanced on the burnline. Between the puppies and the fire, the pachycephalosaurs. Range, three kilometers, target stationary. Trinidad could imagine the big males lifting their blue-crowned battering-ram heads to sniff out the chemical signatures of an unimaginable enemy. Winks of light heliographed from Vaya's weapon as she checked firing arcs.

To the north, a sudden explosion of dust. Digits scrambled down Trinidad's visor as her helmet speakers screamed raw excitement. The herd was up, running at full speed parallel to the kill line, headed due south for the empty spaces of God's country. They were coming down her throat. Trinidad was flung hard against her harness and swung out over suddenly hurtling purple sage as Sula spun wheels kicked dirt accelerated onto an overrun course with the fleeing pachysaurs. She hung on to the twin grips of the big Mackinaw hunting piece like a promise of deliverance as the bushpuppy bounced and jolted. A blur of dust, a streak of movement, of color, shape, mass . . . She swung the Mackinaw, instinctively pumped off an entire magazine before *merda* realizing *merda* that they were only *merda* deinonychuses *merda merda merda merda*. Flat out, solar muscle-capacitors fully charged, they could hit eighty kph and run a bushpuppy past the last drop of gasohol in its tank. Bad hunting. Waste of needles. They were commensal with pachys, despite forty million years and several plate-tectonic shifts between the two historic species.

That's the magic of Disney.

Trinidad ejected the spent magazine and clipped in a fresh cartridge, gritting her teeth in concentration as she tried to balance terrain, velocity, jolt. Dust. Smoke. *Smoke.* Fifty meters from the edge of the burnline Sula skidded the bushpuppy, turned, throwing a wall of dust in the face of the fire and bringing Trinidad helmet to helmet with a raging bull pachycephalosaur. Two tons of semi-photosynthetic self-replicating tectoplastic flat out relative closing velocity one hundred and five kph estimated total contact time 3.33 recurring seconds. Five meters of Upper Cretaceous ornithopod loomed over Trinidad, the electric-blue head almost divinely incongruous. She screamed. She closed her eyes. She fired.

She opened her eyes. Her fingers were tight, tight on the twin triggers. The Mackinaw coughed vacantly, spastically. The bushpuppy slewed to a halt. Trinidad went with the gee forces. The neurotoxins hit the creature's brain. It stopped: dead. It snapped upright: dead. It spun around: dead. Trinidad could feel it fall as if she had shot the moon itself out of the sky. Paleontological voodoo; by destroying the effigy had she caused the sudden, inexplicable death of true flesh, hide and bone in Upper Cretaceous Montana? Extinction by sympathetic magic. Needles and pins.

A second bushpuppy pulled into orbit around hers, its rear gunner punching the air, elatedly shouting "Fuck Trini! Fuck Trini! Fuck Trini!" over and over. She thought it might be Tomas or Benny, the voice was male. They all looked the same with helmets and visors. They all looked the same without. They peeled away to join the greater orbit of the main hunt, south and east of the burnline. The pachy herd—two dominant males, two 'prentices, eight females, four juveniles—had been rounded into a panicked, bellowing corral. The big males lowered their bone-helmeted heads to challenge, to charge, to score coup in a crack of skulls against the circling bushpuppies and the whooping figures behind the big computer-targeted Mackinaws. The dust rose up in a spiral cloud. Lifters sprayed fire-retardant chemicals along the burnline, impatient in the sky, hungry for scavenge. Sula found her mistress a place in the killing ring.

The slaughter began.

Haiku:
A Japanese poem form
of exactly seventeen syllables.

The balcony rail of the ninety-ninth-level apartment is a fifteen-centimeter-wide ribbon of reconfigured carbon beneath Toussaint's feet. Eddy currents spiraling up the chaotic geometries of the San Gabriel spire buffet his body but Toussaint's balance is sure. Before him, a titanic canyon of air at the bottom of which, a kilometer and a half below, flows the blacktop river of Hoover Boulevard; behind him, in the spire-top penthouse, his father's voice speaks to empty air. A recording: it is six years since Toussaint and his father last exchanged words.

". . . estimated contact time for the Freedead fleet to Earth orbit is six hours minimum, fifteen hours maximum. Modal point is eight hours twenty-six minutes, at nineteen seventeen Western Pacific Basin time. *Corporada* orbital industrial installations will be evacuated by . . ."

Communication by sound bite.

". . . preemptive strikes targeted on the Dark Side Tsiolkovski reconfiguration zone will impact six hours after maximum contact probability. Planetary defenses are on full alert, combat readiness estimated in five hours nineteen minutes . . ."

Why tell me this, father, in that always-calm, always reasonable, always *right* voice that you could never understand was guaranteed to raise stubbornness in me? Once heir apparent, always heir apparent, no matter that he rejects his inheritance, still, he must be informed at executive level. Do you imagine that one black sheep returned to the fold, one prodigal repented, can turn back Freedead slamships, sweep away their diggings and delvings, their vacuum forests and sprawling cities naked to the stars, and turn the moon back into green cheese again?

A single black rubber sofa covered in soft spikes is the one object Toussaint regrets having to leave behind the morning he finally flew out of his father's life. He would never come back but for the neatly printed invitation cards that once a year squeeze out of the houseware's hard-copier slit onto the dusty desktop. Six slightly overlapping rectangles where the dust lies a few microns thinner.

Wind tugs Toussaint's light frame. Bodmods (he loathes the neologism but argot is what they mostly speak in Lodoga Eyrie) have given him height at the expense of weight. He possesses the same angelic luminosity you see in famine victims. Angel of Hunger. With Toussaint, you know it is the result of a ruthless paring-down to some esthetic ideal. His white skin—a rarity in the Tres Valles Metropolitan Area—only emphasizes the more radical work beneath it. No human body ever had a bone that looked like *that*, sticking out like *this*. Toussaint's does.

He thinks it's a fair exchange. His bleached white hair is pulled vertical and shorn straight across. His eyes are black: iridial polarizers. Like the eagle, he can look into the eye of the sun. Like the eagle, he surveys creation.

To the north the wooded hills shiver beneath heathaze and evapotranspiration. Even the wind turbines striding along the ridgetops are too exhausted in the damp heat to turn. The familiar orange-brown glaze of photochemicals brews up in the valleys, eddying green and yellow in sheltered microclimatological pockets. Huen claims that there are sacred, secret places where the smog is so old, so dense, so complex and laden with arcane chemicals, it has mutated into a reality-shaping hallucinogen.

Toussaint senses a promise of an end to the heat. Out there over the ocean a great spiral of storm cloud is wheeling in toward the coast, pregnant with the first rains of the winter monsoon. Rain on. Storms upon the earth, harbingers of war and rumors thereof high above the thin film of atmosphere.

Before my face, my destiny,
I set my back to my inheritance

A kilometer due south of the pinnacle atop which Toussaint perches rises the tecto-gothic filigree of the San Miguel spire. A similar distance west the San Rafael tower completes the *Sagrada Familia* of angels. All three towers are rooted fundamentally in the Tesler-Thanos *arcosanti* that has occupied the intersection of Hoover and Third so long that even the long-memoried dead have forgotten the city once possessed a different center. Like Gaudi's Freudian wet-dream, the trinity of pinnacles remains unfinished, and, by definition, unfinishable. Miner tectors constantly dredge the faultline for minerals, transporter tectors haul them molecule by molecule up past the accommodation levels, over the flow constrictors and roughing tetrahedrons and sundry gingerbreads to the summits, where mason tectors manipulate them, mold them, shape them. The younger Toussaint had liked to go naked onto his balcony and press his body against the spire wall to experience the slow osmotic creep of earth stuff over his skin. It is a superstition among both *arcosantistos* and the dead who live in its shadow behind the Necroville gate that the moment the spires cease growing they will start dying, and with them, the Tesler-Thanos *corporada*.

Amen, says Toussaint, *Selah*
The world's but a sandbox
For father's play.

Too many syllables, but in haiku, as everything else, he is a learner.
On the edge, Toussaint lifts his arms slowly at his sides.
And falls forward into the void.

In the absence of air resistance an object of Toussaint's mass (or any mass, didn't you see the hammer and the eagle feather fall on the moon?) will impact the outbound lane of Hoover at one hundred and ninety-three kilometers per hour twenty-two seconds after diving from the rail of the ninety-ninth-level penthouse.

The first second. Toussaint falls past the balconies of inferior apartments. On one of them a woman is sunbathing naked. Scenes from a semi-virtual soap parade across the lenses of her shades. She does not see Toussaint fall past. His eyes are closed. His arms are outspread, crucified on air. He is remembering the day he came to his father's high tower to show him what he had Necroville's meat engineers do to his flesh. He remembers the vastnesses of the room; the great plain of slightly radioactive, mica-flecked granite, the late afternoon light falling through the latticed glass walls, how small his father seemed, seated at his livewood desk, the geneered peacock fanning and frilling its beautiful, vain tail at his right hand, the sapphire-jeweled tectosaur with aquamarine eyes clinging upside down to its roost at his left.

He had been prepared for anything but his father's tears. The arms that enfolded him, the hands that felt out the still-raw skinwelds, the contours of the subdermal packages, had shaken with a genuine affection more hurtful than any rejection. He could not even play Lucifer, declare his great *non serviam* and be damned, fling back the role and inheritance prepared for him within the Tesler-Thanos *corporada* without his father destroying it.

A snapshot memory, wrapped in one single second.

The second second. Twice as many balconies as the first second. A man standing with his back to the sky admiring the interior of his apartment glimpses Toussaint falling, reflected in an ornate antique mirror. Frames of reference. From Toussaint's point of view, it is the Tesler-Thanos arcology that is accelerating past him into the sky. He thinks of the big ships maneuvering up there in cis-terran space. Mass-drive slamships. Sunrunners like spiders in webs of solar sail. They too are victims of relativity. Since the end of the NightFreight War, when meat humanity surrendered the stars to the resurrected, the Freedead have been the demons, the bogeymen, the zombie-flesh-eaters of popular mythology. One man's terrorist is another man's freedom fighter. Planetary defenses, his father had said. Defending what? Orbital manufactories. Corporate wealth. Established power. Privilege. Inequity. The system—to which his father had asked him to be heir—that sets the price for resurrection at the repossession of all human rights. Eternal non-personhood. The law does not presume that such things as the resurrected dead exist. This is what the one-shot rail guns and missile racks and AI-controlled teslers of the military-industrial complexes are defending.

Come, demons, come.

The third second. His velocity is now nine times that of the first second, he falls past nine times as many balconies. Toussaint is thinking symbologies. God and Satan. The temptation of Christ. The All-Seeing Eye of Sauron in the Dark Tower of Barad-Dur. Kronos devouring his children. Oedipus fucking his mother, killing his father. Not for white-boy Toussaint, thankless child of privilege, the sticky, sweaty archetypes of dark-skinned mythologies, their irascible, fickle little gods, their earthy, boogie-ing saints. His pantheon of the Freudian sorrows is a darker, sterner crew. Is there a mythology, he wonders, where the father raises children from the dead and then banishes them to outer darkness, from which they one day return to destroy him and all his works? If not, there soon will be.

The fourth second, Toussaint thinks, a good one in which to check his fall, is not taking him too close to the gradually outflaring flanks of the San Gabriel spire. He shifts his profile to the hurricane of air, changing terminal velocities to give himself some delta vee outward.

The fifth second. The sixth second. The seventh second. Toussaint has fallen beneath the residential zones into the lower administrational and light industrial sectors. His velocity is approaching one hundred and fifty kilometers per hour, at which point it will stabilize at an equilibrium of body mass and aerodynamic profile: the classic freefall semi-spread-eagle. He is calculating load tolerances, gee force maxima, dive configurations. The 'ware in his head makes it as easy and unconscious as the complex relative velocity calculations you make every time you take a car into traffic. Twelve seconds. Thirteen seconds. Hoover is choked with vehicles. The smog layer approaches.

Fifteen seconds.

The gnarled flesh across his shoulders, upper spine and arms deforms. Skin stretches. Skin tears. Curved tectoplastic ribs push through skin and pink and black flightsuit and press through the permeable membrane of the back pack. Datadots, headzups, fragma of information rezz up on his retinas as the systems come to life. Toussaint fights to hold it against the buffets. The margins for error are almost nonexistent. On his back the pack opens like a flower blossoming. Spines and spars of morphic plastic extend and lock into a lattice; the ghost of a wing, a flayed bat. Monomolecular tendrils sniff out anchor points and link, bracing the wing. Interface with his nervous system is complete. It is part of him now, an extra limb.

Seventeen seconds.

Once the airframe has locked into its remembered positions it can withstand momentary accelerations of up to twelve gees. The human skeleton is not tested to such specifications. To deploy the wing surface wide open to the airflow could rip his spine out of his body.

Death on the boulevard is four seconds away, but Toussaint rotates his body head down into a shallow dive. Liquid wing pumps from the reservoirs in the deflating pack, flowing thickly along the channels within the struts, freezing at the touch of naked air into a sheet of molecule-thin steel-strong aerofoil.

Nineteen seconds. He pushes up out of the dive. Mental commands flow out of his spine, along the interfacers, into the wing. Smart plastic warps. Wing bites deep into air. Multiple gees attempt to tear him apart. Blood boiling in his brainpan, Toussaint scores the tops of the palms along Hoover and climbs for clear air.

The twenty-second second.

Hold it. Hold it. *Hold it.* Stall now and you are dead all over again. Wing-tip flexes, a gentle bank toward the technogothic ziggurat of Tesler-Thanos. You need the thermals that flow up its monolithic flanks. The thermal lifts him high above the ragged pinnacle of the spiretop, where tector masons work work work shifting molecules, day in, day out. A kilometer above Tesler-Thanos he comes out of his climb into a long, slow glide down across the dead zones toward Lodoga Eyrie.

Toussaint exalts purity of flight above altitude, speed, aerobatics or endurance. His brother/sister *aguilas*, to whom such things are all flight is, do not understand. In the equilibrim of lift, pressure and gravity Toussaint finds expansion of consciousness.

Adrenaline, Norepinephrine,
In an eagle's eye,
Nirvana.

In this state he knows himself to be an infinitesimal mote adrift in the vastnesses of the atmosphere, and is comforted. The chaotic processes of meteorology and climatology are absorbed into him. Connectedness. On the parapet of his apartment, he had known the heat would end because he is the heat and the heat is him.

Swallowed by sky
I am Thee, Thou art Me.
Climatological Zen.

The dead zones of pre-resurrection Hollywood and Sunset lie beneath Toussaint's belly. Quiet now, for when the hills wake, the valleys sleep, storing the energy of the day to expend on the pleasures of the moist subtropical night. For tonight, when the hills sleep, the valleys will wake, and dance. Tonight the dead hold carnival. High above Necroville, Toussaint thinks of his friends, making their preparations for the Night of the Dead and the annual reunion in the Terminal Café: YoYo in her noisy, busy mess of lawyers, Camaguey in his cool, airy house overlooking the ocean. Trinidad: he thinks of her much, up there in the rarefied social altitude of La Crescenta. This year, will she find the courage to let go of Peres's ghost and join them? Santiago, surrounded by the illustrious dead. Most, Toussaint thinks of Santiago. Year Two: Reseda Private Elementary School. It is Santiago Columbar who braves father's protectors to show Toussaint—another name, then, another life, and few there are who know them—how to make wonderful slow-healing meandering scars on your arms and thighs with a burning lens.

The friendship had always depended on an equilibrium between Santiago's vulnerable darkness and Toussaint's angry, idealistic luminosity. Such relationships are bound by the laws of emotional entropy: ever more energy must be put into it to maintain that balance of personalities against decay. In the end, the investment was too high. They had spun apart, twin planets explosively decoupling. The center of gravity gone, the group had disintegrated.

Once a year, and once only, is enough. Any closer and they would start to destroy each other again. Toussaint has new friends now, new circles, new social orders, yet he wishes it could all be again as it was then, when it was fresh and rich and, paradoxically, innocent.

Up currents at the edge of the hills caress Toussaint's body. He turns his wings into the rising air. It lifts him high, kilometers high, above his city. Glints of light on the outward curve of the immense cylinder of air are fellow fliers, riding the airflow with him, up, up.

Bronzed bodies,
Silver air-riders,
Golden neo-surf-nazis,
Zeig Heil!

Lack of concision. Too much going on. Allusions anachronistic. *Aguilas* have little appreciation for the finer points of haiku construction.

Toussaint's course takes him away from the flocks of fliers toward the Tesler-Thanos *arcosanti*. Like Allah, it bestrides earth and sky, absolute and monotheistic. There is but one God, one resurrection, and Tesler-Thanos is his prophet.

Mile-high mausoleum of black cancer:
my father's house,
Adam Tesler.

Wings catch the afternoon sun, patterned with blue eagles; *aguilas* from Lodoga Eyrie, diving up through airspace to sport with him. Toussaint's forebodings lift like a storm front passing. The sky is big. The sun is warm. The wind beneath your wings is strong. These are the things that matter. Not the moon being converted into a three-thousand-kilometer sphere of nanotechnology. Not Freedead fleets approaching the earth. Not the machinations of the Rim Council and PanEuropa and their masters, the *corporadas*.

Far behind him, his father's dust-dry monologue comes to its unheard end.

Fifty-three hours, twenty-five minutes.

Betrayal the concept was a silver button on the side of a Jesus tank. Stenciled above it: *Flush and Cycle.*

Betrayal the deed was the act of pushing that silver button. The simple application of manual pressure by the heel of the hand. Circuits were activated. Sluices opened. The Jesus tank's contents were flushed into the house drains, the Palos Verdes sewage system, and ultimately, the Pacific basin.

Contents comprising: nine hundred liters of pH-neutral distilled water salted with fifty kilograms of deconfigured tector clusters in suspension. Being the dissolved mass, meat and mind of Elena Eres: *dead.*

Waiter, there's a girl in my soup.

It's girl soup, séor.

He had gone with her into the shallow, womb-warm water. He had kissed her, he had held her hand until the descending lid forced them apart, pressed fingers and face to the translucent plastic so that he might be the last thing she saw as she settled back into the waters of rebirth. All these he had done because he loved her. No degree of love could have made him watch her, over the space of three days and nights, disintegrate into free-swimming tectors. The slow flaying of the outer integuments first: the skin, the hair, the eyes, the soft tissues. Then the muscles, the connective tissues, the veins, the nerve fibers. Last of all, the bones and cartilage, fizzing away to nothing like seltzers in a glass.

Pacing the long, glass-arched arcade, he would often stop to rest his forehead, eyes firmly closed, against the tectoplastic carapace as if it were an immense shell within which the sounds of the ocean were trapped, and imagine he heard the infrasonic seethe and boil of tectors purifying themselves.

Misreplications. Data errors. Soft fails. Transcription glitches picked up from a universe of potential mutagenic sources. Background radiation, ultraviolet, electromagnetic fields, certain toxins, certain chemicals. The mundane cancers of living. Left uncorrected, error would compound upon error; faulty reduplications would multiply exponentially. Aberrant regeneration. Yes. Metastasizing mutagenesis. Oh yes. Bizarre deformities, localized in areas of the body. Certainly. Misreplication had hidden none of its horrors from Camaguey.

Solution: self-immolation. Pass beneath the waters, be reborn. Be reduced to your component tectors, purified, re-resurrected. Reconfiguration. All the dead have to do it, she had said. The first resurrection is the worst.

You did not permit me even that choice, Camaguey thought.

Sometimes, in those latter, insane days, when he pressed his forehead against the tank, it was the molecular seethe and hiss of the things in his own bloodstream that he heard.

"Elena?"

Camaguey removed his hand from the silver button.

Gone.

She was eight hundred billion disconnected particles dissipated by the tides and currents that flowed around the edges of his reef. Elementary biology: take the common marine sponge, pass it through a sieve into water and in time it will reform into that exact same sponge. He imagined tectors passing through the gullets and guts of bivalves and fishes, stirred by tides and currents, intelligent artificial molecules seeking each other out, fusing, knotting, becoming more complex, more intelligent, more aware until on a night of the dark of the moon Elena Eres burst from the surface tension, Venus Surrexit, reborn from nanotechnology and sea foam. In his mind she waded from the surf line and entered the dark, abandoned cliff house: touching, feeling, searching for him. Did she seek vengeance? Pain, confusion, an explanation for waking in dark waters? Love, perhaps, both equals now in betrayal. An apology. She would find none of these. He would be long gone.

"How long?" he asked the air in his ocean room.

"Fifty-three hours, ten minutes," the air answered. "At this stage, the conversion proceeds rapidly toward completion. The predictions are ninety-three percent accurate."

Beyond the curved glass the sea was still, mottled with the subsurface shadings of the reef he had built. Small sailing craft were abroad in the transparent light of early afternoon; sea birds dipped and splashed, hunting. A flotilla of basking plesiosaurs were black and gold lozenges just below the surface; out in the deep water channel great whales would be navigating between the mosquito gantries of the energy stations, moving south with the flow to the breeding lagoons along the Baja coast. The coast guard craft were still out there, quartering, searching, intent upon their enigmatic business. Official channels denied the rumor, which only lent it all the more credibility: that meteor shower? Last month? Uh-huh. That was no ordinary shower, oh no. What they don't tell you is that there was a raid. They dropped Something into the ocean. Darn right I'm getting onto the Palos Verdes Sanitation Department, I don't want God-knows-what coming up out of my toilet.

At least you can still smile, Camaguey. Listen up, you gossips: in fiftysomething hours you'll have story enough to keep you whispering for centuries and every word of it will be true.

Some catastrophes strike too hard, too fast, too accurately for the psychological hierarchies of anger, denial, bargaining with mortality and final acceptance to be played out. Some blows fall so heavily that all that remains is a numb shock, a refusal to believe, like a man shot through the heart too surprised by death to fall.

He knew that somewhere he should be screaming. What he thought—what he felt—was that it was high time he did something about the repainting contract for his fleet of hire yachts.

(*While your body is devoured from within,* screamed the silent screamer.)

Or slip on a gillsuit, take a skiff out to the new seedings and watch the pseudo-corals advancing over the heaped hulks of ancient, windowless automobiles.

Camaguey could remember the precise time, place, weather, clothes he was wearing when he fell in love with coral reefs. 15:28 Eastern Australian time; place: thirty kilometers due east of Cape Tribulation; weather: 32°C, humid, cloudless, wind three knots, low ocean swell; wearing: the Cougar Junior green and gold onepiece that he reckons is his favorite garment of all time. It was the fourteenth year of the resurrection of the dead. His father, down in Queensland Free State on some PRCPS affair, had interrupted his work schedule to give his bored son a treat. They had sailed on a seacat packed with sightseers to witness the hauling out of a three-hundred-meter section of Great Barrier Reef. One of the wealthier of the third-generation Shanghai plutocrats had bought it to decorate his flesh palace twenty meters beneath the South China Sea. As the one-hundred-thousand-ton chunk came up, water shedding from its knobs and protuberances, oceangoing cranes taking the strain millimeter by millimeter, cables creaking, Camaguey-aged-eleven had seen something altogether strange and marvelous. Here emerging from the waters was every fairy tale of sunken cathedrals, drowned cities, lost continents that had ever thrilled a boy's imagination. For an instant the domes and cylinders of coral were the spires of Ys, the chimneypots of Port Royal, the pillars of Atlantis.

Then the coral section, raining seawater and displaced marine biota, had swung free and lurched toward the transport lighters. People had whistled, people had cheered and clapped, but to Camaguey the spell was broken: just another technological sleight-of-hand masquerading as true magic.

The coral city was to haunt his bacchanalic teenhood and beyond; the embodiment of a *something more* which he could never quite quantify—until YoYo's silly comment thrown into a dull evening sitting around on the floforms on Santiago's beach house: *I wonder what we'll all be doing in five/ten/fifteen years' time?* The game is as irresistible as I Spy. They had speculated through the heat of the night into the morning. The other four had all fulfilled their predicted destinies to a greater or lesser degree: Trinidad, ghosting like a comet between lives she found more attractive than her own; Toussaint, young soul rebel, hiding from his father in the shadow of his own wings; YoYo fighting some good fight in micro-second wars out on the virtuality webs; Santiago a brain-burned messiah spewing hallucinogenic revelation to largely baffled humanity. Camaguey defied all prophecy. *Corporada* chairperson *nah* prize-winning novelist *no, not Camaguey* free-lance gigolo *come on* white-water rafter *no* nanotech design engineer *Camaguey?* rainmaker ghostdancer wormrancher cocktailshaker slavetrader sexpartner partnered shacking straight gay bi kids kidfree house home hobbies alive dead . . . *I just can't see him doing anything.*

Camaguey had been handed the key to self-understanding. He now saw that what he had always thought of as a social disability—his desire to be not as others were—was in fact the very essence of himself. If they couldn't predict what he might be in five years, good. Let them go on to fulfill their own prophecies; Camaguey, predestination-free, built a reef. Of his own.

He studied marine biology with a specialism in coral reef ecology. He took nanoengineering and design, primary and intermediary, as his minor subject. He learned to dive. He bought a state-of-the-art gillsuit. He slept his way into the confidence of a Palos Verdes dowager purely because she owned some of the best coastline in the county. While she rubbed his pecs and scapulars with tsubaki oil, he thought polyps and tectors. He bought up one hundred tons of assorted scrap consumer durables, dumped them five hundred meters off Long Point and seeded them with custom-built coral-simulant tectors. All the cool, wet winter as the monsoon rattled the rooftiles and Camaguey gave head in the ivory bedroom, down beneath the tear and surge of waves tectors scavenged dead freezers, micros, dishwashers, vacuumbots, disposable gigabouts for raw materials and fastidiously went about their constructions. When the woman killed herself in February—"the pale season of ennui," she apologized in her note (handwritten, appropriately anachronistic)—Camaguey was gutted. He was of that type who cannot understand how some might find dying easy, the decision to go on living the terrible choice to be faced every morning. He had not suspected what the woman had known the first time she took him to her bed: that what began as barter would end as love. When the silent, solemn women from the Death House came to take the body away, he asked them if he would be allowed to see her after resurrection.

Allowed? the women in white had said. Everything is permitted. Nothing is denied. But you will save yourself much pain if you lived as though she had died permanently.

Why? Camaguey had asked.

Death is not sleep, the women had said. Death is death. We awake, and we are changed. Our lives before, our memories, our experiences, our loves and relationships, are as a night's dream to us; insubstantial, troubling perhaps, but swiftly fading in the heat of day. The ties that bind restrain only the living.

They took the body away in their silent-running white van with the vee-slash of the Death House on the side and left the shattered Camaguey alone in the house by the sea, which the attorney systems told him in hushed, sibilant tones was now his, rooftiles, ivory bedroom, sun terrace and the best coastline in the county. Camaguey went down to the sea to try to wash his guilt away in salt water. Instead, he found himself in a garden of wonder.

Many-branched spires and towers rose on every side; spans and vaults of spiriform pseudo-coral arched over him and guided him across crystalline mosaic pavements into labyrinths of glass filigree and gently undulating fans. Formations like immense marine radiolarin lay scattered like medieval caltrops across the sea floor, the radiating spines five times the length of Camaguey's body. Encapsulated in each central glass sphere was some discarded piece of domestic bric-a-brac: a washing machine, a gardening robot. Elsewhere whip-thin necks rose from deep-rooted holdfasts, undulating in the California Current like browsing sauropods; an appropriate simile, for the head at the end of every neck was an ex–Northwest Pacific aerospace-lines rental jitney encrusted with nanotechnological jewelry and buoyed up by air bladders. Trumpets towers and tenements, palaces and piers: Camaguey explored the architecture of his dream city beneath the sea.

He emerged from the water as the moon rose over the cliff house of the melancholic woman. The lights of the low-orbit manufactories tumbled above him. Somewhere in the convolutions of his city beneath the sea the melancholic woman who had sucked his cock and swallowed one hundred and fifty antidepressants had died and become memory. Memory: in time forgotten.

Possessiveness had never been part of Camaguey's makeup. What had been given to him could not be kept as his own private wonderland. The next day he persuaded two sports divers to forego floating with the plesiosaurs over the drowned hulk of the *Queen Mary* and take a chance that he could show them exactly what he promised. The day after that they were back with fifteen friends. The week after that they were even shipping them down in environment tanks from the Milapa Swimmers colony to visit Camaguey's nanotechnological reef. He was taking ten dives a day with a strict limit of thirty per party; first dive at dawn, the last by the light of the pontoon-mounted floods he had hired from a marine salvage company. He was living in a gillsuit, taking twice-weekly

free-radical bloodscrubs and swallowing fistfuls of wakers, sleepers, uppers, downers and dietary supplements.

Karoshi. Any more successful and they could call the Death House
and book him a Jesus tank. Camaguey hung the equivalent of a Help
Wanted sign out on the dataweb.

Elena came. Dead Elena.

He had found love in dead Elena, and she had killed him for it.
Gently. Softly. Kiss by kiss, without ever once realizing what she was
doing. And now Elena was waiting for him, under the ocean, to join
her. He glanced at his tagalong. Fifty-two hours, forty-eight minutes.
Till human voices wake us, and we drown.

"Recommendations?" he asked the air.

"Where custom and religious observances permit, many victims
prefer suicide to allowing the syndrome to run to its full term," said
the air.

The invitation was the sole object on the slab of raw coral that was
his conversation table. *Santiago Columbar invites* . . . Where better to
burn the last night of your life than in the Terminal Café at carnival;
whom better to spend it with than those people whom, though they
will never know it, you came closer to loving than any other living souls?

Would he tell them? The question assumed a vital importance.
When you have a strictly rationed quota of questions and an entire
obdurate universe to ask them of, each one becomes valuable. He imagined speaking the thing's name, their faces around the wrought steel
table, their reactions.

YoYo would dissolve into shock, tears and emotion and betray all
those humanities and sentimentalities and vulnerabilities that were the
reason she played the case-hardened street lawyer so assiduously.

Toussaint would go dark and silent and worry that whatever words
he said would be wrong or offensive or just insensitive when the truth
was, anything he spoke was precious to Camaguey.

Santiago would shout and laugh and buy wine which he would not
drink and drag them all out into the street dancing and laughing and
raging through the carnival's coils and folds but it would not mask the
envy that Camaguey was doing that thing he most desired and feared:
burning out rather than rusting.

You can have it, Santiago.

Trinidad would not be there. She would hear, and cry, and be des-
olate, and hammer another body to the crucifix of fear she dragged
across her life.

Perhaps he would not tell them. He would drink and laugh and talk with them and go out with them to whatever entertainment Santiago had prepared for them this year. Saint John, Necroville of necrovilles, was big. Room and time aplenty for him to slip away and seek the company of his new brothers and sisters.

He spoke the words in the voice the air could hear.

"I am one of the dead now."

Fifty-two hours, thirty-six minutes, said the air.

The drag queen Carmen Miranda was waiting for YoYo on the eight thousandth step of her monochrome marble stairway to heaven. Tutti-frutti hat—banana, pineapple, oranges, guavas, bunches of grapes—like a *frutería joderi*ng a marquee. Pursed red cupid's bows painted onto thickly plastered cosmetics. Sheath dress slit to the thigh.

"Hiya YoYo!" hailed the Carmen Miranda. "Did you get my little present?"

"Trio's munching her way through it," said YoYo, clad head to toe in stern Calvinist black with just enough silver to look successful but not ostentatious. Ghost winds drew shuddering harmonics from the great staircase; far far below, light gray clouds streamed across dark gray heaven. Not a tiny silver bell on YoYo's earrings stirred. Not a feather on the Carmen Miranda's boa quivered. "She loves marzipan. Now, if you'll excuse me, I'm due in court."

"Just my way of wishing you good luck," the Carmen Miranda said. "Gee, you know, I wish I could come with you."

YoYo turned on the drag Carmen Miranda.

"Listen good, *serafino*. This is a big case. Biggest case of my career. Get this and YoYo Mok is a full partner in Allison-Ismail-Castardi. Fuck it up and she is back bobbing with the sampans in Marina del Rey. Meaning: nothing, including you, is going to be allowed to jeopardize my chances of winning for my clients."

"Eighty-eight point seven percent," said the Carmen Miranda. "Your chance of winning it for your client."

Every hundred steps as far up and down the great staircase as eyes could see, tall statues of mighty lawgivers turned, right arms raised, following the movement of the pure white sun.

"Anything, *serafino*, anything at all happens, and I'll hold you personally responsible. And you know what that means." *The emotional sophistication of a five-year-old,* Ellis had said. *They just like to be liked, go where you go, do what you do, be with you. Feel included.*

"That we won't be friends?" The Carmen Miranda pouted in anticipated disappointment. "I wouldn't like that, YoYo. All I want is for you to love me. Love makes me real, you know."

The step upon which the cork-wedge slingbacks rested, shivered and liquified. Fingers waggling toodle-oo, the Carmen Miranda sank into the marble.

YoYo continued her ascent. Her silver ornaments jingled.

Good karma, bad karma; despite Ellis's dire warnings of what one of them had done to him in Adelaide, she wanted the thing gone. Erased. Expunged. Deleted. Closed. Gone. Not even Iago her 'wareman would sanction exorcising this ghost in her machine, and he was dead.

"Immortal or not, I am not going to get on the tits of something that might someday be the next nearest thing to God," he had said, gently shaving YoYo's scalp with the faithful old Number One as she sat in his roadside barber's chair.

"So you can't do anything," YoYo had said, running her hand over her head. One of the most erotic sensations she knew. Bare female scalp.

"Not can't, won't." Iago flicked off his razor. "Fancy a few serves before lunch?"

The endless marble staircase had been his design. In a previous life he had been the creative half of the West Rim's most exciting indie 'warehouse. Until the company accountants arranged him a little accident for being too original for their own good. Now he shaved heads, volleyballed and 'warehoused custom systems for the dangerous and discerning. Dead or not, he was perhaps the happiest man YoYo had ever met.

"Something like no one else has got," YoYo had said as Iago spiked her serve, again. "And none of your fucking adolescent air-brush chrome-nipple laser-visor mirror-finish cyberwarriorettes either."

"YoYo," Iago had answered, coming up for the smash, "you insult me." Smack. Point.

She got: the monochrome stairway of the dead out of Powell and Pressburger's *A Matter of Life and Death*. Iago took her up it through a tandem consensus link like a real estate salesperson on a virtual-property viewing. Note the wide, shallow marble steps; they go up all the way to infinity. Observe the Parian marble statues of the great lawgivers: mnemonic links into worldweb legalwares and databases from Pretoria to Surinam. Pause awhile on the black marble loggias, designed as social spaces for you to meet and debate with clients and peers. Notice the high resolution and full reality simulation.

She loved it. It would cost her five years of litigation and plea bargains to pay it back, but none of the comrade lawyers she bundled with in the house on Sunset, not even hot-hot, coming-up-so-fast-she's-got-bends Trio had 'ware that could compare with an Iago Diosdado.

And now a poster-paint primary-color transvestite Carmen Miranda was stomping over her beautiful, stark monochrome universe. It pained her soul.

YoYo liked to think she had a beautiful, stark, monochrome soul.

Her room-cum-office was a rigorously minimal cube of white paper shoji wrapped around a bare limed woodstrip floor; all scrupulously neat and clean, partly the legacy of a sampan childhood, mostly because there was no place for flaking skin, shedding hair, stains on the black silk sheets, the stinks and secretions of dirty, messy humans in her black and white world. YoYo Mok, the environment.

YoYo Mok, the woman. Short, solidly built, layers of muscle close packed beneath an Asiatic skin reticulated with the silver veins of body-glove molecular circuitry. American-born Chinese, Drown Town tough. Her face bore the pockmarks of early childhood diseases endemic among the boat people: old killers and maimers thought long dead by the priv-ileged on the hills. Resurrected, like everything else. She wore the scars as proudly as if she had won them in coup fights. She could do so because her true skin was the bodyglove; unmarked, perfect, smooth, silky, her outer interface with the world, its film circuits the nervous system by which she apprehended a brighter, bigger universe than that supplied by her five native senses.

Within the simulation, YoYo looked around, alerted by a neural purr, to see a square of reflective obsidian, flip end over end through the gray sky of heaven toward the stairway. Stars twinkled in black depths: cases at trial, verdicts delivered, sentences effected. The Event Window was a cross-section through the twelve-kilometer-high pyramid of the Zwingli II justice system.

Pulse rising. Palms sweating. Vision blurring. Urgent need to empty bladder. Signs of arousal: Law School, Day One, Lesson One. Calm. Control. Engage the disciplines. Eighty-eight point seven. Remember that. Eighty-eight point seven has to be worth a round for those old friends of mine down in the Terminal Café tonight.

The silent plane of darkness swooped over her. She glanced up, saw herself reflected there, foreshortened by the angle of approach, and was swallowed up.

They had been waiting for her that morning when she went out to Mr. Shoes's *panaderia* for the daily coffee-break *dulces*. On the pinboard, the gilt-edged invitation: *Santiago Columbar invites YoYo Mok . . .* Outside the door, the boatload of marzipan.

"Your guardian angel's still delivering," said Trio, the partner YoYo did not like. She was on her way back with dinner from the all-niter on the intersection: a microwave *crepa* and a decaf in a thermofoam flask. It was not that hard to live out in a different time-zone, she claimed. Circadian activators helped, regular sensdep and disorientation/reorientation sessions played their part but none so much, thought YoYo, nakedly jealous, as the energy of being nineteen, handsome, successful and black.

"A model yacht filled with marzipan?" Trio asked, sniffing suspiciously at the toy boat's contents. Too much to have expected a twenty-meter pleasure cruiser. Even a surf boat would have done.

"Some bully-board court commentator described my submission in the Paulus/Dahl-Esberg-Sifuentes case as like being force-fed a boatload of marzipan. Carmen Miranda picked it up on the web and thought it was a compliment."

"Paulus/D.E.S. You didn't get that one, right?"

Right.

"Say, YoYo, if you don't want the marzipan, can I have some?"

"Have it all. Be my guest." Eat yourself stupid, gorge yourself, except you're one of those damn blessed creatures that can exist on a diet of pure crap: hundred percent saturated fat, sugar and carbohydrate and still bitch and moan about being too thin, too bony, why can't I put on any weight? YoYo said hello to one chocolate *dulce* and presto! instant blimpo. She blamed inherited racial traits. Sino/Southeast Asians carried the memory of the Ice Age in a tendency toward subcutaneous fat: Africa's plains and forests and peoples had never felt the breath of the glaciers.

It had been flowers first, lotus blossoms and bee orchids every day for a week, hand-delivered by a dead courier-girl from Big Occasion Flowers of Hesperia. Next Monday, a bottle of wine. Coonawarra Semillon '88. "Your secret admirer has taste," said senior partner Jorge. "Anytime you're having trouble getting rid of this . . ." By Thursday it was arriving by the case. "I'd be worried someone was going to wise up and want it all back," said Phoenix, the criminal lawyer. The week after that, Belgian chocolates. Handcrafted. Air-freighted. In two-kilo boxes. On the way to her sleeping pouch after another heavy night in Bangkok, Trio answered the delivery company's ring and consequently less than half the box made it to its intended recipient.

"Just be thankful someone out there likes you," said Emilio, the contracts and torts boy, hunting in vain for an orange-flower luocum.

"Not someone," said Ellis, the Australian divorce punk, practicing spin shots off the wall with the hyperelastic SupaBounce WundaBall he had bought from a catalogue of useless gifts. "Something. I think YoYo's picked up a *serafino*."

November 1. 20:30:35:50. Greenwich Mean. Case number 097-0-17956-67:01 is called. Showtime. In a paper room off Sunset, YoYo Mok steps through the Event Window and arrives two kilometers beneath the streets of Zurich.

Zwingli II was impressive. Its Swiss engineers had designed it to inspire respect and reverence for the nigh-divine processes of law. It did. Every time.

YoYo stood on a narrow ledge one-third of the way up the interior face of a pyramid that, had it been actual, would have peaked eight kilometers above her. Four kilometers beneath her its base area would have obliterated most of the Queen of Angels Metropolitan District. The adamant black walls of the pyramid shivered and rippled with flows of colored light: attorney 'wares waiting on the barrier of the arena where only human minds were permitted to clash. She felt Industries Gabonais's legalware at her back as a strengthening, emboldening presence. Heads up, YoYo. Cool. Cool. Keep it cool, cool as Zwingli II's supercore processors bathed in liquid Cee Oh Two. Cooler. Stars flickered in the enormous volume, constellations burning and dying. At any one instant, the Zwingli system was hearing and adjudicating seventy thousand cases.

The black skin of the pyramid rippled beneath her feet and spat a slender pont across the starlit chasm.

All rise. Court in session.

A point of her black-gloved, silver-ringed finger sent her flying across the black bridge. A single star detached from the galactic background and moved toward her, gaining substance and definition.

My enemy. Do not get cocky, do not get swell, do not kid yourself that just because you have two hundred gigabytes of corporada legal software behind you that you can send the country boys running with their jelabas smoking. Zwingli is God here.

She opened her hand and the simulation set her down on the arched center of the bridge. Void above. Void beneath. White stars twinkling. The approaching adversary was now a pentacle of legs, arms, head. Man-star. With the unholy speed of virtuality, he dropped down onto the bridge directly in front of her.

The web is. A domain. A potential. A state. A hallucination. An interzone. A defiance of any glib definition. An act of faith. A *credo*.

I believe in the inviolability of mathematics pure, applied and statistical, the creator and sustainer of all knowledge, the sacred language in which the realities of the universe are most truly iterated. And I believe in physics, chemistry, biology, in quantum theory and general relativity and informatics and chaos (though I can't choose between Gödel's Undecidability and Heisenberg's Uncertainty); quarks and gluons and neat unified theory packages tied up with superstring are a few of my favorite things; I believe in the Holy Informational Spirit, the picture in my television, the money in my bank account, the music in my sound system, the friends in my tagalong screen. And I believe in the nanotechnological resurrection of the body, and the life everlasting, Amen.

I believe in them because they work. I do not need to understand how they work, just that they do. The joy of technojuju is that it requires no especial piety or exercise of faith to make it work. Just money. Yahweh may have sent manna with the morning dew to feed the children of Israel, but for that little bit extra, the virtual shopping channels will deliver the milk and honey to your door.

Like all faiths, it is a product of human minds. And minds change; with them, the doctrines of how the world works. Paradigms shift.

When the big cybernetics *corporadas* failed to produce the Artificial Intelligence it had so long promised, the old Computer Model that Explained Everything from period pains to human consciousness to God in terms of sophisticated digital software and memory systems suffered a massive credibility failure. The street no longer believed that the universe—or even its own self—ran like a very large but essentially reproducible accountancy package. The street put its faith in the Minestrone Universe of the up-and-coming-with-a-bullet Nano-technological Revolution: an amorphous soup of free-floating conceptual entities which, in their natural collisions, made Prigogenic leaps to higher and higher levels of organization and complexity. A disorganized, downright untidy fractal domain, this new world order, where big fleas not only had little fleas upon their backs to bite 'em, but were in fact made up of little fleas themselves. A cool universe in which agile minds could catch a wave and surf from conceptual rip-curl to rip-curl.

The failure of the cyberneticists was now understood as the difference between trying to reach the moon by Apollo 11 and the Tower of Babel. Wrong materials, wrong techniques, wrong approach, wrong wave. The planetary information net they had created was not an embryonic gestalt mind but a primeval ecology analogous to that of planet earth's first few million years; an environment dense with constituent elements in the form of free-circulating shareware, dumped data, viruses dormant and active and clippings and drippings of data-fat from the gigabytes of processing power in motion at any one moment across the worldweb, energy rich, subject to chaotic fluctuations, and approaching a critical mass and complexity out of which an independent, self-sustaining, self-motivating, self-repairing and replicating cybernetic entity—*life*—might precipitate.

Like every suddenly fashionable idea or movement, the *serafinos* were around long before anyone thought to blanket them with a title. For decades they existed as rumors of cyberpixies, invisible brownies in the system who, in return for a saucerful of secrets, would bestow strange good fortune on the webriders who invoked them. By the time they were declared real, actual and, best of all, fashionable, they had accumulated interactive interfaces *(personalities)* garnered from a gamut of sources and inspirations: the great Golden Age archetypes were particular favorites, though with bizarre outgrowths grafted onto the core personalities. The top half of Marilyn Monroe, floating on the datawinds, skirts eternally billowing upward. At least fifteen Humphrey Bogarts, all engaged in bitter internecine webwar to be the sole claimant of the lipcurl and two-fisted drawl. A Marlon Brando intimately fused with a surprisingly well hung Harley-Davidson.

And a drag-queen Carmen Miranda.

Toe to toe. Head to head. Face-to-face. Classic confrontation/gunfight/courtroom-drama stance.

Do not fear your enemy, fear will throw chaotic perturbations into the flow of evidence. Become obdurate as stone, voracious as fire, unpredictable as water, ubiquitous as sky. Become more: become Absolute Mind.

She wished she had had time to pop just one more tranq.

Her opponent wore the flesh and raiment of a poor-trash Gabonais *noncontratisto*. His face, his hands, his shaved scalp, were covered in pustulent sores and the elegantly obscene infestations of parasitical tectors. And she, so cool, so professional, so *corporadismo* in her severe Calvinist black and silver. Clever bastard.

The lawyer extended a pockmarked hand across the short distance between them. YoYo glanced behind her, a nervous gesture against which she always forewarned herself but made every time. Every time. The veils and nebulae of light were there, coiling and twining trapped in the black walls of the pyramid. And something more, a distant splash of incongruous color. Orange. Green. Grape. Fruit?

The Carmen Miranda. Shit. Fuck. Shit. How could it have breached the Zwingli code buffers? *You bitch, you promised!* YoYo caught the scream of outrage before it hit the throat subvocalizers. Not a thing you want yelled through the cathedraline chasms of Zwingli II. She looked into her enemy's crusted eyes (cosmetic cataracts, cunning touch) and took his proffered hand in her own. The trial began.

The writhings trapped in the containing walls gathered into dense knots of star-hot white and launched themselves along the slender black bridge. The shock of uplink blew through YoYo like a firestorm. No worldly thrill compared with this microsecond flicker of penetration, this taste of omniscience as the legal systems pushed gigabytes of evidence along her nervous system.

YoYo made a shit lawyer. YoYo made a class junkie.

Indigenous Peoples of Mayoumba
vs. Industries Gabonais S.A.
Case summary.

Two words. Money. Jobs. Meaning: when Industries Gabonais S.A. (being a cunning disguise for Serious French Money) sets up a plant on the Gabon coast four hundred kilometers south of Libreville to process stuff coming up the pipeline from the mid-Atlantic ridge mining project, the people of Mayoumba are jumping up and down thinking jobs money beer children cars television and pills. Thinking: *future.* The Economic Reality turns out to be that IGSA hauls over two thousand *resurrectois* on long-term contracts from the big necrovilles around Kinshasa and not only do the people of Mayoumba (living and dead) see their bright futures sailing away over the ocean, but within six months waste products from the plant have wiped out half the fisheries on which they depend and accidentally infected the other half with parasitical tectors. They are patient people, the people of West Africa, it is only when the children start to sicken, and weaken, and die that they ask their town webjockeys to hire a lawyer up in Cairo and sue. At which point Industries Gabonais, her mother company and the Truly Serious Money of their mutual Pacific Rim *padrino corporada* activate their legal systems, circulate word and invite tenders. Enter YoYo, with her ambition showing.

After much virtual wrangling between Coast and Delta, the preliminary hearing was assessed and returned for full trial, court availability and compatability pending, in twelve milliseconds by an antiquated but mutually agreeable judiciary 'ware in Ukraine.

It's World Law now. By the end of the Golden Century, legal systems were collapsing under the sheer mass of litigation. Minor misdemeanors were already being heard *in camera* by remote video systems; trial by a jury of peers had evaporated in a miasma of plea bargaining and out-of-court settlements: no great leap of precedent was required to subcontract the public prosecution service to whatever judicial expert systems had slots available. No more the Kafkaesque nightmare of the innocent man standing for long years before the door to the law: you shall have your day in court, provided you don't mind that the court is in Islamabad, the legalware Pakistani, the law by which it is judged Traditional Sharia. Lawyers became international computer-time brokers, attorneys hard-wired webrunners; organic circuitry across which the megabytages of the battling legalwares arced. Justice suffered, the legal business thrived.

In re: Mayoumba: YoYo's preference was for a Pacific Rim court, where Property traditionally took precedence over Person, and her Cairene counterpart's for an African, preferably Reform Sharia. As compromise, a fifty-microsecond timeslot was booked on Zwingli II at 20:30: 35:50 November 1 Greenwich Mean. Plaintiff and defendant contracted to be bound by the adjudication of Swiss Confederal Law, and secretly prepared appeals. The massive law 'wares behind them went tunneling through databases and case law in search of precedent and expert witnesses. The attorneys popped their memory enhancers and neural accelerators and made their peace with their respective spiritual entities.

"A what?"

"A Drag Queen Carmen Miranda." YoYo flopped angrily on Ellis's nasty cracked-leatherette couch. "There I was, going up my staircase to do a day's work, when I see a banana on a step. Next thing I know, a fucking transvestite Carmen Miranda comes up out of the step like something from a Busby Berkeley musical and asks me if I liked the chocolates."

"Excuse me, Yoyo." Ellis wiggled his fingers at her. "Could you move to your left about twenty centimeters or so? It's just that you're merging with Mrs. Badalamente and it's a tad confusing." She shifted. Ellis was in consultation. Wrap-around scanshades glinted as he nodded his head in acknowledgment of the invisible Badalamentes. His lips moved, subvocalizing an apology for the real-world interruption. YoYo considered herself fortunate not to have to deal with gross and fallible meat. The abstract purity of complete virtuality was much to be preferred to the potentially disorienting superimpositions and transitions of interactive overlay. It was no secret in a practice where every partner knew the smell of each other's underwear that Ellis had been forced out of a brilliant potential career in Adelaide into tortilla-and-beans divorce work in the TVMA by a *serafino*.

Ellis concluded his consultation.

"Nothing you can do about it," he said, interlocking his fingers behind his head and stretching his arms. "Not if you're wise. It started the same way with me—little gifts, flowers, things, sent to my apartment. I eventually had to start sending the stuff back as unsolicited goods. Bad move. They like to be liked, and it didn't like this. Started charging the stuff to my accounts. Ended up with debt orders so far up my ass, they were coming out my mouth. And you try earning a rep with your name on fifty credit blacklist files. It cost almost as much to hire a webjockey to hack me off as paying the original debts, and the fucking *serafino* caught wind of it anyway and called the cops."

"Jesus."

"They just want to be liked, that's all. They just want to be with you, go where you go, know what you're doing, be included. If you treat them good, they'll treat you good. There's good karma as well as bad, and they never hang around for long; six months, and this drag Carmen Miranda'll have gone on to someone else."

"Six months?"

"At most. They're like those stray cats that wander into your area and act nice and purr and rub around you and you take them in and they stay awhile and then one day they move on again."

"You're telling me to stick with it."

"Stick with it. It's going to stick with you."

The moment passed. The light failed. The song ended. Moses came down from the mountain.

Under Zurich, on the black bridge across the star-filled void, YoYo's hand recoiled from that of her rival. The legal systems had withdrawn to the walls of the pyramid. Their evidence was presented, their cases made. Zwingli II deliberated. The sloping faces of the pyramid shivered with lightnings and distant half-heard thunder.

YoYo wanted to run. YoYo wanted to hide. But no one may run and hide from the jealous God. The thunder mounted, mounted, mounted. And stopped. The suddenness, the absoluteness of the silence was almost palpable. YoYo looked up into the churning energies at the apex of the pyramid. A few footsteps away, her adversary was likewise looking around him, perplexed.

Something *sehr ungemütlich* with the big Calvinist Jehovah.

Planes of white light slammed into place around YoYo. A fifth glowing square guillotined horizontally above her, sealing her into a cube of milky luminescence. She pointed her finger toward the safety of the boundary and the IGSA legalwares. She remained obdurately put. Zwingli II was nullifying her virtual flight system.

She was under court arrest.

"What the hell is going on?" she screamed in frustration, punching at the unyielding walls. *Hard*, her bodyglove told her, triggering nerve endings. *Pain*.

The Swiss Confederacy finds you in contempt of court, said the still, small voice that lived in the heart of the whirlwind.

"What?" YoYo Mok shouted. "What what what what what?"

Use of unauthorized 'wares within the Zwingli II judicial system. Breach of court protocols, compromise of security codes. Disruption of on-going cases, dislodgment and corruption of evidence files. Introduction of invasive viral material into the Zwingli II operational heirarchy.

"Unauthorized 'ware? Invasive viral material?"

Zwingli II opened a small Event Window in her cell wall.

"Jesus fuck," YoYo sobbed. "I'm dead."

The Carmen Miranda smiled winsomely in the Event Window and rattled a pair of castanets it had never previously manifested.

Advocate Mok of Allison-Ismail-Castardi, acting for Industries Gabonais S.A., is found in contempt of court and is suspended from this legal simulation until such time as her contempt is purged.

YoYo was still weeping in stunned disbelief as the translucent cage rezzed out and the Event Window came swooping down to sweep her back to golden California.

She came out of court on her knees. A film of tears spread across her cheeks in the molecule-thin space between skin and bodyglove.

Finished.

sunset — 21 : 30

november 1

Out in the terracotta land beyond the aerospace port, the liftercraft had picked up the two parallel lines of tire tracks in the dust, and, like a needle to the planet's magnetic core, had turned to align itself with the road that led west. From the cabin window Trinidad watched tracks become road become highway become expressway, attracting the inevitable entourage of tarty camp followers: fuel stations, cheap eaterias, carpet warehouses, discount depots, motels'a'love. Here a town: a neat, well-watered grid of gardened houses, swimming pools glittering, tennis courts red rectangles, and *gone* beneath the shadow of the fan mounting. Hillhopping, the lifter scraped the rotor tips of the ridgetop wind farms, and swooped down into the valley, following the undeviating line of the highway through the big agribusiness orchards, so low the genetweak trees tossed and blew in the backwash and the dead workers looked up at the cool of its shadow on their photochrome-branded backs.

High on killing, the hunters joyfully raided the onboard bar for pourables, smokables, tokables. They laughed, their voices were loud. Bellisario flirted openly with Vaya Montez: those beautiful thighs would soon be opened, Trinidad thought. Death, the biggest aphrodisiac. Ahead of the speeding liftercraft, the grand bacchanale: the Night of the Dead. Why else did the meat come down from their hills, through the luminous gates into the dead town, but to declare the great I AM in a spurt of cloudy fluid, a twitch of ovaries?

Foreplay in horizontal flight. Deep in the valves of her heart, Trinidad was glad that the thing with Bellisario was over. Now that she was free from the pretending, she could start again on her hopeful quest for someone with whom she could find something more than *something*.

Perhaps—as the dead pilot took the liftercraft over the final hilltop and down into the moist coastal plain—it might be that someone was not necessary; that the something that was not *something* was to be found in her, not in the mirror of other's lives.

And at the end of the long westward road was just the tire-smeared concrete of a suburban landing field upon which the liftercraft sat like a pinned bug, legs spraddled, wing-cases spread to show the complex workings within. Turbines whined down to a stop. Shapeshifting tectoplastic clicked and cooled. The cabin door unsealed. The personal musk of the city—her city—rubbed itself on Trinidad as she stepped onto the field: the sweat pheromone of this hypurbation of twenty-something million souls living and dead. Complex hydrocarbons, mostly. But also cypress and ivy. Strange herbs, old Spanish spices. Body heat. Long-tongued blossoms heavy with nectar; slow-swelling fruit on the branch. Citrus and vine, bougainvillaea and Rose of Jericho. Earth smells: dust, dirt, sun-burned blacktop. Oils and essences. Rich tangs of shit and corruption, a jizz of ozone and neon. Woodsmoke and thyme and the inhuman perfumes of the dead. Lasers and steel, all laid over the subtle, omnipresent base of deep, cool, distant ocean.

It insinuated itself into the car as Sula drove Trinidad through the once-prosperous, now-ruinous *favelas* of the *noncontratistos;* districts with names like Pomona and Montclair and Charter Oak that added high notes of desperation, decay and dog spit-roast over charcoal braziers to the heady mix. Through the *seguridado* checkpoints into the leafy loops and meanderings of La Crescenta's hillsides. Different emphasis here: damp green growing, leafmold and tropical fruits weighing down the branches that overhung the car.

City musk. Necroville perfume. It clung to her skin. She tried to shower it off but the heat of the day sweated it out of her pores. It infected the fresh clothes into which she changed out of her hunting gear. In the cool of her La Crescenta *residencia* Trinidad understood that she would cease to smell of fear when she returned it to its native earth, to the place where all *somethings* became nothing. And were reborn.

The terracotta saints of the Ucurombé hagiography—the remix religion of Brazilian animism and Post-Catholicism fashionable among the children of privilege—gazed mumchance from their shrines among the roots of the big bo tree as Trinidad uncapped her silver flask of Mexican courage and poured them generous libations. Around their feet lay the fragile bones and tattered skins of the little living things Trinidad had pettily sacrificed for them to tell her how to make *something* become *love*.

Now they had answered her.

"I can't," she begged them. "Not there."

No other way, said the dumb idols.

She kicked them over in their little shrines and, calling Sula, stormed back to the house, knowing that if even once her momentum faltered, she would be trapped forever by her fear.

The dead did not frighten her, nor crowds. Crowds of the dead did. Their individual, alien smells mingled, amplified into a pheromonal shout of inhumanity. The tectoplastic bubble of her car seemed small protection in the crush of resurrected bodies pouring along the avenues toward the great luminous vee of the Necroville gate. A fragile egg, Trinidad an embryo curled within.

Big articulated electric buses swung arrogantly along their designated lanes; monster truck-trains—three, four trailers long—snorted impatiently behind and before her; pedicabs darted for openings like picadors around a bull, icons swaying from their canopies. Bicycles and alcohol mopeds moved perilously up lines of slow-grinding traffic; everywhere, the press and push and jostle of Necroville's ten million dead, returning to their allotted places before the evening skysign faded.

She could not go back now, if she wished.

The Glendale gate to Saint John—Necroville of necrovilles—reared above the crowd forced beneath its luminous cross-bar. Tesler-armed *seguridados* merely glanced at death-signs and pass permits before nodding the migrant workers through. Their concern was with those trying to get out, not in. Trinidad was squeezed, inexorable as birth, toward the shining gate. A bus passed through, and a flock of pedicabs bearing living revelers to the carnival. The truck train in front of her was waved through, containers barely clearing the slash of the big neon deathsign, and it was her turn.

A securityperson bent to her open window. She saw her face reflected in the datavisor. Was the apprehension that obvious? Digits flowed across the faceless face as identifiers flowed from her carware. Scanners, sensors trained to separate the quick from the dead discreetly sniffed her.

"Going to the carnival?" the trooper asked. Trinidad nodded. A smile appeared beneath the reflective visor. "Well, have a good one and don't drink too much. They may not care who you run down in that thing in there, but you have to come back out again sometime."

And she was through, into Saint John, dead town: Necroville.

No one was old. Everyone was beautiful. There were no children here, only the dead, pressing close all around in their forever young, forever perfect bodies. Some wore the faces and forms of Golden Age of Hollywood stars from the big movie screens that lined the rooftops and overlooked the intersections.

She drove on, into the dead town. The boulevard throbbed like the sounding box of a ten-kilometer-long guitar. By the light of burning tail-gases she glimpsed dancing figures, extravagant costumes glittering. Fireworks climbed and burst against the sky-sign.

She came at last to the Terminal Café. An eclectic miscegeny of juke-box and aircraft carrier, it was anchored on an intersection shaded by dusty almond trees. Strobing neon shouted TERMINAL CAFÉ TERMINAL CAFÉ TERMINAL CAFÉ in shocking pink. *Metropolis* played in silent monochrome on a wall across the square. Fantastically costumed figures—or more than costumes?—hurried to catch the endless parade. As Trinidad stepped out of the car a dead man paused to offer her a handful of twitching spiders. She shook her head: *no*. The man ran on. He had the head of a jackal. At a table beneath the almond trees a heartbreakingly handsome dead woman jammed with the distant drums on a portable boogiebox guitar.

Trinidad paused at the door to adjust her terracotta dress, her boots, her ringing silver bangles. She flicked her hair back over her shoulder, her love-scars livid in the light from the neon sign. No way back now. She pushed open the door and walked into the Terminal Café.

Santiago sat at a mezzanine-level window-booth overlooking the raucous boulevard. The flame from a tabletop oil-lamp underlit his face, giving him something of the character of a repentant Lucifer. In Trinidad's experience, men revealed their truest selves when unaware they were being observed, before the ego-masks were slipped on.

"Santiago."

"Trinidad!" His surprise and delight were genuine. "You came; no, I won't ask any questions in case they pop you like a hologram."

"Pretty damn solid hologram, Santiago."

"Jesus Joseph Mary, you look . . . You look. I'll get you a drink."
He raised a hand to summon a *mesero*. "You look so good. Five years,
Trini." A waitress with Jean Harlow's face maneuvered through the
overcrowded tables to take Santiago's order. "Let's see if I remember.
Sangre Christe? Wasn't that it? Or something a little stronger." His fist
unfolded. Curled in his palm, a bloodred spider slumbered.

Cariño said the graffiti scratched into the tabletop, *Muerte*.

The hand snapped shut. Santiago laughed briefly, theatrically.

"No. Of course not. Not Trinidad. Never was Trinidad. She'll pour
Christ's Blood down her neck until she has to be carried back to her
little home in the hills"—Jean Harlow set a coaster in front of Trinidad
and placed on it a tall red cocktail, rattling with ice—"but the subtler,
more refined nuances of hand-crafted chemicals she denies. Whereas
Santiago drinks only the purest, sweetest mineral water"—he uncapped
the bottle of *gaseoso* Jean Harlow had brought with the Blood of
Christ—"but has sucked the face of God. If it comes to a neuron body
count, I'd much rather them elegantly rapiered than bludgeoned to
death with a baseball bat."

He opened his big hand again. The spider had vanished. Cheap
sleight.

"Don't worry, I'm running on nothing but my own neurochemistry
tonight. So tell me"—he arranged his large frame over the scrap iron
seat in an approximation of relaxation—"why did you come? What
prised Trinidad out of her high castle this Night of the Dead and down
onto Terminal Boulevard? Did you finally manage to lose Peres in that
crowd of beautiful young bodies you've passed through your bed?"

"And I thought you'd be glad to see me," Trinidad said evenly.

Chingar, whispered the scratchings. *Joder*.

"I'm sorry. That was cheap. Note for your diary: Santiago Columbar
apologizes. It's envy, first and last. Pure envy. I scare you, don't I? I've
always scared you."

Yes, she thought, *because, Santiago Columbar, whatever it is the spiders have done to your chemistry, you no longer smell human. Nor do you
smell dead: there are no words for your smell, and so it frightens me.*

*But I have sworn to the saints of the Ucurombe Fé that I will face those
fears down until their true natures are revealed.*

"Don't fool yourself, Santiago. I'm ready for you."

"Glad to hear it, Trinidad, though, personally, I have my doubts.
The teddy bear's picnic I have lined up for tonight, I don't think anyone
will be ready for. Much less ever forget."

The rhythm of the street surged suddenly closer, beating against the translucent shell of the Terminal Café. The open space beneath the almond trees filled with costumed figures, all moving in the same direction like boats flying before a storm. Tables were overturned, chairs knocked down, bottles, glasses and windows broken. The crowd moved around Trinidad's car like water around a rock; firmly rooted to the earth, it was shaken but not stirred. The café swelled with voices; patrons from street tables and carnival refugees crowded in. Someone turned the music up.

The source of the disturbance entered Terminal Boulevard: a pack of wolves, two, three hundred strong: wolf-men, man-wolves. Werewolves, caught in the act of transubstantiating from one state to the other. Beasts that walked erect; what big teeth they had, but sentience shone in their still-human eyes. Clawed feet, dextrous, clever fingers. Many bore large helium balloons, memory-plastic bubbles programmed to display a grimacing Man in the Moon with a space bullet lodged in his right eye. One wolf—a female—looked up and momentarily locked eyes with Trinidad. The naked breasts, sparsely haired as a dog's belly, sent a shiver through her.

"Los Lobos de la Luna," Santiago said. "They support the dark-side colonization. If you can call what the Freedead are doing to the moon 'colonization.' Fifty years, they reckon, until it's all converted. See it as a spiritual home: Ethiopia-in-the-sky. If Ewart/OzWest and Tesler-Thanos and the other big nanoprocessing companies that have the governments in their back pockets don't rock the cradle and it goes down baby and all. What the hell else point is there to those orbital tesler batteries they pushed through the Rim Council Defense Committee other than to keep the Freedead out there beyond the moon and howling. Except"—Santiago leaned forward and grinned a deathshead grin— "they're not playing the game and staying put. Or don't you know there's a fleet of Freedead slamships headed earthward?" He sipped his water, lolled back in his chair theatrically. "Run and hide, run and hide. The sky is falling! The sky is falling!" He glanced under the table. "Do you think we could both get under here, come out when it's all over, be the new Adam and Eve, Trinidad? That's what they think they are, the Freedead. The next evolutionary step; the humanity that will inherit the stars. Tesler-Thanos, the Death Houses, the systems of *contratado* and the ghost economy, the necrovilles, the space-faring Freedead, Watson's Postulate, the Barantes Ruling, they look like one indivisible mass, inextricably interconnected, but you hit it at the right angle, and it splits clean down the middle, all the way. The dead, the future, change; the living, the past, stasis. Simple as that. Fifty years from now those Lobos'll be howling by the light of a ball of nanotechnology. What'll you be doing?"

The wolves of the moon had run on into the depths of the dead town. A sudden gust of warm wind blew dust and discarded streamers and scraps of costume and wastepapers up into a brief dance. A rim of translucent blue cloud edged above the rooftops. On the movie screen across the square, Roman Polanski slit Jack Nicholson's nose with a stiletto and threatened, lips moving wordlessly, to feed it to his goldfish.

"Smell that?" Santiago leaned his head against the seat back, eyes closed, tasting, scenting the night. "Smells of North by Northwest. Big kelp ocean. Wind's shifted. Air's moving. Changes coming."

He looked at her. Against her anger, Trinidad felt herself being drawn into conspiracy. "I'll tell you true, Trinidad. Every fucking word. You deserve it. Honest injun." The red spider reappeared, conjured onto the tabletop. *Coléra*, whispered the table, *futilidad*. Santiago smashed the spider into a bloody smear with the side of his fist. "It doesn't do it anymore. None of them do it. Can you understand that? Wherever there is to go, I've been there. No higher ground. No more mountaintops. As I said, I've sucked God's face, and it tastes of vitamin-enriched high-fiber breakfast cereal. No more mysteries, bread and wine, loaves and fishes.

"It wasn't the money; you know that, don't you? I didn't get into it to get rich. It wasn't fame, friends, anything like that. Fame? Mother of God, thanks to the recreational pharmaceutical *corporadas* and virtuality engineers, every kid on the Rim knows my name. Friends? Every morning I find *amigos* scattered around the house like clothes at a San Jacinto pool party. They're there only for the freebies and the hope that a little celebrity might rub off on them. Famous for fifteen minutes, vicariously.

"I did it because it was a way out. Of myself. It's one of the Big Two philosophical crises of late adolescence. *Uno*, the inevitability of death: *Dos*, the impenetrability of the self. Why am I me? Why am I not you? Why can I never experience another person's sentience, why can I never know anything outside myself? Why am I trapped behind these eyes?"

He tapped the arachniform tector interfacer over his pineal gland.

"Luck? Karma? Am I a ghost in the meat machine, am I God's little seed stored in heaven from all eternity and glued one day onto a blastocyst in Mama Columbar's womb, has this me been recycled through countless previous bodies, previous worlds, universes?" He pressed his forefinger between Trinidad's eyes; adjacent patrons smiled over their glasses, misunderstanding. "This is the final frontier. Here. This curve of bone is the edge of the universe."

He drew his finger down over her nose, her lips, her chin.

"It's my sweet sixteenth: Santiago Columbar's coming of age. I'm four hours into the party; it must be about two, two-thirty; there are a hundred, two hundred? on the dance floor, the temperature's up in the high thirties, the music is so loud it's something you feel"—fingers touched *Tan Tien*—"rather than hear. There's some Thex holding me up, some Hybrid-17 keeping me in touch with the ground and an MDA remix whispering *no limits, no limits* to my autonomic nervous system. They switch on a brain-flicker white flood and the music and the pills and the dancing and the white light come together, become something more, and I'm someplace else. I don't know where, I can't describe it; I don't think it can be described. It lasts only an instant, but for that instant I'm out. I'm free. I'm across the frontier.

"I've been looking for that way through ever since, Trinidad. I want to go where that sixteen-year-old boy went, and this time never come back again. Can you understand that?

"I'm twenty-seven. It's a funny age. I know because my folks sent me an anime card this year. 'Happy birthday from the Milapa Swimmers' it says. There's some nice kelp, undulating gently, and Mommy and Daddy waving flippers and saying, 'Mind now, Santiago, twenty-seven's a funny age.' Have you any idea how many icons passed from mere existence into immortality at the age of twenty-seven?"

" 'Better to burn out than rust.' "

"You have it, Trini, though I doubt you'll ever truly understand. Rust is my inheritance and my destiny. Entropy my handmaid. Slow immolation in the dust desert of irrelevance. It doesn't do it anymore, Trinidad." Wild vehicles were gathering on the intersection for the auto-da-fé, the night races through the abandoned metro system. Tectogothic phantoms they were, all tailfins, streamlines and bones. Teams of uniformed *mecanistos* prepared their *autodores* like esquires their Sir Knyghtes. "It's out there somewhere, in those streets, the exit to the place beyond. The place beyond itself."

He took hold of her chin so that she would have to look into his eyes and see what fire burned there.

"We're going there, this night, to see what is to be seen, to find what is to be found. And if I don't find it . . . There'll be one fewer of us here for breakfast. It's that important to me, Trinidad. If I can't have it, I don't want anything. Death: what's death these days? A quick dip in the cold lake of nirvana, and a good career move. You do your most creative, original, perfect work in your first five years, Trinidad. I've had that; can you see now why I have to find it? If I don't, I am truly dead. Dead in the spirit." He smiled. He had seriously expected her to laugh.

"Christ, Santiago."

"I've got six years on him."

"You're sick, Santiago. You need help, Santiago."

"That's why you're here, beautiful Trinidad. You and Toussaint and Camaguey and YoYo, who will all be here soon. To help. To witness. To take the word back, so that everyone will know, whatever happens. Four good and true witnesses. Four evangelists. The synoptic gospel of Santiago according to Trinidad. And Camaguey. And Toussaint. The Gospel according to YoYo. I like that one. You shall be my witnesses, unto the ends of the earth."

Trinidad's mouth was dry, her heartbeat was strangely loud and close. *He cannot mean this.* A raised finger summoned Jim Morrison. Twenty-seven. A funny age. *It's Santiago, he can mean whatever he likes.*

"Mescal, *por favor.*"

Santiago looked up at her from beneath lowered brows.

"There was a young girl of Nic'ragua/Who smiled as she rode on a jaguar./They returned from the ride/With the young girl inside/And the smile on the face of the jaguar.

"Mind, now, Trini."

"Fuck you, Santiago. Fuck you and your bastard jokes and sick little psychological games. Play them on someone else. I'm going."

She stood up, threw back the mescal in one blazing mouthful and turned to leave. People were staring. She prided herself on knowing how to make an exit.

"No joke, Trinidad. You see me laughing? It's serious. Utterly serious. So serious, I'm going to tell you something, the kind of thing that can be said only by someone who knows he will not have to suffer the consequences of his words."

"No more lies, Santiago. No more games." Against her will, tears filled up the corners of her eyes.

"No more lies. I confess: the stuff Peres took the day he died. I gave it to Michael Rocha. I made it. I designed it. I sold Rocha the specifications. I killed Peres. Now will you believe I mean what I say?"

Fury put a power beyond physical strength into the fist. The heavy twisted iron chair went over backward. Santiago's face was the image of surprised devastation, the wily coyote shot with his own unloaded gun. Nursing her knuckles, she spun on one ten-centimeter heel. The patrons of the Terminal Café parted before her like the faithful before their prophet.

"Trinidad!"

Quemar, Santiago. *Orin*. Words writ in wood.

"Trinidad!"

He called from the main door, but the voice of the carnival swirling into the *zócalo* on a flaw of warm wind spoke louder. He spat blood.

"Trinidad!"

The carnival had once again extended itself into the square, a congregation of exquisite transvestites mingling with a *cuadrilla* of dead men and women with tall gallows fixed to their backs. Several-times-life-size effigies of the presidents of the Rim States hung by their heads: wires connected puppets and puppeteers at wrists, ankles and neck. He saw her turn to look back once, shake her head, and disappear into the crowd.

Santiago picked up a strip iron café chair and flung it at Trinidad's anchored car. The silver tectoplastic remained unmarked, obdurate, immaculate. He could never, never make them understand him. Any of them.

"Stompie footie, Santiago Columbar."

Transvestites and puppeteers melted away before the chrome and midnight bikes. Four of them, like the souls of once-noble Harleys taken down beneath the earth and bathed in fire until skin and flesh were burned away and what remained was glowing, naked bone. Horned and tusked, pared as thin as racing dogs; every teenage wetdream and parent's nightmare of a motorbike. Behind them, gas flares coiled and spasmed into the dark sky: the dance of the damned.

Idling engines suddenly revved in an explosive bark of sound, ear-shattering in the enclosed arena of the intersection. A haze of acrid smoke settled out of the tree branches. Monoxide and musk. Machine pheromones, in combination with seat leather, deeply aphrodisiac. No one *joder*ed in the back seats of fuel-cell cars.

Santiago stood, feet slightly apart, arms folded, smiling, slightly.

"Miclantecutli."

The lights went out. Up on the big screen, Stewart Granger in Scaramouche tights and nose did battle with the silken Mel Ferrer. A woman dismounted from the center bike, propped herself with studied laziness against its still-warm flank. Like her *companeros*, she was dressed in stretch mesh and leathers, all shining contours and tightly pulled little straps and buckles. Her shoulderpads were agonized demon faces in vacuum-molded latex, her bare arms were tattooed from fingernail to collarbone. Studded wristbands, of course. The antique Rolex was slightly surprising. Her hair had been waxed and lengthened with deliberately mismatched hairpieces; the effect fell short of the Gothique ideal because of an inherent vulnerable prettiness in her face.

Any incongruity in Miclantecutli, Santiago knew, was a considered statement of character.

"I'd never have put you down for a temper, Santiago Columbar. Tell me, do you beat up on your girlfriends? Do they like it? Does it get you hot?"

"Death hasn't improved you, I see."

"Why should it, Santiago Columbar? I was jealous of you then, I'm jealous of you now. With you I always knew that pupil would outshine teacher."

"Why did you agree to take me with you if you hate me so much?"

"Who said anything about hate, Santiago Columbar? You've come to find death, that's enough for me. That your car?" She nodded at Trinidad's chrome bubble.

"No."

"Doesn't matter. Asunción . . ." A tall, rangy seventeen-year-old parked his hog to come and lay hands on the vehicle's reflecting skin. The tectoplastic seemed to buckle and strain beneath his touch. "We lost one cruising too close to the edge up by MacArthur. The *mechadors* get trigger-itchy on carnival night. Nice play, trying to lure us onto the teslers. Didn't work, did it, Anansi?" A dead girl riding pillion on Asunción's bike ran her tongue over her teeth and slid three centimeters of steel blade out of its thigh sheath. Matte-black panda patches were spray-painted around her eyes. Under Asunción's transmuting hands, Trinidad's car stretched and deformed, like the bones of the poor beneath their shallow skins. Warped tectoplastic reflected a shapeshifting grin. "So Anansi needs something between her thighs if we're going to take your . . . *compadres* . . . piggyback."

"They're not here yet."

"They've got until Asunción completes his little alchemy. We've four hours to turnaround and only one kill. It's taken me five years to get to earn the coup to challenge the Pale Riders to the *Caza Grande*, we're not letting you fuck that up. When the long knives come out, you and your buddies better stand well back. If you come it's because the idea amuses me, not because I owe you a debt of gratitude for the stuff you run me. Death cancels all debts. We're the Night Hunt, Santiago Columbar, we don't owe anyone anything."

The car now resembled a ramshackle tent barely held upright by its poles and spars. Asunçión's hands moved over the straining mirror skin as if across the belly of an exquisite whore, with greed and desire and the fulfillment of imaginings. The trembling sac of tectoplastic imploded and unfolded like a clever trick of origami into a newborn, unholy Harley. With a mandrake scream, it pulled free from the earth, dark ribs and bonings dripping ichor.

"Time's up, Santiago Columbar. Where are they, your little piggies?"

"Five minutes, Miclan."

"No minutes, Santiago Columbar. The game's afoot. Angel." A sword-thin girl, skin and hair bleached to the color of limestone, stood upright on the saddle of her bike. She threw her head back, closed her eyes in the image of spiritual ecstasy. Her nostrils flared and contracted.

"Pheromone trace, not strong, Miclan. Came through here about two hours ago. Headed north-northeast."

"Male, female?"

"Female. A singleton. Do we split the pack, cover more territory?"

"No. We have to be sure of every kill." The dead woman called Miclantecutli straddled her machine and extended a half-gloved hand toward Santiago. "Surf's up, Santiago Columbar."

The high that would rekindle the ashes of disgust was calling down the streets and flame-lit boulevards. Why wait for those who would not, could not, understand? He did not need them: the revelation always was, always had been, personal. He reached for Miclantecutli's hand, swung up onto the seat behind her. Tectoplastic contours caressed his body, his fingers linked across Miclantecutli's tight-buckled belly.

The dead huntress Anansi slid onto the newborn bike and kicked it into life. The Terminal Café thundered to the hunting song of massed hydrocarbon engines. One by one, the bikes peeled off into single file, Miclantecutli and passenger leading, and accelerated north on Vermont.

Forty-nine hours, maximum, and Camaguey had never felt so alive. The colors of curfew ebbing from the sky, the feel of the ocean wind on his face and hands as he drove open-topped north on Harbor, its undertones of deep water melding with sun-burned blacktop and dried-out day, the sense of velocity, of power over space and time at his command: the serendipitous discovery of the extraordinary in the commonplace, like great wine in a nondescript bottle. Was it the inexorability of the countdown that put the edge on the sensual world, or the cascade of tectochemical reactions dumping strange dopamines into his bloodstream?

Squall lines, faintly yellow on the black sky, clung hulldown to the horizon, like a lost navy, silent running. His amplified awareness colored them with painful nostalgia. In childhood North Queensland, the monsoon had begun as that same thread of darkness on the edge of the world. From the dripping veranda he had watched the *noncontratisto* children dance naked in the rain, wishing beyond desire to join them but knowing that his father would never permit it. Change coming upon the earth, and the hope of new life from burned ground; that was what the rains said.

He called up the house on his carware.

"Have all matters pertaining to the reef and the house passed over to my attorney 'ware and activate my will." The machines made no sound, no response, but a psychic tickle told Camaguey they were hearing and obeying. "Update as follows: the reef is not to be sold to corporate buyers. If no buyer is forthcoming, the reef is to be donated to the State Forests and Beaches Department to be maintained as a public utility. Accountancy systems: contact Stella Maris Immortalidad S.A. and activate my resurrection policy."

"It's done," said the Lares and Penates. What was it the Christians said about faith being the assurance of things unseen? No one ever doubted that when a 'ware said a thing was done, it was done.

Forty-eight hours, forty-eight minutes. One hundred kaypeeaitch in a fifty-kilometer snake of red taillights. Felt good. Felt great. He understood his elation now. Freedom. From the burden of possessing, of controlling, of being responsible. From the opinions of others, of their affection and concern. From reticence, from guilt, from the fear of going after those things you have always denied yourself. From caring for this fragile casket of flesh, whether it lived or died. Nothing could happen to him that was not going to happen to him in forty-eight hours—max— forty-seven minutes. The absolute freedom of the terminal.

Camaguey laughed. Peel out. Nothing can touch you. Peel out. Foot to the boards. The fuel cell engine's whisper rose to a sexual moan. Hundred hundred twenty hundred forty hundred fifty hundred sixty hundred eighty, come on come on come on, two hundred, two hundred. Yes. Yes. Yes. The car shapeshifted, slimming and streamlining itself, pressing itself close to the black skin of the highway, growing spoilers and tailfins. Automated alarms screamed a dozen irresponsibilities; *warning warning you are exceeding the speed limit* whajja gonna do, squeal to the cops? At which instant wham! Fifty kilowatts of white light, straight up in his face, like a Twentieth Century Fox searchlight in the sky, and the hot wind whipping back his hair was the downwash from the police liftercraft dopplering in fifty meters above the interchange signs, pulling a high-gee turn, *you did inform, you bastard carware!* and they'd broken into his com channels and a Standard Displeased Cop Voice was intoning something about séor reengaging full automatic mode and they would pull him off onto the soft shoulder. You say, José? Five well-chosen stabs of the forefinger silenced the machine traitors. The car burbled obscenely in its throat as Camaguey took the Exposiçion slip at one hundred and twenty.

God, the radio sounded good.

He could hear them up there, rattling the sky like a tomcat with a can tied to its tail. At an intersection—traffic lights stoned to death long-since—while he waited for a water tanker truck train to grind past, a skinny white kid of indeterminate gender bounced up at his window with a gamine grin and a fistful of weeds.

This was *noncontratisto* country; hard up under the shadow of Necroville, the land of the worse than dead. The *nouveau* poor. Camaguey stopped at a kiosk under the lowering shadow of a decaying housing pile to buy beer from a tin bath sloppy with melting ice. The deposit on the bottle cost more than the beer. The store woman sniffed his cashcard suspiciously and opened the bottle with her teeth. The cheap beer tasted like the very ichor that ran in the veins of the gods. Kids on city bikes came skidding out of the shadows to run lusting hands over the contours of his car. Hay séor, say séor, *poco dinero*, séor. He could offer them only semi-intelligent *plastico*. They followed him up the street toward the blood neon of the dead town.

A hitherto undiscovered side effect of the syndrome. He could smell trouble. Yellow chevroned signs detoured him away from a crater in the road where yet another section of the uncompleted metro had collapsed, and out of one of many dark entries pockmarking the face of a decaying arcology, it hit him. Trouble smelled red, like a berry smells *red*, or blood.

Trouble looked like three people—one man, two women—backing a fourth up against a steel shop shutter spray-bombed with the names of rival *futbol* teams. The taller of the women seized the victim by the hair—a woman, Camaguey saw as her face was twisted into the light—smashed her against the shopfront and knocked her to the ground. Twin lines of blood ran from the corners of her mouth, but her face was blank, void, pain-free. She did not attempt to protect herself as the second woman, screaming incomprehensible abuse in English, planted the spike heel of her boot between her breasts.

Camaguey knew then that she was dead.

"What the hell is going on?"

One whistle and the black hulks of the *proyectos* could pull a thousand knives on this stupid *rico* who didn't know when to mind his own business. Perversity. Never could leave it lie. If it got him into strife, it would almost certainly be for the last time.

Every eye turned on him. He'd seen the stance—between the twin beams of his headlights, silhouetted by back-scatter—in some old flat-screen television thing. A sense of the melodramatic, even now.

"This is nothing of yours. The *seguridados* have been called."

"For the love of Christ!" the dead woman shouted. "They'll fucking murder me!"

The man drove his foot into the pit of her stomach. Squatting down, he held up his finger in front of her face, as if its phallic implications were more threatening than his boot.

"You shut it, you fucking hear me? Shut it. Shut it. Shut it."

The *seguridados* arrived. Raw meat. Never confuse them with the city cops still quartering the sky for Camaguey's taillights. Those were law. These were power. Like *canabarillos*, they came in packs of tens. Fully armed and armored. Unlike *canabarillos*, they did not carry a health warning. Click-clack of weapons brought to bear, and other sounds: bicycle tires, moped engines, voices. Whither Security goes, goeth attention.

"So?"

The tall woman who seemed to be chief witch-pricker held her victim's hand up to the light and opened it. The deathsign engraved there was like fused obsidian.

"She's breaking curfew."

"I'm on a fucking contract!" the dead woman shouted.

"She's fucking poaching on our territory," the man said. By the lights from the *seguridados* streetpuppies, Camaguey could see the suture lines on the muscles beneath his mesh shirt. Off-the-rack.

"Let her up," said the squad leader. The dead prostitute got to her feet, but not before the second woman gratuitously tugged her hair.

"Enough of that," said the squad man, making clear to all that he saw no distinction between hookers living and dead, between any *Exposiçionisto*. "Let's see your tagalong."

"Haven't got it." A bare wrist, fingers wiggling. "The fucking meat will steal anything that isn't nailed down."

"Mind your language."

"She's lying," the tall woman howled. "Can't you see, she never had one. She hasn't got a john, or a contract, or a curfew pass; anything. She's working our pitch."

That red-heat, blood-berry, hot-stone smell again. And more: sweat, saliva. Sex. They want to see her blown into slag, into a smear of fatally disrupted tectors. In front of their eyes. Prime time, spectator sport.

Do not fear them. They can do nothing to you.

"She's with me." He could see himself distorted in the helmet visors as he went to stand beside the dead prostitute. "I hired her."

"You are?"

The *plastico* glittered scarlet.

"Thank you, séor. Do you have documentation of this . . . ah . . . contract?"

"Nute," the dead woman whispered within mike range of the tagalong on his wrist. The device winked conspiratorially and handed name and image to attorney and legal 'warehouses in Vancouver and Freemantle. Commenced by surreptitious key code while the dead prostitute—Nute—tried to lie her way out of a tesler bolt, the contract was signed and sealed in the three and a half seconds it took Camaguey to unfasten the tagalong and hand it to the security officer.

"Isn't five thousand a little . . . excessive . . . séor?"

"Market economy, *teniente*."

The set of the lieutenant's mouth—the only organ of expression visible beneath his helmet—indicated that he reserved a special circle of contempt, beneath even *favelados* and prostitutes, for those who contracted the services of dead whores.

"On your way."

No séor?

"My tag." The *seguridado* held it at arm's length, as if contagious. Perhaps it was. Camaguey took Nute's hand. It was warm, as he remembered the hands of the dead to be. "Keep quiet. Get into the car with me."

"I'm keeping, I'm getting," she said.

They drove off to a barrage of missiles: beer cans, stones, chunks of fallen *arcosanti*, street debris. Sensing danger, the car unfolded a curving roof of blank silver tectoplastic and activated external video links. Seats slid into low profile; Nute pulled at the hem of her mesh dress as the upholstery rearranged itself around her.

"This is some batmobile, *compadre*."

She wiped crusted blood from her face and hands with a moistie from the car's internal valet. Her external wounds, Camaguey noted, were healing with preternatural speed; as he watched, lesions and bruises faded into her dark skin.

"Why did you do it?"

"It's a life of surprises, darlin'."

"You didn't have to do it."

"You say."

"I didn't have a contract. I was poaching. They had me dead to rights. *Mea culpa, mea maxima culpa*."

"I know."

"Look, can we leave off this sawn-off-gumshoe repartee and converse in sentences of more than ten syllables, like intelligent beings?"

"Camaguey."

"Sounds like it should be some old U.S. marine base in Cuba." observing Camaguey's puzzlement, she explained. "I live in this mental Seven-Eleven of archaic information. Drives some people mad. Nute; but you know that. Though you should call me Gallowglass. Another little anachronism; there're Celtic chromosomes back there somewhere, before Adam Tesler *joder*ed them out of all recognition and the rest of the clan smelled the Push coming and upped and fucked away off to Medicine Hat. Mind you, I was a different color then, but I think I like this pelt better. Blends more with the background."

Camaguey unpolarized the windows. At some point the radio had passed the unseen night-land border between thrash and heartbreak.

"When one of my ancestors saved the life of, say, one of your ancestors, your ancestor owed my ancestor, literally, his life. He was owned: body, mind and spirit, and served his master for life, Gallowglass."

"Like a Death House contract."

"Exactly. So either way you've got me." Nute folded her legs under her, like the nesting reflex of some small feral mammal. "So where are we going, Camaguey?"

"Wherever you want, I'll drop you."

"You paid the money, séor, you might as well sniff the fruit. Five thousand dollars buys a lot of mango."

He laughed. It was bitter but good, like the blood red drop of Angostura that made the cocktail perfect.

"It certainly does, Nute."

"So, Séor Camaguey, where to on the Night of the Dead?"

"Certainly not the Terminal Café."

"You got me there, *compadre*."

"Just some folk I've suddenly discovered I don't want to see." Too much to do, too much to see and hear and smell and touch and taste to waste your final night raking over old ashes that will never burn again. He ordered the roof open. The car reconfigured into a bubble-gum fantasia of running boards, long-horn fenders and owl-eyed headlamps, fins and grilles and yearning silver figureheads hungry for slipstream. Disappointed that it had not changed stations in keeping with the car, to the croons and tunes of an older, soft-focus age, Camaguey switched off the radio.

"Whitewalls?" Nute asked, quietly impressed. Whitewalls there were. "Now all we need are some palm trees to cruise beneath." They went and found some. Two parallel lines of them, each five strict meters from its neighbor, diminishing like a draftsman's exercise in perspective toward the colossal pastel pink deathsign that bestrode the boulevard.

Beyond the overgrown grass verges, the casa grandes and bel air chateaux and Tudorettes stood empty as loveless marriages, windows blinded by stones or boarded up by ever-hopeful realtors to discourage squatters. Feral monkeys jabbered in trees garotted by strangling ficus and tropical epiphytes; dozing tectosaurs floated in abandoned swimming pools carpeted with rotting leaves.

"Gone Hollywood," said Nute. "Life-styles of the rich and famous tour. Look!" Camaguey was that fraction too slow following her finger. "I'm sure that was an ocelot."

"It was probably just a cat."

"With a wardrobe like that? You forget, chico, I worked these streets."

On a movie screen in Camaguey's head: blue filter lens; slow pan. Shredded lace curtains blowing in blood-warm wind from the open window. Many cicadas: nightbirds and vervets chorusing. Moonlight on the swimming pool, in the upper room, furniture covered with dust sheets, highlighting oiled flanks moving together, gleaming hips sliding over each other.

Necroville drew them slowly inward.

"Nute."

"Shoot."

"Why do you run the risk of the seguridados catching you, and probably killing you, to work the meat zones?"

She touched the tip of her tongue to her upper lip.

"High moral standards. Better twenty, thirty years—even paying back the reconfiguration—out on the boulevards than two hundred, three hundred? in some contratista brothel. The big putaradas don't like this, so I have to work the meat on their own pasture. Which means I get shot at occasionally. But I tell you this, *chico*, if I turn tricks solo, it's my decision, understand? My choice. My career path. Specializations like mine cater to a very select marketplace, who can afford premium prices. Your five thousand, Rim, wasn't too far wide of the mark."

Bruises fading, lacerations sealing and healing without a scar.

"You're a transmorph."

"Succubus, incubus, shapeshifter. And you thought it was only your car. The brothers in Saint John are doing things with tectronics you wouldn't believe, meatboy."

Nute looked into a sky pregnant with autumn constellations.

"More stars than there are in heaven, they used to say."

Camaguey did not understand. "Nute, how old are you?"

"Old enough to remember when no gentleman asked a lady a question like that. I'm like the Queen of England used to be, when they had a queen. I've got two birthdays. Well, one birthday, one rebirthday. How old I am depends which one you count from. Count from one, I'm thirty-five: Generation Zero. First born from the dead, or thereabouts. Count from the other, well, let's be diplomatic to an old whore: I remember Reagan. Just."

By either calendar, she did not look an hour over twenty-two. They drove toward the Necroville gate. Until they turned onto this abandoned boulevard, Camaguey had not known Necroville was the place he truly wanted to go. Now no place could be finer.

"Nute how did you die?"

"Language is a funny thing, Camaguey. Fifty years ago, that question would have had no meaning. Nonsensical. The combination of words existed, but the thing they described was impossible. Does our ability to speak impossibilities sow with it seeds of possibility? Simply wore out, Camaguey. Age eighty-three, and everything decided to call time one morning. We don't all die in the fast lane."

I know. I've tried.

"Quid pro quo, Camaguey. That's the way the contract works. So, tell me, how old are you?"

"Twenty-seven."

"Funny age" was all Nute would say.

The glow from the gate obliterated the stars. Life was a series of gates through which you could not return: childhood, puberty, adulthood, partnership, career, childbearing, childrearing. None were as absolute in their implications as this overbearing wedge of luminous plastic. He tried to envision it as Nute might, as a going-home, the seal of safety and security. It defied him. The Final Gate. Forty-seven hours, three minutes.

"Nute, what is it like to die?"

"Can I see your identification, séor?"

Pink fluorescence back-lit the trooper bending over his door. Camaguey squirted identifiers and the contract with Nute from his tagalong.

"This is the dead woman you contracted?"

Sniffers and scanners ran their noses over the car's contours, pausing to turn their full attention on Nute.

"She is."

"Ah-ha."

Nute smiled gaminely at the securityman. The scanners slid over the top of the car and sniffed accusingly at Camaguey.

And the gate howled.

Camaguey sat petrified at the eye of a hurricane of sound, alarms blaring as steel fingers clawed out of the road surface in front of him.

"The fuck out of here!" Nute yelled in Camaguey's ear. "Get. The fuck. Out of. Here."

Whitewalls smoking, the car clawed backward out of the trap. The sirens wailed on. Stunned troopers reached for weapons.

"You watch the road, I'll watch them," Nute shouted. "Jesus fuck, man, what have you done?"

Camaguey scored a swath across the cracked concrete as he swung the car around. His rearviews showed him *seguridados* kneeling, taking aim, their weapons flowing into new, threatening configurations.

"Me done? What have you done?"

He threw the car through the five-meter gap between two palms and went careening along the old sidewalk, scything down the tall grass with his chrome bumpers and hoping that the trees would screen him from tesler fire.

"I done? I done nothing, meat. It wasn't Nute set their darlin' little tectronic activity alarms singing their hearts out."

"What do you mean?"

"Right. Here. Here! It's a warren of service alleys back of these haciendas. We can tie them up with their own bootlaces in here." With the classic Hollywood screech of tires, the car right-angled and plunged through a curtain of Spanish moss. Proximity warnings blared: taking mercy on the car's jangled nervous system, Camaguey switched to full manual as he hurtled along the dark, narrow tunnel of crumbling masonry and overhanging trees. "What I mean is; the gates have an in-built early-warning system to pick up any unlicensed dead trying to get in or out of Necroville. And as, thanks to your largess, I no longer qualify as unlicensed, that leaves one major contender for the title."

He slammed the car to a halt.

"No! Nute, no . . ."

"I could smell something wasn't quite *mechaieh kosher* about you the moment we met. Jesus fuck, I get pulled out from under the tits of the Exposiçion Young Gun and Neo-Nazi Club by someone who it turns out the *seguridados* will happily slag the entire neighborhood to make sure they erase. One hundred and twentysomething is too young and beautiful for Big Death."

"Nute, listen; I bought up your contract. No necro could do that."

"No? Then what the hell are you?" She glanced up, seeing things he could not. "We'll debate it later." Camaguey felt the prickle of re-focused gravity fields brush his skin as Nute grabbed his hand and with supernatural strength dragged him out of the car. "Run. Whatever happens, don't stop, don't look back."

"Will I turn into a pillar of salt?"

"Something like."

They ran. Behind them, the alley exploded in a maelstrom of sus-tained tesler fire.

"My car . . ."

"I'll buy you a whole garageful, honey. Go go go; the alleys restrict their fields of fire, but if they catch us up against a wall, we're *sodai gomi*."

Camaguey glanced behind him. The *mechadors* were black-on-black patterns of navigation lights hovering above a blister of boiling silver slag, heads turning left-right-left, questing, sensing. No more nighthawk radio, no more cruising the boulevards with the top down. He ran.

"Through here, come on, come on." Nute had bent up a corner of rusted chain-link fencing. "The whole district is lousy with old irrigation ditches and watercourses, a lot go right under the wire into Necroville and the *seguridados* don't know one percent of one percent of them." Camaguey rolled under the wire, Nute joined him and together they scurried across the weed-infested red-top of an abandoned tennis court. Ghosts of tramlines; rotting strands of net hung from the posts; a vaguely phallic ball-server-robot corroded politely in the corner. There was a perfume of night-blooming flowers.

"Oh fuck."

The *mechador* floated up over the peeling gingerbread cupola atop the double garage, its black insect-head still scanning: a deliberate, terrifying left-right-left-right. It let itself down onto the brick patio with that same slow deliberation. There could be no hope that it had not seen them.

"Move!" Nute screamed. The mantis head locked into position. The tennis court gate was five meters away. Faceted eyes opened, weapons pods swung into firing arcs. The tennis court gate was four meters away. The *mechador* tilted forward and came flying across the riotous lawn. The tennis court gate was three meters away. The *mechador* hurdled the wire fence in one gravitational bound. The tennis court gate was one meter away.

The tennis court gate was locked, the padlock and chain a garland of solid rust.

The entire hunting cadre were dropping out of the air, soft as thistledown.

With a scream of desperation Nute ripped gate, lock, chain housing away from their mounts and flung them at the lead *mechador*. The robot reeled on its impellor field; in the second's diversion, Nute pulled Camaguey through a tangle of rampant clematis. He fell painfully into a concrete-lined trench in the bottom of which lay a sluggish few centimeters of stinking water. He held up beslimed hands, observed his ruined pants in disgust.

"No one ever died of a bit of dirt," Nute said, pushing past him to rattle a metal grille that barred their access to a concrete culvert. "Right, Nute. Gird up thy loins." She balled fists; it was dark beneath the covering of creepers, but Camaguey imagined he saw her flesh flow and congeal into twin battering rams of white bone. The rusted metal sprang and flaked at the first blow, at the second, the bars bent, at the third, they split. A prescient shiver prompted Camaguey to look up. Lights moved beyond the camouflage of leaves and sickly scented blooms.

"Nute . . ."

She was bending back the bars with her bare hands. Her strength was beyond belief. A useful talent for a prostitute. As was shapeshifting.

"Look at my fucking dress. It never happens to the ones you don't like."

"I'll buy you an entire shopful, honey."

"Can the Hollywood drolleries and just get your ass into that hole." She pushed him in. The culvert was a meter-high circle of absolute black, ankle-deep in vile liquid. "Nute's underground railroad, next stop, Necroville. And remember, *chico*, you owe me an explanation."

Camaguey threw himself into darkness. Behind him the concrete ditch went up in a white rave of tesler fire.

Forty-six hours, forty-four minutes.

Huen's three ambitions:

Uno: to picnic on Mount Rushmore. The Girl Who Flew Up Lincoln's Nose.

Dos: to beat the cross-country unassisted glide record.

Tres: to get inside Toussaint's black and pink helix-pattern flight-suit.

She would pass on numbers *uno* and *dos* if she could get her legs around *tres*. And she would, in time. Even the stone face of *Presidente* Lincoln carved into Rushmore could be worn down, in time, and the Lodoga Eyrie was not so large a place that he could hope to hide from her. The Eyrie, one of twenty that studded the western slopes of Griffith Park, was an end-of-run architectronic housing kit that from without looked like a giant head of broccoli, and from within was like living inside your own left lung. Life beneath the translucent green faceted domes, among the alveoli and ribbing, enforced the same social openness and intimacy found among submariners, circus performers and athletes. No privacy. No secrecy. No body modesty. To a group like the Lodoga Eagles, where individuality was submitted to the greater ideal of flying, this spirit of naked community was a necessary social cement. It stopped people eating each other's faces off.

Huen found the pink and black suit hanging from a peg epoxied to the hygiene center's bubble wall. Sounds of showering. She slipped in, positioned herself in a carefully casual pose against the wash basin and nakedly admired him wet.

"Party tonight?" *(I could slip in there with you, but you'd heave me out.)*

"Dead town, but not a party."

"What for?" *(He's got someone else, bastard.)*

"Just some friends I have to see."

"Anyone I know?" *(I will cut her living heart from her breast and burn it before her eyes.)*

"Shouldn't think so."

"Can I come too? It's boring here. Everyone's boring." *(Try leaving me behind.)*

The hiss and gurgle of water shut off. Toussaint screwed gel out of his ears with a corner of a towel. *(I could do that.)*

"No, it's sort of personal. A sort of reunion. Some other time, if you don't mind."

"There's fireworks, look!" Standing on tiptoe, Huen could see their crimson blossoms spread across the valley below.

"Hey, Toussaint. There's something out there."

Mourn not the shepherd boy
Who, crying "wolf:"
Ends as crunchy lupo-snax,

Toussaint warned.

"No shit, Toussaint. Third time this week."

"Probably just dogwalkers or kids looking for somewhere to fool or pop something." But he came half dry for a look. "Can't see anything." Huen followed him into his space. By no stretch could it be distinguished with the description "room," even "space" asked too much of an ill-smelling dormpod glued to the curving wall and a hanging locker.

"You should wear that, that looks nice on you," said Huen, nodding at his one semiformal outfit, carefully selected to combine with the greatest number of social functions.

Back there, as he thought of it, five-hundred-dollar-a-leg suits hand-tailored by the dead town's finest craftspersons gathered dust and shrank subtly, imperceptibly, year by year. Any business that required the wearing of a suit was a piss-poor expense of a life. He could see the suits, but not the shoes. Never the shoes. Never intended to follow in father's footsteps, then.

Do we merely exchange one uniform for another?

"No, I think this." Streetwear. Kind-climate fashion. Much skin. Huen shrugged.

"I still think you'd look nicer in the other one. Depends if it's folk you want to impress or not."

"Just that *corillo* of friends I used to be in. We meet every Night of the Dead, down at the Terminal Café in Saint John. Appropriate place to meet, I suppose, the Terminal Café; the thing died years ago. We're just toasting a gaudy corpse. We take turns every year to arrange an event, something unusual, a trip, an expedition, something. Last year we went in search of the Cartoon Graveyard. That was my event. This year it's Santiago Columbar's turn. God knows what his idea of a good night out is."

Brother Mohammed, who had been hanging by his heel hooks from the ceiling in his two-by-two-meter corner of the Eyrie, suddenly reached up for his grab bar and deftly lowered himself to the ground.

"You know Santiago Columbar? He used to be my hero. Like every great *futbol* and *movimiento* star rolled into one. There was one he did: Lycanthropeon Mark Three, a time-base Proprioceptor. Every twenty-nine and a half days it kicked in and told your nervous system you were a wolf. Gather ten *compadres* together, one two three down the hatch and you're a wolf pack. Awoo! Werewolves of London. It was very well done, you could watch yourself change as the proprioceptors started to work; with the virtualizer expansion kit, you could program it so you could see your packmates as wolves too. You actually thought and felt and sensed like a wolf. Good stuff. Took a whole year for it to work out my system. By then I'd found flying."

"You should pick your heroes more carefully," said Toussaint darkly. "Does anyone know a cab company number?"

"You'll not get one tonight," Huen said with mildly malevolent relish. "The lives won't go down into the valley, and the deads are all booked up."

To prove her wrong, the phone gave Toussaint a Paramount City pedicab number. *Ten minutes*, they said. Ten minutes, to the second, the pedicab clanged its bell on the gravel outside the Eyrie.

"Well, have a nice time, y'all," said Huen without grace.

"That's not the idea," said Toussaint. The Lodoga Eyrie sphinctered its door shut behind him. Evening: fine, warm, temperature thirty-two degrees humidity ninety-three percent wind west veering north-northwest, light, about eight kph. The last infrared glow of curfew in the sky. Premonitions of thunder. Earth smells; laterites and things that grow in the earth. Fires in the valley below.

"You the guy wants the Terminal Café?" asked the *cochera*, a heavily muscled dead woman dressed in shorts and jewelry who did not seem the least exerted by the steep climb to the Eyrie. Her head was shaved but for five carefully wound dreadlocks at the base of her skull. "Hope you don't mind sharing." The incumbent was a man of indeterminate age, with that kind of face that you are sure you know from *somewhere* and torment yourself the rest of the night trying to hang a name on. He seemed uncomfortable in his slightly-too-formal clothes, like a surfer at a wedding.

"Fine evening," the fare said.

The *cochera* had dismounted and was fiddling with her gears.

A man was walking across the gravel from the dense bamboo that screened the base of the Eyrie.

A prickle, a tickle, of something not totally right.

The passenger leaned forward confidentially.

"You know," he said, "you really should have worn the other outfit. It would have looked much nicer."

Toussaint grabbed the tube-steel frame to swing himself as far away as he could. Land. Run. Hide. Found instead: the chromium emission-head of a tunker, thirty centimeters from his Third Eye, in the left hand of the man who had emerged from the bamboo.

"Back in the cab, Séor Tesler."

Tunker: popular, cheap, mass-market antipersonnel weapon, comprising a hi-watt maser and a supply of energy cartridges. Short-ranged but anti-social. Works on the poodle-in-the-microwave-Urban-Legend principle, except this version, it's your brain that flashes to steam and blows your head apart. Can't beat the good old exploding-head scene.

Séor Tesler. Séor Tesler. Séor Tesler.

The seam along his hump felt raw and red and hideously vulnerable.

"Who are you?"

"That's Texeira"—the man with the tunker smiled shallowly—"this is Shipley"—the well-muscled woman nodded, a glitter of silver a second tunker half-hidden in her fist—"and my name is Quebec. Which doesn't tell you a lot. And isn't meant to, Séor Xavier Tesler."

"I don't go by that name anymore."

"We know. As you've by now guessed, we've been keeping an eye on you. And an ear, and several other, subtler, senses."

"You intercepted the call to the cab company."

"Of course we did."

A pause. Then: "You. Who are you?" Toussaint used the intimate pronoun. *¿Qui es tu?* The man who called himself Quebec smiled. Suddenly angry, Toussaint launched himself out of the pedicab.

"I'm not playing this anymore. You won't shoot me. You need something only Xavier Tesler can give and if you kill me you won't get it. So, I'm walking."

He turned his back on the tunkers. He felt as if the seams in his skin gaped wide and the intimate mechanisms of his soul were displayed to human view.

"You're right, of course, Toussaint." Toussaint stopped, suspecting that he had been let this small tactical victory only because it secured them a greater, strategic gain. "Your friend, Huen, the one who gets wet when you're around, call her out. Tell her you've changed your mind, you'd like her to come down to meet Santiago Columbar at the Terminal Café.''

How long had they been watching listening smelling that they could flay his life so bare?

"Or?''

"Three armed desperadoes against twelve unarmed, peace-loving flyers?''

"Fuck you, Quebec.''

The woman called Shipley grinned. Texeira accompanied Toussaint to the door. Huen answered.

"Decided you couldn't bear a night in the dead town without fun-loving me?''

Toussaint forced a smile, a flippant answer.

"Man's prerogative to change his mind. So, you coming?''

"Try stopping me.'' He felt sick as he watched her return wearing her very favorite silk jacket. "So, let's party.''

Even *aguila* reactions were not enough to save her. The man who called himself Texeira took a step forward. And his face peeled off in a spurt of liquid silver *something* (a ghost of a smile still on it) and launched itself at Huen's eyes, ears, nose, mouth. Huen opened her mouth to scream. The silver liquid poured in and choked it in her throat. Her eyes were blind ovals of mirror. Her hands waved spastically, help-lessly. Her pants darkened with urine.

Texeira toppled like a broken marble caryatid to the carefully rake-sculpted gravel and did not move.

Toussaint fell to his knees and retched dryly, uselessly. Black bile. Bitter acid. A hand touched his shoulder.

"Séor Tesler.'' The voice, the touching hand, were Huen's. The words could not possibly be hers. Her crotch was wet, the fabric dark red where she had pissed herself.

"Now do you understand who and what we are?'' Quebec asked. "I think you should know that I deeply regret having to use this form of leverage on you, Toussaint. I had hoped that your particular . . . per-sonal history? might give you a sympathy for our cause. Your friend Huen will be returned to you, intact, on the completion of our assign-ment. Texeira has taken control of the higher cognitive and motor func-tions but has left his replication systems inactive. A coup de tête, you might say. To settle any doubts there may be in your mind, noncom-pliance with our instructions will result in Texeira fully reconfiguring her. As with conventional resurrection, the process is irreversible, and fatal. It will still look like her, sound like her, but it'll be dead inside. Real zombie stuff. Ask our friend there." He indicated Texeira's discarded erstwhile body.

"You bastard."

"Not so, Toussaint. Not at all. Shipley." The big woman—whose body had she stolen, with its proud big muscles and careful dreads?—moved around the pirated pedicab, stripping it of nontectoplastic ornaments and artifacts. Eventually satisfied, she placed her hands on the rickety contraption and immediately the nanoplastic blistered and melted under her touch.

"Careful, Shipley, there isn't much mass in that, we can't afford to waste any." Shipley dealt Quebec a sullen over-shoulder look and continued with her warping and weaving. Spars stretched, bars elongated between her cajoling fingers into monomolecule fibers, struts unfolded into dripping sheets of film. Suggestions of wings. Suggestions of airframes.

"As you've no doubt guessed by now, we are not your garden-variety dead," Quebec said silkenly. "Likewise, ours is no ordinary assignment."

"You want me to take you to my father, and kill him."

"Right in the first part. Wrong in the second. All we want is to meet Adam Tesler."

"And?"

"Convince him of the impossibility of his position," said the Huen-thing. On the gravel lay three microfoil wings, folded like soft gray moths. The dead woman called Shipley smiled, proud of her work.

"Fly now," she said.

YoYo on a moped. Wearing: leather cutoffs, sleeveless jacket, Garçon Garçon hat, fingerless gloves, serious footwear: over filmskin virtuality bodyglove. The Illustrated woman. Putt putt putt: the moped's alcohol engine puts out fifty kaypeeaitch max, looks good in traffic, or the mob-pedestrian dynamics of the dead towns. Going: downtown, dead town, to a street-corner cantina to meet Martika Semalang the dead woman.

"I've got a brief, if you want a shot at it," Jorge, the investigating attorney, had said, finding YoYo slumped in the corner of her black and white room, staring at three-quarters of a bottle of José Cuervo.

"Fuck it, Jorge, I'm finished," she'd said. "And Ellis tells me this *serafino* following me everywhere I go like Mary's fucking little lamb is good karma? Well, Carmen Miranda, you going to send me a truckload of dead turkeys tomorrow, that make you feel good?"

"Come on, YoYo. You're a good lawyer. The contempt citation wasn't your fault."

"This is meant to make me feel better, is it, Jorge? I know I'm as fucking good as anyone out there, but they still threw me and hired someone who isn't going to be haunted by a Drag Queen Carmen Miranda all her life."

"Talk to me when you're talkable to, YoYo."

Which, after telling Trio her long-standing wish was granted, she was free to do whatever she wanted with the stairway to heaven 'ware, was three hours later.

"This brief."

"It's a private investigation," Jorge had said, passing YoYo a beer from the communal coolcabinet. "It's not your kind of thing, I know, but I'm up to here with the Margolis case and I don't like to turn down work."

"It's my kind of thing when I lose the biggest case of my career," YoYo said.

"Her name is Martika Semalang. You're to meet her here . . ." Jorge scribbled a location in the Saint John necroville on an adhesive notelet and stuck it on YoYo's wrist. Writing. Jorge and his quaint anachronisms. "You can read this okay?" YoYo nodded. "She'll be at a street table between eight and nine-thirty. Order the *camarónes español*. They're really good."

"Face-to-face?"

"Meat to meat. No virtuality. Raw law. Where's your gumshoe instinct?"

"I don't have a gumshoe instinct," YoYo said bitterly. "Perry Mason is my Hollywood archetype. Was. Can I borrow your mope?"

"Don't forget to fill it up. One thing I can tell you." Jorge smiled theatrically. Actors and lawyers have always been soul brothers. "This Martika Semalang: she woke up one morning to find herself dead and wants to know why."

The Sunset *seguridados* check YoYo's tagalong and wave her through with the usual male testosterone ritual chorus of coyote yips and slow, sly upcurlings of the tongue to meet the bottom lip of the visor. *Sit on this, mi hermana.* Diseased assholes. She's through, into Necroville.

Street life. It's wonderful. That hot baked blacktop smell. That horn section on the corner, saxes down and swingin' low. That spice of *carnival*! And because it is wonderful, and because it hangs from a hair over a very great height, it makes the anger and the hurt of the Industries Gabonais case so much sourer and sharper. "How did I lose it?" is not so much further along from "How could I lose it?"

Ambition overvaulting ability. She could hear her parents snickering all the way down in Marina del Rey. Why could she not have taken their advice and become a third-generation welfare bum? If it was good enough for them to rock their days away on a sampan down in the Floating World blissfully immersed in Mah-Jongg, cheap television and state handout *bhang*, shaking their heads in sorrow at the wicked wicked ways of the wicked wicked world, it should have been good enough for her, but oh no, not her, not their willful Number Two Daughter, she had to go and Be Someone and Do Something with her life. Time enough to work after you're dead. All eternity to work, then. We tell her, but will she listen? Quiet now, it's time for *Camino Real*, your mother's favorite.

YoYo could not understand the concept of *getting above your station*; egalitarianism was as tightly wrapped around her DNA as fatalism was around her parents. So: squat on your haunches with bilge water lapping at your ankles smiling smugly as if you know something important about the character of the universe not given to other mortals.

Smile, nod, tilt the teapot spout, *so.* Meredith Mok's reckless daughter is on the up again. This Martika Semalang's going to get Number One. YoYo Mok twisted the throttle. The little streetbike coughed up a flat-out fifty-five. Race on, steel juggernaut.

YOYO, a videowall on the side of the U-Bend/We-Mend suddenly said, I'M SORRY, I DIDN'T DO ANYTHING, HONEST. Carmen Miranda's apologies followed her up the avenue, leapfrogging across the street from screen to screen. YOYO, AM I STILL YOUR FRIEND? By the time she parked the mope in the rack outside Tacorifico Superica's, the *serafino* had resorted to pleading. PLEASE PLEASE PLEASE

YOYO, said the side of the Banco Nogidaches. Suspicions of tropical fruit ghosted among the corporate pixels. TALK TO ME, YOYO. People in the street looking up smiled, thinking lovers' quarrels, sudden and hard as summer rain; reconciliation, romance and roses.

"Listen, you fucker," YoYo whispered into her wrist tagalong, by means of which she supposed the *serafino* had tracked her to the necroville. "I am on a brief. I am very lucky to get this brief. By rights, I should be out on my ass. I should be thumbing my way back to Sampan City. That I'm not is because I have good friends. This is my last chance. Absolutely. Categorically. Unequivocally. So I do not want anything to prejudice this. Like my client getting suspicious because I am on first-name terms with advertising billboards. ¿*Comprendes?*"

Banco Nogidaches's corporate smiling Angeleno with halo of orbiting dollar bills spasmed and morphed into the carmine leer of La Miranda. The disgraceful old queen winked and regurgitated a talk-bubble reading SURE THING YOYO. YOU EVER NEED ME, JUST WHISTLE. The last thing to vanish was the pineapple that crowned its tutti-frutti hat. A scattering of *carnivalistos* applauded politely.

Tacorifico Superica's was of that school of vernacular street eaterias that, through absolute rejection of change, eventually becomes the pinnacle of fashion by the Kalifornia-Karma principle of what goes around, comes around. YoYo lined up at the tin counter, received her exquisite food on a plastic plate for a pittance, bought a bottle of dead town beer—freed from the exigencies of eating as a chemical necessity, the dead ate well, drank better and always managed to make it taste exactly the way it smelled—and took her tray out to the table in the dusty yard, where a handsome dead woman sat beneath a dead tree, poking at a dish of bean salad with a fork.

"Martika Semalang?" YoYo felt conspicuously teenage; smiling and spotty. Face-to-face. Meat to meat. I can't do this. What if there's bean skin on her teeth, or I can smell her breath? Just think sampans bobbing on the high tide. "I'm YoYo Mok, from Allison-Ismail-Castardi. I've been assigned to investigate your case."

Can she tell I'm making this up as I go along?

The dead woman shook her proffered hand. YoYo pulled up a chair.

"Do you mind if I record this?" She slipped the tagalong off her arm and set it on the table. "I don't write very well, I'm afraid." Slap hands on thighs. Right. So: "Séora Semalang, what exactly is it you want me to do?"

"I want to know how I died," Martika Semalang said. Her voice was very soft and low, barely audible over the street noise beyond the clinker-block wall. "And, if the answer is as I suspect, I want to know why I died, and who killed me."

"What is it you suspect?" YoYo asked.

"That I was murdered."

Murder as a means of information suppression had been rendered largely obsolete by resurrection technology. Murder of the heart remained as popular and widespread as it had since Cain Had a Bad Day, and was considerably safer to commit. Convicted culprits could look forward to at maximum a ten-year banning order, at minimum a suspended sentence. After all, their victims were still engaged in some form of walking, talking, eating and shitting.

For this dead woman not to know who had murdered her, if indeed she had been murdered, to even suspect the nature of her own death, implied so many impossibilities that YoYo felt her nostrils dilate at the very thought.

"You see, Séora Mok, ("YoYo, please") YoYo, I have no memory of anything prior to the lid of my Jesus tank lifting and the Death House technicians helping me out."

"You didn't know you were dead?"

"Can you imagine what it was like to learn that?"

No. She could not imagine. She doubted anyone could imagine it. Though YoYo understood intellectually that this woman's estate would inevitably be hers also, she had never been able to accept emotionally the darkness of death, the eternal light of resurrection. In her shorts and jacket, Garçon Garçon hat and bodyglove, YoYo Mok shivered. Clouds edged over the ebbing red glow of the skysign.

"There have been instances of this kind of absence of memory," YoYo said. Her dinner on its plastic plate gathered flies. "If someone dies in childhood, or infancy, there can be a continuity gap. But, as you say, they generally remember the death. In more extreme cases, there are antenatal resurrections; miscarriages or abortions. In those, there would be no memory of death, no memory of any previous life at all. There was an incident last year, the Sifuentes case, quite famous: a woman up in San Yaquinto was convinced her houseboy was her aborted son returned to haunt her because he had no memory of any previous life. The woman was a complete fuckup."

The dead woman said, "No, I don't think that can be the case. As you probably know, when you are resurrected, you are permitted a few small personal effects of your prelife if you wish them." YoYo didn't know. "When I came out of the tank, I was given this." A self-seal plastic envelope. She tipped the contents onto the tin table. Contents totaling one old, flat videostill, creased at the corners, toners cracking and fading.

A girl, pubescent and slightly self-conscious in the fashions and styles of twenty years ago, sitting on the bottom porch step of a twentieth-century wooden suburban house, knees drawn up and encircled by her arms. Ivy front gardens and no fences. Weather sunny, as it always was in childhood. The girl was hugging an unhappy tabby cat and squinting into the camera; the photographer, eager for a homesy shot, had forgotten the sun was behind him and cast a shadow on the gravel path. The house bore both name and number: 1345: Sunnymede. Some of these old developments went way back. Half a vehicle in half a drive. Looked like an early Nihan Cityhopper. The half of the license plate YoYo could read carried a Tres Valles code. Possibly a San Fernando suffix. That narrowed it down to only three million licensees.

The girl bore a passing resemblance to Martika Semalang, but in the mutable world of dead flesh, such significances were slight.

"When you came out of the tank, did you have to be taught things? Toilet training, or how to walk, or talk, or read, things like that?"

"No. None of that. Everything was intact, except my memories of my life. I know what the world's like, it's my part in it that is missing. You can understand my suspicions."

"That your memories were deliberately erased."

"Which in turn strengthens the case for murder."

"Your name, it sounds Southeast Asian, Malayalam."

"Means nothing. It's not what I was called. I've checked."

YoYo sucked in her lower lip. In virtuality, the unconscious moue generated a pleasing dermal tingle, like an allover kiss.

"It's possible that it's not gone, merely buried deep," she said. "I'm no expert on the neurochemistry of memory, but as far as I know, the engrams that encode our memories are hardwired and can't be totally erased, but the chemical codes that locate them can be disrupted. In which case, the right stimulus might be enough to trigger an association, which in turn could start an avalanche of remembering. A smell would be good; it's the most powerful activator of memories, so those who know about these things say."

"I have considered this," Martika Semalang said. A lift of the finger summoned a *mesero*, a talent YoYo had never possessed and envied in others. "Another beer for the séora, and I'll have a *minerale*. However, I don't know how to start, or even where to start."

YoYo lifted the old snapshot. Summers were better then, even in boat town. You swam, you ran about, you got brown and lithe.

"I can run crossmatches on the vehicle make and license with the relevant municipal directories and architectural archives. That should tell us where this picture was taken."

"Is that hard?"

"No problem at all." The tagalong on the table dutifully extended a filament which YoYo grafted into a film circuit in her wrist. "Excuse me a moment." YoYo flipped up her bodyglove hood. Her eyes blurred with tears as the optic interfacers burrowed around her eyeballs and hooked into the visual cortex. She blinked them away, and was In.

The tagalong's cel-link was narrow and mollusc-slow, the virtuality low grade and grainy—at times idiosyncratically monochrome, as, she thought, all good gumshoe movies should be—but it was In. Boogie Street. It felt so good even in scratch monochrome that she momentarily forgot her purpose, forgave even the low-resolution poster-paint blobs of the Carmen Miranda lurking on the edge of the field of vision.

The protocols were swiftly and easily established, though she gritted her teeth when the databases interrogated her business account on its creditworthiness. She should have asked for cash up front.

Question: (she created a small file for future reference, nested within a cage of orbiting interrogatives) how does a dead woman afford Allison-Ismail-Castardi's class of investigation? Even that of its most junior sub-sub-probationer? If she was uncontracted there should be an account in one of the big *Immortalidads* that would contain identity, employment, health records and other valuable information toward coloring in the life, death and resurrection of Martika Semalang.

Later, YoYo. Defying gravity five kays above the luminous net of the city, three windows were opening in the red night before her. The transitions were a little jerky, the rendering crude and, to her jacked-up senses, interminably labored. Thirteen thousand No. 1345s in this city of twenty-two million angels. Forty thousand Nihan late-model get-arounds, and that was the finest she could slice it; the photograph had missed the year prefix. Six matches of model with house number in the estimated timeframe. Getting hotter. Three failed at the first fence. Not the right valley. Smelling good. Smelling *blood*. Her accelerated synapses caught the snap in the architectural archive one microsecond before the geriatric 'ware binged her. A flicker of her finger superimposed archive over photograph. *Correlation 92%* the computer told her in gauche chrome letters tumbling out of the infrared sky. *Where's your gumshoe instinct now?* YoYo crowed triumphantly at it, hovering above the virtual city-web like Peter Pan.

And *out*.

Total elapsed real time: eight point three seconds. Opticals and aurals disengaged. She pushed the hood back from her head, tried not to look pleased with herself.

"We think the photograph is of 1345 Enero Heights, Mission Oaks. It's about thirty-five kays north of here, up beyond San Fernando."

"We?"

YoYo shrugged. "We." The waiter returned with the drinks. *Minerale* and Red Hat. He uncapped YoYo's bottle with his teeth. Martika Semalang paid with a *plastico*. Red rockets rose above Tacorifico Superica's rusting iron roof and exploded with muted, soft reports. Sweet novas.

"Wait. Séora Semalang, wait. Just one moment."

YoYo intercepted the card between hand and scanner. The waiter raised his eyebrows in the way that says *as long as someone pays and leaves a suitable propina.*

"Can I check something?" Without waiting for permission, YoYo ran the card through her tagalong. With her best Thursday Night Poker Face, she asked, "This card, where did you get it?"

"What do you mean?"

"There are five and three-quarter million dollars in credit." The waiter, equally poker-faced, recalculated his tip. "What I mean is, a woman wakes up and finds herself dead one morning with no memory that she ever lived, never mind died, and the guts of six million dollars in her little black card and isn't a little curious as to how she came by it?"

"I presumed it came out my *Immortalidad* policy."

"Séora, only the very rich and the very beautiful get that big a pocketful of small change from the Death House. Did you never query this, check with the bank? Who are you with anyway?" YoYo flipped the card over between her fingers. The Earth-Wind-Ocean-Fire quadranted circle of Pacific First Consolidated. "You shouldn't even be with these people. You can't be with these people."

"Shouldn't I? Can't I?"

"PFC don't have a necro division. Lawyer talk time. The Barantes Ruling established that the dead—you'll pardon me using the expression—were not human, and therefore could not be afforded the protection of and responsibilities to human—living—law. It cuts deep, the Barantes Ruling, it's the bedrock of our socioeconomic system. The financial sectors are no more immune from it than anything else; technically, being dead, you should have no need for, and no entitlement to, money. The no-pockets-in-shrouds principle. However, our system requires that there be a Ghost Economy; I pay José here and José pays a whack here to his landlord, who is some *blanco* meatboy floating around in a swimming pool up in Copananga like the Great White Whale, and a whack there to the power and water and municipal services companies—which, though their workers are all deads, are owned down to the last rivet by meatboys—and a big whack right down the middle to the Death House. The power companies aren't obliged to sell José electricity, the landlord has no formal lease naming him as a tenant; it's all one big gentleman's agreement.

"And where there's an economy there will be banks sure as scum on a shower curtain. The big meat banks set up independent dead subsidiaries—ghost banks—that do all the things they do but don't actually exist. Our world is as dependent on things unseen, on articles of faith and accepted premises, as medieval Catholic Europe. And only then by consensus. Because thee, and me, agree it should work this way.

"Pacific First Consolidated claim the moral high ground in not being party to hypocrisy of the Ghost Economy. Demeans the law, they say. Truth is, they're strongly Pro-Life. A lot of New Millennium Born Agains on their board."

The irony amused Martika Semalang. Like her dress, her demeanor, the manner in which she addressed a trauma beyond the imagination of the living; like everything YoYo had seen of her, it was graceful. Elegant. YoYo felt lumpen and unfeminine. So: she liked zips. She liked clothes that did something. She liked her leather. Wasn't it resurrected skin? Nothing more natural than skin. YoYo held up the card again.

"I could find out where it came from. The five and three-quarter million."

She evaded the Carmen Miranda *serafino* hanging in the imaginary sky and slipped into the embrace of her stairway to heaven 'ware. She would need powerful familiars to penetrate the arcana of Pacific First Consolidated. Disguised as a debit transaction, she approached the bank's Shinto *tori* icon. Again, the slowness and jerkiness of the tagalong's low-resolution link frustrated her.

The spirit gate gradually opened up before her.

No wonder Iago's erstwhile business partners had knocked him off the corporate perch. Within three point two seconds real elapsed time his 'ware had Open-Sesamed Martika Semalang's bank account and was scrolling statements down a small event window.

She shopped *there*?

She spent *that*, on *that*?

She bought *those*?

She fetched up hard against an opening balance. Six million dollars, Rim. Hard as they come. Sniffing true trails from false, YoYo checked foreign transactions. The enormous gyrations of transnational banking spun up a credit transfer from the Purmerend Bank of Lucerne. Swiss. The Gnomes of Zurich, extended family. Tighter than a Calvinist's ass.

"Well, Iago, let's see if you're as good as you say you are."

The bodyglove stacked her in sensory deprivation for a few seconds while the laboring tagalong exited Pacific First Consolidated and, disguised as an international money-market gambit, uplinked to Lucerne.

All this from a backyard table at Tacorifico Superica's, with a half-drunk bottle of Red Hat and a plate of cold *camarónes* in front of you. Is there seriously any other way to do business?

Rezz up. Purmerend Bank was a rather old-fangled and fuddy-duddy *corporada* ziggurat. Swiss conservatism apparently extended to their web iconographers. Setting behind her what happened last time she stood in the shadow of a similar Swiss pyramid, she rode the wave in.

Her insane surf in behind three million imaginary Rim Dollars looking for a little fiscal convertability set alarms jangling in security systems she had never imagined existed. She ignored them. By the time they traced her, she would be up and out with the loot. Iago's 'ware hauled out of hiding the account from which Semalang's six million had been transferred and ripped it open like a Navidad present.

Digits flowed across YoYo's cerebral cortex; her jerked-up CNS moving from entry to entry, assimilating, synthesizing, connecting. Black money. Payments. Payoffs. Payolas. The Semalang six million was gravel beside the Matterhorns of the big corporate bribes. And behind it all . . . The name in the frame . . .

Alarms yelling in her audial nerves, YoYo pointed her finger and pushed forward.

A nova of brilliant white light exploded around her, so bright it went beyond sight into other senses: a cacophony of taste-smell impressions, a wave of heat that seared every nerve ending as if she had been dipped in molten lava, a pulse of white noise, and a screaming that she realized was not Purmerend's cybernetic watchmen, but her own body burning in sensory agony.

It ended. It ended. It. Ended. She blinked open the physical world and saw that the filament connecting tagalong to bodyglove had melted through. Martika Semalang was beside her, offering a glass of water and concern: "Are you all right, YoYo? All of a sudden you cried out. . . ."

Patrons at Tacorifico Superica's other tables were staring. YoYo pushed back her hood, ran a gloved hand over her bare head.

"Jesus. Jesus. I'm all right. I'm okay. I think. Someone took rather a strong objection to my eavesdropping." As she spoke, she realized that the destroying energy had merely brushed her. Whatever—whoever—had struck had not known she was operating at a distance, through the slow, low-grade tagalong link. Its very inadequacy had saved her. The target of the assault had been her black and white room off Sunset. The sheer power of the attack would have shattered her Powell and Pressburger stairway and all its cunningly concealed subroutines into dust.

Oh Jesus. Oh Mary. Oh fuck.

The tagalong queeped. Its tectoplastic skin peeled back to reveal Ellis, with the face of one who has just been *joder*ed by the angel of death.

"YoYo. Oh Jesus. Get back here. Oh Christ. There's been an accident. Trio. Jesus, I don't know . . . There was an accident, I don't know, some kind of power blowback, I've never seen anything like it. . . ."

"Ellis. What happened. Tell me what happened."

"Trio was riding your 'ware. I hear this scream, I know something's wrong. Some sort of blowback, maybe. I come running."

"Ellis. Trio. Is she?"

"Burns. Like her bodyglove overloaded. Jesus, how could it happen? A crash team's on its way."

YoYo cut transmission. Martika Semalang's distant grace was gone, erased by fear.

"What is it? What's happened?"

"I have to go. There's been an accident. Your friends have just upped the ante."

"What do you mean? What friends?"

"The ones who paid you six million dollars, Séora Semalang. The Tesler-Thanos *corporada*."

Valery Kuznetz's 2012 version of *The Virgin Soil Upturned*.

The unreleased post-Tien An'men Square director's cut of *The Red Detachment of Women*.

These films looked down from their rooftops on Trinidad, running. High-heel boots. Red dress. Swinging earrings.

Trinidad did not care where she ran; she did not know she ran, only that it was away from Santiago.

Demon. Monster. Murderer.

She found herself on the corner of Somewhere and Anywhere, cast up by the crowd, all run out. Across the thronged intersection, *2001*'s dumbbell space station waltzed across a twenty-by-fifty wall screen, prisoner of gravity. The end of the street seemed to be burning.

She had no idea where she was. Lost in Necroville, on the Night of the Dead.

(Trinidad: her earliest, worst nightmare. Age four. First trip with Momi Luv to the Mall. Somehow the grip falters, the hand slips and she's alone in a universe of legs and voices *Momi* she screams *Momi Momi Momi* but in the legs and shouting no one can hear one little girl age four. She's lost. Utterly lost. Terrified. All those legs. All those voices. And then a hand reaches down to her. She takes the hand and arms lift her up onto a shoulder and carry her to a safe place, a quiet place, a place with no legs and voices where a kind man entertains her with magic tricks until Momi Luv comes. And when Momi Luv comes she pulls Trinidad to her and slaps her, hard, and screams abuse at the magic man, because he is a dead magic man, and everyone knows what the dead do to little girls age four.)

A trinity of tailgas flares lit the crowd congregated around a black pool. Dark viscous ripples caught the light: oil. Back before the dead claimed the intersection of 3rd and La Brea for their own, a tectronic oil extractor installed by TejCo Hydrocarbons had malfunctioned spectacularly one night, melting a fifteen meter crater in the blacktop which slowly filled with black gold. What had been a geochemical curiosity was now a shrine; a holy place of Ucurombé Fé, where the spirit of Sieu JabJab, Prince of Deceptions, stirred the dark liquid. Five, six hundred had gathered there. Against her will, Trinidad was pushed by the internal dynamics of the crowd to the edge of the oil lake. Unseen drummers maintained a rock steady righteous rhythm with dub bass and roots guitar; the congregation swayed from foot to foot, murmuring the names of saints: *JabJab JabJab*. Lector and preacher traded lines from the *Chanson Saint Jacques*. The cantos were well-known to Trinidad.

Impelled by the kick of bass guitar and drum, the edges of the congregation constantly broke into spontaneous dance. Beneath the surface of the oil lake nightmare figures moved; hands, arms, heads pushing out of the viscous liquid, glossily highlighted by the red gas flares. A woman so tall and thin she could only be dead ripped away her constricting clothes, shivering as the electric power of the Lordly Ones arced across her synapses. Her friends laid hands on her and passed her from hand to hand to hand around the circle. Her eyes were shut, her legs and arms pressed tightly together, but her lips seemed to be moving. The hands rolled her into the lake of black oil. She made not a noise, scarcely even a ripple as she vanished beneath the liquid velvet surface.

Preacher and teacher howled praise to each other, the bass and the batteria scooped it up and fed it into the master dub, the congregation moved to the rhythm of the lords and Trinidad found that fear was a gateway to subtler, more profound emotions. There had been danger in the pachysaur hunt, there had been exhilaration, but they had been controlled, managed, predestined. In this claustrophobic cauldron of oil and bodies nothing was safe, nothing was predictable. It was wild. Everything was permitted. More than anything, Trinidad wanted to run. More than anything, Trinidad wanted to shake off her self-preconceptions like sweaty clothes and join the dance.

" 'Meat can't dance,' that's what they say," said a voice. Behind it, a face: young, male, dreadlocked. Living. "Too bound up by the inhibitions of living to be able to truly lose themselves. The dead have no inhibitions, no restraints, no limits, and so they can dance." The newcomer was shorter by a head than Trinidad in heels.

The surface of the oil pool erupted as the dead woman was thrust up by submerged hands. For a moment she seemed to be standing on the black liquid, then her colleagues came wading into the shallows and dragged her to shore. They crucified her on the concrete. The red light gleamed on her oil-black skin. She was a saint, an icon, a black madonna, then she disappeared beneath swarming hands and tongues, touching, tasting, licking the sacramental oil.

"Chosen?"

"Ridden. *Los Caballos*, the Ridden Ones. Mounted and penetrated by the Lordly Ones, riders of time, space and the quantum universe. The theory is that the Logra are a future humanity from a time when nanotechnology is so pervasive that it can manipulate the substance of the universe itself. Reaching back through time, the Logra are retrosculpting the continuum through their human mounts, using their quantum technology to select between the potential universes that might collapse out of a particular event for the one most favorable to their wills. Quantum miracles. Like the La Brea pool; those who bathe in the crude take some of the reality-shaping spirit of the Logra. After midnight, all cats are Schrödinger's, so to speak. It's all bullshit, of course. Pseudo-science. But it sounds good."

On the farther shore of Lake La Brea a dead man with the face of Clark Gable was being baptized under the oil by two female acolytes. Drops of black oil ran in hydrocarbon tears down his face as he threw his head back and shouted at the moon.

A voice cried out. An upturned face. An arm pointed at the sky.

High above the city the night was ripped apart by parallel slashes of ruby light. As Trinidad watched new glowing lacerations lanced across the sky, ten, twenty, forty, more than she could count. Silence and stillness was absolute. All Necroville, all the TVMA's twenty-two million, held silence. The *caballos* stood waist deep in the sacred crude, staring at the sky, black oil dripping from their fingers. The sky was a loom of light, hundreds of ruby-red threads. A dim rumble passed over the congregation, like a premonition of thunder. It echoed, it resonated, it took hold and grew into a growl of anger.

"What is it, what's happening?" Trinidad shouted.

"Launch lasers," the man shouted back. "Ion trails. Deep-space weapons leaving orbital command. MIRVs. Microtoc warheads. Grasers, teslers with AI jockeys. The whole fucking fleet. Pretty high acceleration too."

"War?"

"Don't you listen to the newschannels? No, you probably don't. The Freedead have been raiding the orbital manufacturing platforms for the past year or so. Space is theirs, they say, and they've assembled this fleet to prove their point."

The suck of wind at her clothing warned Trinidad an instant before the pressure wave hit her. Heat kissed her left side: the flame danced fifty meters tall, momentarily outshining the orbital display before subsiding into greedy tongues of fire licking across the surface of the oil lake.

"Jesus. They torched the pool. Come on. They'll tear apart any meat they get their hands on."

The dreadlocked man pulled Trinidad through the pressing, hostile crowd, sheltering behind porches and flights of steps until they reached the relative sanctuary of a service entry. Sheer black walls of masonry reduced the sky to a CinemaScope band of black laced with red beams.

"This makes everything a lot more difficult," the small man said. He pulled up his right sleeve to reveal a small tagalong which he held up to his ear. Trinidad watched the fireshadows on the red-lit shopfronts.

"The *seguridados* are shitting themselves. I'm on their communication channel. Triple fucking red alert, and the scanners on the San Vicente gate picked up some kind of Freedead trying to sneak in. They're too chicken to come in in force and restore order, so instead they're going to seal the perimeter. Hoping maybe with nothing to rage against, the violence will burn itself out. In the meantime, we're down at street zero with no way out. Why tonight of all nights? Why, God? It was tough enough to begin with. Now . . ."

"You mean we can't get out?" Hot night, but she felt cold in her red dress, cold and nightmarish. Wake me up, Momi Luv, take me into your big warm bed that smells of manmusk.

"Not until dawn curfew. Shit. This makes things really complex."

"Complex. Difficult. Tough. Jesus, man, you tell me the dead are rising up, we're trapped in with them and can't get out, and it's complex? It's difficult?" She punched the dreadlocked man on the thigh, hard, in the hope it would make her feel braver. It didn't. He did not notice.

"Good thing I chanced along to rescue you," he said. "Look, I'm supposed to meet up with some friends in a bar over on Willoughby. Might be safer up there. This was a wild area you took yourself into, meatgirl."

"Trinidad."

"Emeliano Salamanca. Friends call me Salamanca. Friends, lovers and the lost and lonely."

"Which am I, Salamanca?"

"That," he said, "remains to be seen. Trinidad. Looks like it's quieting down out there. I think we could make a run for it."

"Have you any idea how much running I've done tonight?" She caught herself almost smiling.

"You'll do a lot more before we're clear of this." He was already halfway to the street. "You coming?"

The network of alleys took them away from the Dondé Yap riot, ducking along twisting passages between parasitical outcrops of shacks and housing pods. Thunder growled out west, Topanga way, the storm front the forecasters had been promising all day.

"I think I'm heading in the right direction," Salamanca said. "All this building and overbuilding, the old grid system's gone to hell." The intestinal coil of passages and runways evacuated them into a claustrophobic courtyard. Lowering architectonics: all ribs and bones. Darkness visible. Rotating crucifixes of airco fans high above only redistributed the heat. The air stank of rotting vegetation and the odd secretions of the dead; beneath the black slick of leafmold, markings on the gritty surface underfoot betrayed a previous incarnation: tramlines on a tennis court.

The dark-adapted eye can see the quantum universe at work. The rods and cones of the fovea are sensitive enough to register the impact of a single photon. More than sensitive enough to distinguish those shadows which move from those which do not.

"Shit, Salamanca."

Whatever they were, she and Salamanca were encircled. She heard the rustle of fabric, the tiny rodent squeak of damp skin on rubber jacket.

Blue lightning illuminated two things, and two things only.

The Wolves of the Moon, all around, eyes filled with a curious sentience, like the embers of humanity. Salamanca, arms held out straight before him. Gripped in his hands, a tesler. Aimed square between the eyes of the big werewolf that barred their escape along a black-on-black alley.

An impression: in the eyes of the man-wolf at which Salamanca had aimed: a light, a knowing, a *recognition*.

The wolf-man seemed to know her.

Salamanca raised the tesler. The Lobos danced back; not fast enough, the targeting laser of the tesler pressed its monochrome accusation between its nipples.

Shot and action were simultaneous. The trigger finger, Trinidad's sweeping hand, knocking the weapon out of arc. In the narrow passage the muzzle flash was blinding, report was deafening. The tesler bolt chewed a path to oblivion through the ribbed roofvault. The werewolf had fled.

Out on the street she turned on him.

"They weren't going to hurt us." She punched him on the sternum. "They weren't going to tear us apart or suck the marrow from our bones or make wardrums out of our asses. Maybe shake us up a little, maybe give us some of their political tracts to read, but not hurt us. Until you pulled that piece." She punched him again. And again. It felt good. Stupid *male*. "Jesusjosémaria, you would have used it, wouldn't you?"

"Yes!" he shouted, seizing her wrist to stop her hitting him again. "Yes, of course I would, what other reason is there to bring a tesler into Necroville if you're not prepared to use it? Yes, big bang, yes, Big Death, yes."

"Let go of me," Trinidad said evenly. "I didn't give you permission to touch me."

He stared at her, released his grip. One finger at a time.

"And don't treat me like a twelve-year-old. And yes, I'm coming. You don't have to drag me."

At some time in the flight from the burning oil pool through shadows and fear she had snapped the heel of her left boot.

21:30 — midnight

november 1

Forty-five hours. Dead.

At the root of Nute's love of towers lay a childhood steeped in three-volume wonderlands of pot boys who were Kings of Lost Realms incognito, politically right-on princesses with names that ended in *iel*, Dread Dark Ones whose evil seemed to lie in their opposition to absolute monarchy and the feudal system, and 'prentice mages in wind-swept stone towers. Especially the 'prentice mages. She'd practiced the part in a pair of leggings and a belt-bag magic-pouch over a T-shirt jerkin but Resenza Heights Apartments ran only to four stories and Security, mindful of insurance claims, would not tolerate eight-year-old girls running around on the rooftop at dead of night.

She was not dissuaded. She would find taller towers. The Watts Trash Towers. The Coit Tower. The Tower of London (a disappointment). La Tour d'Eiffel. The Toronto Television Tower. Most of Manhattan. Various pagodas minarets stupas and sundry religious phallic symbols. They were fine but they were other people's towers, inhabited by other people's magics.

In the early years of the Disunification she went up to British Columbia and built herself a tower of driftwood on a beach by the edge of the ocean. It was hers. It was magical. She lived there five years with a man who cheated on her and was never happier. Then the gringos came north riding the Push, the Pacific Coast from the Olympics to the

Aleutians became one extended Displaced Persons Camp, she realized that the man she had been living with for five years was a complete bastard after all and, stunned more by her stupidity at it having taken her five years to discover this than his zealous infidelity, she came south to the city of her birth, learned a new language and took up a new life among people whose cultural heritage had no place for the magician in her windswept tower.

Until now.

The Greeks built their temples and theaters, the Romans their baths and roads and bloody circuses. Generation upon generation of medievals raised cathedrals from the shit to the glory of God, the Renaissance doges and Princes of the Church scattered casas and palazzos across the north Italian littoral. The Georgians set their elegant Palladian mansions in vistas of landscaped Arcadia, the Victorians erected their railway stations and public conveniences. The architecture of each age embodies the spirit of its times.

The late-twentieth/early-twenty-first century built malls.

Los Robles Galleria had been an Atlas among titans. Four square kilometers of rentable retailing opportunity, covered secure parking for five thousand cars. Interior climate-controlled and environmentally engineered using state-of-the-art nanotechnology into five (*five!*) ecological tropes from Siberian taiga to Mayan rain forest—the only rain forest Los Robles's visitors, or anyone else, was ever likely to see. The metropolitan area's largest range of quality retailing, catering and servicing outlets. Plus a full range of recreational resources and entertainments for all ages and socioeconomic groupings.

For ten years it ruled Queen Bitch of Malls, then came Watson's Postulate, and Tesler's epochal Corollary. Within three years it was a hulk, abandoned as the demographic map of the TVMA was hastily redrawn, its leisure pool matted over with reefs of quasi-algae, state-of-the-art ecological tropes bursting the vaulted glass roof in a riot of mis-replicated foliage. Dead prospectors came, picking a cautious path through the overgrown detritus of shopping civilization. They liked what they found. They stayed. They tamed the mutant taiga, they re-configured the rampant rain forest, they restarted the leafmold-clogged escalators and people movers and warmed up the hibernating power and environment controls. They broke the retail units into comfortable apartments, the flat roofs they turned into truck gardens and orchards, while the parking opportunities for five thousand cars became a multi-story market where every night the resurrected of Saint John came to trade their negotiables on the oil-stained concrete. Housing kits were grafted onto the mall's skeleton and tweaked into fantastical spires and oriels. Los Robles became a walled city. Fortress California. A city within a city within a city.

Down on the boulevards the woman who loved towers got off her back one day, looked up and saw against the westering sun the turrets and pinnacles of her Avalons and Minas Tiriths and said to herself *this is the place*.

Nute's Tower rose five floors from the rooftop gardens above the nocturnal hum of the nightmarket. Appropriately, it bore a strong resemblance to an erect dick.

Nute never took clients there. For magic to remain magic, it must not be sullied by gross worldliness. Until Camaguey.

She apologized for the shower: "Sorry it's an ultrasonic, but there're too many people after the water supply to swill it over the body beautiful." She left him a mesh shirt and a pair of smartleather pants that could stretch around any torso, kicked off her working dress and good shoes and slipped into a stretch lace onepiece.

Nute's tower had four windows, each for a cardinal point, each a cat's eye circle of tectoplastic slitted by a variable oval iris. Warm night winds rustled the hanging bouquets of dried flowers that ornamented her room.

"Big burn down on La Brea." As she spoke, ten powder-blue puffball novas detonated in the eastern sky and faded, then ten more, then another ten. "God's tits. They're shooting back at the Freedead. Laser shows, fireworks, *son et lumière*: this is war in space?"

"One-shot rail guns, probably," Camaguey said, standing beside her in the window alcove. "Superconducting fieldcores powered by micronuke detonations accelerate the warheads to point one lightspeed in a fraction of a second. There must be slamships out there, close to earth."

"Micronukes. Slamships. Jesus. War by sound bite. The people who are shooting at us are our children, Camaguey. Our babies. Why do they hate us so? What is the meat so shit-feared of?"

Long fingers of cloud reached across the sky, silver-edged like knives by moonlight. Outriders of the approaching front. At the dark end of the street a solitary movie screen glowed: the eye-slicing scene from *Un Chien Andalou*. Lights moved on the greater luminous tapestry of the dead town; by their shifting configurations Camaguey realized they were airborne.

"Someone up there, flying," he said. Nute pressed the palm of her hand flat on Camaguey's chest, gently but insistently.

"Quid pro quo, Séor Camaguey. Nute got you through the wire.

Now you tell Nute how come this homeboy looking for a piece of trim manages to set every alarm in the District of Saint John jingle-jangling?"

"No, Nute . . ."

She was a head and some smaller than Camaguey but she moved with the speed of a mongoose killing a snake. The left hand gripped the back of his neck, the right his jaw. Slowly, slowly, she tilted his head back.

"You've seen what I can do, so you know that if I want to I can tear your head clean off. It wouldn't be difficult, it might even be enjoyable."

The fingers were carbon steel, the inexorable leverage behind them so powerful that his greatest strength was no more effective than a child's. Tendons strained, the breath fluttered in his barely open windpipe. Vertebrae grated, bone on bone.

"Old ladies of a hundred and twentysomething like to live in ordered and peaceful times—okay, so they go poaching on meat territory, but at least it's my risk, Séor Camaguey, my assessment of the odds." She wrenched his neck, a few millimeters of gratuitous torment. "So pay me my due. Give me my quid pro quo. Tell me who, what, why, where."

"I am not dead, Nute," Camaguey whispered. "I'm meat. Flesh and bone. Alive, Nute. Come on, have you ever met a necro like me?"

"So, there are certain irregularities about you, but I heard with these very ears the border alarms go ring-a-ding-ding. And so did the *seguridados* and so did the *mechadors*. And they may not be curious, but I am. Why?"

"I don't know." *I do know. Why lie? What purpose would it serve when the truth can hurt no more than you are hurt already?* "Nute, have you heard of Human Infective Tectronic Syndrome?" The steel fingers flowed into flesh; the omnipotent grip was relaxed.

"Oh fuck Camaguey," he heard her say. "Oh Jesus. Man . . ."

"Of course you would have in your line of work. The tectors in my system were obviously enough for the sensors to conclude that I was not human. No longer human, Nute, but not dead. Half alive, half dead. The living avatar of quantum theory." He crossed to the kitchenette blister, picked a knife from her block and ran the serrated edge from the tip of his left thumb down across the ball to the rounded boss of the wristbone. Wonderfully cold, the blade, awakening, invigorating, like a dawn dive.

"Do I not bleed?" In fat, fast drops onto her vinyl flooring. He knelt, examining minutely the growing pool of blood. "Look, Nute, look, you can see them. In the blood. Just on the edge of visibility. They must be clustering. That comes near the end, clustering."

Nute's powerful grip on his wrist forced his hand under the cold tap. Bright cold sapphire pain. Wonderful. I am alive.

"How long, Camaguey?"

"Forty-four hours twenty minutes. Maximum."

"Jesus, man . . . How does it . . . how do you . . . feel?"

"Liberating, mostly. Can you understand that? That nothing can touch me. Nothing has any power over me."

" 'Neither principalities nor powers, neither thrones nor dominions, has any power over me.' Sorry. Brought up a good Mass-going girlie. Frightened?"

He nodded. "You always think you'll have time; when it comes, you'll be ready for it. You'll be prepared."

"That's why you asked me, at the gate, what it was like to die."

A nod, head bowed. Eyes averted.

"What is it like to die?"

"Do you want to know?"

"Not really. What I want; what I want most is to talk about it. Tell someone. You understand? Talk about it at great length, in great detail, totally selfishly, brooking no interruptions, and demanding much sympathy."

Nute grinned.

"That is seventy percent of what my job is about." She indicated the bed. Camaguey lay on his back, hands behind his head, staring at the quasi-organic folds and ribbing of the ceiling. Nute curled beside him, his maimed hand pressed between hers. Hot wind entered through the open windows, setting the dried flowers rustling. Clouds covered the sky, the atmosphere was charged with premonitions of thunder. Camaguey's blood thickened and curdled on the kitchen floor.

"Her name was Elena. She was the only woman I ever loved and I killed her. But not before she killed me. You see, I had a reef in Palos Verdes . . ."

He had found her by the street gate when he went out for his predawn run. She had been there all night. She was dead.

"Are you the man who has the garden at the bottom of the sea?" she asked.

"I am," he said. "What about it?"

"I want the job."

"Oh. So?"

She held up her left hand in front of his face and slowly spread her fingers. They were webbed to the final joint.

"I want out of my contract, séor. Buy me out."

Bodmods were simpler for the dead than the living—a matter of deconfiguring and reconfiguring into the desired format—but the full subaquatic adaptations her spread fingers hinted at would not have come cheap.

"Who's your current contractor?"

"Ewart/OzWest Mining, SubPacific division."

Deep water, dark pressure.

"Those bastards," Nute hissed. "You know Ewart/Western Australian's at the root of that *muy machismo* military lightshow up there. They have a policy of buying up your contract while you're still swimming in your Jesus tanks. 'NightFreighting': shipping mining plants and crew out to the asteroids in the form of cheap light-sail drivers with slap-on tector packages. Two seconds from impact they detonate and envelop the target in a cloud of tectors. Slamships. It's not just some adboy's buzzword. I tell you this, give me a century on the street and another on my back rather than dying and waking up five hundred million kilometers from earth with no idea of how I got there. It's the press gang, and not even a king's shilling in recompense. Sorry. You were probably still in disposables at the time of the Farside mutinies and the NightFreight Wars, but like we say, long life, long memory. Go on."

Even before extraterrene space was surrendered to the mutineers and their slamships and nanoprocessors, Ewart/OzWest had turned to the mid-ocean trenches, seeding them with machines and dead configured for deep-water labor.

"Ewart/OzWest will crucify me if they catch me moonlighting you," Camaguey had said.

"Cheaper to buy me up, then," said the woman waiting at his gate.

The sky was graying beyond Palos Verdes's skullcap of desirable housing. First dive within an hour.

"If you're still here when I get back, I'll try you out," he said, moved by cool spirits.

She was. He did. She moved through the cold, still-dark waters of the reef, like some minor Greek sea deity.

"I let her take her first tour party the next day. By the end of the week, I had the accountancy and attorney 'ware buy her contract off Ewart/Western Australia Mining. It was more expensive than my worst guesstimates, but by then I was a little and something in love with her."

He never considered that society had conventions on living/dead relationships. To Camaguey, *attachment* could bury its barbs as deeply in the dead as the living. *Necrophilia* was not a word in his vocabulary. *Love* was.

He could not bear it when the curfew forced her away from him back to the sprawling dead communities in Long Beach and Normandie. He asked her to stay; she refused: the *mechadors* and their Big Death weapons she had cheated once to meet him, she would not test the grace of the saints twice. The ocean house felt big and empty around Camaguey, too full of space and air. The glow of the skysign seemed to work its way into every dark corner. One day in early autumn, while the city still seemed fresh and clean after the August short rains, he followed her in his shapeshifting car. She lived in a converted trailer huddling with fifty others under the hump back of the disused Terminal Island freeway. Lost and lonely hypertankers rusted broken-backed and broken-hearted in the tidal lagoons; chain-link shock fencing and security drones warned of decommissioned but untrustworthy submarine reactors.

"This time you'll come home with me," he said. "I'm buying residency rights. You'll come home, and you'll stay, this time."

She didn't do any of the things he had hoped she might; embrace him, kiss him, open her thighs to him, but she meekly accompanied him to the car, where he punched into his houseware and let her watch the security clearances go through.

That night he was wakened from his sleep by disturbed moonshadows to find her beside him, curled tight against his side. She pressed her hand over his mouth. He licked the dark vee-slash of the deathsign in her right palm. They made love. Each night after they lay together, Camaguey sleeping lightly, the dead woman by his side, eyes wide, the waking dreams of the resurrected flickering across her eyeballs.

"Sex was the only point of contact between our different understandings of love; sex the bridge over which we could cross between life and death."

Curled against Camaguey's side, Nute nodded.

"Sex is death of a kind. Mortality is coiled around every twist of our DNA. We don't die, we're murdered by our own genetic imperative. Every sperm is a bullet, every egg a timebomb. God's not a crap shooter, God's a used car salesman."

As they lay in the afterglow of the evening curfew, Elena had tried to communicate the nature of her experience to him. "Death is nothing, not even darkness, not even timelessness, yet the nothing touches every part of you, wraps itself around every cell in your resurrected body: *you have been dead, you have been nothing, you have been utterly annihilated, and now you are again.* No way around it. No escape. No plea bargaining. The tectors destroy what they touch. There is no immortality; there is death, and resurrection to eternal life. That's why the Zoo Cults with their promises of deathless immortality are such dangerous and glittering lies."

"But how do I know that what is resurrected is me and not merely a walking, talking, grinning, pissing replica of me with all my memories and all my experiences and all my abilities but no *me*, no sense of self-awareness, animating it?"

"That's the big fear, isn't it?"

"Yes."

Elena had pulled him to her, wrapped hungry legs around his waist.

"Does this seem like a walking talking grinning pissing replica?"

That night he had dreamed that they made love in the coral city under the sea while the winter monsoon broke above them. Whalesong and the beat of robot bulk-transporter engines kept rhythm as they coupled among the wafting fans and undulating necks of Camaguey's pseudo-corals. At the climax Camaguey dreamed that the floating globs of his semen fused with and fertilized the tector-polyps of his reef and that as the warm wet winds from the southwest shook the paper walls of the ocean house a new humanity gestated in water-filled wombs and glassy nodules, deep down among the anchorholds.

"You said God was a used car salesmen, Nute. God's a whole order of magnitude crueler than that. When I was at elementary school, two guys got suspended for cutting the tail and back legs off a cat and throwing the poor bastard thing onto a bonfire. That's God's kind of cruel, Nute. They did it with a knife, God did it with a mole. A damned spot."

Camaguey knew Elena's flesh intimately enough to be sure there had been no mole on her left shoulder before. New, and growing. Throughout the month of March and the equinoctial gales he watched the mole expand and take on a definite shape: an oval mound with two lips of blue-black skin above and below. At first Elena refused to be concerned about it; later, after the hairs had appeared on the lips, she refused to mention it. In mid-April the central mound developed a longitudinal fissure. On the night of May 5, the fissure split. A baby-blue eyeball regarded Camaguey from the scapular hollow of Elena's left shoulder.

"Christ, Camaguey . . . You knew what it was?"
"I knew."

After the vomiting and the trembling and the tranquilizers, he asked her, "It's a misreplication, isn't it?"
She would not answer. He followed her around the cliff house, asking the same question over and over and over until she answered him: yes, it was a misreplication.

"How long had it been since her last deconfiguration?"

"Eight, nine months. Just before I bought her from Ewart/OzWest. She wasn't due one for another six months, at least. She said. Spontaneous misreplications sometimes occurred; nothing to worry about, they usually cleared up of their own accord."

"And you believed her, Camaguey?"

In early June came the clusters of black, lustrous crystals under her finger- and toenails that left bleeding scratch marks on his belly and back where she stroked him. In July her skin developed a pattern of dark blue patches, like a giraffe's reticulations, which gave off a powerfully attractant aroma; in August her hair started to thicken into ropey, Medusalike strands. To Camaguey she became more beautiful and exotic with each aberration. Over the summer he had learned that kissing Elena's shoulder eye gave her a powerful and unique orgasm, and he himself had found a strange excitement in the bloody caress of her crystal needles.

"By September we couldn't lie to each other any longer about what was happening and what was necessary. But I couldn't bear the thought of the long separation Elena's visit to the Death House would entail. She was the first one I loved, Nute. The only one. I wanted her with me. I . . . I refused."

"You what?"

"I refused to release her from her contract to me for deconfiguration."

By the start of October only Camaguey would have recognized Elena as a woman. Deconfiguration could no longer be delayed. He arranged for the Death House to install a Jesus tank on the ocean terrace. The carapace sealed over her and Elena Eres was reduced to a soup of deconfigured tectors. Every day Camaguey would go to look at the static, featureless, obdurately immobile tank for hours at a time.

"In the third week of the deconfiguration I started to suffer from an unusual lethargy, a disinterest in every worldly thing. Even the reef bored me. My appetite vanished, what food I ate I could not keep down. I thought it was depression, I thought I was missing Elena. But that wasn't the end of it. I started to experience heart palpitations and shortness of breath. And at night: Nute: the dreams!

"The medical houseware was state-of-the-art; it pondered the symptoms, accessed databases and expert systems as far away as Rio de Janeiro and Srinagar and told me there was nothing conclusive, we must watch and wait. Watch, and wait!"

Ten days later, while trying to urinate, Camaguey was paralyzed by excruciating pain, as if a glass rod had been inserted into his penis and snapped. When his vision cleared, he saw the yellow piss-water fizzing with darting motes of miroscopic motion.

Tectors.

Camaguey became very, very afraid.

He fed a sample of his piss to the computer doctors. The doctors spread it and sectioned it and chromatographed it and analyzed it and sent the results to a medical research simulation system in Free Queensland which they said was the Best in the Field, though they declined to tell him in what Field it was the Best.

He could guess. Two days later they were back.

"Sexually vectored symbiotic Human Infective Tectronic Syndrome, they said. They couldn't lie, they couldn't even soften the truth. Rare but increasingly common, they said. Fifty cases last year, they said, all living individuals having sexual intercourse with resurrected dead past deconfiguration date. Whack whack whack. Fact after fact after fact. Transcription errors cause a tector to misreplicate into a form symbiotic with living cells. The rate of conversion of biological matter to tectronic is exponential, starting slowly, one cell at a time, accelerating into an avalanche of transmutation until at the end the victim is reduced to a mass of tectoplasm."

"Always?"

"Always. Mortality is one hundred percent."

"Fuck, Camaguey . . . How long?"

"At the time of diagnosis, a maximum of fifty-six, a minimum of thirty-two hours, Nute. On average, forty-eight."

And Camaguey had gone out onto the terrace filled with the sun and the wind, the cries of the seabirds and the sound of the ocean, and hit the silver switch marked *Flush and Cycle* on the side of the Jesus tank.

"I loved her, Nute, and I killed her. But not before she had killed me." The darkness was total now. The storm front was a lens of black cloud peering down onto the shining city. By the blue shiver of street cinema, Camaguey studied his left hand. All that remained of the bloody laceration was a line of puckered scar tissue.

"They've started to repair themselves. It's further advanced than I thought."

"This is Necroville, *chico*, death is life, life is death, light is dark, dark light. Everything can happen here." Nute beckoned him up from her bed, out into the deep blue night. "Come on, man. Whatever the state of your internal biology, you still paid five thousand Rim for a night of my services. So, I shall play Virgil to your Dante and maybe in one night I can show you enough of living for you to be ready for dying. I'm still your Gallowglass, I owe you my being. Come on."

He came. Lightning shivered the streets; the sky gods muttered out over the Santa Monica Mountains.

"One anatosaurus, two anatosaurus," she counted as the hydraulic elevator lowered them toward the night-blooming flowers of the roof garden, "four anatosaurus, five anatosaurus. It's not here yet. We've still got time." Parrots rose with raucous voices and clattering wings from their roosts. The clouds crawled blue silver. "One anatosaurus, two anatosaurus," Nute shouted at the sky. "Come on you bastard, count!" Thunder bawled, closer, shaking the air. "Here! This'll do." She ran her thumbnail up the seam and deftly wiggled out of her lace onepiece. "Take your clothes off, it won't work unless you're naked. Hurry up, there isn't much time."

"Nute, we aren't going to; I can't . . ."

"No, nothing like that. Come on, man."

Devil-forked lightning struck among the ridgetop windturbines, the swelling shout of thunder came only two anatosauruses behind. Dazzled, dazed, not knowing why he should be doing what he was doing, Camaguey pulled off the mesh shirt, slipped out of the smart-skin jeans. Nute drew him down to lie beside her on the crushed poppy stalks.

"All my life I was terrified of thunderstorms—strange premonitions of mortality, you know?—until John the Bastard showed me the secret of it on a beach up in Canada. If it shouts, you shout back. If it shouts death, you shout life. Whatever it is you fear, whatever dark thing it is the storm wakes in the cowering, rodent part of your brain, you shout it back to the storm."

The sudden blue-hot bolt burned between heaven and earth for an eternal instant. Every contour of Nute's body, every leaf hanging limp in the thick air, the whole chaotic surface of the city of angels, was limned in ultraviolet.

"Shout!" Nute cried. "All the things you feel, all the things you fear, all your hopes and dreads and wishes and desires, shout them, Camaguey, shout them." The cataclysm of thunder silenced her. Nute threw her head back and howled at the sky, a roar of defiance and great *I Am* of being. Emotion balled in Camaguey's throat, demanding iteration. He was seventy kilos of protein; naked, vulnerable, exposed to the anger of the Thunderbird that spread its dark wings over the city, but he could not release. The echoes died away among the canyons. Nute leaned over him, held his face between her hands.

"What are you, twenty-six, twenty-seven? You're young, you're beautiful, you're going to die. Forty-eight hours. No appeal, no remittance. You've been cheated out of your life before you've had the chance to properly appreciate it. How does that feel? Come on, Camaguey, you don't want to die, but you must. How do you feel? How do you feel?"

"Angry," he said, "hurt . . ."

"Fuck you, Camaguey, do not lie to Nute. Shout it out, boy, it's in there, I can hear it, I can see it, like a bird in an egg. Let it fly, boy, shout it, set it free. How do you feel? How do you feel?"

His body dripped sweat, the warm electromagnetic air seemed to press down on him. He could not speak. He could not breathe. The sky lit, silhouetting Nute leaning over him against a cosmic silver screen. Hard behind it, thunder cracked and boomed, vast and close as a personal apocalypse. The storm was on top of them. Primeval terror seized Camaguey; the shell around his spirit cracked and shattered.

"No!" he roared at the sky. "No! No! No! No! No!" The words became a senseless bellow that blended with the greater bellow of the storm, his voice a conduit along which all his pain and fear and rage and confusion and doubt and dread flowed into the storm to be absorbed and earthed in spasms of electricity among the boulevards of the dead town.

He lay panting beneath racing black clouds. The storm towered over him. He felt luminous, filled with light. Muscles clenched tight, then released. He felt dark, beating wings pass over him.

A raindrop burst on his face. Another on his belly. Two. Twenty. Summer rain pattered on the leaves of the roof garden.

"What did the thunder say, Camaguey?" Raindrops dewed Nute's skin, slid sensuously down the valleys of her bodyscape. "Nothing is ever taken that something isn't given in return. So John the Bastard said. Only time he didn't lie to me. What did the thunder give?"

It was before him the instant he turned inward to seek it.

"Grief," he said, and as he spoke the word he felt it well out of him like deep buried water. "For my life. For me. For the complete, utter injustice of it." He could scarcely finish. Nute took him in her arms and the sky opened. Cloudburst. Rain punished the nested, naked bodies. Fetus-curled against the dead woman's breasts, Camaguey cried the salt tears he had withheld for so many years.

They ran the first one down on an abandoned industrial site back of Paramount City. A girl, hundred-year-old eyes in a sweet-sixteen face, with clever clever skin that melted into the background but was not quite clever enough to save her.

With pheromones they hunted her, with those same subtle pathways of chemicals in the air that guide the luna moth across tens of kilometers to sex and death. In the warren of service roads and backlot alleys they found her, frozen in their headlights, skin the exact color of night and concrete, eyes twin pools of glitter. The eyes of the cornered animal. By the light of a thousand launch-lasers they trapped her between high walls of fire escapes with ten meters of razor-topped chain-link fence at her back. Crouching like a cat, the girl screamed at them, the wordless scream of the final frustration of the hunted, and threw herself up the wire fence.

Blue steel, unsheathed, gleaming in the neon light. The hunters were fresh, the hunted run to exhaustion. In two bounds Anansi and Duarte overtook her and neatly hamstrung her. She screamed the pain scream which is unlike any other cry of man. Blood streaked her beautiful hexagon-patterned skin, but she clung, she clung to the mesh, howling at the unreachable stars wrapped in razor wire.

They broke her fingers to get her down. She could not stand, so her mutilators held her. The girl did not struggle, did not make a sound. Her eyes were dull and unfocused with the terminal passivity of the animal that understands it has seconds to live, hypnotized by the play of light along the edge of Miclantecutli's blade.

Miclantecutli gently lifted the girl's chin, opened her mouth. She kissed her. The tip of her tongue traced the girl's lips.

"I love you," Miclantecutli whispered. The point of the knife rested on the angle of the jawbone. With a short, sharp tug Miclantecutli slit her throat.

Santiago cried out, an emotion thirty parts dread, thirty parts tension, thirty parts horror and the rest pure excitement. He retched, suddenly nauseated.

Miclantecutli crouched beside him, cradled his jaw in the gloved palm of her hand. She stank of blood. "Tell me," she whispered in his ear, "tell me true, Santiago, tell me how you feel?" She rubbed her cheek against the side of his head, whispered once again, intimate, obscene. "I know, Santiago. It was like that for me, the first time. Too much, too complicated, a thousand things going on in my head at once; emotions I had never experienced before. Emotions I had never thought existed. Let me help you. You feel horrified, yes, you feel disgusted that you have been party to what you see as a piece of gratuitous butchery, you feel afraid, you feel fragile. Fear. Loathing. Dread. Nausea. Guilt. All these, yes, Santiago, but most of all, you feel alive. You feel alive as you've never felt before. Every part of you, every cell, every atom, is singing. Sweetest song you'll ever hear, Santiago, the great song of existence. The first human languages were songs of the Dreamtime, no words, no meanings, just that same Amen of self-existence proclaimed against an inanimate, dumb universe."

The body lay as the hunters had let it fall, kneeling, head bowed, arms outstretched. An attitude of supplication, of prayer. The beautiful, clever skin had faded to matte black: a murdered shadow. Blood spread in a circle around it.

"You think I'm a monster, Santiago, but do you not sustain your life by the death of others? Carnivore, omnivore, herbivore; whatever, your capacity for life is dependent on another's death. Life goes in one end, shit comes out the other, merely to keep the middle ticking on through day after day of mundane existence; she died that we might be lifted out of the mundane into the extraordinary. Rejoice, Santiago, she's dead, you're alive. I'm a monster, you're a monster, we're all monsters together, celebrate it."

"You said you loved her," he mumbled.

"Miclan!" The hunters were remounting their bikes. "You coming? Angel's got another lead."

"If we hurry we might get one in before midnight," pale Angel shouted.

"At the end, you said you loved her," Santiago repeated.

Miclantecutli stood up, wiping imaginary street dust from her pants.

"I did love her, Santiago. At the end." She called back to him as she kicked the bike into action, "Come if you're coming, stay if you're staying, but the clock's running, Santiago, the game's afoot."

Within seconds the alley's sole occupant was the dark, drained thing praying to its own blood.

Following airsigns, Angel led the pack westward along boulevards throbbing to carnival and political unease.

"Diff'rent strokes for diff'rent folks, Santiago," Miclan shouted back to her pillion passenger. "For Angel it's the thrill of the chase. Pursuit is all, the kill is anticlimax. Angel can detect a concentration of one molecule per million, she hunts for the joy of using her skills, her talents, her senses. Angel!" She waved to the pale rider, Angel grinned back. "Anansi now"—Miclan's lieutenant, picking her name by cocktail-party effect out of the snarl of engines, flashed her dark-rimmed eyes over at them—"she actively enjoys the pain. To you, pain is a thing to be feared, for it warns of irreparable—possibly fatal—damage to the physical organism. But we cannot be irreparably damaged, even destroyed, and thus pain is transfigured. Pain goes beyond mere physical distress into an altered state of consciousness. Pain is revelation, ascension, enlightenment. That girl, back there in the alley, she died—believe it, Santiago—in terrible agony. Hideous pain. But who knows into what heights her consciousness peaked before fading into the Big White Light? Tectors never sleep, Santiago, even now the same processes that lifted us all out of death are repairing her wounds, restoring her body, reawakening her mind and memories, and she'll remember. She'll remember the pain, she'll remember the slow dying, but she'll also remember what it was she found beyond the pain on the borderlands of death."

Pressed hard against Miclan's rubber-clad back, Santiago shuddered; some dark, unclean, cold current in the hot stormwind had sought and found him.

"Anansi has made a religion out of pain. You could call her a Transcendental Sadomasochist. More blessed to receive than to give, to pervert Holy Writ. She's one sick fuck, honey, but I love her. Anansi!" Anansi waved a gloved hand and kissed the night air.

"And you, Miclan?" Santiago said into her ear. "What do you get out of it?"

"Love," she said. "What other reason would there be to do this fell thing?"

Angel circled her fist in the air and stopped. The platoon drew in around her.

"Cold?" Miclan asked. A handful of hundred meters down the street the edge of the night party pulsed and throbbed. Angel spread her hands in exasperation at the costumed revelers. "They been through here?" Angel nodded.

"Fucking Chanel," she said, wrinkling her nose in displeasure. "I hate doing this. It's so undignified. Meatboy, take my hog."

Santiago straddled the warm leatherette. The machine purred deep in its cylinders.

Angel went down on hands and feet and pressed herself close to the ground. Eyes closed, she swept her face across the street at a range of mere millimeters. A hand shot up. Fingers clicked, impatient *come on come, I can't hold this pose all night*. The bikes formed up, two two and one behind her as she darted down the street. The crowd parted—some kind of Jolé Blon, it seemed to Santiago, semiseduced by the endorphin jolt of the hunt. The pale specter of Angel wove between the couples caught in three-four time.

"What the hell is going on?" a drunken voice asked close as Santiago crept past.

"Hey, *cher-ami-o*" he heard the whispered answer, "A wise boy keeps his tongue still in his *bouche* when the Night Hunt passes."

Angel paused a moment, rose from her crouch and pointed up at the roof of an apartment unit part covered by a movie screen on which prehistoric biplanes did battle over Mons for the glory of the Blue Max. She took the rungs of the rusted fire escape two at a time, clung a moment to the parapet, air sensing, and then was sliding over the flat rooftops, along stone copings, leaping the spaces between buildings with the unselfconscious arboreal ease of a ghost gibbon. The hunt followed.

"Tell me, Santiago"—Miclantecutli had allowed Duarte to take

point so that she might fall back and waste some badinage on her aco-
lyte—"isn't she the most purely beautiful thing? You know when
women love men most? When they're working. When their attention
is absolutely given to what they are doing and they're so absorbed in it
that they forget the peculiarly male self-consciousness that is the root
of masculine vanity. You forget the pureness of being. An old Greek
Orthodox theologian once told me—this was back in my Christian
phase, long before you knew me—that a tree, by being a tree, is, and
so worships God. The sacrament of the present, he called it. The holi-
ness of unselfconscious being. That is the nature of Angel's beauty, up
there, doing what she was built to do, being what she was designed to
be. Thought and action, one unity."

"All hunting is an act of love. The identification with the hunted,
the merging of mindsets, pursuer with pursued, vice versa, until they
become one mind; the inevitability of the surrender; the grace of the
dispatch. As all love is an act of hunting. That first scent, the cutting
out from the herd, the slow pursuit, the investment of ever-increasing
degrees of yourself in the chase, the running down, the cornering, the
equally inevitable surrender and symbolic thrust and stab. I did love her,
Santiago, that girl. I knew her spirit, Santiago. I chased her, I hunted
her, I became one with her. And I consummated that love in a way
vastly more intimate and profound than a quick interlocking of biological plumbing. She didn't struggle, she didn't fight, because she loved
me. Because I loved her, I couldn't withhold the blow."

"Miclan!" Poised on the lip of the parapet, Angel spread her arms,
shook her head.

"What do you mean?" Miclantecutli shouted up. Sporadic bursts
of flame, invisible at street zero, lit up Angel with hell light. She mimed
a neat piked dive with her forefinger.

"Interesting," Miclantecutli mused. "He would have had no idea if
we were behind him or not, so how would he know if he could afford
the five? ten? minutes it would take him to put himself back together
again?" All the time, her eyes moved from building to building. "It's a
pawn sacrifice. Throw a player to the wolves in the hope that they'll
get us all close together come turnaround."

"Turnaround?" Santiago asked, but Duarte spoke louder over him.
"Should we leave him then?"

"If we had three kills, I'd say yes. But two . . ."

"But you said if they catch us all together . . ." Anansi interjected
uneasily.

"They may be the Pale Riders, but we are the Night Hunt, Duarte."

The shaven-headed Afro-Chinese deadboy donned a pair of rollscreen sensory shades. He slowly scanned the local environment with his spectrally enhanced vision.

"Angel!" The pale girl mock-saluted her leader and stepped into twenty meters of air.

Santiago screamed.

Santiago was still screaming when she hit the street a second and a half later and burst in a moist crack of flesh and fluid.

The fallen Angel-thing lay crucified in its own liquids, broken, smashed. It seemed a far longer scream than that to Santiago.

"Yes!" Duarte exclaimed. Teeth white beneath the *el bandido* mask of the scanshades. "Pattern-recognition systems throw up a definite spook," Duarte said, eyes a blur of digits. "Range this, bearing that, exactly *there*."

The Angel-thing moaned, pushed itself on splayed fingertips up out of its own wreckage.

"Anansi, Asunción, Duarte, find another way around and seal the end of the street," Miclantecutli ordered. "He'll know you're there, but damn he can do about it." Anansi drew a long, pistol-grip weapon from a thigh holster with the blue-velvet languor of one who enjoys using it.

Grimacing, wincing, gasping, Angel rose to her knees. The dark pseudo-blood of the dead stained her ivory dress; as Santiago looked on the pale puckerings of scar tissue faded like shadows in fog; shapes and stretchings like bones realigning moved beneath the lily-white skin. She sniffed the air. "He's back of the row on the your right, Miclan." Wind rising from the west streamed her bleached hair out behind her. Santiago returned her bike to her.

Dying, and living. For a few seconds before the tectors shifted into trauma reconfiguration, she had been dead. She had willingly walked off the roof into death, and been reborn. A cold, gusting wind spiraled up the streets, driving before it a vanguard of litter and papers. Power cables sang in Aeolian mode. Jesus, he was alive. Thank you, Jesus.

Miclantecutli glanced at her antique Rolex as Santiago mounted behind her. "Shit. Come on come on come on you guys."

A raindrop stung Santiago's face like a needle of ice. Another. A volley. He shook the clean cold shock from his skin.

A shot. Another. A volley. Flat. Thin. Not the heavy male yakker of guns; a subtle, feminine snigger.

"Heads up!" Miclantecutli shouted, but Angel's engine was already gibbering. Lights came on behind windows up and down the boulevard, blinds twitched. A figure burst from the dark mouth of a serviceway behind a row of tall, cable-strewn *apartamentos* on the right. Young. Male. Waist-length hair blown on the wind as he glanced wildly about him, checking for escape, for cover. His clever camouflage tried to blend him into the streetlight and rain-spattered concrete but found the challenge too much.

"Oh, you beautiful beautiful child," Miclantecutli whispered for herself.

The clouds opened.

In the same instant, the boy saw the two bikes.

Rain thundered down.

He tried to run. He slipped on the wet surface, scrabbled for grip, found it, sprinted away, arms held high, legs driving, not daring to look back.

"Mine!" Miclan roared as the bike leaped forward to her desire in a plume of spray. She reached back to draw a long, curving blade from a sheath beneath Santiago's right thigh. The blade skimmed his ear as Miclan brought it down, tip to the blurring concrete. Blue-hot sparks screeched back from the hurtling blade.

The boy heard it. The boy stopped. The boy turned. The boy stood, hands outstretched. The bike bore down on him. A flick of the wrist, Miclantecutli lifted the blade. The Kendo *Men* stroke, most masterly of attitudes. Blade held perfectly horizontal. The beheader's stroke.

The boy closed his eyes, a look of beatific ecstasy on his rain-streaked face.

And the Rolex on Miclantecutli's wrist chimed. Once. Twice.

Ding. Ding.

Her wrist moved. A fraction of a centimeter. The blade skimmed the left side of the boy's head by millimeters. Miclantecutli threw the bike into a skid turn. Blinded by spray and rain, Santiago buried his fists in the rubber demon faces down Miclan's back and held on for the love of all the saints.

The boy stood smiling. His hair was plastered to his body, his skin the color of cloudburst. Very slowly, he bowed, still smiling, and applauded slowly. Miclantecutli dismounted. Rain streaming from her leathers and latexs, she bowed to the naked boy.

"Saved by the bell," she smiled. "May I be so lucky, next time."

Piece by piece, she laid down her weapons: the street-honed killing blade, the knife with which she slit the girl's throat, a spread of five *shuriken* from sundry zippered breast pockets, a monofilament bola weighted with a chromium death's head wrapped around the ankle of her right boot. All set down on the wet, reflecting avenue with the sacerdotal slowness of a high mass, or a Noh drama.

The others also set down their weapons of the hunt.

Afar, something bellowed; the cry of the damned on the night of the dead.

"What are you doing?" Santiago asked. "I don't understand."

"You will," said Anansi ferally.

Miclantecutli waved her fist in the air and shouted to her brothers and sisters of the Night Hunt, "Okie-dokie team! Let's go! The game's afoot!"

Without, the Café Posada on Willoughby was the usual Necroville miscegeny of Christmas decoration *jodering* an old Spanish mission church. Within, nave, chancel, choir and cloisters were a shell supporting a domed roof of glass-clear tectoplastic. Much of the floor space was occupied by immense potted plants between which squeezed elegant white-painted cast iron tables. Tropical birds wee-ooed and sirened, macaques shinnied down trunks of well-concealed roof pillars to scavenge under tables and stuff cheek pouches. A blue macaw cocked its tail, chuckled and shat twenty centimeters from the toe of Trinidad's wobbly boot. The walls were decorated with curious murals of skeletons in frock coats and wedding dresses; peons fleeing public *zócalos* in gibbering terror from strange lights in the sky.

Every square centimeter of available floor space was occupied by refugees from a night of revelry and grand debauch that had suddenly, catastrophically, turned dangerous. Someone had rigged a rollscreen from a crossmember between two roof piers; concerned newschannel anchorconstructs tried to keep abreast of the torrent of events.

A young woman—hardly more than a teenager, Trinidad guessed—came bounding up to Salamanca, aglow with excitement. She had a lot of crinkly black hair, her face was pretty (pretty was first in the bodmod shop catalogues) but held a subcutaneous potential for fat she would have to fight the rest of her meat life.

"Salamanca! Salamanca!" she shrieked. "They got a ship! I heard it, on the newschannels, isn't it fantastic!"

Salamanca, she called him. Which was she, friend, lover or the lost and lonely? Or just another poor waif needing rescue?

The anchorperson on the rollscreen dissolved into the lambent blue quartersphere of Earth. The ocean hemisphere: hints and allegations of the Coca-Cola company's monstrous colophon formed by dye-secreting seaborne tectors were visible beneath the spirals of cloud.

A sudden supernova lit screen upper right. There were gasps and scattered cheers. Something half shadow, half jewel and mostly delicate solar vanes tumbled across the eye of the lens. Another, and another, and another followed.

"Fighters," Salamanca said. "Close order defense systems. They accelerate at three gees toward a high-velocity pass and try to inject corrupters into the slamships' self-regeneration routines. Twenty milliseconds combat time, three months in sensdep waiting for orbital mechanics to bring them the long way home." He seemed transported by the pavane of lights on the screen. "Twelve-year-old kids, mostly. Hooked into real-time virtualizers. They've got the speed, they can take the acceleration. They last eight, ten months, tops. They fit them up myelin-enhancer pumps, for the speed. I helped design the combatware; before."

Before what? Trinidad wondered.

The actinic blink faded rapidly toward the infraspectrum.

"One less of the bastards, though," said a tall, middle-aged woman with severe, scraped back hair.

"I doubt it," Salamanca said. "Those ships of theirs aren't much more than mass-drive units embedded in ice/nickel-iron cores; they'll have nanoprocessed the stuff into a halo of decoys and deflectors long before they reach high-Earth orbit. My money says it's a hit on a Wild Weasel."

A second brief star illuminated heaven. A third, a fourth, a fifth spread in a gentle arc across Earth's luminous terminator.

"Christ," Salamanca breathed. "The fighters. They got them. They're gone." He stood, staring at the screen that had changed hastily to material fresh in from Paris: aerial shots of rioting in the La Défense necroville, imagining the cries of the beautiful burning children up on the edge of space. No resurrection in heaven. Not even Adam Tesler could scoop a handful of plasma and shape a man out of it. "Suicide. Fucking suicide."

"Hey. Salamanca." Kid crinkly-hair pulled gently on his arm. "Hey, come on, before you say something that gets us all in trouble."

The girl—Salamanca introduced her as Rosalba—led them to a table beneath a tall locust-bean tree enveloped in strangling ficus.

Rosalba stood behind the oldest woman with the bluest eyes Trinidad had ever seen. Her hand rested on the back of the wrought iron chair in which the woman sat in the way that says *property protection affection respect*. Mother, grandmother, lover? *Cerristo* society was built upon as many sexes as there were hills.

"Montserrat, may I introduce Trinidad, a friend. Trinidad, I'd like to introduce Montserrat Mastriani."

The Malcopuelos thought themselves well-established *La Crescentistos*, but Trinidad's father admitted that he would have Made It only the day a Malcopuelo was invited to cocktails on the terrazzo with the Mastrianis. They were the first of the pre-Push Italo-Hispanics to have made it to serious money in Old Los Angeles, and thus jealous of their position. Sensing the climatic shift to warmer and wetter, they had invested in improved genetweak editions of the tropical fruits that now grew in the big agribusiness farms over in the eastern valleys. The biotechnician's natural prediliction for the small and perfectly organized led them to invest in the emerging nanotech *corporadas*. They had employed Adam Tesler in their Culver City R&D facility. Chairman-for-Life Marcello Mastriani decried Adam Tesler's research into Watson's Postulate as being of no conceivable commercial application, and had canceled funding. Adam Tesler terminated his contract with Mastriani SimuLife with extreme prejudice, charmed six million dollars out of a consortium of Rim banks and venture capitalists and set up his own shop. Three years later Marcello Mastriani died from cancer of the larynx. Two years after that, Adam Tesler raised the five-day-dead corpse of Ronaldo the chimp to everlasting life.

The Mastrianis thus joined the Hollywood talent scout who described Fred Astaire as "Can't act, can't sing, can dance a little" and the designer of the *Titanic*, who reckoned they probably had enough lifeboats in the Valhalla of Considered-in-Hindsight; nonetheless they were the closest thing La Crescenta had to royalty.

Something lifted the séora out of her chair. Something extended the séora's hand.

The exoskeleton was a transparent shell enclosing every part of Montserrat Mastriani except head and hands. A-glitter with neurocircuitry, it was a virtuality bodyglove with ambitions to be a lifeguard on Silicon Beach, pumped up with translucent tectoplastic musclemotors and sinewy veins along which gritty clear fluid pulsed. Of course Trinidad had heard of such things. She had never before known anyone sick enough to need one. The Mastrianis themselves had been among those who had trumpeted the miracles that nanotechnology could offer medical science. The reality was that tector treatments were so monstrously expensive and the prolongation of life they offered so fleeting measured against the effective eternity of the resurrected that a tacit euthanasia had become accepted medical convention in cases of terminal disease. For Montserrat Mastriani to refuse the bottle of Seren-I-Tee and submit to the indignities of the exoskeleton was either unspeakably courageous or unregenerately cowardly to Trinidad's worldview.

She took the proffered hand, exchanged introductions and tried not to think of rotting gumbo. Trinidad glimpsed the array of raw red socketing at the base of her neck, the grasping tendrils of the suit interfacers.

"Yes, I am an absolute horror," Montserrat whispered confidentially. "However, I always feel an irresistible urge to piss in the face of anyone who uses the words *physically challenged* within my hearing. Salamanca!" This in the mannerly imperiousness appropriate for faded nobility. "Get Séora Malcopuelo here something to drink."

"Actually, thank you, I've got my own." She pulled out the silver flask.

"May I?" Montserrat took the flask with her dreadful hands. She sniffed the contents, took a sip, wiped her lips, returned the flask to Trinidad. "Riding the jaguar, so?"

"Grandmother," Rosalba protested.

"I am eighty-three years old, I am dying of tertiary metastasized spinal cancer, I think that entitles me to do what I like, Rosalba."

"So, is Jens here yet?" Salamanca asked.

"Out looking for his contact," said Rosalba. "Doesn't know when he'll be back."

"In the meantime," said her grandmother, "tell us your story, Trinidad. No one comes to Necroville without a story. It'll be good to hear a fresh story, we've all heard each other's so many times. Jens is a gambler and this is the ultimate bet; Salamanca is tired of living but scared of dying, like the ol' song says; me, you just have to look at me, my story is written all over this hideous exo; Rosalba here is the dutiful granddaughter who loves her *abuela* so much she will contemplate the uncontemplatable for her. Old bones, gnawed over. Tell us your story. Give us the whos and the whys, girl. Confession is a sacrament. Why not?"

Why not? Why? Flip that mental centavo and see which side shines in the blue stormlight. A shadow passed across the curving glass roof. Clouds. Wings of the Thunderbird. Candle flames flickered. Trinidad moistened her lips.

"My name is Trinidad Malcopuelo, I come from La Crescenta and I am here tonight because I made the mistake of falling in love with Peres Escobar."

I met Peres the winter we went up to the Overlook.

We went to the mountains because we wanted snow. Marilena's family owned the lodge and had told us it was empty every November to April. Unlimited winter sports, if we didn't mind the dead. We chartered a lifter, filled it with food, friends, fuckables, ski gear and Navidad presents and told it to fly us until we hit snow. Peres was there among the baggage. As he was not wearable, edible or huggable, he was either beddable or smotherable in gift wrap and hangable in a stocking above the real-wood fire. More probably both: Arena, with whom I shared a tax-dodge apartment, had rustled him out of the social circle that orbited Santiago Columbar and was making ready for a very long, cozy winter.

We discovered what Marilena meant about the dead. We ran into them everywhere for the first few days, all in the same pose, seated in a chair, hands on thighs, head slightly bowed, completely immobile, cold and hard as glass. Shut down like Overlook itself. Deader than dead. Someone suggested moving them all into the garage, but no one ever quite got around to it. Someone else suggested thawing one out against a heater so that we wouldn't have to run the daily risk of ptomaine poisoning from what we called our "cooking." We never quite got around to that either.

Peres did not share Arena's idea of winter sports. He dismissed her invitations to the giant horizontal slalom and women's downhill in front of the log fire and went out alone at first light to surf the frozen ocean. Lonely myself—the partner I was with had turned out to be a hysterical bore—I watched him carve sidewinder curves in the snow as he wove his board across the face of Weeping Woman Mountain. Always when he returned there was a brightness about him. Peres shone. Board, snow, sky, spirit: the elemental essence of his self.

"The Art of Zen Surfing," Peres tried to explain it to me. "Grand Unified Theory teaches us that all things contain the wave nature. Our universe exists on the ripples where the ten-dimensional nature of superstrings intersects with the four dimensions of our universe. Reality surfs. Snow is just one endstate of water, at the other are clouds. In the middle, *ripcurl*. Surf water in all its forms, and you understand water, you become one with water, you attune yourself to the wave nature."

"New Revelation Buddhism makes more sense," I said.

He laughed. "I know. I say it only to get into girls' pants."

"So why do you do it?"

"Get into girls' pants?"

"The snowboarding. Riding the great wave."

"Same reason. It tells me I'm alive, *hermana*."

Overlook was the beginning of the end for former relationships and the end of the beginning for new. I went west with Peres to learn the Art of Zen Surfing.

The first time I saw him vanish under the roar of a collapsing ten-meter-er I knew that all I could hope for was to be a shallow-water neophyte.

"Christ, Peres, I thought you'd drowned," I said, hugging him cold and wet and shivering and *real* to me. He felt good in wet neoprene.

"So? They'd just stick me in a Jesus tank and when I came out I'd try it again, only this time I couldn't drown."

I thought he was being glib and male and was angry and hurt. He wasn't. He was hopelessly addicted to his own adrenaline. Experience was the only valid reality; the kick of neurochemicals was the way he knew he was alive. When the cold fogs came down for days and the ocean was flat as milled steel and a brassy amber light filled up the wooden beach house where we lived weekends, he would play Bruckner at joist-shaking volumes, and *listen* with such intensity that it became almost dynamic.

"That's living," he would shout over the surge of strings. "Can't you hear it, in every, single, note? Bruckner dedicated his symphonies to God. I can interface with that."

Even in those early days I knew he wasn't happy. Me, the surf, the music; we weren't enough. He wanted, he needed, more. He grumbled, he growled, he howled. His capacity for unhappiness was truly Byronic. It would have been frightening but that it was ultimately pitiable.

Then he disappeared. None of the others in the *corillo* knew where he was. He evaded YoYo's legal 'wares; not even Santiago could find him in the ghostlands of virtuality. After a week the bastard turned up grinning and smiling and loving and so *happy* that I was not cruel enough to torpedo it with my anger. He had found the thing that was greater than the deep sea wave.

To the casual eye it looked like any other surfboard, perhaps a little flatter, a little narrower. Only on close examination did you notice the flarings and curvings and streamlinings that hinted that it rode a quite different medium.

"It's more than freefall, more than flying," he said. "It's surfing the sky. There are currents and waves in the air as much as in the sea, and you ride them. You feel them, you sense them, you go with them and they carry you forward. Like running a wave, you can outstrip terminal velocity on this thing. You are no longer a prisoner of gravity. You become one with the sky. Jesus, it's the hardest thing, to pull that ripcord, kick the release straps, let go of the board and surrender to the pull of the earth."

"And does it do it, Peres?"

"It does, Trini."

He got rid of the beach house and moved east to the desert, where the land was as pure and absolute and empty as the big sky. I went with him. Every day the skysurfers would zip up their skin-hugging flying suits, stash their boards on the readyracks hooked to the fuselage of the liftercraft, go straight up to five thousand meters, and when the plane configured into glide mode, hook their feet into the straps and bail out.

I know this because I went the first time. And the only time.

It was as if they disappeared, they fell so fast. One moment, Peres's grinning face outside the hatch, thumbs-up, A-OK, hair streaming out beside him; the next, a glittering speck of light against the immense dun geometries of the desert.

"This is insane," I shouted to the dead pilot. She agreed.

The crashing restlessness of those beach-house days when the surf wasn't up had gone. Terminal vee was the one true faith. Peres seemed content, deepened, present. He seemed to have realized that the thing for which he had been searching in the great waves had always been within himself. I never loved Peres more deeply than I did that desert spring.

Desert spring; desert summer: when the heat dessicates, the light blinds, blasts, kills. I had been rummaging through Peres's drawers for a T-shirt to borrow, when my fingers felt a clik-top plastic tub that rattled when I shook it. Gentle, gentle. Don't want to wake the alphamale turning in his sweat-soaked sheet. Peres snored on. I pocketed the tub and presented it to him over the melon at breakfast.

"What are these?" I asked, tipping a small pile of wriggling blue spiders onto the tabletop. Their tectoplastic legs clicked and clacked.

"Oh, these ones. Neural accelerators." As matter-of-fact as if I'd asked him the name of one of the little blue birds that nested in the eaves.

"What are they for?"

"Can't you guess?"

"So it doesn't do it anymore."

"It does with these."

"What do they do?"

"They slow down time. You can't go on indefinitely reaching for higher and higher states of arousal. Even with adrenaline enhancers, like you get in any main street *farmacia* there comes a point when the brain supersecretes serotonin and neutralizes the dopamines. Either that or goes into shock. Which can be somewhat unhelpful at terminal gee. What these do is not to make the highs higher, but longer. More of the burn. Transmission speeds along the axial sheaths are accelerated by a factor of ten. Can you see the implication? If internal time is speeded up, world time slows down. A ten-minute surf can seem to last . . . an hour, two hours. Trini, you can't believe it; it's falling, but like in a dream, nothing can touch you, nothing can hurt you, everything just . . . floats. But your mind is working at normal speed—that's the incredible thing about this stuff—so it's as if you become hypersensitive to the thermals and air currents and temperature gradients and winds; you can do things with the board you never dreamed you could do before. Because your mind is moving faster than the world, it's as if you're controlling the world, you think, and the sky responds. You feel like God; with a click of your fingers you could send tornadoes to the ends of the earth, you could create thunderstorms with a wave of your hand. Incredible. And the adrenaline burn becomes . . . It can't be explained, Trini. Only experienced. Like surfing your own brain chemistry. One with the quantum universe."

"You've used this?" I asked.

"We've all been using it for over a month, Trini."

"And what will you turn to when even that doesn't do it anymore?"

It took less than a month for the most sophisticated neural accelerator not to do it anymore.

I went into town to make the call. Peres had been growling around the house for days, staring out the windows, lifting his silky-sensuous surfing suits out of the drawer to feel and sniff them, reading a few lines of a magazine before throwing it away, hopping from channel to channel to channel on the television; his favorite Bruckner raging from the soundpanels while he ate voraciously, two-fisted, from the refrigerator. A call such as this needed the security of knowing no one was going to come creeping up and peer over my shoulder.

When I saw the ocean rezz up on screen, with the tropical island a low green smudge on the horizon, I'd thought I'd misconnected except that I knew Santiago's code like I knew my own birthday. The viscous slowness of the waves gave the clue; and the fact that no sky was ever that electric blue.

"Don't fuck me around, Santiago."

The island grinned. The island morphed into the head of an Archimboldo Santiago Columbar and rose from the ocean. Shoulders, torso, legs followed; a green colossus emerged, waves breaking around his ankles. He was hung with what looked like most of the Malay peninsula. High cirrus wreathed his brow.

"Yo, Trinidad. As you can see, you've got me in the middle of something, but I'm always willing to make time for my favorite ethnic minority."

His humor found me even less appreciative than usual.

"Leave Peres alone, Santiago."

"With a body like his? And a body like mine? We could make beautiful plate tectonics. You can keep his attitude, sulky boy."

"Fucking leave him alone!"

Patrons of the Desert Stop (Last Gasohol for Fifty) were looking up from the magazine racks and ChowPresto! Bar.

"I know about the accelerators, I know how they work, what they do, I know all about them and that's all right, there's nothing I can do about it but I know you know that they couldn't keep Peres up there with the angels forever. He's down now and he is one sad bastard when he's down and I know it's only a matter of time before he gets in touch with you and says *Santiago, make me something new, make me something good, that'll do it like the adrenaline enhancers or the accelerators, only bigger, only better* and because you could never ever resist a chance to prove what a fucking Jeen-Ee-Us you are, you'll do it. Except this time you won't, because it has to stop, Santiago, there has to be an upper limit, or he will kill himself looking for the big one."

"Maybe killing yourself is the Big One," the virtual-Santiago said.

"Just leave him alone, please? Say no for once. For me. For him. Please." The hallucinatory ocean lapped and broke in full sound simulation.

"Okay," said the dripping green behemoth. "Since you ask so nicely."

"I'm serious, Santiago."

"So am I. Look me up next time you're over in the Tee Vee Em Ay, Trinidad."

Peres and I snapped and bickered continuously; the heavens shook to our arguments. The frustration energy was building inside him; soon it would kick him onward, upward to a new level of experience. It was the classic can't-live-with-or-without-you scenario, and in the end I resorted to the classic endgame. I moved out of the beautiful desert home, and in with YoYo in her cheerfully squalid 'prentice-lawyer squat in Los Estudios. Angels and consciences were whispering that it was the very worst thing I could have done, but I had reached the point where all that mattered was that I, and I alone, got the psychological life raft, and sharks take the swimmers.

Hindsight hunts for signs and omens; coincidences, synchronicities, meteorological events, odd animals and strange people crossing your path. There were none that morning. No bolts of lightning, no plagues of tectosaurs, no noticing that the last three letters of the license plate ahead of you in the morning traffic spells your initials. No forewarning at all of the message that Teniente Rosa Montalban of the San Bernardino Police was to leave on YoYo's houseware asking if Trinidad Malcopuelo was resident at this address and if so could she call her at her office on the following code?

I knew he was the dead the moment Teniente Rosa Montalban's face rezzed up on the screen.

She had bad news, she was afraid. There had been an accident. Peres Escobar, the whole team, were dead.

Something to do with the aircraft? I asked mildly. Shock, grief, disintegration, depression: these were the reactions proper to the death of lovers. All I felt was distance, as if this were a news report of a war in another country. Because I had not been there, it had not happened. I could not believe in it.

No, it had not been the plane. It was the skyboard team itself. There would have to be post mortems, of course, to determine if there were any contributing factors, but they all seemed to have (I felt the world kick into slow time, as if I had taken one of Peres's neural accelerators). Simply. Forgotten. To. Open. Their. Chutes.

I saw them, falling through the sky, balanced on an ever-breaking wave of air, imagining that the power of their augmented wills could somehow twist gravity ninety degrees so that it would draw them on forever around the curve of the world. All the time falling faster, closer. Had there been a last-minute revelation, a frantic deploying of parafoils that they realized with horror were too low too late? Or had the real world simply lifted up its hand, reached into their dreams and smashed them into oblivion?

"Séora Malcopuelo? Séora?"

I had been trying to calculate the terminal velocity of a human body massing sixty kilos falling from three kays.

I must have mumbled something about coming out to identify Peres and settle up his things—all I remember are the words *how calm you are how clear you are* screaming over and over and over in my head—because the next day I suddenly found myself eastbound on Ten three kays out of Banning with a pale, tearful YoYo in the passenger seat and no clear memory of how I had gotten there.

Grief should have destroyed me. What I felt was guilt that it had not. A line from an old flat-screen monochrome Hitchcock movie kept going through my head as I drove: *in a few days you're going to have the most wonderful breakdown, darling.*

Teniente Rosa was cute and kind and prepared us with Desert Tea and a little homily. The post-mortem scanners had picked up traces of what seemed to be a custom-built cortical damper cut with an acetyl-choline accelerator in the brainstems. Simulations indicated that it would have had the effect of slowing chronoperception so much that time effectively stood still while disabling the cognitive filters that pre-process sensory data into comprehensible forms according to hard-wired a priori cognotypes. They had overdosed on reality, undifferentiated data pouring in through ears eyes nose tongue skin in an unstoppable torrent of sense impressions that had lasted no time and forever simul-taneously.

Satori in the sky.

At that moment I wanted to see Santiago Columbar hung from a hook by his own intestines.

"The thing about these designer drugs is you can always trace them back to the motherhouse. These little beauties came from a necro sweat-shop in San Fernando growing smartgenes for one Séor Michael Rocha of Sherman Oaks. Our city sisters are having a few well-chosen words for him even as I speak."

Forgive me, Santiago. You were honorable and true.

The Death House had prepped Peres for the Jesus tank. Done things with tectors, put things back together again, made him look something like the Peres Escobar who had tried to teach me the Art of Zen Surfing up at Overlook. Teniente Rosa asked me if it was him, I nodded. YoYo looked in and got very emotional and had to be helped to a chair.

Even in death he looked discontent.

Then the five dark, beautiful women from the Death House low-ered the plastic lid of the Jesus tank, and a thought struck me.

"Has he got an *Immortalidad*?"

One of the woman checked a tagalong.

"Nothing here."

I'd never known anyone who had not been insured for resurrection. These five fates would take Peres away into an eternity of indenture;

stateless, dispossessed. Peres's sin was always that of Satan's: *non serviam*. Pride. Yes, he had been a stupid vain bastard—more—but at that moment I felt he deserved to find in death the freedom he had never known in life.

"How much would it be to . . . you know?"

They named a sum that drew an involuntary gasp from YoYo.

"It would be cheaper to buy his contract," the dead woman with the tagalong said. Of all the words spoken in the last twenty-four hours, it was those eight that penetrated the insensibility that had surrounded me. I saw Peres restored, repaired, relit with that strange black heat that shines out of the dead. I saw him moving around my La Crescenta home, attending, serving, caring, working, executing his duty to his contract holder. I saw myself covering him with kisses, taking him to my bed, to the hidden places of the gardens, to the warm waters of the pool, filled with love that the one I had seen lost was found again, was mine again.

It could not happen. Death was stronger than love. He would remember Trinidad Malcopuelo but not the love she had given him; it would be just another lost relationship in a time that seemed to him like a long and highly detailed dream.

"Have his resurrection charges made to my *Immortalidad* account," I told the dead women. "I never want to see or hear from him again."

"That is almost certain," the dead women said.

YoYo drove me back to the city, for by then I had started that most wonderful breakdown I had promised myself.

"It's one of those inverse laws that seem to govern human pain," Trinidad said. "The bigger the bastard, the more the love. Peres had defined my life. Everything I was was a reaction to him; without him, Trinidad did not exist. Even before the shrinkwares had finished with me I was hunting the hills for another Peres to hold the strings of my life. Everything the 'wares told me not to do, I did, because at worst they didn't hurt and best they felt like warm flesh. The year I took myself out of therapy I had thirty affairs, the shortest twelve hours, the longest three weeks. To find myself, I had to lose myself in others."

The *Posada*'s many candles had burned down to a softly glowing constellation concealed in the drooping greenery. The storm had passed, the rain that had come in its wake was a gentle tapping on the roof.

"And have you found yourself yet?" Montserrat Mastriani asked.

"Perhaps," Trinidad said.

"Is that why you're here, to find Peres?" Rosalba asked.

"No, no, of course it's not, stupid girl," Montserrat interrupted tetchily. "Didn't you take in a word of what you were told?"

"No, I know I can't find him, I don't want to find him, not anymore. I came here on this Night of the Dead because Santiago Columbar invited me."

"Why did he do that?" Salamanca, now, perched on the edge of the table. "More to the point, why did you do that?"

"Because I wanted to prove I wasn't afraid; of the dead town, of him. And because I felt he might know something about Peres's death I didn't."

"And did he?" Salamanca again.

"He couldn't resist it. He promised me, but he couldn't resist it. The San Bernadino County cops traced the spiders back to Michael Rocha's operation; what they don't know is that Rocha built the stuff from designs and blueprints created by Santiago Columbar. He killed Peres as surely as if he had cut his heart out."

"Fucker," said Rosalba unexpectedly.

" 'Better a live rat than a dead lion,' they used to say in old Singapore." The new voice was directly behind Trinidad, so sudden she shivered as if physically threatened. "Better still a live lion. Instead of courting the reaper, your friend should have come with us to shake the hand of eternal life. True immortality. Excellent story, séora. Makes our little litanies of cancer, cowardice and probability sound quite mundane. This is not a criticism, far from it." The speaker was a tall, spare man dressed in a dripping green stockman's coat. A matching hat concealed his face, what Trinidad could see of it seemed weary and gray. He was not young, but not as old as he looked. He was Santiago, decades from now, worn away by the unbearable gravitation of being. "May I introduce myself, séora? My name is Jens Aarp, mentor, seeker, searcher and, at last, discoverer of the way to true eternal life."

Concealed by shadows, YoYo saw the mobile trauma unit pull away. Ellis stood in the street, watching until the flashing blue lights merged with the traffic before returning to the house. Jorge, senior partner, had gone in the ambulance. Thunder growled after the ambulance, like a bad dog chasing cars. Hidden among the trash cans and garbage sacks, YoYo suffered agonies of guilt. She should go to them. She should have been with them. She dare not go near them. She had drawn demons to her. They had declared their indiscriminacy over seventy-three percent of Trio's skin surface.

People had died from less than that. People had gone into the Big Dark. Trio had hardly been able to afford the medical insurance, let alone an *Immortalidad* policy. Don't die, right? So, you were taller prettier thinner more successful than me, but don't die.

YoYo sniffed, knuckled tears back into their ducts. She raised her tagalong to her lips, then froze, words unspoken, paralyzed by the realization that the universe was no longer fundamentally trustworthy. Her tagalong could be a little wrist-mounted Judas. A legion of bugs could be hiding out in the crannies of the streetbike. Her bodyglove could be informing unseen monitors of her every twitch and tic. Only her own smooth-shaved skin could be trusted, and that could not be relied on to remain intact indefinitely.

"Ellis," she whispered. His private colophon, a surfing kangaroo with improbably sized genitalia, rezzed up on the tiny wristscreen. Come on come on come on. "Ellis, stop pissing about and get on the line, I need you."

Ellis appeared. Not a virtuality construct, not an interactive icon. Himself.

"YoYo. Where the hell are you?" Gone the laconic surf-heaven.

"I'm . . . I better not say where I am. Sweet Jesus, Ellis, they knew my 'ware, my access codes, my locators, everything."

" 'They?' This wasn't a random blowback?"

"Ellis, I . . ." Ellis, I can't tell you. Ellis, I daren't tell you. Ellis, I must tell you. "Ellis, I'm in trouble."

The flash was too bright for lightning, the boom too close, too flat for thunder. Ellis's image disintegrated for a few seconds into a blizzard of interference.

"Jesus, Ellis!" Down beyond the Sunset gate, fifty security alarms were screaming as one.

Ellis glanced off focus. "Something's coming in, all channels. Excuse me a moment." He turned into his surfing kangaroo. An aircraft passed overhead, so low she could feel the downwash of its fans. Ellis returned. His face looked freshly embalmed.

"Where did you go when you went down to Saint John?"

"An eateria called Tacorifico Superica's. Why?"

"Tacorifico Superica's has just been destroyed by what appears to be a shaped picotok charge." YoYo staggered back, the cheap cinderblock wall reassurance and solidity in a world melting into insanity. "All the hallmarks of a classic *corporada* war hit. Shaped charge chucked into a containment field. Total vaporization.''

''Survivors?'' Patrons enjoying a plate of *camarónes español* and a Red Hat. *Chefs de parti*. Bar staff. The silently eloquent waiter. Martika Semalang.

''YoYo, it was a mass conversion charge. The place is a twenty-meter crater of bubbling glass.''

The aircraft she had heard swept low once more over Sunset Strip.

''Ellis. Listen to me. Listen to me. Who's in the house with you?''

''I'm on my own. Why?''

''Listen. Just listen. Dump everything into safe storage. And get out of the house. Now. Don't look back. Just get out and go. You are going to die, Ellis.''

Looking up, she saw the liftercraft turn above the palms, flashlit by a shaft of Hollywood Gothic lightning. It came in for the third time.

Third time is the witching time.

The eye of her tagalong was filled with the nightmare-blue fuzz of dead webchannels. At least the 'wares were safe.

With a shatter of ducted fans, the liftercraft swooped down and aerobraked directly over YoYo's hiding place. Curious neighbors came into their gardens, clothes flapping, leaves storming around their faces. A figure burst from the house: Ellis. He screamed warnings to the gaping neighbors. Some few heeded. Most did not. YoYo glimpsed the containment field as a pale blue cylinder of electrified night and turned her back, covered her head with her arms, closed her eyes.

The picotok blast shafted sheer white light through her sealed eyelids. White heat stroked her back, her arms, her hideously naked scalp. Burning leather. And *boom*. YoYo screamed as a sound louder than any sound could be stretched her eardrums to breaking point. Her bones rattled. Blood ran down the sides of her face where her fingernails had pressed through skin into flesh. Most of the blast had gone straight up, channeled by the containment field, yet when the field collapsed, the pressure wave punched the wind from her lungs, rolled her with tumbling trash down the alley.

It ended. She opened her eyes, blinked away swarms of afterimages. The cheap Barato-Mart terracotta paint that decorated the walls had been bleached white. She saw the assaultcraft lift straight up on its fans, spin on its vertical axis like a bug on a pin and slide away across the night.

The blast had sent Jorge's moped skidding along the concrete. Its plastic shell was scraped and lacerated, Jorge's hand-custom paint job of deathsheads and *vampiras* half jaguar, half large-breasted woman wrestlers was abraded away to almost nothing. She picked the machine up. Its alcohol motor kicked into instant life.

She mounted the streetbike and rode off through alleys and service-ways. Convoys of emergency vehicles came slamming along the avenues, a conga line of sirens and blue lights. Flames lit the night behind her. Heeding her own wisdom, she did not look back.

Brave gesture, bold gesture, to shake your fist in the eye of a God on High who has shown no compunction about shredding you to atoms, but where do you go, little lawyer? What do you do next? You stand alone in your bodyglove and cute/expensive streetgear on a friendless boulevard where any who offer aid of shelter draw the divine wrath upon them. What can you do that is not merely a protracted way to die? Give it up. Surrender. Bare the soft, pale skin of your belly to the blade.

Concealed in backstreet shadows, YoYo saw her parents sitting over the alcohol stove in their Drown Town sampan, muttering muttering muttering: *told you so told you so told you so. Now, tell me, what was the point of all that?*

Every expression of self she had ever attempted, every stand against their monstrous fatalism, every personal hope and ambition: met with that question: *Now, really, what was the point of that?*

Her ferocious will to succeed that had driven her out of the foot-rot and salt-burn of the sampan suburbs to the languid Spanish-speaking hills had been a need to find the answer to that indifference. Now, at the nadir of isolation, fear, defeat, danger, she knew what it was. The universe doesn't owe us a reason. You just do it.

YoYo Mok is not going to die today. Where do you go? What do you do? I don't know yet, but I'm a Starchild. I'll think of something.

"It is not over. Believe me. Tesler-Thanos, God, I don't care who you are, how big you are, I will destroy you." Mighty Fine Words. What is the point of being a lawyer unless you get to utter Mighty Fine Words at some crucial point in your career? Brushing grit and shit from her leathers (if those bastards have scorched them, I'll add it to costs) her fingers found a forgotten rectangle in her left tit pocket.

Santiago Columbar invites YoYo Mok . . .

Santiago Columbar. Trust him to turn up at a time like this. District of Saint John. Necroville. Where all the dark things end up. Down among the dead men. Where else? Santiago. Sant Iago: Iago, her 'ware-man.

Dare she admit it, or was there a tiny fetus of gumshoe instinct, down there, curling its fingers and gestating in the dark? Lightning poured blue heat into the alley, thunder hard on its tail. YoYo turned her streetbike. And her tagalong sang on her wrist.

She hesitated one long moment, listening for liftercraft engines, before she answered.

"Ellis? That you? You all right? Jeez, *compadre*, you shouldn't be calling me on this . . ."

"Séora Mok?"

Those cat-cool features, that graceful languor should have been veins of trace elements in a pool of cooling obsidian.

"Séora Semalang."

"I've been trying to contact you as you said in the note. Is everything all right? The diner, it's been . . ."

"I know, I know." Think. Think. Perry Mason always knew what he was going to do. His scriptwriters told him. Think. "Note? What note?"

"The note the *patrón* brought me, asking me to call you from a public 'fon point at the end of the street. Séora Mok . . . ("YoYo") . . . YoYo, the restaurant . . ."

"I know. I know. They threw one at my house. My fucking *house*, my home, my friends. Your *compadres* play the professional foul game. I need answers from you, Séora Semalang, I want to know just what the hell is going on."

"I don't know; believe me, I can't remember. It's not there to remember. YoYo, I don't exist. And I am very frightened. But for your note, I'd have been at the table . . ."

"Séora, I didn't send any note. It's not my style." Her client did not Need to Know that YoYo was a functioning dyslexic.

"Then who did? Why? What did they want?"

"Working from easiest to hardest, I'd say 'why' "—she counted it off on her finger—"you out of there, 'who': someone who knew Tacorifico Superica's was going to get hit and that you were there, with me; 'what they want': I don't even know how many teams are on the court, let alone what game they're playing."

"The people who destroyed the diner and your house," *(And burned Trio, never forget)* "are hardly going to send their target a warning note."

"Which immediately puts another team on the field." Sporting analogies again. You watch too much of the damn stuff, YoYo Mok. The new opiate of the people. "Someone who wants you alive as much as the away team wants you dead. Permanently." Little doubts nagged, like persistent mosquitoes. Later. She would marshal them, train them, make them perform little tricks for her, but later. "Séora Semalang, I know you can't remember anything that might be important enough to get you killed, but the people who're trying think it's not just possible, but probable, that you will. Which is a good thing and a bad thing. Good for us in that maybe I can find out just what that is, bad for us in that these *hijos* aren't going to give up." *Think. Yes!* "Listen . . . Hello? Hello? You still there?" Martika Semalang had vanished from focus; the camera eye showed a street in which not one window remained intact. Fire glowed off camera. The dead woman ducked back into shot, smoothing her hair with her hands.

"I'm sorry," she said. "I can't stay here much longer. The wind's shifted and the fire's coming this way."

"Listen! Listen! Listen!" YoYo yelled. "Just stay there awhile longer. I'll send someone to you. He'll take you to a safe place where we can meet. But just stay where you are until he gets there, all right? You'll know him because he'll say . . ." (what'll he say what'll he say what'll he *say*?) " 'Stairway to Heaven' and you say to him 'Bloody David Niven.' " Well, what could you expect. "Got that?"

" 'Stairway to Heaven.' 'Bloody David Niven.' "

"And wait, wait, wait, just one more thing, Séora Semalang, whatever happens, do not call me on this tagalong number again. I can't guarantee it's secure. I'll find you." How? Worry about that later. Later. Always later.

YoYo carefully rode the mope over the tagalong. The cracking of its plastic carapace was the sundering of her last link with the electromagnetic ecstasy of the web. She shuddered, alone and clammy in a filmskin bodyglove suddenly gone cold and dead.

Thunder boomed and rolled over Copananga. YoYo maneuvered her streetbike between long columns of armored security vehicles, lined up all the way to the pastel glow of the gate. A *corporada* picotok hit, it could have been, but did they need to call out the marines? Something even bigger in the air tonight. Might as well make a few calls while they finish doing whatever it is they do. The telecom point was in the lobby of a deserted café: all neoned up but no sweet-sixteens swinging their legs in the Naugahyde booths. All down over the border dancing with the dead. *Necro Mambo.*

The 'fon choked on YoYo's cashcard but decided it could take it. On a wallscreen across the street, Janet Leigh drove furious furious, faster faster, furious furious, faster faster glancing into her rearview, imagining pursuers. They're in front of you, honey. At the Bates Motel.

Llamado llamado said the 'fon, *Llamado llamado YoYo.*

"Iago."

"YoYo."

"Iago?"

Shaven head powdered with 'lectric-blue mica dust. Eyebrows plucked, falsie-lashes mascaraed, baby-blues kohled and shadowed. Earrings long and pendulous. Chin shaven to the bone. Lips pouted and pretty-boy-pink. Wet and puckered as a split persimmon. Makeup, not bad. Not bad at all. Centavo-store glitter and costume jewelry: the bigger the better, "gaudy" is considered a compliment in this esthetic system; nails decuticled and lacquered to match the keess-mee-hombre lips. The hands worked; usually they were the part that was hardest to change, but these worked. Pay-by-the-night hire-shop subdermals; the tecto-silicon would have all squeezed out through the pores again come morning, but they looked good. Better than hers, dammit. All poured into a sheath of sheer liquid Lycra. Like a home-brew Popsicle.

He looked, YoYo had to admit, *fantastic.*

"Iago?"

"Every man should have a hobby, YoYo."

"You look great, Iago. I would kill for a complexion like that."

He smiled. The smile worked too.

"Thanks, YoYo. Aren't I a bitch? The guys and I have been busy on this all year."

"Iago, is this, ah, a bad time for you?" (And it's not for YoYo?)

"Only in as much as I've got to be down in the *zócalo* in five minutes. Something you need?"

"Yes. You could say that. Can I ask you a couple of favors?"

"Oh YoYo, YoYo," he groaned, his big night out with the boys shimmying down the boulevard toward oblivionville.

"Have you got a copy of the 'ware you ran up for me?"

"Never throw anything out."

"You couldn't load it up?"

"YoYo, have you any idea what volume that program occupies?"

"Iago"—the name just didn't fit this vision in drag, like a pair of workboots slipped onto pedicured feet—"I need your help." She told him why.

"Fuck, YoYo."

"I want you to find something out for me. Tesler-Thanos transferred the six million into Martika Semalang's ghost account, but I want to know exactly who authorized the payment. If I can find out *who*, I can find out *why*. Can you do this for me, Iago?"

"Surely can, *querida*." Cleopatra eyes glanced off focus. " 'Wares up and running."

"I'm squirting the parameters to you. The suit's got them stored. I don't need to tell you, but mind your sweet ass."

Iago smirked coyly.

"Little old *moi*, pussyfooting around? Shoot, YoYo."

YoYo extended a filament of bodyglove into the 'fon datatransfer interfacer. Bored staff, propping their elbows on an empty counter and playing finger games with steak knives, craned their heads to look-see what was going on in their lobby. None of your damn business, *favelados*. The glimmer of linkage to her old, beloved 'ware was like a lover's fingers on her spine.

Pleasure and guilt. She had never been able to admit to herself that her sexuality was connected body and soul to the machine by an unbreakable umbilical. The limbic purr of data, the lift into the cybernetic cloud of unknowing, the dissolution of too solid flesh into the liquid multivalence of the morph; these were of it, but also the sleek embrace of the bodyglove, the street clothes she chose, the sensual slide of Iago's razor across her scalp, the small penetrations of the interfacers.

Why could she not, like the dead, deconfigure her sad, confused monochrome YoYo and emerge renascent, reconfigured, happy, honest, manycolored, cybersexual? It was who she was. It was what she was. It did not make her anything less than she was now. The measure of a person was not who or what they liked to *joder*. The package of loves, hates and vulnerabilities that was YoYo Mok would not change.

"Yo? You all right?" At the image of Iago, free to do and be and celebrate whatever he felt his Iagoness consisted of, tears welled up. Dammit, *no*.

"Yo?"

"I'm all right. I'm all right. Shit. Iago, one more thing I need you to do."

"Anything, *querida*."

"I need you to go to this place"—she squirted him Martika Semalang's location—"pick up my client and take her back to your place. I know it's asking a lot"—the outrageous face pouted flirtatiously—"but there's no one else I can trust. Oh, you need to tell her: 'Stairway to Heaven.' " Iago rolled his head and arched his exquisitely plucked eyebrows in high-camp despair. "Sorry, it was the best thing I could think of. I was under certain pressure, you know? She'll tell you 'Bloody David Niven.' "

"I hope you know he's a teevee icon."

"Iago."

"Aha?"

"It could be dangerous."

"So? Who wants to live forever. By the bye, that search? Got something for you. The name in the frame, the face who slid six million Rim into your client's account on behalf of Tesler-Thanos, is Lars Thorwald Aloysius Maguffin."

"You got an address on that?"

"I've got an address but I don't think you'll find anything, or anyone, there. Someone's playing games, YoYo."

"What do you mean?"

"Do you know what a maguffin is?"

"Should I?"

"A device for catching lions in Scotland."

"But there are no lions in Scotland."

"Exactly . . ." said Iago, and disappeared in a blizzard of static. The white data-roar that is the true voice of the web hissed in YoYo's ears. Nothing on all sensory and virtuality channels. A message rezzed up on screen.

Las Encinas Seguridad regrets the suspension of all communications channels into Saint John necroville for the duration of the current emergency.

Out in the street armed and armored *seguridados* were running to their vehicles; patrol carriers were firing up in vaporous blue detonations of biodiesel. Technicians were working over readyracks of powered-down *mechadors*, the rising hum of impellor systems warming up set her teeth on edge as harmonics clashed.

YoYo disengaged her bodyglove from the 'fon point.

YOYO, WAIT, said the message on the scrawled-over screen. IT'S ME, YOYO. I CAN HELP, TRUST ME.

"Leave me alone," she hissed into the mouthpiece. "Get away from me, Jesus Joseph Mary, have you any idea what you have done to me? Everywhere I go, you're there, like one big spotlight lighting up everything I do."

I WANTED ONLY TO BE YOUR FRIEND, said the Carmen Miranda.

"Your friendship is going to get me killed."

I'M SORRY. I'M SORRY. I WAS SENT TO HELP YOU.

"I don't need your help." *Sent? Sent?*

REMEMBER, IF YOU EVER NEED ME, JUST WHISTLE. YOU KNOW HOW TO WHISTLE, DON'T YOU?

The 'fon returned YoYo's cashcard. Fifty centavos left to her name in the world. How much worse could this get? Don't answer that, YoYo. At least the bike started the first time. Dodging *seguridados* and curious carnival-goers in a range of costumes from nothing to drag that made Iago look dowdy, she passed under the luminous crossbar of the gate.

"I'm sorry, I can't let you through," said the pale lips beneath the datavisor.

"I have to get through, I'm a lawyer, I have to see a client."

"A client? In Necroville?"

"You've got to let me through. It is a matter of life and death. No shit, officer."

"I'm sorry, orders are the borders stay closed. No one gets in, no one gets out."

The steel teeth grinned out of the blacktop at her. Hah hah *abogadito*.

"How can I make you understand? I have to get through. Just me, eh? Just one, is that so much?" Were Las Encinas *seguridados* bribable for fifty centavos? All right all right, I'm a closet cybersexual, but you can do it with me any way you like if you'll Just. Let. Me. In.

"How can I make you understand, séora? All security units are on maximum alert during the current emergency. Nobody gets in. Not you. Not God. Not anyone. Now, either you turn your little bike around and go back where the hell you came from, or the *muchachos* turn it around for you, which they would like very much, but I can't guarantee that you will."

So much for chummy little sexual flirtations and harassments. Condeming the *male, sexist, muy machismo* lot of them to endless genital torment in the one of her grandmother's Confucianist hells reserved for those who denied the needy justice, YoYo found herself on the street again under the watchful eye of Anthony Perkins peeping at Janet Leigh stripping for the shower scene. Can't phone in, can't ride in, can't run the wire without getting slagged by some *mechador* with only slightly more brain than its controller, no client, no clue, no ideas, no home, no friends, no place to run and you haven't even the price of a cup of coffee on your cashcard. What now, little lawyer?

What the hell. It was worth a try.

The whistle made even the *seguridados* flip up their display visors to look. It dissolved into a distant mutter of thunder, moving east. Cold wind swept the street.

The telephone rang in the lobby of the Last Chance Diner. For some reason, the staff all stared at their hands.

"Hello?"

"Hello YoYo. I'm glad you called. I didn't like us not being friends."

"I need a favor."

"Name it."

"I need to get into Necroville."

"I'm sorry to have to tell you this, YoYo, but the security companies have sealed off the dead towns and won't let you in until morning. Can't it wait?"

"No it fucking . . ." *Uno dos tres cuatro cinco seis* . . . "I have to get in immediately."

"It may be a little difficult. But I will try, because you're my friend."

The image froze, the equivalent, YoYo guessed, of a *busy* symbol. *Uno dos tres cuatro cinco segundos*. It must be difficult, even for something that inhabited the Planck-time interstices of the dataweb. It returned with a revolting grin.

"YoYo, if you go down the next access lane on the left, just behind the café where we're speaking, you'll find it runs through into the District of Saint John. There is a chain-link fence that you could climb quite easily. Unfortunately, it is fitted with passive and active sensor systems and alerts, self-targeting tesler weapons, and the fence is electrified. I know it sounds bad, but don't be upset, YoYo. I said I would try to get you in, and I will, I promise."

"Just do it." Manners. Remember, these things are the emotional equivalent of five-year-olds. "Please."

"I'm so happy you're allowing me to show I'm your friend, YoYo. Probability significant precipitation in the next fifty-three seconds is ninety-eight percent. That would be a good time to move. I can take out the main, backup and tertiary level systems, which will give you thirty-three seconds guaranteed before they can reroute backups from other areas. Hope we can get to talk again soon, YoYo. Bye . . ."

Section by section, block by block, street by street, the lights were going out. Darkness descended like the open hand of God upon West Hollywood. The confused *carnivalistos* in their many costumes flurried in consternation. The café was extinguished like a glass ornament shattered by a hammer. Janet Leigh turned, screamed at Mother's descending knife, and flicked into nonexistence. The luminous vee-slash of the Necroville gate coughed twice and died.

And the rains came down. Vehicle headlamps and *seguridado* flashlights cut seething arcs through the downpour, voices shouted to make themselves heard.

"YoYo, now," whispered the voice of Carmen Miranda, but YoYo was already gone. She hit the wire, threw herself up up up. *Come on YoYo.* And over.

The lights came on, two by two. A teenager waiter replaced the voicepiece on the lobby 'fon, puzzled by the on-screen message: MISS-ING YOU ALREADY . . .

Toussaint could feel the rising thermal as a vague warmth on his face. A stroke of his mind: the wingtips curled, the aerofoil warped; he turned into the thermal. It had taken time and patience for the neural pathways to properly imprint, but now the commands were as unconscious as a concert pianist's to his fingers in a Debussy étude. Glancing back, he saw the line of three 'foils bank to follow. The familiar blue condor pattern of Huen's wing was like a long, cold claw in his heart.

Retinal telltales flashed five kinds of datapanic. Big storm coming; these updrafts were merely its outriders. Toussaint blinked them away. The tug and flutter of the wing against his spinal spars told him all he needed to know about the state of the sky.

Quebec spoke in his inner ear. The earbud Shipley had forced into him received but he had been given no means of transmission. Its only purpose, he suspected, was for him to hear—without interruption—the story Quebec was unfolding.

Call me Quebec.

I awoke from my second rebirth as the sun rose over the twenty meter horizon of Tessier 813 stroke 18 stroke C, a cratered potato of carbonaceous chondrite eight hundred meters long by seventy broad following an elliptical orbit that took it within three hundred thousand kays of Martian orbit at perihelion and just short of Jupiter on the return lap. While I was still coughing the gluey placental fluids out of my lungs, the sun set. Twenty-three minutes fifteen seconds from dawn to dusk, and it was the first day. We were twelve—seven men, five women—the crew of Tessier 813, reconfigured by Ewart/Western Australian for deep space work. All were contractees, some were nightfreights. I can imagine no crueler punchline than awaking into resurrection life sixty million kilometers from your last memory. Our skins were fully photosynthetic pressure membranes, capable of supplying all our energy requirements given an insolation less than that of Mars; our metabolisms capable of functioning as anaerobic sealed units for several earth days; our bodies implanted with wide-spectrum analyzers, data hookups and subaudial communications rigs. We were the future humanity: as at home in vacuum as in the environment blisters the nanotech package had created out of Tessier 813's carbonaceous chondrite. The solar system was our front room.

We were a state of supernumeraries with enough to do to require our presence but not so much as to keep us occupied. Checking the command 'ware, monitoring the construction of the mass driver, adjusting the attitude jets to stop Tessier 813's rotation—my first EVA. I had died and been resurrected twice, but I could hardly bear to bring myself to the brink, to step through that pressure membrane onto the surface. Yet I did, and the glory of it, the sheer ecstatic vulnerability of knowing yourself naked beneath the universe—but aware, conscious, capable of declaring your self-hood, your existence back to its infinite indifference—was an experience of such intensity that it made all the sins and hurts that had brought me here worthwhile. Vacuum-rapture, they call it. Communion with the infinite. Some have been lost to it, forgetting to tether themselves while the ship is under micro-acceleration, they drift into space and are lost. I imagine them alive and aware, unable to die, flying on forever lost in the wonder of the universe.

The crew are among the last things manufactured by the slamship: the conversion of Tessier 813 was already well begun by the time we emerged from our Jesus tanks. Tectors never sleep; while over half of Tessier 813 was fired out the ass end at a goodly fraction of light speed, the nose end erupted into a bubonic mass of bubbles and pods within which asteroid-stuff was ripped apart and forged into microgee smart fibers and mnemopolymer chains. Six months into the flight, with three months left to Ewart/OzWest's high-orbit manufactories, Tessier 813 had been transfigured into an array of processing tanks linked together by nanofiber webbing balanced atop the slender spine of the mass driver. Halfway between nanotechnological hell and the electromagnetic kick-back, our cluster of habitation modules clung like overripe grapes to a fifty-meter boom. The whole ungainly mass was in turnaround mode, firing a twenty-kilo pellet of the rapidly dwindling reaction mass reserve every thirty seconds to bring us to Earth orbital insertion vee.

It was in those long reaches between Mars and Earth that they jumped us. Within a few minutes of its appearance on the long-range scanners we knew that this was not another chunk of deep-space debris. We knew we could not hide. The navigation 'ware told us we could not run either. We spent the fifteen days to intercept hanging free; luxuriating in the waxing sunlight and watching a small, dim star to the left of Mars grow ever brighter and sharper.

Their ship was a lean black widow lying at the center of a web of radiating light-sail panels. A small shuttleboat, little more than a grid of construction beams and a hydroxy engine, clung to its mother's belly. Our image enhancement 'ware picked out impossibly agile figures scrambling over the subship. We received one message: *Prepare to be boarded*, transmitted in Spanish, English, Cantonese, Hindi, Arabic, French and Japanese.

If beauty can be rationalized as fitness for purpose, then they were the most beautiful creatures I have ever seen. They were shaped for space as a bird is for sky. Their hides were patterned and dappled with recognition markers; their features annealed into blank masks that nevertheless seemed possessed of all sensory faculties. Their legs had been completely replaced by long, powerful arms; fully articulated and terminating in large, grasping hands. Those lower hands held the heavy laser cutters with which they had opened our habitat blisters. Gender identifiers had been stripped away by the vicissitudes of reconfiguration, yet I gained the impression that their leader—rather, the one closest to us—was a woman.

"Welcome to Tessier 813," said Marianne, our captain. "Please accept our surrender."

"Thank you," said the leader in badly accented Spanish. Spots of polychromatic skin on her shoulders, nipples and buttocks glowed blue when she spoke, identifying the speaker. "I'm sorry."

She shot Marianne through the belly with a short harpoon connected by monofilament to a weapon in her upper right hand. Body stuffs and fluids fountained out under internal pressure. While we screamed, Marianne died twisting and spasming on the end of the line, the raiders opened fire. I was the last to die.

I awoke from my third resurrection in darkness. I called out the names of the friends I had seen slaughtered.

"It's all right," a woman's voice said, so close as to be unnerving. "You have been dead a long time, come a long road. Those Ewart/OzWest slamships are buckets, even with lunar slingshot. I'm sorry you and your friends had to be killed; it was much more convenient that you be stored before we began the course corrections; shortly after we finished we suicided anyway."

"Who are you? What is this? Where am I?"

You can hear a smile if you have the ear for it.

A faint blue glow suffused the enclosing darkness. A four-armed angel floated beside me; above me, stars. The light brightened. A dazzling speck of sun rose. I cried out in wonder.

The tectoplastic globe that enclosed me was only one of hundreds, an amorphous frogspawn of habitation modules kilometers across. Yet even this seemed insignificant compared to the objects that filled the sky above me. Vast nanofacturing complexes devoured asteroids whole, spinning them out into webs and sheets of construction materials or clusters of gleaming organochemical processors. The more brilliant stars were lunetta mirrors and moored light sail units: old O'Neill can utilities were ensnared in rooty holdfasts of more recent nanotech additions. Dome farms and agriculture tubes turned their transparent faces to the suns, their curved inner surfaces checkerboards of crop seedings.

I watched slabs of rough-hewn asteroid-stuff turn into the sunlight and saw to my amazement their naked faces softened by the unmistakable dappling of leaves. More marvelous yet: a spherical mass of dark green drifted across my field of vision. I estimated it to be almost a kilometer in diameter and, in the same instant, I understood what it was. A tree. Enclosed, self-sustaining, a thing of vacuum and starlight. Figures moved among the huge leaves.

Yet wonderful though all these things were, they were mere ornaments for the centerpiece. I had seen a shadow eclipsing the stars, glints and highlights hinting at some immense unseen object. Now that object turned full into the light and I was humbled.

From its smaller companions, I judged the great wheel must have been twenty kilometers across. It was not complete; only three of its five spokes were connected. Haulers and construction crews maneuvered massive chunks of processed asteroid toward the exposed ends, where ferocious architectonic systems dismantled and annealed them into the ever-growing circumference. Some of the longer established sections were shaggy with the extraordinary vacuum mosses and plants.

"We're already tectosculpting the interior," said my nameless companion. "Ten years we've been working on it, since the first ships mutinied and set up here in the Belt. Ten more before it's finished. If the meat let us."

"It's beautiful," I said.

"It's called Neruro, and this is the Neruro Clade."

The spin city wheeled out of the light into darkness, and awe welled in me so that I felt that pricking in the corners of my eyes that is the prelude to tears. Yet no tears came. No salty spheres swelled and drifted away in the microgravity.

"What have you done to me?" I exclaimed, conscious of strange new sensations in my old familiar body. I looked down. "Oh Jesus Joseph Mary!"

I stared in numb outrage at the outspread fingers of my new hands. I touched them with my upper hands; they curled reflexively. Without knowing how I did so, I bent my new arms so that my upper fingers could explore them.

"We did it while you were dead in transit," the Neruro woman said. "You are a *quadro*. You are of us now."

More had been done to me in my third death and resurrection than physical evolution. New neural pathways had been burned in; new kinesics enabled me to use my new arms and hands with the same facility as my old; my senses had been extended into new, broader, spectra of perception; my radio implants opened my mind to communication more intimate by far than spoken words, one that encompassed emotion and unvocalized prethought, and subtler mental states for which language has no names.

The dead are the true humanity. There was no environment that we could not conquer, given time. And time likewise served us. With our ability to die, to step outside time, and be resurrected, the months—years—of space travel did not exist. The gulfs between planets, the centuries between stars; no difference to death. I was shown the manufacturing installations where slamships to the stars were planned. Accelerated to ten percent C by powerful mass drivers, the ships could reach the nearer stars in a handful of decades, decelerating by solar sails hundreds of kilometers across while searching for a suitable target body out of which it could reconfigure crew, biomass pods, exploration and communications equipment. Research tectoengineers—a mob of wildly colored, wilder-speculating outlaws raided from orbital factories in the early days of the NightFreight Wars—theorized human slamships reconfiguring extrasolar planets and satellites, filling up the energy-rich spaces between the worlds, transforming entire star systems: a universe seeded with life, a universe becoming life, tied together by webs of lightspeed communications and C-fractional space vehicles. One human being might colonize and in time become an entire world, the human time sense could slow to the point where C-limited communications would seem almost instantaneous. The galaxies, the clusters, the super clusters, would shrink to the perceived size of a single world. Engineering of the universe at its fundamental level would become attainable. Space, time, entropy: reality, all these could be manipulated; humanity would no longer be tied to the physical universe, but merge with the underlying isostructure.

They showed me their engineers' joke: an old Earth-style fire alarm. Etched on the glass were the words *In Case of Emergency, Break Laws of Physics*. A short chain floated in the research facility's microgee; the hammer with which to smash the glass was missing.

The great work had already begun. Sister Clades were sprinkled like shining dust across the solar system: in the tectosculpted chambers of Phobos the Ares Orbital Clade watched the dark green gloss of tecto-forests advance across the red deserts and planned the courses of Martian canals. The Pale Galileans were two hundred pioneers whirling around Europa in a ragged encampment of environment pods, mass drivers and processing units clinging precariously to a thirty kilometer web of tectoplastic cables and spars. Yet their ambitions were as vast as the planet that dominated their horizons: nothing more than developing tector strains that could reconfigure humans that could live *down there*. They never called Jupiter by name, it was a point, or a nod, in *that* direction. On the very edge of possibility, the Shepherd Moons Clade dreamed of sculpting floating iceberg cities on Titan and sailing on the solar wind through Saturn's rings.

No secret could remain private for long in a community as intimate and interconnected as Neruro. When the facts of my prelife became public, I was commissioned into Neruro's fledgling Diplomatic Corps.

As the NightFreight Crisis edged toward outright war between Earth and her rebel teenage children, Neruro's anarchic government had been forced to resurrect face-to-face diplomacy, as well as other, less exalted archaisms. My mission was to liaise with Dark Side, oldest and most powerful of the Clades. Their monumental excavations beneath Tsiolkovski were the most vulnerable to attack, and most likely to receive the wrath of Earth. Furtive communications flickered on the tightbeam; a ship was readied: HS 1086 C—*Jesus* from the image of the crucified Christ spray-bombed onto the lightsail fans. Its primary payload, a captured cometary head of water-ice to the lunar tectoforming, was to be augmented by a few smears of dirty pseudocarbon: the reduced souls of crew and diplomatic mission.

It was a considerable surprise, then, to be resurrected not in the cathedral-like vastnesses of Dark Side, but with my crewbrethren in a clutch of atmosphere cells starkly illuminated by sunlight reflected from a deployed lightsail. For some reason *Jesus* had decoupled from its payload, reconfigured its crew and was decelerating as hard as photons could push it.

The explanation awaited us on the main memory. While we were a month out from Neruro, a fleet of hastily militarized commercial ships under joint PanEuropean and Rim Council command had invested the Marlene Dietrich Clade's eponymous asteroid base and destroyed it. An outrider of that fleet had been probing us with long-range sensors for over two months and was warping orbits to intercept in five hundred and twenty hours. The phony NightFreight War was ended. *Jesus*'s navigation 'ware had cast off the payload, reconfigured for battle and was asking for evaluations and strategems. We did not tell it that in all probability the Earth ship would be rendezvousing with a diffuse cloud of gas cooling toward the 3k universal background: for the last eight of those twenty-two days we would be within range of their high-gee microtok massconversion weapons with nothing to swat them with but a close-in-defense pulse laser designed for turkey shoots with errant space debris.

Better to have stayed dead.

We had one advantage. While *Jesus* rode in the comet's emergent tail, we were effectively shielded from their weapons' guidance radars and they had no way of knowing we had separated. We furled the sail, commenced silent running some five hundred kays down the comet's shadow and asked *Jesus* to reconfigure some of its hydrocarbon processing mass into close range weaponry. Sophisticated tectocompounds spun out into Stone Age technology. We were out on the skin practicing with our monofilament bolas the day they destroyed the comet. It must have been visible over most of the inner solar system. Twelve million tons of dirty ice went from an undistinguished eighth-magnitude star to a supernova. It was the seventeenth day. We hoped the meat *capitán* had been arrogant enough to have played his entire hand. Certainly, the sneak we dared with our scanners revealed nothing remained of the comet but jagged shards of ice tumbling erratically through space and a rapidly expanding nebula of dissociated hydrogen, oxygen and trace elements. It had taken a full alpha strike, but instinct nagged me.

"Deploy the sail," I ordered *Jesus*. "Full spread." Within three seconds the crucifix-painted sections had fanned out to their fullest extent and locked. Fifteen seconds later we hit the shock front from the comet. The hail of ionized particles struck the tectofilm sail like a typhoon. Christ hung crucified on nails of blue lightning; *Jesus*'s body of girders and bubbles glowed with Saint Elmo's fire and screamed in travail. A dozen systems were failing, environmental integrity was compromised in a dozen places, yet we held. We survived. We maintained. Neruro's technology held in the teeth of the storm; *Jesus* decelerated.

Had I been looking sunward, it is possible that the heat flash of five hundred grams of matter converting totally to energy fifty kilometers ahead of us would have melted my eyes in their sockets. On the principle of never underestimating the enemy, I had gambled that the meat captain had left a couple of missiles ahead of the comet to catch anything that might have been hiding in its shadow. Had we not used the cometary hydoxyl cloud to brake, we would have been exactly where he had calculated and instantly vaporized.

The plasma front struck us like the fist of God. In that first primary shock wave the three, seven and ten o'clock sail panels were stripped away: *Jesus*'s abused rigging systems struggled to furl the remaining vanes in the teeth of an electromagnetic hurricane. We should have died. We were intended to die. *Jesus* rode the lightning. Its pods blistered and blackened, its booms and antennae fused and melted in a welter of arcing, but the sail reefed. Maimed, the ship survived. We lived. We and *Jesus* repaired ourselves.

We waited on the hull for the Earth ship to draw within boarding range. Like all space vehicles, it was an ungainly construction of girders and booms, but someone—perhaps the very captain I had successfully outguessed—had squandered precious ground-to-orbit mass on a vast flag, a sheet of electrically stiffened monolayer polymer one hundred meters on a side that trailed behind the ship on cables. The gold-on-blue starry circle of PanEuropa caught the distant sunlight. The marine waves were camouflaged night black but shone bright as stars on our retinal displays, as doubtless we did on theirs, for all our dermal merging. Two battle groups, fifteen in each. Heavily armored, heavier armed. Exactly as we had expected.

The earthmen approached. Rijo, my battle partner, gave *Jesus* the order. The open lightsail rippled, flashed blinding white. The screams on our radio senses were mercifully brief as the focused beam of reflected sunlight swept across the second battle group, melting tectoplastic combat armor as if it were ice.

And they were upon us.

Space marines. The military elite. Trained to perfection. Battle-hardened. Armed with Earth's most powerful weapons. Merciless warriors. As well have put them naked in a tank of sharks. They were out of their element. And in ours. Our first volley of monofilament bolas claimed four. The molecule-thin edge of the lines opened up the resilient plastic of their suits, sectioned and sliced their soft meat as the weights wrapped themselves around them in a death embrace. The marines returned fire, but in those few moments of shock that they had taken casualties we had disappeared, hiding among *Jesus*'s specially grown nooks and crannies. The marines hovered overhead on their motility units, still psychologically tied to the gravity-bound dogma of controlling the high ground.

It made them better targets for our harpoon guns. The barbs could inflict little real damage on the battle suits; their purpose was to web the victim with enough line to leave him hog-tied and helpless for the close-in defense laser. The marines lost three before they destroyed the laser and relinquished the high ground. By now the fifteen of the battle group had been whittled down to five. Our losses were four; two with ghastly laserholes punched through them, two to tesler fire. The laser victims would at least rise again.

We had our enemy where we wanted: pinned down and helpless in a confusing chaotic environment where the partnerships could come into play. One would draw fire while the partner, attached to the other end of the monofilament line, would swing wide around the back of the ship, slingshoting around girders to make a more difficult target, picking up enough momentum to punch a stone spike clean through a faceplate. There is a particular horror about death in space. No one dies cleanly in vacuum. They fight for life and air and hope. They lose, screaming silently, bodily fluids erupting from every orifice, blood pumping from eyes and ears, lungs spewed out in a cough of depressurization.

After the last marine was dead we jumped over to the Earth ship. The mainframe vibrated beneath our feet, the captain vainly trying for engine relight. We overrode the hatch 'wares and went through the ship, killing everyone on board. I found the captain—a sad-faced woman—at the control decks, trying to key in self-destruct commands with clumsy suit-gloved fingers. I shot her through in the stomach. She died like all the others, badly, screaming in vacuum.

We returned with the bodies to *Jesus*, where we tended to our casualties; four Big Dead, three for the Jesus tank, five flash-burned or otherwise injured. Then we stripped the meat naked. Six of them were women, their heads shaven, which made them look at once brutal yet strangely vulnerable. When the warriors were stored for resurrection, we docked *Jesus* with the Earth ship and flooded it with construction tectors. While *Jesus* cannibalized the ship and reconfigured itself, we went to our Jesus tanks, swallowed our suicide pills, and woke up among the vacuum forests of the moon trying to adjust to having *legs* again. That, and the news that Ayali, the woman who had resurrected me, was dead.

While we were thirty-three days dead from the moon, twenty-five meat ships had attacked Neruro. The Clade's picket-line of shuttles and inter-orbit tugs had been swept from space within three minutes of engaging. They had met a new kind of ship for a new kind of space warfare, little more than missile racks clipped onto high-gee thruster units piloted by teenage singleton jockeys floating in acceleration gel sacs, hooked into virtuality nets and stretched thin on neural accelerators. Ship and crew were designed for no other purpose than to find and kill the enemy. The Neruro crews had watched in shock each of the five target schematics suddenly split into five sub-ships, completely overwhelming their defenses in a barrage of microtok fire. They had died unable to believe what was happening to them.

The Clade lay open before the Earth fleet's alpha strike of two hundred microtok missiles. Ayali, I learned from the fragmentary data coming down the hotline, had died in the first wave when the N-17 Habitation cluster was vaporized. There was no hope of her resurrection. Hers was one of countless thousands acts of courage and sacrifice that day. The orbital forests were raved away in balls of plasma; the O'Neill cylinders and agriculture cans split open, their precious cargoes seared and spilled freezing across the asteroid belt. The fight was not wholly one-sided. Neruro's mass-driver rail guns swung on their jets, seeking firing arcs; their unseen target ships suddenly unfolding into ultra-blue blossoms of hard radiation. Warrior squads took fifty, sixty, seventy percent casualties, but the handful of survivors that made it to the meat ships cut their way through to the pilots, hauled them out of their virtuality dreams and slaughtered them. Close-in defenses might take out ninety percent of the slamship warheads, but even one releasing its cloud of tectors immediately in front of a frantically decelerating meatship was enough to reduce it and its crew to bubbling plastic slag.

The twenty-five Earth ships dwindled to seventeen, to twelve, to eight, to five. In the end, three soloships rolled on their attitude jets and accelerated away from Neruro on the long loop back to Earth. Story has it that when they pulled the pilots out they were all insane from sensory deprivation and neur-acc withdrawal. That is legend; fact was that sixty percent of Neruro's infrastructure had been destroyed, eight hundred of its population of ten thousand were Big Dead, and another seven hundred awaiting resurrection.

It was the last and greatest battle of the NightFreight War. Thereafter the Earth *corporadas* and their political puppets withdrew and conceded all the solar system outside the orbit of their planet to the dead. Earthspace was humanity's, they said. It would never be surrendered to the dead. It was the final frontier. The line in the sand.

I was recalled to Neruro. In the three months it took to match orbits, the Clade had healed itself of some of the outward scars of war, but the absence of many familiar landmarks spoke of the true scale of the devastation. The freefall trees had burned, every last one. Above my accommodation pod, Neruro the Great Wheel still turned.

Diplomats and representatives had been summoned from all the scattered Clades to reevaluate strategy now that the NightFreight Wars were ended. Our opinions polarized into two factions. The Isolationists pressed for the immediate expansion of the extant Clades across all the solar system, the establishment and recognition of a dead transhumanity that had severed all ties with planetbound humanity. Separate speciation was their watchword. The Interventionists opined that the NightFreight Wars could never be truly won while the dead of Earth, who outnumbered us many thousands to one, remained bound by the twin chains of the *contratado* system and the Barantes Ruling. The proper task of the Clades was to fight for liberation by whatever means. The arguments were heated. Both sides had cogent cases. What carried it for the Interventionists was the simple truth that the Isolationists' vision of a universal transhumanity could not be achieved by just five Clades, the largest of which had lost an irreplaceable ten percent of its population, the least of which had exactly fifty-seven members. Now that the *corporadas* had retreated under their atmosphere, the only place where such numbers could be found was in Earth's teeming necrovilles.

The motion was passed by the narrowest of margins. The liberation of the oppressed would be the major work of the Clades. Volunteers were spun sunward to run the planetary exclusion zone and take the temperature of earthdead society, liaising with whatever organs of resistance existed.

Feelers were extended to the radical Freedead and the various small terrestrial liberation organizations. Behind them was an unexpected ally; the Death House itself. Connections were made, contacts established, but subtly, delicately, like the finest spider gossamer that blows away on the least puff of wind. If Tesler-Thanos were ever to find their own left hand was plotting murder, they would have cut it off without a thought. In practical terms, it would have embargoed supplies of coded tectors. Big Death would have returned to night-walk the cities of men.

Out in the Clades new techniques were perfected, new technologies realized, new strategies developed. Slowly, Neruro and the Death Houses drew their plans together.

It was magnificent to fly in such a storm. There was a poetry to it that could not be contained by any *haiku*. All artificial senses shut down,

Toussaint flew by instinct alone through the atmospheric chaos beneath the storm toward his father's dark tower. He banked into the updrafts that permanently ascended the *arcosanti*'s flanks. A blue dot pulsed on Toussaint's retina: a security code interrogative over-riding his display-down command. Now was the Judas moment. One error in the security code patrol lifters hovering out in the indigo night would lock on missiles and launch. Emotions distilled into complex motivations within the curve of his skull. The query was repeated. Toussaint chose. A touch of his mind activated the subdermal transponder. The invisible curtains of watchfulness parted. The gliders soared upward to the spires. Aircraft warning beacons pulsed, pressed up hard against the lowering cloud ceiling. Following Toussaint's lead, the quartet of gliders wheeled in the air above the chaotic pinnacle of the San Gabriel spire. Warning bee-baws fluttered on Toussaint's retina; schematics red-lined, screaming proximity and velocity alerts as he came in hard, fast. The adamant black wall of the spire loomed before him. At the last instant he lifted up into a stall, cupped his wings to spill lift and dropped softly onto the balcony from which he had so spectacularly departed that morning.

Let them try that, if they dare. He allowed himself one small vain smile as his wings folded back into their casings and the neural interfacers retracted into his back.

Huen/Texeira dropped onto the balcony beside him with a rush and rattle of moving air.

"Point to prove, Xavier?"

The houseware opened doors and put in lights for him as Toussaint reentered the penthouse. A rattle, a clatter, a thump and oaths from the balcony. Quebec and Shipley coming in for competent if less-than-esthetic landings.

We're all together again,
We're here, we're here,
We're all together again

The sentiment of the childhood rhyme was apt, but it failed to make *haiku*. Thunder bawled, terrifyingly close in the dimly lit towertop apartment. Toussaint's weather sense told him the worst was past. Big rain coming. He could feel it, like the cool of blue on his skin.

"So, Quebec, what is the Neruro Clade's master plan? Blow away Adam Tesler and hope the whole shebang will fall apart? *Corporadas* are bigger than just one man these days, no matter whose name is on the corporate ident."

The squad leader was moving around the apartment, examining the decor as if it should somehow be familiar to him.

"Xavier Tesler, you have no soul. A man bares the whip marks on his spirit, takes you through the mirror maze of his life. Humor him a little. Let him tell it his way, no? He's waited a long time to tell it to you."

Again, that assumption of familiarity.

"There was no shortage of volunteers, though the mission required only four. My background made me an automatic choice. Texeira, Owens: both commando-squad veterans of the Battle of Neruro and experts in the new technology. Shipley: a trained warrior in her own prelife. We four.

"Can you believe that there are deeper deaths than others? To run the interdiction we were reduced to a nutshell of tectors locked onto a Krebbs twistor that held our encoded personalities and memories. Four lives in the palm of one hand, loaded with an environment-construction system into a knob of nickel steel the size of your fist and sent down with fifty decoys in an artificial meteor shower. First time anyone had cause to be thankful for mass-driver meteor pollution. You remember five months ago there was a brief panic when a couple of Dark Side slamships tested the orbital defenses? Running interference for us. Decoys. *Lion of Zion* and all her crew died merely to draw fire from us."

"And the current fleet up there? What fire are they drawing, or this time do they actually get to blow us to shit?"

"Maybe," said Shipley, "maybe, meatboy, they just want to talk. Human to human."

"We came to rest sixty kilometers out in the ocean. The environment system went to work immediately. Pressure means as little to it as vacuum, but it was still four whole months before we woke to consciousness in our dark, cold, oppressive pressure bubbles. On the next dark of the moon we rose up from a kilometer deep and came ashore just north of Malibu. We knew what we were to do. We knew what we wanted, and who. We knew who you were, what you were, what you had become, how to find you. Everything, Xavier. Everything as planned. Everything was perfect. And then Owens accidentally alerted a stupid *segurarido mechador* patrol up in Copananga. There was a firefight, he got separated. They shot it out. He died. I felt it, Xavier. In here." Quebec touched forefinger to pineal gland. "Like I've felt every one of those who died, who were killed by your father. In here. Every one of them, Xavier."

"Don't call me that. It's not who I am. I am Toussaint. First, last, everything. There is no Xavier Tesler. Not anymore. Adam Tesler's son is dead."

Quebec laughed much too hard, much too long.

"Hey, Xavier, Toussaint, whatever the hell your name is," shouted Shipley, reclining among the soft black rubber spikes of his lounger. "This is one hell of a sofa."

midnight—
4:00 a.m.

november 2

Fingers of rain, stroking YoYo's face, caressing her five-o'clock-shadowed scalp, running over her closed eyelids, along her cheekbones, down the muscles of her neck, under the close-fitting collar of her bodyglove.

Lawyers, like all creatures that make a living in the arena, are a superstitious people. As a Hong Kong Chinese Sampan City lawyer, YoYo's life was doubly governed by obeisance to unseen spirits and personal observances.

Always bodyglove-up the left side first, on those occasions when she reluctantly had to take the superskin off. Always begin on and end on an odd-numbered step on the stairway to heaven. Always remove clothes in the following order when entering the virtualizer: cap (optional), jacket, shirt, pants, boots. Never commence or conclude a case on a Tuesday. Never expect great revelations on a cloudy day, or after eating Indian food. Never expect satisfaction from anyone called José, or Mercedes.

Always be wary of bad karma in heavy rain.

Sector by sector, street by street, the Carmen Miranda restored power to the dead town. On top of a street-front apartment *cuadra* Gene Kelly sprang to restored life and capered beneath a downspout. YoYo wiped her face. It's only water. No one is asking you to dance and sing in it, just live with it. She pulled the bodyglove hood over her exposed head and emerged from the dark backstreets. The main marches seemed to have broken up. Costumes wilting in the downpour, groups of dancers gossiped and laughed, splashing heedlessly through the brimming gutters. Families of musicians traded breaks under shop awnings, sheltering their precious drumskins from the rain. A glitter of horns in the streetlights, a sway of rubber breasts: a party of elegantly disturbing *desfigurados* moved through the crowd; lofty sin-black demons that towered over the mundanes, brilliant with satanic arrogance.

The overemphatic normality, like a divorcing couple hosting their last dinner party, did not disguise the unease of both dead and living. The glow over at La Brea was obvious to YoYo, even through the rain.

"YoYo."

The voice was a bloody gurgle, the hand extended toward her a shatter of torn flesh and exposed bone. The nails were snapped and broken. YoYo recognized the polish.

"Iago?"

"Fuck, it hurts, YoYo. They told me nothing would ever hurt me again. Bastards."

Bodyglove downloaded rudimentary first aid from its small intrinsic memory. YoYo carefully maneuvered Iago from his hiding place behind empty fruit boxes and massive commercial garbage hoppers and laid him flat. His chest heaved beneath the sheer Lycra sheath, his breath steamed in the warm, neon-rich air. Passersby passed by. Blood on the blacktop did not warrant a glance in Necroville.

"Jesus Joseph Mary, Iago."

Blood trickled from the corner of his mouth. Seeing his distress, YoYo knelt and wiped it away with the paisley lining of her leather jacket. They had gone for the head. Baseball bats, metal piping, claw hammers. He had covered his face. Hands, forearms, shoulders, had taken the brunt of the attack. The left eyebrow bled inconsolably, both ears were terribly swollen and bruised. Blood and glitterdust. YoYo wondered if it was toxic.

Iago laughed. Ribs grated audibly.

"I'll be all right. Humpty can put himself together again. They weren't meant to hit me that hard. Bastards." He examined his ruined hands. Rain smeared the blood down his wrists. "It took me hours to get those right."

"Who did it, Iago? Was it meat? Teevee-phobes?"

Iago shook his head, retched, spat into the gutter.

"Oh for God's sake help me up. This is so undignified." YoYo assisted him into a broken-doll slouch against the wall of an electrical goods shop. Classic four-a.m. pose. A bottle and a friend and me.

"YoYo, listen. Martika Semalang. They've got her."

"They've got her? Who's got her? What?"

"First sign of a good lawyer, an inquiring and disciplined mind." Iago grimaced. "The people who did this to me. I met her like you said, on the corner, all the right passwords, 'Stairway to Heaven,' 'Bloody David Niven,' all the five-year-old's shit. She's asking questions I don't know the answers to and I'm trying to tell her this when this big black car comes up alongside and these six bodmod shitbags step out, smack me up the face with a bat, haul this Semalang woman in, smack me around a bit more because they seem to enjoy it so much."

"Oh Iago." Did this have to happen? Was it mandatory in every private investigation case, all this running around not knowing what was going on? Did it ever happen that all the pieces fell together like some exercise in continental drift and the investigating lawyer could sit back and solve it in the peace and quiet of her porch with a few beers and some nice contemplative music?

"If it had been you, *carnito*, they'd have called you up a Jesus tank. Which is what I am trying to say. This big black car, yes? It was a Death House cruiser. Little vee-slash on the door, yes?

"I recognized the suit giving the orders. Big turd, name of Van Ark. Everyone knows him. Chief executive of Saint John Main. Hey. Hey, YoYo. Before you go running off in your cute boots with a list of wrongs to right. We got cut off, remember?"

"Something about someone called Maguffin?"

"Lawyers. Get them without their memory enhancers . . . A maguffin is a device for catching lions in Scotland."

"I remember: 'but there are no lions in Scotland.' "

"Therefore, there is no maguffin. And certainly no Lars Thorwald Aloysius Maguffin. Never was, outside of Alfred Hitchcock movies. Good thing you have your cute boots on, YoYo, because someone is playing the running man game with you." Iago waved his hand, grimaced and panted painfully for a few moments. "Ah, shit. Don't you find that it never happens to the dresses you don't like?"

"I don't have any dresses, Iago."

"Your loss. The point of the maguffin, in classic Hitchcock theory, is that it has no point other than to keep the running man running."

"That's me?"

"And whoever tried to 'tok you. And whoever lifted your client off me. While you're all running around like headless chickens, the real action is someplace and something else entirely."

"And Martika Semalang?"

"*Querida*, she is the maguffin."

Things They Don't Teach You at Law School, *abogadito*.

"I think I have some questions I would like to ask this Van Ark. Will you be all right, Iago?"

He held up his hands. The naked bone had already been overlain by bands of pink synthetic tissue. Scabs hardened, scar tissue puckered, bruises faded as YoYo watched. "Told you I could put myself back together again." A lop-sided half-smile, ghastly among the ruins of make-up, was the most he could manage. "YoYo!" She was already half a block away. "For once, take a cab."

Up on the fire escape of the Saint John Main Death House, YoYo picked a lock, *poco a poco*. All professional bodygloves possessed an innate rudimentary processing capability; the finger filaments moved through the molecular lattice of the lock, the nanocircuitry threw schematics onto her retinas and crunched out the permutations. To YoYo, myelin nerve-sheathings hiked up to the hypervelocities of *corporada* processors by years of neur-acc habituation, it was as painfully slow as the bonsai her grandfather had grown in cunning wire cradles suspended from the boat's gutters, safe from careless bodies and polluted seawater. Tiny trees in tiny pots, bound by copper wires. YoYo-age-nine had felt sorry for them, seeing her own past and future written there. "You see as a human, to understand properly, you must see as a tree," he had told her, for he was a Chinese grandfather, and thus wisdom was expected of him. "You see souls in torment, bound by tight wires, trapped. They see spirits struggling to be free, to grow, to express themselves, to find a path to perfection. It may take many lifetimes, you and I may be gone to the dead town by the time they achieve perfection, but they know that one day they will be free."

The bodyglove spread a slow green web of capillaries across her visual cortex: a graphic of the Saint John Main alarm system, her location flagged with a crude and unflattering female colophon. *System burn-through estimated in seventy-eight point six seconds*, the bodyglove printed on the inside of her eyeball. Growing wisdom teeth had been quicker. A viridian icarosaurus no longer than her hand watched her from its dry roosting place under the door lintel, glider membranes folded tight against its body. YoYo scowled at it; dirty, trash-eating vermin.

After her grandfather had died in the sampan fire she had removed the copper wiring from all his trees. *Be free, grow!* she had told them.

She did not know that a twist once put in a tree can never be taken out again. The warped trunk cannot straighten and grow true to the sun. Within a year all her grandfather's bonsai had died from neglect, but YoYo never forgot their lesson. She had escaped the wires that bound her; sheer will to succeed, to grow toward the light, had taken her into circles Drown Town could only dream of, but the twists and maimings of a Sampan City childhood had permanently marked the growth rings of her soul. A tree that is bound too tight, her grandfather had said, will wear the marks of the wire forever. YoYo was an expert on wire marks.

Burn-through effected, said the bodyglove. The web of informational veins and arteries rezzed down; the micron-thin tracery of extruded circuitry withdrew through the molecular interstices into YoYo's fingertips. The bolts shot back with a satisfying clank. Wiping rain from her face with the back of her hand, she kicked open the green door with one deeply serious boot.

"Oh," said YoYo.

"Hello," said the man with the very large gun who was waiting on the far side of the green door. "Séora Mok? Please be so kind as to come with me."

"Are you Van Ark?"

"I am Van Ark." Taller than she, darker, better spoken. Younger, save for the eyes. Like transvestites' hands, the eyes of the dead betrayed their true identities.

"You lifted my client." The dead man did not reply. "Your goons smashed up a good friend of mine."

"So sue me. It would have been much simpler if you had knocked on the front door, Séora Mok," said the silken Van Ark. "After all, you are expected."

"Like I've got a long tradition of detective fiction tropes to uphold," said YoYo, surprising herself at her sass with a slug thrower in her left ear.

Van Ark took YoYo to a room. The only light was a wan green glow from a datadisplay desktop and stray street-shine through a rain-streaked picture window the width of the office. Good soundproofing; not one scream or drumbeat from below broke the silence of the Death House. YoYo's vision was slow to adapt from the antiseptic glare of the corridor. Two figures were silhouetted against the window, one seated, the other standing just behind the seated figure, both women. The seated woman was Martika Semalang. The ghastly light from the desktop underlit her face. She looked like what she was: a dead woman.

"YoYo," she said. Her voice was a ruined creak. "I know who I am."

YoYo's attention was entirely focused on the silhouette of the woman who stood behind her. Nothing living had that many hands. Not there, not like that, not open, fingers spread, along each shoulder and over the skull.

"Jesus fuck," YoYo whispered.

"Some Death Houses would have balked at the modifications Aylita demanded," said Van Ark, holstering the gun inside his immaculately cut suit and switching on a discreet reading light. The look in the dead woman's eyes challenged YoYo to stare. Her head and neck were covered with clasping hands, fingers interlocked, which slowly released their mutual grips and opened like obscene fleshy blooms. A reef of gently rippling fingers saluted YoYo. "The specifications were unique, the tectoengineering parameters exacting; still, I think you must admit the Saint John Main design team met the challenge in a highly creative and original manner."

"What challenge?"

" 'Oh, 'twould be the gift tae gie' us/ Tae see oorselves as others see us.' " said Van Ark. The woman with hands for hair smiled. Her face was angelically beautiful. Some of the hands stirred away from her head on ropey muscular tentacles. "Telepathy, Séora Mok. Breaking the barriers of selfhood. Entering another's thoughts. Knowing that the other truly exists."

Martika Semalang was weeping, head bowed, face buried in her hands; destroyed.

"Impossible."

"This from a lawyer who spends half her life strung out on the web? You felt your way molecule by molecule into our security system—which, by the way, is neither so old nor so decrepit as it seems—you became one with it, you became a physical extension of it and it of you. It is the same for Aylita, molecule by molecule, memory by memory, she extrudes her tectocircuitry through the skull into the brains of her clients, becoming one with them, thinking their thoughts, feeling their emotions, reliving their memories, transferring them to another. You'd be surprised what a market there is for a living empathic link between minds. *Corporada* security companies who like to know if their employees are telling the truth. Sex partners who want to exchange bodies. Of course, she doesn't come cheap, but she does owe us a certain indebtedness. Would you care for a demonstration?" The dead woman took a step YoYo-ward, tendril hands outstretched to their fullest extent. YoYo scrambled away.

"That bitch comes near me, I break her fingers. Every single one of them." Wearing knowledge as a perfect skin, a meniscus between self and world; that was comfortable, that was safe. Letting that knowledge through the skin, into the body, the self, was a penetration YoYo could not sanction.

"I'm sorry," Van Ark said. "The Linker did not mean to frighten you. Really, our purpose in bringing you here was not to banter film noir clichés but, because we have almost everything we need, I see no reason why Séora Semalang should be denied her attorney."

"YoYo, she took me back," said Martika Semalang, her face streaked with tears. "She took me back, she made me remember. Before, YoYo. Before."

"Your petshop Medusa here went into her head and peeled apart the hard-wired engram codes."

The Linker dealt YoYo a lofty stare: *little scurrying leather-wrapped meat.*

"Everything, YoYo. The photograph, the house, everything. I know it all now." YoYo could not remember ever having seen one of the dead cry.

"Seeing as how we still have a little work left us, perhaps it might be better if you were to experience it firsthand," suggested Van Ark. "It would save a lot of repetitious explanation."

"You want me, with her?"

"I'm not asking you to fuck me, honey," said the Linker. Her voice was surprisingly deep and resonant. "Just ride tandem. You don't even have to let me into your head; I can patch into that cute suit you're filling and rezz it up for you in virtuality mode." She pulled up a swivel terminal-operator's chair and sat directly behind Martika Semalang. Tendrils extended, hands surrounded Martika Semalang's head. The laying on of hands. YoYo caught her gorge rising and forced it down.

"As your legal representative, I have to advise against this," she said.

"YoYo, it's all right. I want this, please understand. I want to know." Palms and fingers pressed down on Martika Semalang's head. Her eyes were closed, her lips parted in an expression part religious rapture, part pain. The Linker extended two surplus hands from the base of her skull to YoYo.

"You comin' in with me or not, meatgirl?" YoYo reluctantly took the proffered hands, but could not suppress the shudder as the prickle of synesthesia ran across her arm. Contact. Tector systems clashed and passed through each other like medieval armies, molecular bridges and scaling ladders thrown across the moats and trenches of selfhood.

And YoYo Mok fell into another lifetime.

In her imagination she was the drowning man who sees, so the legends go, his whole life projected onto the sky for which he so desperately claws. Going down going down going down down down: a life lived at zip speed, jump-cutting over the tedious and mundane: edited highlights of the great chain of being: womb to tomb in twenty-three minutes with ad breaks. *This life was brought to you courtesy of . . .*

An eighth birthday party she had never had with friends she had never known in a house she had never lived in but which was as familiar to her as the five tethered barges in which she had been born and grown. The house in that photograph with the fragment of license plate in the drive. Eight candles on a cake. *Happy birthday to you, happy birthday to you . . .*

First fumbling fuck with Marco from across the turning circle while Mother broke in a new boyfriend up on Tahoe.

Diving on the Barrier Reef, with tall, beautiful giggling girlfriends shipped straight from paradise, afterward sprawling around on a veranda smoking resin and talking about men and the future and men and their careers and men and men.

Graduating in theoretical nanoengineering and design summa cum laude. Stepping off the express career elevator right at Tesler-Thanos's R&D department. The twenty-fifth level outside-edge apartment with panoramics all the way to the ocean, and the *corporada* this-year's-model shapeshifter. The suborbitals to nanoengineering conferences in Singapore and Shanghai and Valparaiso. The sun holidays in the shadow of Kilimanjaro and the snow holidays in the shadow of Mt. Erebus. The parties. The partners. The promotions.

Codex 13. Tiered memories sprang into being behind that simple name, like a door behind a lock, a wall behind a door, a labyrinth behind the wall, an emerald citadel within the labyrinth.

The Idea: turn away from the cancer-cell model Adam Tesler had used as the basis of his bioreplicant tector, that destroyed what it touched; turn to a template less voracious, more life-engendering: the human sex cell.

Five explorers hugged up in bodygloves, hooked together through affinity links, moving through the fullerene domes and vaults of their tector like atheists in St. Peter's, cooing and muttering at the angels in the architecture.

Deathless immortality, YoYo whispered in her dreams of a life she could have wished for herself. The Great Grail.

And, with the realization that Adam Tesler, having been savior of the world once, was not prepared to be that again on grounds of cost accountancy and market penetration: the betrayal.

The coded tagalong calls. The clandestine meetings at mountain resorts and desert spring hotels. The droppings out, *no, not me, this is not my kind of thing what if they ever find out?* The trip to the floating gambling complex two hundred kays off Pacific Mexico, when the Nameless Buyer with No Face finally took a face and a name. Roland Carver, Special Projects Executive of Aristide-Tlaxcalpo.

The money. The deal. The hustle. Fragments of memory, a room, a color, a certain perfume attached to the skin of a personal assistant, the condition of light, the awareness of deep water.

The height of the sun above the horizon, the song that was playing on the radio, the smell of the coffee, the scent of the bath oil, the gurgle of the hot water running into the bath as the men in 'flage *corporada* battle gear open the door that only you are supposed to be able to open and sweep aside your protests and defenses and pick you up, stifling your screams with their gloved hands, holding your legs, your arms, carrying you out onto the sun-filled balcony with its view of the distant sea, holding you out over the edge while you kick and kick and kick hopelessly, helplessly, and one of them wipes the traces of your piss and shit off the rail. And they tumble you naked out of your raw silk kimono into half a kilometer of empty air.

"Oh Jesus Jesus Jesus Jesus," swore lapsed Taoist YoYo, surfacing from virtuality sweating and shivering and pale like the crash after drugs. The Linker folded her many hands like demure fans around her head.

"They killed me, YoYo," said Martika Semalang. "They found out about the deal I had made with Aristide-Tlaxcalpo, and they killed me."

"But they did more than that, Séora Mok," said Van Ark. Only his hands resting on the desktop beneath the reading lamp were illuminated. "Tesler-Thanos had to be sure that the secret of Codex 13 died with Martika Semalang. Unfortunately, it proved more difficult than they had thought to merely erase one set of related memories: engrams are stored on a multiple-redundancy quasi-holographic array in the brain. As Linker here will confirm, it is difficult to run down every nook and corner where memories may be stashed. Simpler by far to erase everything, every memory of the woman you call Martika Semalang."

"Madrilena Fuentes," said the dead woman, her face the only clearly lit object in Van Ark's shadowy office. "I was Madrilena Fuentes."

Thick rivulets of rain streaked the window, fingers of wet neon on the glass. "What Tesler-Thanos had not bargained on was the disloyalty of their Death House staff," said Van Ark.

"Aristide-Tlaxcalpo are payrolling you."

"A deathless immortality renders Tesler-Thanos dead as the dinosaurs. How long do you think the *contratado* system and the Barantes Ruling will hold on when everyone becomes immortal, both living and dead? Certainly, Aristide-Tlaxcalpo have been slushing me handsomely for years, little thinking that I would be on the spot when Séora Semalang failed to keep a certain important appointment with them. But when all is said, we are the dead, we serve our own ends."

"How did you find me? her? us?" YoYo asked.

"A persistent Carmen Miranda *serafino* tends to be something of a giveaway in a game of hide-and-seek," said Van Ark.

Aircraft engines penetrated the office's soundproofing, close enough to be felt. It must have come in high, reconfigured into vertical mode and be dropping straight down on its fans for a street landing. The building shook. The sound pitched to a shattering crescendo. A blur of colored lights hovered for a moment outside the window; engine backblast smeared the raindrops into fans and deltas of whipped spray.

"Ah, Séor Carver," said Van Ark, standing up as if to receive a guest. "Come to collect. On time, as he said. Punctuality is such a timebound obsession, don't you think? Séora Mok, if you wish to accompany your client, I really don't think Aristide-Tlaxcalpo will have any objections. After Linker gives them what they want, you will both be at liberty to leave."

And the ever-circling question marks that she had set orbiting around her from the moment she sat down at the outside table in Tacorifico Superica's came crashing down on her like plummeting comsats.

"Van Ark!" Feet, distant but approaching, amplified by long, echoing corridors. "Something doesn't figure, Van Ark." Feet, a steady tramp, tramp, drawing nearer. "They tocked the restaurant, they tocked the practice because they didn't want to leave anything that could be resurrected. Van Ark, why didn't they toc her? Tesler-Thanos must have had a dozen opportunities to blow Madrilena Fuentes and Codex 13 into plasma, why didn't it?" Feet, outside the door, waiting a moment for the back-markers to catch up. "Van Ark, why go to all the trouble of making it look like a fall and then wiping her memories?" The door slid open. The light behind the silhouetted figures was dazzling to the dark-adapted eye.

"Why indeed, Séora Mok?" said the voice from the open door. "Why indeed."

The muzzle flash lit the big office like lightning, freezing thoughts, actions, deeds in green ice. Flash-printing forever on YoYo's visual cortex, like the painted shadows of Hiroshima victims, the image of Van Ark as the MIST 27s blew him into something hideous and terrifying and revolting and unimaginable and *dead*. Spirit hands spread wide in terror, the woman called the Linker leaped for the window. In a second flash of lightning, the tesler smeared her into a splash of dripping tectoplastic across the rain-streaked glass. Lights came on, blinding. Blinking through a blur of afterimages, YoYo saw the chitinous, mantislike datahelmets, the flageskin combat suits turning a gentler shade of corridor, the muzzle of the big tesler in the hands of the lead *asesino* turned on her.

"Oh no," she whispered, "no no no no."

The assassin made a little choking noise. Murder temporarily forgotten, he looked down at the new thing that had commanded his attention: thirty centimeters of barbed aluminum rod protruding from his breastbone.

His *compadres* seemed not to be at their posts.

He fell to one side like a toppling sequoia.

The corridor was full of werewolves sporting what looked, to a YoYo now convinced she had gone out of her mind, like exceedingly large underwater spearguns. A human figure came through the mass of fur, fang and fury: a tall man—good volleyball height, thought hallucinating YoYo—poured into a flageskin suit switched incongruously to Mandelbrot Sets. His shaved head glittered; a little dusting of mica? And around the rim of the wrapover scanshades; a little cracked foundation, a little dab of blusher.

"Iago?"

"YoYo!" Her 'wareman beamed with undisguised affection and swept her up in a bone-cracking bear hug. *"Querida!"*

Beneath a canopy of rain
Mylar wings
circle, trapped by green glass.

The elevator platform had risen above all but the most daring of the gliders who flew the spaces of the *arcosanti*'s cavernous main mall. Bright wings, brave deathshead and shark's jaw paint jobs, sharp turns, dazzling aerobatics around the lighting clusters and overhanging executive level apartment stacks. Trapped, sterile. Caged birds. Tame sky. Wings flashed across the face of a thirty-meter hologram of Adam Tesler anchored to the curving glass roof. Look upon thy chosen people, Yahweh Pancreator. The most fundamental level of political attachment is that of the individual to the authority figure. The Tesler-Thanos employee is contracted not to the *corporada*, but to the person of Adam Tesler. He had always boasted that his *contratistos* knew who they were, what they were, to what and whom they belonged.

A feudal city-state, he had said. *Daimyo Tesler.*

No, a family. A dynasty.

A Cosa Nostra, he had said. *A Mafia.* This little birdie had refused to tumble and sing beneath its father's smiling face, but spread its wings and flown away from all the things it had been promised.

Quebec studied Adam Tesler's monstrous features.

Know your enemy, Toussaint thought. *Know him like you know yourself. Know him better. Know him better than even I know him, know me, know this place. You know unknowable things.* The look on Quebec's face was that of a man returning after a long journey to his home.

The upper gallery, never as bustling as the lower levels of the *arcosanti*, was virtually deserted this Night of the Dead. Your labor resurrects them, your habitation overshadows them, you eat of their sweat, and on the night of their carnival, you party down with them.

Up on the catwalk: behind them the glittering spaces of the mall levels, before them the nanotechnological hell of the manufacturing zones.

"*Muy imponente*," Shipley whispered, pulling tight around her the spiked rubber jacket—the match of the sofa—she had liberated from Toussaint's penthouse.

From the geothermal cores that sucked seismic energy out of the Los Angeles fault zone to the *millefeuille* wafers of the atmosphere plant radiating waste heat to the night sky in a thermodynamic plume visible from the moon, was a vertical kilometer. From the high causeway across the tectofacturing core to the lighted windows of Management and Production Control was the same. The interior of the enormous cylinder was two-thirds filled with evolution machines; globular fermenters each a hundred meters across enfolded in an intestinal tangle of conduits, ducts, power lines. Toussaint had always imagined he could hear the boil and seethe of the tectors within as they replicated themselves out of their chemical feedstocks. Great gurgling organs in the body corporate; glands leaking out hormones that brought oil from rock, water from stone, built roads from desert sands, raised cities from dust, smelted cars from slag, computers from trash, pharmaceuticals from waste plastic, fertilizers from clouds. And resurrected the dead.

"Shit," he said. "The organic base for the Tesler process is human sewage."

" 'Between the shit and the piss are we born,' " Quebec quoted. "The Clades use cometary ice. Dirty water."

Toussaint remembered the last time he had stood here: the figure of his father approaching from the spire shaft doors.

"Son." That dark, old-fashioned suit, the eyes black behind the polarized contact lenses, the precision of the manners, the softness of the voice that many mistook—to their cost—for deference.

"I am not that person anymore."

"Ah yes. Toussaint. Isn't that what they call you, your friends? Is that what you want me to call you?"

"No." Suddenly he had felt ashamed of the name and identity he had chosen for himself. Self-conscious. Adolescent. "Xavier. If you must call me anything, call me what you named me. Not 'son.' "

"Xavier; drug designers, skysurfing bums, bored society girls with their brains between their legs, Drown Town gold diggers looking for a way up and out: I really don't think this kind of company is helpful for you."

"I don't choose friends because they're helpful."

"Indeed. Indeed. But, for want of a better cliché, 'all this will be yours someday, my son,' and *corporada* man has a long memory for scandal.

"I know you don't want it, but it's yours. It will always be yours. The succession demands it. The executive codes are keyed to your DNA matrix; it was done at your birth. All you have to do is touch them, anytime, and they will serve you.

"I can understand how daunting it must seem at twenty-one. Go out into the world, go wherever your *wanderjahr* takes you. Join the *aguilas*—it's a good, healthy life, they're good people, what I know of them—go and fly with them, live with them, be one of them. You need equipment, modifications, whatever, I'll pay for them. You want to go to them, go to them, and when you're ready, however long that takes, come back and take your rightful place."

"I don't need your permission. If I join the *aguilas*, it's because I want to be something other than the king in waiting. If I asked you to set me free, to let me go and never come back, would you dare grant it?"

"Freedom is an illusion. Ask your *aguila* friends. They achieve freedom only by the meanest of compromises with laws far more implacable than any you would find here.''

That same day Toussaint went and asked Santiago to lend him the money for the body modifications to become a true *aguila*.

"Daydreaming, eh?'' The obscene familiarity of Huen/Texeira's touch on his arm jolted him into the present. "Come on, meat, we got things to do. People to see.''

Were the sins of the father so great that the son could casually contemplate his murder?

The executive elevator 'ware accepted Toussaint's identification code.

"Take us to Data Traffic Control,'' Quebec announced. The elevator heard but did not obey.

"It needs a security code,'' Toussaint said.

"Please enter it.''

The elevator disc obligingly rezzed a ten-digit grid out of its limed-wood central column.

Toussaint imagined the verdigrised brass doors opening onto the plain of mica-jeweled granite; the angle at which the moonlight would strike through the walls of latticed glass. The peacock would open its hundred eyes, the ultramarine tectosaur on its perch would stir lazily. He could imagine his father roused from his sleeping quarters, wondering, perhaps fearful, always immaculate and prepared, descending the stairs to the office below. What he could not imagine was the look on his father's face when he recognized who it was that had brought the soft assassins to kill him.

He stabbed out the code. Oh. Two. Three. Seven. Six. Seven. One digit. One digit was the difference between betrayal and salvation.

Quebec caught his wrist as he brought his finger down on the final six. The dead man's strength was astonishing.

"Be careful,'' he said.

Toussaint pressed six. The roof iris above them opened and the elevator platform lifted into the transparent shaft that clung to the side of the spire.

"He's my father, for God's sake, I'm not going to stand by and let you cold-bloodedly murder him,'' Toussaint said flatly.

"Haven't I told you that we don't want to kill him?'' Quebec answered, looking out at the ever-expanding vista of city lights.

Rain ran in hundred-meter tears down the outside of the containment tube. Half a kilometer above the translucent green dome of the mall roof, the lift platform came to an abrupt halt. A constellation of winking lights hung in the night; a patrol lifter, weapons armed, hovering on its fans in the space between the three towers. The elevator's simple-minded 'ware jangled with identification interrogatives from the faceless security crew.

"My my, but they're jittery tonight," said Quebec. He looked at Huen/Texeira. "One can hardly blame them."

The control column signaled recognition of Toussaint's override. The lifter swooped away in a green glow of jets through the steadily falling rain. The elevator continued its ascent toward the lowering clouds. Fifty meters from the towertop penthouse it stopped and opened an iris in the spire wall.

The bored young woman on the desk looked surprised to see anyone but maintenance staff abroad in the computer center this time of the morning. Surprised, and suspicious.

"Ah, I'm sorry, Séor Tesler, but I'm going to have to check this with main security."

"Even the president's son?" asked Shipley slyly, resting her elbows on the desk, bringing her face down to the *recepçionista*'s level.

"Even the president's son, séora."

A sick thrill of foreknowledge paralyzed Toussaint as Shipley took the receptionist's face in her hands.

"No!" Toussaint shouted as Shipley's face erupted into rams of silver tectoplasm. The *recepçionista* struggled, gurgled as the Shipley-stuff invaded her by eye and ear and nose and mouth. The hands released her face; the big, muscular *cochera* body slumped open-mouthed, open-eyed over the desk. The *recepçionista* walked around the desk, stripped the discarded body of the black-spiked rubber jacket and slipped it on over her working-girl suit.

"Well, I like it," she said in the voice that was hers and not hers. She cocked a thumb at the body. "Do we dump it over the side or risk someone finding it?"

"Stash it behind the desk. By the time they find it, it'll be too late for them to do anything about it."

Bioluminescent markers guided them inward along spiraling corridors. The few tech and cleaning teams they encountered spared them hardly a glance. Anyone who was here should be here. If not, then it was somebody else's problem. Quite probably they did not recognize the face and figure of their own heir apparent.

No dead. All meat-trash *noncontratistos*. Alone among the mighty Rim *corporadas*, Tesler-Thanos was not based upon an army of contract-bound dead. Their place on earth was in the Death House, Adam Tesler's shadowy left hand. Toussaint had never been certain whether this rejection of its own creation was an act of supreme contempt or unparalleled magnanimity.

In heaven, of course, things were very different. Heaven was the place of the dead: Tesler-Thanos's orbital factories ran on the labor of the nightfreighted. Shanghaied to *Paraiso*.

Toussaint had always appreciated the cloistral simplicity of the computer core; the austere surface that alluded to the potentially infinite complexity beneath. The big angled roof screens each subdivided into a fifty-by-fifty grid of images and icons; the wall-mounted virtualizers curled shut on their omnifit bodygloves like day-blooming flowers in the moonlight; the inner ring of floform chairs. The semivirtuality audiovisualizer helmet balanced atop the datacore spine and the open claw of the manipulator glove on the armrest had made the young Toussaint think of skeleton knights seated around a rotting Round Table.

Beneath a single spotlight, a bony hand flexed, a skull moved. An undead skeleton lived. Motors purred as the chair turned to face the door. The occupant, a male in one of the old-fashioned suits that were de rigueur among Tesler-Thanos's higher executive echelons disengaged the manipulator and pushed up the audiovisualizer visor. Porfirio Kazantzekes: one of Toussaint's father's closest advisers. Six years older. Grayer. Wiser. And shocked to the core of his being.

He rose from the chair.

"Séor Tesler . . ."

"Shipley." In the submarine, sacramental hush, Quebec's voice had the edge of a shark's tooth. Hunters from deep waters.

"Easy come, easy go," said Shipley, taking off her rubber jacket. Five steps took her to the old man's side. He would not know. He could not suspect. He saw only a receptionist, an employee, the recipient of his unthinking daily flirtations.

"For the love of God, Shipley," Toussaint cried.

The *recepçionista*'s body fell heavily to the floor. Huen/Texeira hid it in one of the dormant bodygloves.

At no time had Séor Porfirio Kazantzekes been looking or speaking to Toussaint.

Shipley shucked off the long frock jacket and slipped on Toussaint's sensual spiked rubber.

"Nice pants," she said in her stolen voice, feeling the crease. Her fingers encountered her genital bulge. "Hey, ho," she giggled.

The Freedead took positions in the data chairs. Huen/Texeira wiggled his fingers into the manipulator and turned his chair to face the leftside roof screens. Digits cascaded down his visor; one by one the screens blanked. Shipley hooked in, Quebec played five-finger virtuality exercises. As guilty by default as any of them, Toussaint took the chair beside Quebec. His questions would find no answers here, now.

One by one, the wall screens filled with aerial views of the cities of Earth.

The La Défense necroville was still smoldering, sending smoke up into the Paris morning.

The perimeters of Moskva 12 and St. Petersburg had failed. Government troops were falling back, their withdrawal hampered by panicking, fleeing meat.

Labor strikes had paralyzed most of the western European hypurbations: Brussels, Berlin, Barcelona were black holes in the planetary dataweb, power supplies shut off: deafened, blinded, struck dumb.

North Africa. Tripoli was under curfew, Casablanca-Rabat a battlefield, Greater Cairo a smoking morgue. Sub-Saharan Africa was a sandstorm of data-noise, interrupted by sporadic hallucinatory revelations of burning cars in downtown Lagos, jack-knifed streetcars blockading the avenue of Khartoum. The gracious towers of New Harare were burning. Vee-slashes had been spray-bombed on the Dutch gable-ends of Pretoria.

"Transatlantic?" Quebec asked. His crew obliged.

"Minor disturbances in Core States, PanAtlanta, Minneapolis-Saint, Montreal and Phoenix Metropolitan Axes," Shipley reported. Fragments of television news strobed across Toussaint's field of vision. "Private and metropolitan security seem to have it contained: what fighting there is seems to be dead versus dead."

Havana was burning, the Cojimar ablaze, all those beautiful, crumbling houses of Ayuntamiento dying.

The TVMA partied on. Vivid insanity: rainsoaked *autodores* gathered in an abandoned *metropolitano* cutting around their adored streetracers.

"Mexico, Central, *El Sur*, pretty much the same pattern as *El Norte*," Shipley continued. "Sporadic violence, mostly internalized feuding; the rest just wondering what the hell is going on and getting on with it."

"Tesler-Thanos is on crisis alert," Huen/Texeira cut in. "Disengage

from sensitive areas, secure company property and personnel, bring mar-
shaling areas up to yellow alert and prepare evacuation plans, prospect
the transnational markets to extend the corporate holdings base and buy
gold and Rim Dollars at the money mart. Not quite the global uprising
of the dead."

Toussaint yelped as his visor went white and then blanked. Sensory
shutdown: the light had been so bright as to be audible: a keen white-
hot whine.

"What the fuck was that?" Shipley asked. Never, ever, in his
twenty-one years within his father's house had Toussaint heard Porfirio
Kazantzekes's voice swear.

"Newsnets are claiming a hit on a slamship." An oleaginous news-
person construct appeared against a background of gently expanding
thermonuclear nebula, the fatuous bread-and-circuses jaw-jaw tuned to
sub-conversational volume.

"FYIO Military Intelligence routed from orbital command to the
Rim Council and the *corporadas* confirm a hit on a hostile," Shipley
reported. Toussaint heard worry, concern, care. These were their
friends, families, lovers, out there, riding those ungainly jerryrigged con-
flations of ice and iron. "The probability spread that it's a decoy duck
is ninety-two percent. Every time they probe with their high-resolution
radar interferometers it's like writing 'shoot me' on your ass and sticking
it out of the window."

"Can we go orbital yet?" Quebec asked.

"We're in," Huen/Texeira said. "They're evacuating all civilian
units. Going to real time transmissions from the Tesler-Thanos *Paraiso*
Orbital Manufactory."

Pressure-skinned figures scrambled along webbing-lined tunnels,
darkside identity lights flashing, carooming from the sides at improbable
angles, pouring upward toward the green-lit maw of the exit lock.

"They're evacuating all non-contract units," Huen/Texeira said,
cutting to a new view of shuttles blasting away from the docking booms
in the blizzard of ice crystals and assorted space garbage. A woman's
visored face, bloated by microgee and all the more alien for being inverted, screaming soundlessly at the lens. Cut to: a sprightly gavotte for
magazines, plasticfoam drinks canisters and sweatbands in an abandoned
control room.

Cut to: a shot from a solar panel monitor, of tiny stars bright against
the penumbra of the curving hull. Dozens of them, catching the light
as they orbited the orbiting factory. So pretty. Bright green stars. Bright
green five-pointed stars. Strangely irregular pretty bright green stars.

"Quebec," Toussaint heard himself say, "what are those?"

"Hold, magnify and enhance please, Texeira."

"It's risky, running Tesler-Thanos's image enhancement 'ware under their noses," Huen/Texeira warned.

"Do it please."

The image froze and leaped to twentyfold magnification.

As the manufactory turned into the light, more and more bodies became visible: men and women, all dressed in green coveralls, all alike, arms and legs spread, crucified on vacuum. All young. All, despite the ropes of flash-frozen blood that trailed from their eyes, ears, nostrils, mouths, beautiful.

All wearing the vee-slash stain of the deathsign on their green coveralls.

"They're not vacuum-adapted," Quebec whispered. "They're as vulnerable out there as meat."

"The whole dead crew," Huen/Texeira said. "Jesus and Mary, a thing like that, there must have been hundreds of them working on it, and they vacced every last one. Only the meat get off *Paraiso* alive."

"Quebec, I've got you a secure beam to *Marcus Garvey.*"

"Patch her through, please."

Relocation. Dislocation. A quarter of a million tons of kilometer-long slamship balanced over your head by a single, slender boom. The wide-angle lens sends the perspectives racing away from you. Vertigo. But you can see how the balancing act works. At one end of the accelerator spine, a knobby sphere of nickel-studded water ice, ghostlit by plasma kickback as the slap-on engines throw out waves of decoys, each with the radar signature of a slamship. Counterbalancing it, the luminous opal of earth from the orbital approaches, southern Africa an inverted, accusing finger, periodically obscured by the blue-white stutter of the mass driver matching orbits. And in the middle, directly above your head, at the center of the radiating power, weapons and communications booms, among the clustered environment pods, nestle soft-edged, incongruous globes of greenery. Vacuum trees. The forests of the night. Figures move with agility of monkeys through the trees, over the pods, along the shafts and booms. Toussaint does not need his father's image enhancement 'ware to show him that they are four-armed, self-contained, naked to space. Long chains of lights strung out against the night are sister ships, silent running; hard, fast-moving blinks of actinic light are pickets, decoys, fighters, missiles moving ahead of the fleet.

It is magnificent. It is beautiful. It is all the things Toussaint flew away from his father's house to find and never has.

Dislocation. Relocation. The environment bubble was transparent to space. In the background: brilliantly pelted *quadros* grouped every which way around freefloating instrument clusters. A handsome, ageless dead woman occupied foreground center focus. Her skin was patterned a dark-on-light dappling of leaves.

"Looking good, Marie-Claire," said Quebec.

"Thank you, *compañero*," the woman said in slightly accented High Spanish. Bioluminescent patches on her shoulders and nipples glowed as she spoke. Soft blue flowers spread across the sky behind her and faded. She glanced down at an unseen display. "Gunline attrition rates are thirty percent per hour. We estimate them maximizing to seventy percent as we approach perigee. We lost *Babylon and Ting*—a rail gun hit early on—and *Susie Q*, a semiautomated lightpusher manufacturing core in the van, took a strike from a logic-bomber squadron. Our own rail guns took out the bombers, but *Susie Q* is a flying hulk until we can get a full tech team onboard her to debug her. Otherwise main fleet penetration is forty percent below estimates. The gunline is absorbing their rail gun and tesler fire and the interceptors are taking out their missiles and fighters. We are holding them, Quebec."

Brilliant sparks climbed away from *Marcus Garvey*'s skeleton: virtuality-control interceptors, a subtext informed Toussaint, rezzing up specifications, weapons suites, delta vees and fractional orbits.

"They're evacuating the manufactories, Marie-Claire. Phase one is complete. We're through to their intrasystems channels. Show her, Texeira."

Fragments of atrocity at squirt speed. The dead woman pursed her lips. Her skin darkened, sudden autumn. An aura of deep-space detonations momentarily haloed her. "We have mass resurrection facilities back in the auxiliaries," she said grimly. "Some of the meat will just have to wait their turn. Have you got the line in?"

"Ready to go," said Huen's voice. "You're through into Tesler-Thanos's executive command system. The channel is tightbeam, encoded, it can be broken into only from this end. They've got links into the Rim Council and, indirectly, Orbital Command. Also, you have noninteractive read-only access to the complete Tesler-Thanos management hierarchy, and newsnet search-and-compilers." The view from space dissolved into a collage of low-resolution shots of freight shuttles blowing free from manufactory docking teats, aerial views of burning cities, orbital weapons turning on their jets to take aim on still-unseen targets. "Failsafes will warn you if Tesler-Thanos catches you eavesdropping, so you don't end up being the one spied on rather than the one doing the spying."

The helmet returned to the dead space captain and her silent, elegant fleet falling earthward.

"Good work, Quebec." Again, she glanced at out-of-shot displays. "The 'wares are running up revised probabilities right now. I should say with the intelligence you've given us, we're home free. Thank you, *compañeros*. On to phase two." White light flooded the bubble; and hard behind it, a red pulsing. The image shook violently. On-screen alphanumerics screamed twenty different dangers. The dead woman grabbed overhead support bars to steady herself. Her lower hands came into view, encased in manipulator gloves. "We have a red-alert situation here," she said calmly, pulling down an audiovisualizer hood from off camera. "One near-miss and six, eight, my God, twelve incoming." In the background her beautifully marked crew were diving from their perches around the control clusters to take up combat stations.

"See you in heaven, Marie-Claire."

"See you in heaven, Quebec," the woman said as she smiled. "Good luck with your father."

The visor blanked. The cochlear buds whispered white noise. The link was broken. Crashed, despondent, earthbound and painfully mortal, Toussaint disengaged from the data chair. He had been shown true flight, absolute flight, flight as poetry, and at the apex of the climb, his pinfeathers had been pulled.

Truth and mystery. All the questions Toussaint had told himself to ask when the time was right declared *now* was the time, *here* was the place.

The true name and the true nature. The familiarity of things he could have known only in abstract. Knowing six was right. Porfirio Kazantzekes, good and faithful servant, unable to take his eyes off him even as death folded its fingers around his skull. And the dead space captain's casual farewell.

"Quebec; I want to know now. Who are you?"

The man who called himself Quebec looked to his deputies.

"I've secured the room," said Huen/Texeira, last to come out of virtuality. "It'll take heavy-duty cutting gear to get past the overlocks on those doors. The penthouse level is effectively sealed off. The man upstairs isn't going anywhere. You've got all the time you need."

"Tell him, Quebec," said Shipley, rubbing old bones, stiff joints. "He deserves to know. Everything."

Quebec indicated an empty chair beneath a shaft of white light.

"Come, sit, Xavier. I know you've heard many stories this night, but I'd ask you to listen to just one more, and then you will understand. Everything."

Forty-two hours twenty-seven minutes.

"Living is easy, it's dying that scares me to death," Camaguey said. He stood on the edge of Los Robles, blown by the wind, soaked through. Beneath his feet, Necroville began. "Like that line from the old song, 'Tired of livin' and scared of dyin'.' I once saw this repeat of an old Judy Garland show from way back before I was born. The first half was all numbers with Sinatra and Dean Martin, duets, trios. Stagey and kind of lifeless though the songs are great. Then, the second part, it was just Judy, on this stage in front of her name in lights: *Judy*. She sang that old song, *'Ol Man River*. I never heard anyone ever sing it like that, before or since: when she got to that line, 'Tired of livin' and scared of dyin',' I tell you, it made the hairs stand up all the way down my spine, because of all the people who ever sang that line, she was the only one really meant it."

Seated beside him, Nute munched a peach filched from the roof-jungle. She flicked the pit out into the night. The market in the old parking levels beneath them had struck its last deal on the stroke of midnight. The sounds of the carnival had moved to a different quarter, distant and liquid.

Nute swung her legs over the street.

"To understand mortality is to be adult. Teenagers can't die. Teenagers live forever. Adults die, and knowing it changes them. Out there"—she hooked a thumb back toward the distant lights of the meat city—"it's a teenage culture. Because we see nanotechnology bring people back from the dead, we think we can live forever, and so we no longer believe in our mortality. And so we live like we are never going to die. We regress. We become a civilization of teenagers. But Watson's Postulate—that the first thing we get with nanotechnology is immortality—is unproved. The Tesler Corollary is something quite different. We haven't got immortality. We have resurrection. We haven't beaten death. We've found something on the far side of death that sounds and smells and tastes and looks and feels like what we know as life on the near side, but the only way to find out if it is is to pass through death. A hope of immortality is all the living can know. I could tell you that my lifespan, barring pretty cosmic-league catastrophes, is now measured against the universe. I can sense the continents move. I can hear the mountains being ground down to dust. I can see the stars move in their courses. I can feel the sun grow cool on my skin and the galaxy turn beneath my feet. The moon will fall from the sky and shatter and I will be there. The sun will swallow the earth and boil Jupiter away like a double-chocolate-mint sundae in plasma beam, and I will be there. The solar system will nova and collapse into a neutron star, and Nute shall endure. That's the kind of creature I am, Camaguey. The kind of creatures we are."

Departing storm clouds glowed along the eastern horizon, hemorrhaging lightning. All Camaguey was was a fistful of hours trickling out of his hand.

"In India the yogis used analogies to express the vast periods of time that made up the divine cycles of the Upanishads," Nute continued. She plucked wet apricots from a genetweak tree that grew out over the drop and shared them with Camaguey. "Imagine a cube of stone a million kilometers by a million kilometers by a million kilometers that is a million times harder than diamond. Imagine that once every million years some passing angelic being brushes it with the hem of his robe: imagine how long it would take to wear away that block of stone."

"Then imagine that happening a million times," said Camaguey. Rain and apricot juice ran down his face. "I know the story. My people were Old Catholics: they used to use it as an analogy of hell: all that time *and still not one instant of eternity will have passed.*"

"I always thought that was rather exciting in a kind of kinky way." Nute tilted her head back to let the rain fill up her closed eyes. "Great for masochists. A billion trillion years in chains with spiked iron rings around your dick and it hasn't even begun yet. Ecstasy. Though I suppose if you were enjoying it, it wouldn't be hell. If God really wanted to punish you, you'd say *whip me, whip me* and he'd say, *No.* That's real sadism."

Forty-hours, ten minutes, and we are debating fine points of comparative theology and sado-masochistic practice.

"I need something more than just a hope that my me-ness, this sense of *being a person*, of being uniquely behind this pair of eyes and no other, that this comes out on the far side. Since I found out, since the medical 'wares confirmed the diagnosis, I've tried to convince myself that it will be like falling asleep, that you drift, that you become unconscious, that no time passes until you awaken. But I can't, Nute. Death is not sleep, a voice tells me. Consciousness blinks out and never blinks on again—never, ever—and my too-conscious mind reels in terror from that. I want to believe, Nute, but I can't."

"Camaguey, I won't lie to you. Now, there's a novelty, a pro who doesn't lie to her john. Death is not sleep, not a slow submerging into unconsciousness. Death breaks through sleep, shattering dreams, dispelling unconsciousness. It is a light brighter than any other, an awakening into a moment of utmost lucidity."

"And after that moment?"

Nute did not immediately reply, but plucked a palm leaf and, trapping it like a reed in her cupped hand, blew through her thumbs. The vibrating leaf lamented like an animal in torment.

" 'I went to the Old Man of the Earth to ask him to show me the Way,' " she said. " 'He lifted a huge stone from the floor of the cave, beneath it was a dark hole. "That is the way," he said. "But there are no lights, no stairs!" I cried. "You must throw yourself in," said the Old Man of the Earth. "There is no other way." ' John the Bastard used to write reams of that sort of stuff, which I used to think was pretty fucking profound until I discovered it was all sampled and remixed from other writers, with the serial numbers filed off."

"I'm not ready."

Nute stood up. "Who is, Camaguey? Who can say to death, *I'm ready now, you can have me?*" How many people are going to die out there tonight, not ready? In a burning wreck on the highway; in an aerospacer falling to Earth at ten kilometers per second; with the sound of their own vomit rattling in their lungs; at the end of a blade in a coup fight; with a lover's bullet in your left ear; with your brain turned to gravy by some mugger's baseball bat; at the bottom of your own swimming pool, screaming with cramp; in burning houses; in sinking ships; in caving accidents and climbing accidents and gliding accidents; in elevator accidents, in construction accidents, in manufacturing accidents? Do you think any of them are ready, any of them had one second's warning that they were going to die? Do you think any of them can stop the car two seconds from the crash barrier, or hold the plane twenty meters from the ground, and say to death, *could you hold it just a minute. I've a few things to sort out first?* They would envy you your ration of hours, your chances to say your farewells, make right your relationships, settle your affairs, even, as you keep saying, *make yourself ready.*"

"Relationships. Affairs. I don't think any of those could be put right now. It's me I need to make ready. I need to prepare, I need a way to go, a path to follow, that when I come to the end of it, I can say, *now, I'm ready now, I can go.* I want to start again, I want this eternal life you tell me about to begin now. Even while I live, I want to be part of the dead nation."

" 'If the agents of the Emperor come to your house at midnight, is it not better that they enter as your invited guests than break down your door?' "

"John the Bastard."

"In Kafka modality. You want a foretaste of the dead nation: there's a place I can take you where you can have that. There'll be a Shattering someplace in the city tonight, if we can find it. And on the way, who knows who or what we might bump into. It's the way gone that matters, as much, or more, than the destination."

The cars are steel-jacketed high-velocity assassin's bullets; ten meters of verdigrised gold-bronze slung between fat dragster's slicks. Fins and fairings, Mach bumps and streamlines; are those liftercraft ducted fan engines Camaguey hears, running up and down the harmonic spectrum? Weatherproof team jackets glittering in the rain, mechanics and technicians scurry about like workers attending some bloated termite queen. No, the analogy fails, Camaguey thinks standing on the parapet looking down the sloping concrete sides into the uncompleted *metropolitano* cutting. There is something altogether too predatory and beautiful, too mantid, about these street racers. As if they might turn at any instant and devour their courtiers; squeeze out blood and lymph and marrow for their fuel.

"Let's get closer," says Nute, clearing a path through the racegoers. The green and gold brocade coat she grabbed from her tower flaps out behind her like a banner. Spectators line both edges of the cutting three, four, five deep. Behind the bookie's parasol is an inspection ladder. The rungs are slippery in the rain. Camaguey, careful of his life until the moment he chooses to let go of it, takes them slowly, one rung at a time. The revving engines reverberate deafeningly between the high concrete walls.

"Luis!" Nute shouts over the screaming engines. A tall Afro-Hispanic man in an Equipo Raya Verde jacket turns, spraying raindrops from the peak of his cap.

"Nute!" They embrace, they kiss palms, as the dead do.

"This is Camaguey!" Nute yells. "He's a friend. I'm showing him what life can be if he's got the *cojones* to grab hold of it." The man Luis looks suspiciously at Camaguey: living, dead, paying, nonpaying? "How's it going?"

"Running a new mix," Luis shouts. Team attendants step back as he brings his guests to look at the car. "Should give us a two point two percent mass/energy advantage over the opposition. Also, we're the only ones figured on it raining." Luis runs his fingers over the notchings and corrugations of the man-high driving wheels.

"What use is a prophetess unless she can get the weather right?" shouts Nute.

A meter section of hull clamshells open. In a bed of soft impact gel lies a Chinese woman in a VR bodyglove. Team Manta technicians check interfacings, hookups, remotes. Test patterns and output grids rezz up on their portables.

"There're hundreds of kilometers of abandoned metro tunnels and culverts and buried rivers under Saint John alone, all as dark and black as sin," yells Nute. "It's all done through virtuality simulations. Radars, proximity sensors, image amplifiers, night-eyes."

The woman driver is kissing the hands of each one of her team. Nute is last in the line. "Crash and burn!" she shouts. The Chinese woman smiles and grips her hand in solidarity, genuinely blessed. Unquiet in spirit, Camaguey watches the opaque lid close and seal over her. He is thinking of them lying in their coffins as they race blind through the city's underworld. The engine roar rises to a steady scream. Race marshals shepherd the tech teams away from their vehicles. Nute drags Camaguey to a wet bleacher set into the side of the cutting. All conversation is lost as the cars kick in their turbofans and taxi in clouds of spray to the start line. Rudders flip side to side, ailerons up and down.

"They can use the aerodynamics to go up the walls and pass each other," Nute roars in Camaguey's ear. "Isn't it fabulous?" Halfway down the kilometer-long cutting the five cars turn and line up. The tunnel mouth is a plane of unremitting darkness. Stalactites leached from the concrete hang from the upper lip; calcite fangs. The engine notes merge into one shattering shriek. The concrete cutting is shaken to its very molecules. Spray and steam plume from fan exhausts. Up on the podium, built into the cutting wall, the starter has her flag up. The cars tremble, straining at the constraints that bind them.

The flag goes down. Five spears of tectoplastic and energy launch themselves at the tunnel entrance. In a second they are past the team bleachers. And against himself, against all that he knows about himself, Camaguey is on his feet with the rest of them, jumping up and down, shaking his fist, shouting and roaring soundlessly into the great howl of engines, *vaya vaya Raya Verde!*

And on, through the rag-end of carnival; the processions returning home, victorious or dejected, after the judging. Nute steers Camaguey between wire mesh and spray plastic St. Anthonys the size of tenement blocks and dancers in rain-streaked luminous body paint tethered to helium balloons in the shapes of cherubs in shades. Exquisite tranvestites push past; Maria Earth Mother and *Infante* Jesu, *Rey* and *Reina* of the Night of the Dead, stoop low to bless them. Seu Obuluwayé, the Night Traveler, slinks past in jaguar-striped Lycra.

"The night is ours, Camaguey," Nute declares. "We rule: the night, and the future. Every second of every day, there is another one of us. Dozen of us, hundred of us, thousand of us. We grow. The people on the outside of the wire will be on the inside, one sure day. In another seventy years this city will be all dead. Hundred kilometers long, hundred kilometers wide. All dead. How long before the state, the Rim, Mother Earth, is a dead nation, a dead planet? No wonder those Freedead are fucking up the moon: after twenty years at current population replacement rates and no one dying, the demographic charts go asymptotic. Our future is out there, this planet cannot hope to contain all the life that depends from it. I remember a scary old Malthusianist parable from back then: no matter how small the percentage, any unchecked population increase will eventually run away until it reaches the point where the universe is nothing but a sphere of naked human flesh expanding outward at lightspeed. The constraints put on dead society make no effort to answer these questions; they just fudge them for a future generation. I'll be there. You'll be there. The ones who were our enemies will be there. We'll all be there, when those questions have to be answered. We can wait. We have time. Tomorrow belongs to us."

"But," says Camaguey, "what happens on that day a thousand, ten thousand, million years from now when you wake up and there is nothing left to look forward to? What do you do on that day when there is nothing new left under this or any other sun?"

"The old 'heaven is boring' argument." Nute sighed. "Eternity is one big Sonoma Consciousness-Raising Interaction Group. Bat shit. It isn't even good theology. What the hell kind of heaven is it you end up wanting out of because it bores the tits off you? That's not heaven, that's hell. Any self-respecting heaven should just keep getting better and better. It was great this morning when you woke up, you just wait until you see what it's going to be like tomorrow.

"You met anyone who thinks they'd be better off dead? Who's worried about being bored a couple of million years down the line? Who isn't madly in love with the idea that it doesn't have to end? Meatboy, resurrected life is no different from flesh life: we both live it one day at a time. You can't contemplate eternity, we can't contemplate it either. All we know are our memories of yesterday, our hopes for tomorrow, our joys and pains of today. And so we'll get there, day by day. In an infinity of time there's room for an infinity of joy and surprise. And there'll be pain, there'll be sorrow, there'll be heartbreak—no maybes about it—but that's good too because it's feeling, it's emotion, it's living.

"There's a guy I know, runs money for me through some black Rim 'ware, you know, *caballeria* stuff. Heaven is a golf course to him. God's truth, Camaguey. He looks at the future and sees an ever-unrolling fairway; he sees bunkers on the moon and greens in the calderas of Olympus Mons and clubhouses on Pluto. He'll quite happily spend eternity playing golf, and do you know why? Because he'll never be perfect at it. Because if he practices for a billion years, the limits of his humanity mean he'll never be able to play a complete round of holes-in-one. Not even on Pluto. If he did, it would destroy it. All he could ever hope to do again would be to match it. Perfection is stasis and death. Imperfection is change and life. It's our humanity that makes living this way if not heaven, often infinitely preferable to death.

"Come on. In here." Here being a dripping, decaying multi-level carpark from the glory days of cars and girls. "If there's a Shattering anywhere in this city tonight, Florda Luna will know where. Knows all, sees all."

Moonflower, Nute goes calling through the dripping upper levels. *Flower of the Night, a question for you.* A steady stream of water flows down the ramp, falls in glittering strings and droplets through the interior spaces of the carpark. They emerge onto the roof. To Camaguey the dead town is a dimension of silver screens, stardust memories left in the rain. Clark Gable, Bogart, Maureen O'Sullivan. Gutman and Mr. Joel Cairo. The Thief of Baghdad. A black body—too large, too irregular for humanity—is silhouetted against Spencer Tracy in *The Old Man and the Sea*. Spaced around it are portable satellite dishes and uplinks; swaths of cable drape it.

"Hey, Florda Luna, it's Nute! How ya doin'?"

Camaguey sees the prophetess by movie light and green bile gags him. Elena. It is Elena, who never went that final time into the Jesus tank, who was never flushed away to the sea of forgetting, whose mis-replications doubled and redoubled and multiplied geometrically, loga-rithmically, until nothing recognizable as Elena was left.

"Jesus Nute!"

"Hey. Shh. Think of other people's feelings."

If Shirley Temple were elevated to Aztec deity, she might be the moonflower prophetess. A girl of nine, ten, eleven sits on a plastic chair. Her head, her shoulders, most of the upper part of her body is surrounded by a halo of tectoplasm outgrowths and deformities: horns, tendrils, extrusions that look like feathers cast from obsidian, animal masks and bird beaks, ruffs and frills and geometric shapes that have no biological simile. Cables and coils of interface connector twine from underneath the fans and crests and plug into the attendant communications equipment. At some time in the process of misreplication her legs and forearms have fused with the plastic chair. The seat itself has grown roots and locked itself immovably into the concrete roof of the carpark. She can move her head just enough to nod to Nute and Camaguey. The fantastical halo clicks and clinks. She smiles very beautifully, like a nine-ten-eleven-year-old girl should. Rain runs down her face.

"They're trying to jam but they can't keep me out," she says. "Jam tomorrow, jam yesterday, but never jam today." Her voice is perfect, but for that quartertone of too-knowingness Camaguey hears in all the voices of the dead. "Their newschannels are lying to them. All their hits have been on decoys. The main fleet is intact, while the automated defenses are being steadily eroded. The defense crews are being evacuated by intraorbit tugs to prearranged drop-shuttle rendezvous points. The Rim Council, PanEuropa and the orbital *corporadas'* estimates of tactical victory are currently forty-three percent."

"Tactical victory?" Nute asks.

"Forced disengagement of the Freedead ships at the cost of seventy-five percent defense casualties." The prophetess blinks. Rain drips from the many peaks and points of her halo. "I see the slugfest's spreading out from La Brea. Elements are clashing with Adamist cult members. Nasty."

"Adamists?" Camaguey asks.

"They think Adam Tesler is God," Nute says. "Their creator, redeemer, savior, friend, messiah. They are his children, resurrected to be the new humanity of the new Eden: sinless, perfect, immortal. Like I keep telling you, this is Necroville, meatboy."

The dead child continues. "I'm trying to correlate this with reports I picked up from the *seguridado* channels of a mysterious power outage on the Sunset Gate and two nanotoc blasts in the same area, one inside, one outside the Saint John district boundary."

"You see everything, Moonflower," Nute says, seating herself on the parapet. "Want to find the Shattering. I know there's one tonight, there always is every *Noche de los Muertos*."

"Too easy. Delong and McCadden. There is a small community of craft workshops. Back of them. Now ask me something worthy of the one true prophetess."

"All right. Can you see if we'll still have a world this morning?"

The prophetess closes her eyes. Camaguey shakes a sudden high-pitched whine out of his head; a static charge of sympathetic magic.

"Death is a timeless time," Nute whispers. "All the dead, past present and future exist simultaneously. What Moonflower does is recreate the time when she was dead and pass the information she gleans from her weblinks to the future dead, who cross-reference it with their memories of what happened. Will happen, to us."

"You don't believe this stuff?" Camaguey says.

"Not unless it says something nice about me."

The Moonflower speaks. "Wheels within and wheels without. Play of the day is Oedipus Schmoedipus but only the man in the high tower knows it. What none of the principals suspect is that the bit players may yet upstage them. It all ends in fire. Pain and warm leatherette go well together. There is a town where the walls are made of compressed memory. Those who lose their lives will gain them, those who love their lives will lose them." She smiles. "So the dead of tomorrow's tomorrow say."

"Moonflower, you know these things can mean whatever the hell you want them to mean," says Nute.

"Truth is hidden, only the ear of faith can hear its voice."

"Old cynics like Nute would be more convinced if they could hear the voice of truth without faith. Clear and unequivocal. Come on, *compadre*, to the Shattering."

"A Shattering?" Camaguey asked as the dukduk navigated a course around Necroville's ever-shifting trouble spots toward Delong and McCadden.

Nute was evasive. "'Verily verily, I say unto you, you must be born

again.' Or words to that effect. Roughly translated into the Angeleno."
All the bells fringing the taxi's canopy jingled at once as the moped hit
a rut in the road.

A Shattering.

Behind the shut-up craft units was a warehouse. Steel pillars, ribbed
aluminum roof, poured concrete floor. Candle brackets had been epoxied to the roof uprights. Hieroglyphs covered roof and walls: hands out-
lined in green spray-paint. Eye symbols, an oval containing a black iris.
Red spirals, winding anticlockwise.

People sat in ranks along each side of the warehouse. Camaguey
guessed their number at upward of six hundred. Seated cross-legged,
the two groups faced each other across a four meter gap.

The four meter gap was not empty. Twenty-five roughcast cylinders
of yellow adobe set side by side occupied the length of the warehouse,
decorated with the ubiquitous hand, eye, spiral symbols. Camaguey estimated each was three meters long and one and a half wide.

Hand music filled the warehouse, beat its metal and concrete like
a drum. One half beat out a complex, five part clapping rhythm on
hands, floor, walls, pillars while the left half, eyes closed, stretched their
arms out in front of them, leaned forward and then slowly swayed from
side to side, sending waves across the congregation. Every five repeats
of the hand music, the clappers would suddenly shoot out their arms
and point at their counterparts across the divide who, without skipping
a beat, would take up the rhythm while those on the right side would
begin the movement. Back and forth the music and the dance went,
across the divide. The five-upon-fivefolds of its rhythms found resonant
frequencies in every part of Camaguey: heart, lungs, the swash of the
digestive tract, the twitch of synapses, the flicker of eyeballs.

"They'll have been at it since nightfall," Nute shouted into his ear.
"Pretty soon they lose track of time. Altered states of consciousness,
and all that."

She found him a place on the floor at the end of the third rank near
the door. To his right a shaven-headed black woman clapped her hands,
oblivious of anything but her part in the greater music. Camaguey struggled to catch the complex rhythm, shook his head in frustration.

"Clap whatever comes into your head," Nute said. "No one at a
Shattering ever knows in advance what the music will be. Anything can
be the seed: traffic in the street, the sounds of insects, the rain on the
roof. It's always improvised, always different, always changing over the
course of the night. Let go. Lose yourself. Permit yourself to be sur-

prised, hurt, terrified, killed: whatever, it's all right. It's your choice. Let it go. Don't let it be taken from you."

But how . . . he prepared to ask but the clapping music was scooped up and handed across to him and he caught it in his hands. He rolled it about. He used it, any old way, any old rhythm, and as he clapped it out he found echoes in the hands around him. That *Americano Indigena* woman two rows in front and six down. That man with Bogart's face twelve along. That man/woman with the jackal head of an ancient Egyptian god in the back row directly behind him. As he listened, the rhythm of his hands matched theirs. As his rhythm matched theirs, so he heard them less and less. There was no black woman to the right of him. There was no Nute to the left of him. There was no Camaguey. Only the rhythm. Without knowing how, he had counted out the complex cycles of five by five, he handed the clapping music back across the gap.

A tremor shook the third clay cocoon. Its adobe shell flexed and cracked, shedding scales of yellow clay.

The rhythm passed back, and returned.

The third cocoon split. A dark movement within: something, stirring.

A hand thrust forth. Black back, white palm. A second hand. The cocoon split down the center, tore, fell in two halves.

A young black woman lay in the split cocoon. She was naked. Her chest heaved from her exertions in breaking the clay. Her eyes were closed, her face was in turn puzzled, suspicious, hopeful, frightened, excited. The black woman sat upright, brushing clinging clay from her breasts, the backs of her hands, her face. She rubbed the sealant gel out of her eyes and stared at her hands. Her self-exploration moved from hands to arms, from arms to legs, from legs to body, from looking to touching the undeniable reality of flesh.

"At first you think it's a trick, a dream from the underside of death," Nute said. Every cocoon had now answered the summons of the hand music. From some, resurrected men and women were struggling, some were splitting and cracking, others merely trembled in time to the clapping. Without sign given or word passed, the hand music changed into a subtler song of fingers: clicked, rubbed on concrete. Camaguey slipped into the rhythm like a pair of old leather gloves. "Then you wonder if the life you remember before was only a dream, like the *Indigenas* who believe that the world ends on the third day and what we imagine is reality is only the dreams of the final night. Then you start to realize everything they told you is true. Yes: you have passed through death and needn't fear it anymore. Yes: you have the body of your young days, but made perfect, with all those things that made you so unhappy put right. Yes: it will never grow old, it will never grow ugly, it will never fail you the way your old meat body did. Yes: you have a full lifetime's experience and memory and sophistication and wisdom poured into that body. Yes: it's all true, it's all yours. Look at her, Camaguey, look at her." The black woman knelt among the clay shards. She hugged her own body, rocked unconsciously in time to the finger music. Tears of uncontainable joy ran down her face, glistening in the candlelight. "You don't think about the price to be paid, Camaguey; however much that price is, it's worth it, and more." A look of decision crossed the resurrected woman's face. She wiped her tears from her face and tried to stand up. Once, twice, the newborn muscles failed her. The third time she heaved herself up into an ugly, awkward straddle-legged stand. She dripped sweat, her body trembled from the effort.

Dead people rose from the first rank to take her, hold her, embrace her. From the other cocoons the dead were rising, taking their few faltering, exultant steps. The congregation was coming apart as the resurrected were welcomed into their new families.

"She'll need father, mother, sisters, brothers, lovers: she's so much to learn about herself, her society, the world into which she has been reborn. So much hurt and loss and confusion to be guided through. So much fear to be overcome. Not everyone chooses this way to come into life, the clay and the Shattering, but to those who do, it's the most powerful experience of their lives." Nute broke off in a choked sob. "I'm sorry. I hadn't thought it would do this to me. I thought you should see the mystery and sheer joy of it and maybe it would help you not be afraid. I hadn't thought it would hit me so hard, so deep."

"You've done it," Camaguey said.

"It was raining that night too, the night I came out."

"I want that for me." Camaguey was decisive. "I don't want to be just another load of Jesus-tank fodder, decanted, scrubbed down, hustled out into the streets. I want to celebrate being a member of the Dead Nation. I feel like one already. Can you live a life all in one night? Birth, adulthood, love, death?"

"Let's try," said Nute. Out on the boulevard the rain had stopped. The air was fresh, cool; the air of early morning that feels so rich and fine-edged in your lungs, like snorted diamond dust. Every sound was as clear and sharp as a needle of crystal: the rush and swish of the few vehicles along the wet avenue, the sounds of drums and marimbas from those *cuadras* celebrating carnival victories. With the clarity, sudden pain. Camaguey saw that the subtle, sibilant rhythm of the concrete had scraped his fingertips bloody.

And he saw another thing. In the palm of his right hand was a large white pimple. Without knowing why he did so, he pushed at it with his left forefinger. The blister burst and collapsed. Protruding from the skin was a needle of black crystal.

So: it begins.

"Nute, what I said about living a life in one night?"

"Birth, life, death."

"Sex?" He showed her the thing he had found in his hand.

"Jesus, Camaguey."

"Nute, don't hate me."

"I understand, Camaguey. You can't shock Nute. Everyone knows death is the big aphrodisiac. Lovers worth the name always fuck after funerals. You paid for me, Camaguey; you saved my ass from the *non-contratistos*, I'm your Gallowglass, remember? I know a place, not far."

Thirty-seven hours, twelve minutes.

The bellowing cry sounded again, closer now. Santiago shivered, chilled by something colder than the rain. Nothing had the right to sound that damned.

"Standard dispersal pattern three," Miclantecutli ordered. "Report back at oh two hundred. Angel, you with Duarte. Call me from Taco-rifico Superica's. Asunçion, feel all right about going on your own? Anansi, with me and Santiago."

"Are we not taking the bikes?" Santiago asked, seeing Asunçion's clever hands stretch out cables of hog stuff and bond them into the boulevard.

"It's not how it's played," said Miclantecutli.

The voice in the night cried out again and was answered by a second bellow. By then the rain-slick street was empty.

They loped east through a labyrinth of new housing projects. Those few out in the narrow streets—mostly misplaced *carnivalistos* and lovers seeking the privacy of dark entries—gave the hunted wide berth or touched fingertips to head, lips, breast, belly, loin: the fivefold self-blessing of Ucurombé Fé. Miclantecutli led, as relentless and tireless in being the stalked as the stalker. Santiago lagged some distance behind; Anansi dropped back to keep him company and taunt him.

"Pace too fast for you, meatboy? This all a bit too dirty, too sweaty, too physical? Too real? I don't suppose you burn too many kilojoules *jodeing* a computer, do you?"

Panting, Santiago turned on the hectoring, panda-eyed woman, grabbed two fistfuls of stretch mesh, lifted her up to eye level. Lifted her. Held her. Said nothing.

"Can't even tell me what you'd like to do to me, can you?" she said. "*Querido*, there's nothing you could do to me that I haven't enjoyed more from someone else."

"You are one sick fuck, woman," Santiago gasped. He set Anansi down on the rain-spattered hood of an electric pickup. Anansi grinned and righted her clothing.

"Sick fuck is better than dead fuck," said Miclantecutli, waving them down a narrow street choked with parked trucks from a short-order *panadería*. "They'll never get those unholy things down here."

As if in answer, the unholy thing roared again. The canyon walls of masonry focused the sound, amplified it, beamed it straight into the heart and mind of Santiago Columbar. A second call joined it, a third, a fourth, a fifth. In front of them.

"Mother of God, the whole pack is after us," said Anansi quietly.

"They haven't wasted their reconnaissance time," spat Miclante-cutli. "Rats in a shit pipe." She looked up into the falling rain. "These roofs look like they interconnect."

Miclantecutli climbed up onto a truck hood, and then onto the roof. She found a foothold on a gushing downspout, swung herself up, leaped and caught the bottom rung of a fire escape descender. The ladder rattled down. Anansi swarmed past her and was three flights up by the time Santiago had even scrambled onto the roof of the truck. The cry, like something long dead woken from its sleep, shook the narrow alley and found an answer from the far end.

"What is that?" Santiago paused to catch breath on the fifth-level landing.

"You'll find out soon enough." Miclantecutli's face was a study in savage glee.

She loves it, thought Santiago as he followed Miclantecutli across the roofscape of homebrew chickenwire satellite dishes, airco ducts and rusted, dismal carousels of saturated laundry. *There is no difference between hunter and hunted. Pursuer becomes pursued: that is the mystery of it. And pursued, pursuer?* He found himself on the lip of a narrow brick parapet, the streets of Saint John a dizzying thirty meters below. Don't look at the rain. Do not follow the drops down into the chasm of streetlight. Miclantecutli ran along the very edge to join Anansi beckoning them from an arch-backed wooden bridge—clearly home-made—that spanned the gap between rooftops. She was magnificent, feral, careless, calculating, appalling. She inhabited with blithe unconscious ease the place beyond for which Santiago had sought since the dark revelation of his sixteenth birthday party. There was no other way it could be inhabited, he realized. Consciousness destroyed it, for it was the unconsciousness of pure physicality. The moment you were aware you possessed it and reached out to seize and keep it, you lost it. Animal awareness. It was not to be touched by hands and minds.

Behind, below, the hunter screamed again. There was no mistaking the harmonics of pure frustration within the bellow.

Across the bridge, and into the smack. A full hectare of the stuff, arranged around the *cuadra*'s central lightwell. Some of the plants were over head height, gamy and potent on Angeleno sunlight, Angeleno smog, Angeleno monsoon rain and generous applications of night soil. The early harvest was hung out on racks sheltered by a roof of transparent plastic sheeting that bulged beneath its catchment of rain.

The hunting voices roared as one.

"Bastards are still onto us," Miclantecutli hissed. "Santiago, front, Anansi, right. I'll take left. I want to see what they look like. Anyone skylines, I'll have their nipples."

Santiago's section of frontage commanded a radiating network of wide streets down which anything capable of such a scream would have been visible for the better part of a kilometer. Nothing. But they were out there. The absence of Necroville's ubiquitous nightlife betrayed them.

"The only other way down apart from the main stairs is a rope hoist for shifting the weed," Anansi reported. "Unless we want to go back the way we came. Nice, Miclan. Clever."

"Too far to jump on my side," Miclantecutli said. Anansi and Santiago concurred for their sectors. "Well well. So here we are all on our little rooftop up to our asses in sensemillia. Now, Anansi, as you expressed doubt concerning my leadership, tell me, what do you think we should do?"

"No, Miclan. Not me. Send him. I'm not doing it. It's suicide."

"That's why I can't send him, Anansi. And, having seen your open animosity toward my old friend and fellow artist, I couldn't trust you to look after him if I went. He's meat, remember, and meat's delicate. You're quick, you're good; you might get away. You probably will get away. And if you don't, isn't one better than three?"

"Fuck you, Miclan, Fuck you to hell."

"Thank you for your cooperation. Some people, Anansi," Miclantecutli said as her stalking horse climbed into the rope sling of the smack hoist, "would relish the opportunity to give a virtuoso performance in a specially commissioned concerto for solo pain." She thumbed the switch and sent Anansi down. Santiago watched her spin slowly on the rope as she descended through the rain; a Foucault pendulum weighted with a single life. "Of course, they may not be convinced that there was just one quarry up on the roof, but it's exactly those little imponderables that spice the game." Anansi touched ground. She knew better than to look up and wave. She disappeared into the warren of streets west of the *cuadra* at the hunter's steady, tireless wolf-jog.

"It's a good thing your *amigos* missed the bus, Santiago." Miclantecutli lay supine on the coping, watching the street. Rain ran from her rubber jacket; the vacuum-molded faces seemed to be crying. "They never had the *cojones* for strong meat like this. I could never understand what you saw in them. Two glasses of tequila, a snort or two of the white stuff and a quick bisexual fumble under the mosquito nets and that's life on the fast and loose. You were always worth more than that. Than them."

"You, for example?"

"I was touched when you decided to make our relationship more than just supplier and supplied. Nice to know that I'm still an inspiration to you. But I'm curious: what made it this Night of the Dead of all nights of the dead? Wake up this morning and find it just didn't do it anymore? I warned you, Santiago. Those clowns couldn't hold you: you and me, Santiago, it was always special. Always looking beyond."

The roar stopped her before she could say any more things Santiago did not want to hear. After the roar, running footsteps. Anansi came into the open intersection. Thirty meters up, Santiago could sense the fear, the single-minded concentration on escape. Sudden death was knotted tight in every muscle.

"Whatever happens," Miclantecutli whispered, "do not say a word, do not make a noise. Whatever happens."

Glancing over her shoulder, Anansi rounded the corner of the apartment house. Black shadows in the foliage, Miclantecutli and Santiago followed her. Anansi ran for the cover of the labyrinth on the west side.

A Pale Rider emerged from Anansi's intended escape route.

"Dear Jesus," whispered Santiago, forgetting Miclantecutli's injunction. Miclantecutli hissed through her teeth; admiration not admonition.

She pulled herself as close as she dared to the edge to watch the showdown.

The creature stood three meters tall on its hind legs: the alley was barely wide enough to accommodate its bulk. The hooked steel claws on the short, powerful forearms struck sparks from the ironwork as it squeezed between fire escapes, the heavily clawed feet gouged scrapes in the road surface. The head was a heavy ax of bone and skin; the thing's night vision had been augmented by two spotlights riveted to the bone behind each eye. It quested left, right, up, down, scenting, hunting. Sighting prey, it split in a grin of a hundred steel daggers. The rider occupied a saddle that seemed to Santiago to have grown out of the creature's shoulders. Ribbons of datacore connected skullplugs to a joystick control unit: the hunter, a shaggy-maned angel of a woman whose flageskin matched the reticulated green on green of her mount, pushed the lever. The monster took two steps toward the paralyzed Anansi.

"Dwarf allosaurs," Miclantecutli whispered with undisguised admiration. "Early Cretaceous variant that used to hunt the South Victoria littoral when Australia and Antarctica were *esposo* and *mujer* at the South Pole-io. They brought them down on the flight from Seattle-VanColumbia in can form and paid the Death House to brew them up. These people have money as well as class, for gringos. Now do you understand why I had to play hardball with them?"

The Pale Rider woman pushed a control on her board. The tectosaur threw back its head and screamed at the night. Its headlight beams lanced through the falling rain. The cavernous bellow shocked Anansi from her helplessness. She turned and ran. The allosaur came after her, devouring distance in two-meter strides. Up on the roof, the watchers followed. As Anansi entered the open intersection in front of the housing unit, the hunter stopped. The pursuing allosaur reared up and roared again. A second allosaur stepped out of an access alley in front of Anansi. A third, a fourth, a fifth. All the exits were closed.

"She's dead," Miclantecutli whispered. "She is dead meat." Santiago found her viscous note of lust disgusting.

Anansi stood alone on the concrete, spotlit by headlight beams. The woman Pale Rider who had cornered her unclipped a long lance from beside her saddle. The allosaur lowered its head, leaned forward. The Pale Rider leveled her lance. Her mount scraped twice at the concrete with its claws, and exploded forward. Anansi stood unflinching. The shock of bursting flesh, the cry of terminal pain, were simultaneous.

The lance took her in the breastbone, ran a full half meter through and out of her back. The force of the impact carried her halfway across the intersection before the Pale Rider released her grip on the lance and let Anansi fall. Her fingers fought for purchase on the smooth wet shaft as she slid agonizingly down it to the wet concrete. The huntress turned her mount, frighteningly agile on its huge, clawed toes and wrenched free the lance. Anansi's fingers slowly relaxed and opened. The Pale Riders circled their mounts around the dead woman.

Unable to take his eyes from the thing lying on the street staring at the falling rain, Santiago released a shocked, bubbling wail.

An allosaur lifted its head, sent its twin beams racing across the flank of the *cuadra*. Miclantecutli pulled him off the parapet and under the wet weeds.

"Say nothing. Do nothing," she whispered viciously. "I don't know what those things are using for targeting but we take no risks. Hopefully, the *bhang* will cover our scent." She rolled onto her back. "Certainly, we don't move from here until I'm satisfied it's safe." She peeled off her left glove and slipped the fourth finger into her mouth up to the first knuckle. "*¡Ay!* Anansi!" she whispered, and cleanly bit the last joint off her finger. Santiago's heart hammered. Miclantecutli whimpered in pain and spat the dismembered thing into the dark. "One to you, my enemies." For a few seconds the only sound was the drip of blood onto leafmold, then Miclantecutli's supernatural powers of regeneration staunched the flow.

Spirit guide. Lover. Tormentor. Muse. All of these Miclantecutli had been to him. All of these he had let her be to him.

Lightning-bolt memories: like hallucinogen flashbacks. Their first meeting at the Gallery Behind the Wire on Wilshere, where you could do the things that you did not dare in the meat world because in Necroville there was no law to draw a limit to art. Santiago Columbar: three days off twenty, painfully self-conscious in his painstakingly chosen streetsmarts among people whose names were his gods. In the tit pocket of his tectosaur skin vest: the disc containing the molecular schematics and predictive models of New Worlds, his first original piece. Miclantecutli: outlaw *virtualista*. Old enough to be responsible for half of Santiago's chromosomes but bodmods gave her the confidence to wear only a black-fleshtone bodyglove and a strategic vee of riveted aluminum. They met outside the plastic bubble inside which a dead woman surrounded by her own eviscerated intestines waited to die.

"New Worlds?" she had asked, running her fingertips over the leather thongs around his wrists.

"Alien worlds," he had said. "A perception-linked tailored hallucinogen. It reprograms the brain's pattern recognition systems: the familiar becomes the alien. A tree could be a fountain of liquid helium, a cloud a living blimp-being, a human a sentient crystal harp."

"You, *muchacho*, have been sent here by God," Miclantecutli outlaw *virtualista* had said, shepherding him away from the crowd into the cool of the gardens where acoustic sculptures whispered. She had told him her wetdream where virtual reality *joder*ed custom hallucinogens and spawned a terrifying, magnificent miscegeny: a virtuality that created itself from the hallucinating mind and in turn fed those hallucinations made actual through the bodyglove's sensory links. "Self-sustaining feedback loops. Full interaction, but on a wholly unconscious level. The ultimate inner-space trip. Something that burns the skin off the private pornocopias and daytrips through Van Goghland and Boschworld and Gilbert-and-Georgian life-as-art fly-on-shit hyperrealities that call themselves art virtuality. Something spontaneous. Something with *here be dragons* written above the gate. Something that leaves you so changed when you climb out of your bodyglove you may not recognize yourself. Something you may never come back from."

She had taken him home with her that night. They had stayed up until the dawn skysign, she drinking rye, he drinking bottled water, blinding each other with new revelations. The next day he had dropped out of the university and moved in with her.

To buy expensive computer time while he modeled molecules for the virtuality project, Miclantecutli had put Santiago's New Worlds spider into production. Because he had always been honest about his art, if nothing else, Santiago insisted they test the prototype. They had popped the spiders and taken a pedicab out across a city that, before their eyes and ears, changed into a numinous, symphonic dimension of chiming glass icebergs and neon trees, of hydrocarbon reefs and flying manta rays, of grazing herbivores that reared up in front of them and exploded into fountains of thistledown and patterns of light that danced in the peripheral vision but fled when you tried to look at them. They had fucked that night in Miclantecutli's glycerine bed; two delicate, crystalline aliens, coming together in a rustle and whisper of glassy cilia.

The first million, they say, is the hardest. A legend in less than ten days, Santiago had worked blithely on, spinning off a dozen best sellers in as many months. By then he was Miclantecutli's; body, mind and spirit.

The party had been a crashing bore. They had gone only because their celebrity demanded it. Santiago had handed out free scratch'n'sniff euphoriant patches to everyone who came up to him to tell him how brilliant he was. The sooner they got out of their heads and stopped bothering him the better. Behind the sound stacks he had pulled Miclantecutli to him, kissed her. She had started, surprised, as she felt his tongue push something into her mouth. Then she had felt the spider cling to her upper palate and familiar warm liquifying of the ego as the chemicals spread into her brain.

"Here be dragons," he whispered. They had barely made it back to her house. In their excitement they had stripped each other; obscenely expensive Beverly Boulevard party clothes ripped and torn. The bodygloves had sealed around them.

On the rooftop, in the rain, beneath the Indian hemp, Santiago remembered the lift into another place.

He had been a seed buried in cold earth. Cold earth pressing around him, cold earth holding him in suspension, in abeyance, a potential buried in cold earth, blind deaf dumb insensate.

Months passed in the cold earth while the virtualizer read the things the spider was sending through Santiago's brain, amplified and returned them, enhanced and improved them. The synesthetic passage of worms questing blindly through the soil was a shiver of sensor circuits on naked skin. Spring warmth he felt as a coil of heat wrapping itself around his body; unfolding him to the light, the heat. Soil slid from his shoulders as he burst from the earth reborn, renascent, bright shining like Blake's Adam crowned with the sun.

Glad Day.

Santiago Resurrexit stepped forth onto the judgment plain. Called out of the earth by the new sun, the army of the just emerged to walk with him toward the mountains of God: Marilyn and Jimmy and Buddy and Jimi and John and Wolfgang Amadeus and Wilfred and Janis and Jim and Mama Cass and Billie and Bird: the blessed company of those who had lived and died young and now lived forever.

Miclantecutli's virtualizer 'ware pulled found sources and ephemera and fitted them to Santiago's hallucination.

Time uncounted the army of the just crossed the red earth plain toward the mountains. They saw a cloud above them and as they went up into the hills so it drew nearer and they saw it was full of faces. Farther yet, into the valleys with the Christ-light shining upon them and each knew that within the cloud was the exact duplicate of his or her self. Santiago understood then that the bodies within the cloud were the lives they had left on earth; the imperfections, the failures, the sins of commission and omission. He understood that the name of the cloud was Unknowing and that, up ahead, where the lower slopes of Zion swept down to the encircling hills, it touched the earth and veiled the naked presence of God. He pushed through the gray, whisper-filled cloud, cold with inadequacy and compromise, and out into the primal light that takes away all speech and thought and vision. Tectors migrating through the glions of Santiago's brain sought out and ignited the human talent for religious ecstasy and the sensory skin poured overload down his nerve endings.

Time is, time was, time shall be no more.

And he had awoken and found himself on the cold hillsides of Old Hollywood.

Their two-person show *Dangerous Visions* had run on twelve virtualizers day and night for fifteen weeks at the Gallery Behind the Wire. With his share of the rights package Santiago bought the *residencia* in Copananga and moved out of Miclantecutli's Malibu stilt house with its feet in the cool green ocean. The partnership was ended.

In the Cloud of Mystery he had seen his relationship with Miclantecutli spiral downward, inward, each turn of the screw more claustrophobic and incestuous. He had turned outward and upward, to childhood friends, to college acquaintances, to new relationships rooted in mutual affection, not need and desire, demand and supply. He took back the reins of his life.

Three months later Miclantecutli was dead. Neat OD in the home by the sea, but Miclantecutli had not left a clean corpse. T17 had been marketed as a high-order euphoric. It was not. It was the ultimate euphoric. The trip it took you on was so good that nothing could ever compare with it. Users came down from it, looked at the rest of their lives, saw only fear, loathing, ashes, shit and darkness, and overdosed in a fit of suicidal depression.

Santiago heard of the story of Miclantecutli's death in a precis from his mediaware, programmed to keep watch on the global newschannels for stories which might have some bearing upon him. He went to her valedictory to be certain it was her inside, that death would make him safe from her affections. Over the weeks in which the Jesus tank took her to pieces and rebuilt her from the bones out, that certainty faltered. Santiago discovered a new reaction in his neurological alchemy: guilt. He had not loved her, he had come to fear her, even hate her, but he knew she had taken the stuff because he was gone from her life. His hands were unclean. He needed her forgiveness.

Received wisdom was that among the dead towns' swarming millions no one could be found who did not wish to be found. There is one rule for money and one rule for everyone else. Santiago sent out his spies physical legal informational virtual. They combed through the living and the dead, they bribed their way into zealously guarded Death House files, they surfed into *corporada contrada* and *Immortalidad* company records. They found Miclantecutli Resurrexit. They made her an offer no street girl could refuse. Work for the man who had abandoned her. Agent for him; run his stuff onto the streets of a Necroville badly in need of anyone's dreams.

She accepted because her memories of a man called Santiago Columbar amused her.

He could never, never keep away from self-destructive, yearning people, the ones who were brave enough to go to the very edge and look over.

That same summer, Peres fell, mind frozen in nirvana by a neural accelerator customized for him by Santiago Columbar. The circle of friends dissolved: the strain Santiago's personality placed on its strong nuclear binding forces was always going to be too great for the people he attracted to him. He found himself alone among a host of acquaintances—his natural lot—looking down the entropic slope of disillusion and decay. It was at this time that he started to talk to Miclantecutli. It was at this time that he learned the thing that had replaced outlaw virtuality in her desires, and step by step drawn closer to that edge he had never dared approach before.

Up on the roof, Miclantecutli glanced at her antique Rolex. She rolled out from under the hemp plants to crouch, poised like a hunting cat, on the edge of the roof.

"Come, *corazón*."

"They're gone?"

"There are people in the streets." She brought up the cargo hoist. "After you, séor. We've got a rendezvous to make." Santiago rode the rope down. Sky, wall, rain, spun around him. The sole fixed point seemed to be the neat stump of the last finger of Miclantecutli's left hand.

They moved through the backwash of carnival, safe among floats and teetering costumes from Pale Riders. Miclantecutli's maimed hand clamped around his wrist pulled him against the flow of bands and danc-ers. The young Santiago had once seen a fresco in some Old Mexican basilica. Lords and ladies were dragged into the fugues and figures of the Dance of Death by smiling skeletons, their hands linked together in an unbreakable grip of bone.

Daft Eddie's was a plastic-roofed quadrangle between four chro-mium luncheonettes, each dispensing a different ethnic cuisine from roller-skated serving staff. Rain drummed on the plastic; despite the odd leak, the tables beneath were busy.

"The original movable feast," Miclantecutli said, catching a maître d's eye. "When it gets too popular in one place they hitch the whole thing in a conga line and move it somewhere else." Daft Eddie himself brought her her margarita. "Just a water for my friend."

"How's it going?" Daft Eddie asked, who was none of the things his name implied. Miclantecutli held up her left hand.

"Who?"

"Anansi."

"¡Ay!" sighed Daft Eddie. "Those Pale Riders: I seen a lot, Miclan, but those *norteamericanos* . . . I hear those things of theirs; Jesus Joseph Mary, Miclan."

"Halfway to morning and we're only one down. Surely I'm still worth a bet, Eddie?"

"You have my hundred, Miclan, as always." He summoned a *mesero* to bring Santiago his water.

"No calls for me, Eddie?"

"Nothing yet."

"We're early."

The thunder of an allosaur, unmistakable, clearly audible over the rumble of the rain, stopped every conversation. Daft Eddie glanced nervously at Miclantecutli. Santiago found his fingers were gripping the edge of the table.

"Oh ye of little faith." Miclantecutli sipped her margarita.

A waiter carrying a telefon wove agilely between tables. Miclante-cutli set it on the wicker table and flipped open the display. The picture was gritty with interference, the sound weak. The Angel caught in the booth's wide-angle focus looked twenty days dead and buried.

"Miclan." She could scarcely speak. "It's gone, Miclan."

"What's gone?"

"The diner. The whole fucking diner. Tacorifico Superica's is a twenty-meter crater of molten glass. Like someone tocked the whole fucking place. I'm in a booth up near the Sunset Gate."

"Duarte?"

"He's bad, Miclan. He's bad. The Pale Riders; they don't stop, Miclan. They don't give up. They just keep coming, and coming, and coming. They almost had us back of Lexington. Duarte took a javelin through the foot. Tore off two toes trying to get loose. We threw them in the warrens up there; some of those tunnels are barely big enough for a person, let alone those fucking tectosaurs. He's lost a lot of juice, Miclan." Angel spun around suddenly. The audio picked up the bellow with deadly clarity. "You hear that, Miclan? I can't hang around. I may have to leave Duarte."

"Angel, Anansi's gone." Miclantecutli reported the chase and kill, flat and factual as a news bulletin. "How long since you encountered them on Lexington?"

"Twenty, twenty-five minutes. There were three of them."

"We heard one about five streets away a couple of minutes ago. How can they move so fast?"

The hunters up on Sunset roared again. That little bit louder. That little bit nearer.

"Jesus, Miclan. I'm leaving Duarte. He either makes it or he doesn't. Say one for me." She turned to leave and reeled back into the tectoplastic *cabina*. The picture shook. Angel grabbed the edges of the door, looked up. She screamed once as some massive indistinct object bore down on the top of the booth. Blackness.

The callback code returned a fizz of white noise.

"If they have got Angel, then Duarte is gone too." Miclantecutli spread the fingers of her left hand on the wicker tabletop. The drum of rain on the plastic roof seemed to have eased.

"Asunción?" Santiago asked. For the first time Miclantecutli's vast arrogance seemed shaken; Miclantecutli uncertain. Afraid.

"I'll call him up. That's what I'll do." She tapped in the code for a vehicle repair shop off Western. *Llamado llamado* said the little smartplastic screen. *Llamado llamado*. "He might not have gotten there yet," Miclantecutli said. *Llamado llamado*. "The whole place is falling apart, I've never known a *noche* like it." *Llamado llamado*. "Freedead ships; riots, a nanotoc attack on Tacorifico Superica's. The world protesteth too much. I don't want the world. I don't want change. Give me back my streets, let me hunt my boulevards, that's all. That's enough."

The telefon chimed.

"Asunción?"

No answer.

"Asunçión?"

No answer.

"Asunçión? Answer me you bastard. You all right?"

An image rezzed up on the screen. Pale skin. Pale eyes. Pale hair. Pale Rider. Santiago recognized the boy who had been saved from Miclantecutli's blade by the stroke of midnight. "Good morning, séora," he said in appalling Angeleno. "Unfortunately your friend is not able to take your call right now, but if you leave a message, we will make sure he gets back to you." An allosaur screamed. Not through the audio channels. Not five streets away. Not two streets away. Outside.

"Go!" shouted Miclantecutli, kicking over table, chairs. The 'fon fell to the floor. The Pale Rider smiled at the sudden and significant change of image on his screen.

"No," said Santiago. "No. I won't go, Miclan." He defended the upturned table like a besieged hillcity. "I've had enough, Miclan. It's not fun anymore. It never was fun; all it ever was was vile and cruel and painful and sick. I don't like it. I don't want it. It's not what I was looking for. I was wrong to have ever imagined that I could find it in this. I want to pick up my toys and go home now. You play out your perverted game. You run. You hide. You die. Not me. Game over."

Daft Eddie's clientele drifted away from their tables. The rain had stopped. The allosaur shrieked again.

"Go on then, Santiagito. I never was one to hold you against your will, you always knew that. You're free. Walk out that door. Call a dukduk. Go back to the Terminal Café and tell your friends about all they've missed and what a brave, bold *muchacho* you were to go riding out with the Night Hunt. You won't make it to the end of the street, Santiago. And if you stay here, they will get off their high horses and come in and drag you out and slit your throat in the street like a fiesta goat. You are in the game now. You always were in it, from the moment you climbed onto the back of my bike. You wanted death or glory; you have it. They have your scent, Santiago. They have your DNA spread, they have your biofield resonance, they know your starsign and shoesize. They will not stop until you are spitted on a lance, or the sun comes up. You have one hope of seeing that, and that is to come with me." She extended a gloved hand. "Maybe I'm lying. Maybe every word is the truth. Do you trust me? Dare you not trust me?"

A third time the allosaur roared.

"You bitch," said Santiago Columbar. He took the offered hand. Miclantecutli smiled.

Jens Aarp set his saturated hat on the table and kissed Trinidad's hand in the old Spanish fashion. "So, Séora Malcopuelo, are you here to play the great game, or, like our Rosalba, merely kibbitzing? Not that I mind an audience—I've played some of my best under the gaze of onlookers, the urge to impress a beautiful lady puts an edge on my play." Then, to the others, he said, "They'll pick us up at the back in half an hour and take us there."

Trinidad studied the new arrival. In an age of while-U-wait bod-mods, no one needed hair like that, a face like that, hands like those. Unless they were part of an elaborate front. Unless everything said and done and meant by these people was part of an elaborate front. Trinidad heard the distant click of existential cogs meshing and turning. Coins dropped, neons lit, the mental jukebox played.

"Salamanca, can I talk to you a moment?" she said. She drew him into a secluded bower between roof-scraping potted palms. "Why didn't you tell me you were a Zoo Cult?" The rain thundered on the roof.

Not even Santiago would sanction the Zoo Cults.

When it became evident that the Tesler process could only resurrect, not bestow immortality, stories appeared like the flies that were once believed to spontaneously generate from dead matter; stories of experiments in resurrection that had resulted in obscene hybrids half biological, half tectronic, half living, half dead; immobile chunks of tectoplasm within which the mind and memory and spirit of a once-living person was trapped. The half deads, the zombies, were incorporated into the landscape of popular horrors, the bogeymen and Freddy Kruegers of children's nightmares and slumber party ghost stories. Then the story came out of the sprawling fetid necrovilles of Viejo Mexico that these half deads possessed the great chimera of resurrection society: deathless immortality. In the midst of the slagged death that was their bodies there existed a few misreplicated tectors that had the ability to incorporate human DNA and convert cells to its molecular matrix without destroying them.

Resurrection while still in the body, or Big Death, molecular disruption beyond any hope of resurrection. That was the deal, you gambled your life on which tector system would invade your body. Eternal life, eternal death. Aztec roulette. Seekers and fools poured into Coyoacan Dead Town driven by myths of secret cabals of laughing, golden immortals moving and shaking the world tree. The universal silence into which the gamblers vanished only reinforced the myth. Whatever they chose, *Suerte* or *Muerte*, they would never be heard from again.

They forced one admission from Tesler-Thanos. Those urban legends? The ones you used to scare yourself with when you were incinerating marshmallows around a campfire out in the big wild and one of your friends said *let's tell ghost stories*? The ones about the *mediomuertos*, the living souls trapped in eternal torment within twisted columns of nanotech? They're true. Here're the pictures.

Trinidad's father thought the pictures on the news of the things that looked like tree stumps covered in hands and beautiful dead movie stars floating in plastic tanks too frightening for Trinidad age eight but Trinidad's friend Yolanda had videoed it for them to watch every time Trinidad came over to play.

No one believed Tesler-Thanos's official line that they were acting to preserve their corporate image from contamination by association. If they were taking TacTeams loaded for bear with full *mechador* support into Coyoacan, it was because they wanted the secret of deathless immortality for themselves. They found nothing. No surprises. The Zoo Cults heard the heavy plod of boots, stepped into the closet and pulled the door after them so that only the tiniest strip of darkness shone out. Those who wished could always find them, following that line of darkness into the hearts of a thousand necrovilles. If there never were as many as in the glory days down in Mexico, still there were always some who found any chance of eternal life, however slight, preferable to the Death House and their Jesus tanks. Discreet questions would be asked, confidential bulletin-boards consulted, secret meetings arranged. One night they would walk out of their lives, set the stake, make the play, and never be heard of again.

Tesler-Thanos, still picking the P.R. scabs from Coyoacan, left well enough alone. More people overdosed in a week than were vanished by the Zoo Cults in a year. Tesler-Thanos and its representatives on the police and *seguridado* boards prided themselves on their sense of proportion.

"Jesus Joseph Mary, Salamanca, what kind of suicide game have you got yourself into?"

"Trinidad, you don't understand . . ."

"I understand that no one comes back. Ever. I understand that you either live or die: forever. This is what I understand, or have I missed something? What is it you're so frightened of that *this* seems like a good deal?"

"I can't explain it to you. Please, just trust me."

That word. *Trust.*

"Can't explain what, *hermano* Salamanca?" Jens Aarp, stepping through the parted palm fronds. Behind him, Montserrat Mastriani, embraced by her exoskeleton, behind her, like a domesticated shadow, faithful Rosalba. "It's quite simple, *hermosa* Trinidad. We are all cursed. We are all mortal sinners. Salamanca's is the medieval sin of *accidie*, pushed toward the love of death by the tedious mechanics of living, drawn toward the hope of eternal life by his fear of dying. Séora Mastriani's is the sin of pride; the sin of refusing to submit to the disease that is killing her, the hubris of taking hold of her destiny in her two hands and saying *this is what I chose for myself*. Mine is the sin of gluttony: the addict's sin, the gambler's sin, the sin of a man who has been cursed by probability never to lose and thus sets the stakes higher and higher until at the end he comes to the ultimate bet; eternal life or Big Death. Will Séora Suerte favor me, or at the end will she prove just another faithless woman? What gambler worth his toss could resist the highest game of all?

"So, has that explained it for you, Séora Trinidad? I do hope so, because our guides are waiting. Listen! I do believe it's stopped raining."

Trinidad looked up. Through the green fronds, through the rain-speckled dome, through the fleeing clouds: stars. In that instant, Salamanca slipped away.

"Salamanca!"

He hesitated, torn.

"Salamanca . . ." Jens Aarp's voice cut through the café sussuration.

He looked like a man between heaven and hell. Between heaven and hell was Necroville. He raised one finger.

"One minute!" he shouted to the pilgrims. "I'll see you out back in one minute. There's something I have to tell Trinidad.

"We asked you to tell us your story because we said we all knew each other's too well. That's not true. I was economical with the truth to them. Hell, I lied. Not one word of what I told them was true." Salamanca seated himself on the rim of a large terracotta palm pot. "I am not what I seem. I am not a pilgrim, a supplicant, a beggar of mercies from something that laughs at our hopes and fears; something that delights in our despair and destruction. I am an executioner. I am judgment. Nemesis." He drew the tesler he had pulled on the Lobos and set it on the cocoa-pod mulch beside him. It gleamed like oiled skin. "Sounds good, doesn't it? Much-rehearsed words: Nemesis. Judgment. I've got it all worked out, all plotted and scripted, every weighty word, every significant gesture, so why the hell is it so hard to tell you this?" He glanced at the time display on his tagalong.

"I'd always felt responsible for Leon. That, or guilty. I always was my brother's keeper, though, by rights, Leon should have been mine, he was three years older than me. But our father had entrusted me with the responsibility, and the guilt. On the day he died, he called me in to see him and told me that Leon might have been given the looks and the wit and the charisma and the sun would always shine warm on him but I had been given the brains and the determination and the gift of worrying and so I was to look after him because he wasn't safe to be let to look after himself and yes, life was a three-legged one-eyed bitch but he was dying so he could ask whatever outrageous thing he liked and we would have to do it. Then he died and went to the Death House and we tried to forget that our father was out there somewhere in a new body and life, because, I told Leon, our father would have forgotten he ever had two sons, except as memories in a long and involved dream from which he had just awoken." Salamanca checked the time again. "I was sixteen, Leon was nineteen. Too young to realize that responsibility without authority is a pure cell culture for guilt. I could no more have stopped Leon from moving into the wrong social circles, doing the wrong stuff, *jodering* the wrong people than I could have blown out the sun. It was a great relief when he found God. It was not what I would have chosen for him, certainly not what our father, a career atheist, would have thought responsible living, but it kept him out of the scandal boards."

"Ucurombé?" Trinidad asked.

"No. Older and darker than that. Evangelical Christianity."

"I thought Watson's Postulate and the Tesler process were the final nails through the hands of the old Evangelicals," said Trinidad. The suspended rollscreen rippled in the wind; complex CAD-graphics of earth near-space warped, suddenly translated into non-Euclidian space. "Tectronic jam today rather than theological pie-in-the-sky."

"They're a resilient breed," Salamanca said. "The sect Leon fell in with believed that though the resurrected dead had committed a grievous sin, all sins were forgivable through acceptance of Jesus's saving grace. They would be denied the blessing of physical death, but when the end of the world came, they would be taken up bodily into heaven with the other faithful in the Rapture and given true resurrection bodies. Trapped on earth, they could still aspire to the same Christlikeness that their mortal brethren achieved in heaven."

"I was told that the reason that Old Catholicism was taken over so easily by Ucurombé was because of the Papal Bull that the resurrected were no more than nanotech robots and that the souls that once inhabited them were burning in hell for all eternity for the sin of pride. Scared the piss out of me when I first heard it."

"There are some *Viejo Catolico* orders that hold that the dead are capable of salvation, like these *Evangelicos* Leon joined. They baptized him in the Los Angeles River. Washed his sins away, supposedly. Kind of hard to tell, with all the turds. Became one of their missionaries; going around the Necroville hives handing out tracts and buttonholing people, singing on street corners, that sort of thing. Tried to convert me too, but I made it clear that I didn't want any of that sort of thing. The truce between us held until he told me one day that one of his *compadres* had been in the Spirit—as he called it—and been given a Word of Knowledge that Leon was to go into the dead town, where he would be guided to his father—our father—and save him from eternal death by the redeeming love of Christ. That was it. I'd tolerated the rest—just—because though I didn't agree with it, it seemed right for Leon. This was just sick. Picking at scabs. True necrophilia: digging up the dead and *jodering* them. Our dead. My dead. My father, as much as Leon's, and certainly more than the Maranatha Assemblies of God. We argued. I argued. Leon just went on and on and on at me in that hushed, calm, wheedling, *reasonable* convert-a-sinner voice—'but Emilio, don't you think, now Emilio, I'm sure you must agree,' Jesus Joseph Mary, it makes you want to spew—until in the end I threw him out. Bags, books, cant and credo, out of our father's house.

"His chair wasn't even cold before I had convinced myself that I was to blame for the bust-up. I went to look for him, of course. The Maranatha Assemblies of God had schismed into two conflicting subsects, as these *Evangelicos* inevitably do when someone in them doesn't get their own way. Neither knew of Leon's whereabouts: it seems he had already been attending another group before the split took place. I must have contacted fifty Christian sects. The search began to interfere with my defenseware work.

"He turned up at the house six weeks later. Breezed in out of nowhere and helped himself to the contents of the refrigerator. I was too guilty to be angry, too relieved to ask him just where the hell he had been. He told me soon enough.

"The *Evangelicos*? Phuh. Tedious. Sanctimonious. History. The Tribe Called Zoo; that was truth, that was life, that was his spiritual family, the resting place for his soul. I had no idea of what my brother had gotten himself into, except that I was instinctually distrustful of anything that enthused him to such a degree. I hired a webjock and asked her to check out this so-called Tribe. She told me what she'd found, and Leon and I argued again. Compared to this, our argument over the Maranatha Assemblies was a candle flame next to a fusion drive."

"They're a Reform Buddhist Zoo Cult," said Trinidad.

"Obviously you move in the kind of circles where these things are common knowledge," Salamanca said.

"I had some friends moved on the fringes of their cult." As Trinidad had herself, briefly, in her world where, because everything was permitted, it must be explored. "They believe that only the pure in heart receive the gift of eternal life from the half deads. They practice Jodo-Tendai chanting and meditation to attain freedom from worldly affections and so earn the favor of Seu Guacondo."

"Seu Guacondo, Seu Guantanamo, Dougou Feray: Lord of the Crossroads, Yinyip Dédé, Baron Sabado. Many names, many places."

She offered him a burning kiss from her silver flask of mescal. He refused.

"You fought," she said.

"He left. It was the last thing I wanted. I tried to convince him not to go—all the time, I heard my father's voice telling me I was responsible for Leon. I went back to my webjock, contracted her to find him. It nearly bankrupted me, but after three days she came back and said she had found something. Someone. Carmina Sung, in the psychological trauma clinic at Santa Monica.

"She told me Leon made contact with the Guacondo *corillo*—at that time they were operating in the Santa Monica necroville—and took her with him.

"Leon always had to impress. He went first. He made the choice between the *Muerte* and the *Suerte*, Carmina Sung watched. *Look!* he said, all smiling and proud *it's nothing!* and he turned around to look at her and it hit him. Five seconds, that was all it took, but she told us it seemed like forever. *Burning* was the closest she could describe, every cell in his body burning from inside, melting, changing, becoming something so obscene that she could not bear to look at it but she knew it would be branded into her brain forever. He died. She ran. The *seguridados* caught her at the San Vicente gate and called a trauma unit. The psych team unpicked her memories all the way back to the teat and still could not stop her screaming.

"It's five years since Leon's death. Five years to turn myself into this avatar of retribution, this avenging angel. Five years to learn, to study, to arm myself, to cover myself, to infiltrate the Zoo Cults, earn their trust, work my way through them, find the ones that lead to Seu Guacondo, and bring myself here, to this place, this time, and destroy him. That's the true story of Emiliano Salamanca. Call me sentimental, but I didn't want us to part with you believing evil of me. At least now you know what I'm afraid of."

"Seu Guacondo?"

"Of something preventing me from doing it." He picked up the gorgeous black tesler. It responded to his touch, rippled like stroked skin. He holstered it next to his heart and glanced at his wrist tagalong. "Damn. Still, they won't have gone without me."

"Salamanca." He had stood up, pulled his jacket around him, ready to march out into legend. "You can't do it for Leon."

"I know."

"You can't do it for you either."

"I know."

"You won't ever stop feeling guilty."

"I know that too."

"Salamanca." He obviously did not have a firm grasp of the rules of the game of heroes if he was prepared to leave without a good-bye, without one word for her. "I'm coming too."

4:00 a.m. — sunrise

november 2

Thirty-six hours, thirty-six minutes.

With the years the strangling fig had invaded the room on the fifth floor until every centimeter of the walls and ceiling was covered with a dense mat of leaves. Stems and vines grew thick and strong: the *patrón* hung tin and glass alcohol lanterns from them. The effect was of fallen stars caught in the branches of a tree. The bamboo blinds had been rolled up to let a little night heat out of the room; intrusive roots had long ago jammed the windows open. Jewel-bright birds of paradise perched on the overgrown balcony rail fled Camaguey's approach with a hand-clap of wings.

"Zoologists used to believe that birds of paradise lived, loved and died without ever touching the earth," Nute said, looking down after the birds. "The dead specimens they were sent didn't seem to have feet. What should have been obvious, but wasn't, was that the trappers in Borneo used to cut the feet off."

The apartment *cuadra* opposite was a geometric exercise in fire escapes and backlit window blinds. A different shadow-play behind each blind. Someone had tied five happy colored balloons to their fire exit.

There were eyes and small, furtive rustlings among the canopy of leaves. Apart from the bed and its potential clients, the room's only other occupant was the ice bucket, the bottle and the two glasses slung with casual care through the wrought ironwork.

One of his favorite years.

They drank the wine. It was very fine. It knocked him loose inside, like the cruel/kind fingers of a masseur, knocking loose the knottings and writhings of living.

Two movements and he was free of his borrowed clothes. He touched the sensual universe and was touched by it. His own physicality stunned him. With raw fingertips and lanternlight and the first glow of dawn, he explored his body.

The blisters formed oval patches on shoulder blades, inside elbows, small of the back, inner thighs. His examining touch was gentle, fearful, but even that was enough to burst the blisters and release the spikes of black tectoplastic within. For the first time he noticed the scaly encrustations between toes and fingers and on the backs of his knuckles.

"The marvelous thing is that it's painless," he said. Camaguey felt the warm press of Nute against his back. Her body moved against the needles and sent waves of sensual pleasure crashing into his limbic system. The nerve endings beneath the needles had become hypersensitized.

He went to stand by the window to look out at street, city, sky, the waxing glow of the dawn skysign. Genetweak monkeys no larger than the palm of a hand foraged through the mass of vine and creeper that covered the front of the hotel, eating moths. Somewhere above him, lost in the foliage, the neon sign dripped yellow light on his chest and belly. "But do they not frighten you, these outward and visible signs of inward and physical changes? I'm not even fucking human anymore."

"You're forgetting Nute's specialty, meatboy. Outward and visible signs are her stock-in-trade."

Camaguey looked up at the thin tendrils of high cirrus that barred the skysign. The promise of another gorgeous day in heaven. And the sky went white. For an instant he thought the sun had novaed. For an instant he thought his eyes had melted in their sockets. The white light lit up the inside of his skull. The monkeys in the foliage, the dead in their apartments or out on their streets, Camaguey at his hotel window, all were struck motionless by the white light. The world held its breath. And slowly exhaled. He could see.

"Earth's last stand," said Nute. "Either the militaries rolled the bones right and got the slamships, or they threw snake eyes and the slamships got them. Either way, that was a real industrial-grade mass-conversion strike."

"Does it matter?"

"Not a damn."

The blast faded. The dawn stars appeared through the veils of the skysign. Birds frightened by the sudden change of night-to-day returned to their roosts. The warm shadows of the room seemed deeper and darker and more inviting. Nute invited him onto the bed. Its covering was a hadrosaur hide; desert-colored, sand, tan and shadow, sensuously soft and silken. © *the Walt Disney Corporada* whispered the upper right corner. Some strangling fig leaves had fallen on it.

Kneeling, they kissed.

She stopped him.

"One thing, *mi corazón*. You want this to be any good, you got to tell me what you want. Don't be afraid, you can't shock me, I won't privately despise you for dark and secret dreams. You tell me what you want to do to me, what you want me to do to you, and we'll do it."

He did, in small, furtive whispers, afraid, despite Nute's assurances, of the dark things that came creeping out of his mouth, his penis. She ran her tongue around his lips. He ran his tongue around her lower lips as she bestrode his face. She ran her tongue around the corona of his penis. He whimpered in fearful pleasure. She pulled at the fine black needles between his thighs. He collapsed panting and sweating, beyond speech, on the tectosaur skin. She tugged at the tectoplastic quill in the palm of his hand with her teeth. He almost fainted. She ordered him upside down, spread-eagle against the leaf-covered wall. When she let him down, delirious, feeling twelve kilometers long, she executed a neat handstand and wrapped her legs around his neck. He laid her facedown on the bed, lifted her legs and fucked her. She flipped him onto the silken skin with a twitch of her thighs and straddled him, riding hard, hard. He buried his fingers in her breasts—surely they had not been so large, so full?—that the nipples thrust hard and dark as ripe loganberries between his scabbed knuckles. She caught his penis, squeezed it hard to keep him from coming. She slid two moistened fingers into his anus, flexed them to show she meant business and with her free hand directed the scaly, ridged backs of his fingers toward her clitoris. Three, four, five times she brought him to the edge and sent him back before finally taking him over with her.

"First time the john ever faked the pro," she said, returning from the bathroom.

"What do you mean?"

"One hundred and twentysomething gives a woman a certain perspective on the sins of men. You didn't laugh. Great sex isn't sweat and tendons and arching your back and going *God, yes, God, yes God yes!* That's Old Hollywood sex. Silver-screen sex. I mean, what the fuck has God got to do with it? Great sex is laughing: maybe out loud, but always in here, silently. Always, laughing in here." She touched the place over her heart. "And you didn't laugh. You didn't let go. It wasn't real. You faked it. Good, mind, but fake. You suddenly remembered where you were, who you were, what you were doing and who you were doing it with and it killed you. Dead, Camaguey. What did you remember, Camaguey? What was it you didn't tell me? What was it you couldn't trust me with?" She rolled into an all-fours kneel, straddling Camaguey, trapping him between knees and hands. She looked down into his face. "What was it you thought I couldn't accept? I can be anything, Camaguey. Anything." Resting her weight on her elbows, she took his face between her hands. A span of centimeters separated their eyes. Nute frowned. A shiver crossed her face. The skin puckered and flowed into a chrome metal skull.

Camaguey screamed. Bone fingers, inhumanly strong, held him down, looking up into the naked eyeballs.

"This what turns you on, Camaguey?" The voice was Nute's, issuing from locked, grinning jaws. "You'd be surprised how popular this one is. Lot of real necrophiles out there, ready and eager to pay top dollar for their particular vice. No? Maybe the Mark II will satisfy your little peccadilloes."

The silver skull flowed to liquid. The liquid shivered and stretched into a sheet of putrescence. Shreds of decaying skin. Lips shrunken back to reveal green teeth, shriveled gums. Nose gnawed away, a gaping dark cavity. Legs and arms were bones wrapped in stretched taut, torn skin, yet the rotted fingers, nails curling and splintered held him in rigor mortis. The breasts were withered sacs of shit-colored leather. Camaguey gagged, struggled into the corpse grip. The rotting cadaver flowed, and he was looking up into Marilyn Monroe's pert features.

"I can never remember the lines where they rhyme 'Finnan haddie' with 'heart belongs to Daddy,' " she said in exactly the voice. "Not that it works in Angeleno anyway. So: does real necrophilia, with the truly dead, do it for you? No? Hell, I think nothing's going to do it." As she spoke, Monroe's itchy-coo features were reabsorbed. Pencil-sketch mouth, nose, eyes stretched, elongated and dissolved into a face that was no face. A mask of skin, blank save for a single central orifice, hovered over Camaguey's face. The hands that held him were soft, featureless mittens of flesh. Camaguey closed his eyes. He felt Nute's skin shiver against his, betraying shapeshifting. He hardly dared look. Nute's own ugly/cute face looked down into his.

With all his strength, he pushed her off him. For her size she was phenomenally massive.

"Fuck you, Nute. Fuck you to hell."

"I'm sorry, Camaguey. I'm sorry. I didn't mean to . . . Yes, I did mean to. I meant to shock you. I meant to hurt you. I meant to make you hate me."

"Why should you want me to hate you?"

"Because"—lying on her side on the tectosaur throw, she curled her knees up to her breasts, wrapped her arms around them, pulled in her head like a reluctant tortoise—"I think I'm in danger of falling in love with you, you dumb meat bastard."

"*¡Ay!* Nute!"

"*¡Ay!* Nute."

"Why should that be so terrible?"

"Because all those things I showed you, I am. I'm a monster. For money. Sick people's money. And good, stupid, vulnerable, dreaming, honest, cute, scared, damaged people like you deserve better love than a monster's." Before he could interject, she went on. "Do you know what they ask me for most? The clients? They show me a photograph of someone they loved who is gone down to the dead towns and ask me to be them. Most of the time it isn't even sex. They just talk, or do things that they liked to do together—play tennis, swim, read the papers together, go for a walk, eat out—or sometimes they just sit and look.

"Touch that." She extended an arm toward him. He took the offered hand. "Isn't it hot, doesn't it feel strange? My epithelial and subdermal layers are doped with hypervelocity tector systems: my outward self is shapeshifting realtime memory tectoplastic. Like cars, with half a dozen basic programs built in only Nute's a much better ride than any ol' Daddy's Caddy because she can reprogram her molecules at will. They've got nanocircuitry fibers strung like colored lights through my visual and audial cortexes. Show and tell, and Nute will be it." She gripped his hand. "Camaguey, I can be her if it's what you want. I can be Elena. You can tell her you're sorry, you can tell her you'll love her always, you can tell her she's a fucking diseased whore. It doesn't matter. Tell me what will set you free."

Camaguey rolled onto his side and pressed his lips to Nute's ear. Newschannel liftercraft thundered low over the apartment *cuadras*. A few brown leaves drifted down onto the bed. Camaguey turned away and marveled at the way the planes and shafts of shadow moved across the building opposite as the sun rose. He felt the shiver of transubstantiation transmitted through the pine bedframe. Looking back, he saw himself lying at his side.

With eyes and fingers, with lips and tongue, he explored his duplicate body. Breathlessly he moved his hands over biceps and pectorals heavy from underwater swimming. Fingertips flirted with the small, hard nipples before moving on across the close-packed, lightly furred muscles of the belly to the pubic vee and its soft protrusions and pouchings of flesh and skin. He pressed cheek to thigh, feeling the bunching of muscle fibers beneath the skin, the thrum of blood and life through their arteries. There were differences. Differences of limitation: the teeth were not right; the hair was changing color as he watched; the body double was a good twenty centimeters shorter than him, but it was himself as he had been, before Elena, before Human Interactive Tectronic Syndrome. His fingertips brushed the smooth, uncorrupted flesh of the inner thighs, the small of the back, the shoulders, the inner elbows. They felt good. They felt right. They felt old and innocent. Lifting the hand, he sucked the fingers one by one. They were good fingers. They were his fingers. He caressed the head, feeling the familiar skull contours beneath the seal-short hair, the characteristic cervical knob at the base of the skull. He felt out the facial features; he looked into his own eyes. She had even mimicked the day's growth of sharp black stubble. He gently opened the lips and kissed them.

The tears surprised him, so sudden they were a physical pain. He turned away from the mouth, pulled his double to him. He could hardly speak.

"I'm sorry," he said. "I'm sorry. I didn't mean to do it to you. Hurt you. Maim you. Make you ugly and sick. Kill you. I didn't mean to. I'm sorry. I'm sorry. Oh Jesus, I'm sorry. Can you forgive me? Please, forgive me."

"I forgive you, Camaguey." The words clucked and croaked in the Nute-double's throat as her vocal cords sounded for the right voice. "I forgive you everything."

He did not speak or move. After many minutes he went again to the window. The sun had risen over the shops at the eastern end of the street. Hot golden light poured unstintingly into the narrow alley. Nute joined him, folded an arm around his waist. Standing beside him, the differences were more apparent. She seemed less his double than a beloved younger brother, the one graced by the TVMA's capricious gods.

"Nute, I think it's time."

"They can book it downstairs," Nute said. "Any preferences where you'd like to go? I'll need you to authorize the *Immortalidad* policy number. I presume a *cerristo* like you isn't going to be reborn a Wednesday's child. Hang on a second." The voice, Camaguey thought, was his, the language, the slice'n'dice inflexions, the jackhammer delivery were incurably Nute. He felt her melt against him, shiver, and reform. The perfect Camaguey who, he knew now, never existed, was gone forever. "Jesus Joseph Mary, that's better. These transsex morphs . . . Sorry, but that voice is just not me." She spat his tongue out like a wad of phlegm. "You ask me, all this masculinity, *machismo* bullshit is far too heavy a load to hang on just fifteen centimeters of erectile tissue."

Nute leaned against the balcony railing, back to the street, chin raised, hair trailing, drinking in the sun. Camaguey wondered how much energy her shapeshifting cost her, especially at the end of the night, when the reserves were low.

"You see, Nute, I could grieve for what I had done to myself— that's easy—but I couldn't forgive myself," Camaguey said. "I needed to have it made visible, audible, tangible, so I could understand the magnitude of my crime. That's why I asked you to do what you did. And in the end, it was easy. Can you understand that? I looked, and I saw, and all it was was a mistake. One mistake. That's all there was to forgive. There's nothing living or dead that doesn't have one mistake in its life."

"John the Bastard once thought he'd write his autobiography," Nute said. "He wanted to call it *One Hundred Thousand Mistakes*."

"But it's all right to make mistakes, Nute. It's human. Like your friend the universal golfer: he'll never be perfect at it, but he isn't going to refuse to forgive himself every time he misses a putt. So, my mistake cost me my life, but I'm not the first to have died from one mistake. Maybe I'm making a mistake here, now, saying *I choose, this is the time*. It doesn't matter. I have a right to make mistakes, and keep making mistakes. I am allowed to be wrong. I have permission to fail.

"I'd like a place where I can see the ocean, if that's possible.

"I miss the reef. I worry about it. I imagine storms, wrecks, boat props, divers with geological hammers. I hope Florda Luna is right in her prophecies, I hope those ships up there fuck the Rim Council and PanEuropa and Tesler-Thanos and Ewart/OzWest and the *corporadas* right up the ass. They're the true dead. If the Freedead do it right, if the world does end this morning, maybe I can go back there someday. Maybe I'll find Elena waiting for me." Deep water. Long-stalked nano-blossoms waving slowly in the cool currents. Tropical fish, tame and colorful as flowers. Overhead, the passing shadow of a basking plesiosaur, photosynthesizing. Light poured across the verdant balcony into the empty room. Mundanities. Formalities. "I've already notified my insurers, Nute. The company is Stella Maris *Immortalidad*. All you'll need is my name. I presume the Death House will do the rest."

"A cigarette is the more usual final request. Sure. I think I can arrange that."

"And, Nute?"

She looked over her shoulder from the door.

"Put some clothes on."

She tutted, grinning. "Don't be so damn bourgeois. You're in Necroville now, *muchacho*."

On the night of the feast of Corpus Christi in the Dominical Year 1719, Fray Juan de Dios of the Society of Saint Francis founded the Mission San Ysidro after Our Lady Queen of Angels appeared to him and his dusty-footed friars in a small dell at the foot of what would one day be the Santa Monica Mountains. As sign and seal that this was the appointed place, a spring of clear water burst forth where no water had been before. Fray Juan de Dios washed himself three times, once for the Father, once for the Son, once for the Holy Spirit, and began forthwith with his brothers to seek wood, red adobe and cheap Indian labor to build a small scriptorium.

For almost five hundred years the Friars of San Ysidro resisted the encroachments of the world. Palaces of Mammon in Hacienda, Georgian or mock Tudor besieged it; the shrieks and moans of pool parties and the smack-crack of suburbia's little sadomasochistic diversions broke into the brothers' meditations. And the dead came, house by house, garden by garden, street by street, creeping up and over San Ysidro like strangling fig, driving the *cerristos* from their Haciendas, Georgians and mock Tudors. The Franciscans, an island of anachronistic belief in an ocean of refutation, held on. Theirs was a resilient creed, and accepting. The end came when TVMA Group Areas Committee drew the ne plus ultra across the map and placed Mission San Ysidro firmly behind the wire inside the Saint John necroville. The brothers moved out. The Death House, with knowing irony, moved in.

"You can see the ocean if you go up the tower," Nute said, lighting a long, tapering candle and setting it on the rack before the statue of Our Lady Queen of Angels. Resurrection machines filled the long narrow nave: a mass requiem. Machinery hummed a low Gregorian chant: souls awaiting rebirth. "On a clear day. With no smog. Or haze. In perfect observing conditions. The steps are a bit rickety. Not recommended if you suffer from vertigo."

As Camaguey did not, they went up the tower. Whitewashed

arches gave views over the four cardinal points. The wind carried on it the smell of ocean: for a moment Camaguey thought he saw through the heathaze the silver glitter of waves breaking on the distant, unattainable shore. In the valley below, columns of smoke rose from the dead town, ranks and files of it, following the gridiron of streets and avenues. The palms would smolder for many days, thought Camaguey. Aircraft buzzed low over the burnzone, churning the smoke into coils and spirals. Looking from the east window he saw the black triple spires of the Tesler-Thanos *arcosanti* rising from the smoke and gathering amber smog. At the south window he looked up. He could not possibly make out the ships he knew were up there, yet he hoped that he might see a handful of black specks beyond the fading skysign, or maybe a falling hulk, burning up, drawing the long charcoal streak of its own destruction across the sky. The driver's radio in the dukduk that had brought them there had gabbled about the Freedead fleet breaking up the orbital factories and spinning them into some enormous spacefaring construction.

Some questions would have to go unanswered.

They went down from the tower through the darkened, pregnant nave into the mission garden. White clad young women, the Death House's operatives, met them beneath the tall shade palms that arched over the chapel's red rooftiles. They shook hands, the meat way.

"Séor Quintana." Camaguey's Resurrection Guide was a tall black woman, silent and graceful as seemed mandatory for all the Death House's employees. "There have been a number of very recent changes in Death House operating procedure of which I must inform you. The Death House is no longer acting as agent between its clients and Tesler-Thanos. Therefore, we have deposited the contents of your *Immortalidad* policy into the San Ysidro Death House account on your behalf. The full amount, plus interest, will be available to you on your emergence to dispose of as you wish."

"Jesus fuck," said Nute.

"Exactly. Now, here is the tank we have prepared for you, Séor Quintana."

Suddenly slamships, space battles, mysterious orbital artifacts, renegade Death Houses and crumbling *contratado* were paper lanterns in a tropical storm. Dashed, smashed, bowled over, swept away. Their small flames extinguished. Death was near, death was here, death was the open shell of a Jesus tank beneath the ancient roof-timbers of a mission refectory.

"Do I have to? Must I?"

"You don't have to do anything you don't want to," said Nute firmly. "Here, give me the fucking thing. We'll do it our way." The tall black woman hesitated before passing a small cylindrical plastic vial to Nute. Camaguey had spent too long in the shadow of Santiago Columbar not to recognize it. "I'll call you," Nute said. The women in white bowed and withdrew to their cloisters.

"Nute, I'm scared."

Nute sat down on the dew-damp grass and leaned against the sloping trunk of a mission palm. She opened her legs, patted the grass. "You come and sit here." He sat down cross-legged. Nute loosely wrapped her legs around his waist and drew him back onto her. Needles bent on his shoulders and back, each one a minute kiss of pleasure. Nute folded her arms around him.

"I'm here. I'll be with you all the way. I won't leave you. When the clay breaks, it'll be my ugly face that'll be the first thing you see."

"Nute."

"Yah."

"I understand now why you did it, back at the hotel. The shape-shifting tricks. You didn't want to make me hate you, see you as a monster, a vampire of men's desires. You wanted to shock me, you wanted to challenge me to a love beyond my flesh-bound ideas of what love should and could be. You stripped yourself down to the bare bones of what you are and asked me if I could love that. I can accept that, Nute. I can love that."

"Those aren't the bare bones of love, meatboy. You want to see them? I'll show you them." She opened the vial, shook the thing it contained into the palm of her right hand. She held it up before Camaguey's face: a single tectopharmaceutical spider; sin black. "That's love. That's the marrow of it: one question. Can you love it enough to kill it? Can you love it enough to end its pain?"

She held the spider out in her open palm, offering it to Camaguey.

"I can't Nute. I can't take it."

"I know. But I can." She lifted her hand, touched palm to his forehead. The briefest of contacts, the most fleeting of touches.

He inhaled sharply, exhaled slowly.

"I expected to feel something."

"It's very gentle. That big Death House bitch promised me it would just be a slow falling-asleep." Nute touched her head to his. The spider was a black castemark on his brow, leaking subtle poisons into the forebrain. Camaguey nestled up against her. The points of his needles ripped her lace suit, left neat parallel contusions on her skin.

She felt out the new outcrops of blistering: the nape of his neck, the backs of his hands, the hollows of his collarbones. The delicate pimples burst, the tectoplastic spines within were hooked into sharp thorns.

"I wish my father could have been here. I'd like to have said good-bye to him. Maybe, afterward . . ."

"It would only hurt him and confuse you."

"That's what I can't understand; how all the people we love are utterly lost. Why we have to start again, build new lives, new loves, find new friends and families. The hurt it must do to those who are left on the other side."

"The hurt it would do to those who go through if they were to watch their loved ones, their partners, their children, grow old and weak and die while they remained unchanging."

"Sweet Jesus, it's a terrible thing Adam Tesler did."

"You can't expect to battle and outflank death without some casualties."

Camaguey stretched, smiled, reached back an arm to touch the side of Nute's head.

"It's so warm, so peaceful here. It's starting, isn't it?"

She ran her fingers through his hair.

"Nute, there's something I'd like you to do for me. Go to the Terminal Café. They'll all be there: Santiago and Toussaint and YoYo and maybe even Trinidad. All my old friends. It's a sort of tradition, I suppose, to meet there once a year on the Night of the Dead. We begin and end at the Terminal Café. Go to them. Tell them what has happened to me. Please."

"I'll do it. Of course I'll do it."

"Thanks. Isn't it warm, Nute?"

Nute held his hand. The sun rose higher, pouring raw heat into the cloister garden. There was shade beneath the palm fronds. Close by, a fountain—the same waters that had shown Fray Juan de Dios where Our Lady Queen of Angels wanted him to build his monastery—gurgled luxuriously into its moss-covered stone basin. Vapor contrails were moving I-Ching lines cast onto the sky: aerospacecraft falling from their fractional orbits toward the big port in the desert. Thinking she heard faint murmurings from Camaguey, Nute bent forward to listen. She imagined he whispered *the light, the light*. But she was never certain.

After a time, his hand fell from hers and rested palm-open, fingers loosely curled on the cool grass.

"Don't. You. Dare. *Querida* me, you bastard!" screamed YoYo Mok, attorney at law of Allison-Ismail-Castardi, throwing her heavy left fist at Iago's head, and, as he danced back, genuinely alarmed, her whole self at his throat. A detachment of werewolves caught her in midleap. Their fur was spiky with rainwater and smelled of washed dog; their only other covering was a modesty pouch just large enough to fulfill its purpose and sport a Mister-Moon-shot-in-the-right-eye-with-a-space-bullet colophon YoYo felt she should recognize from *somewhere;* that maddening tip-of-tongue phenomenon that always afflicted her where Jorge played one of his so-who-did-star-opposite-Fred-MacMurray-in-*Double Indemnity?* games.

Blood spread in an ever-widening apron from the impaled *asesino*. The remains of the hit squad lay similarly speared, clutching at the harpoon shafts, mouths open in pain and anger. This was not a game of film noir trumps.

"Séora Semalang, or whatever you call yourself, you would be advised to come with us, if you please." Iago extended a hand toward Martika Semalang/Madrilena Fuentes.

"As your legal counsel, I'm advising you not to do this until we know just what these people's intentions are," YoYo shouted. Iago crouched down to YoYo's level and flipped up his combat glasses. His lashes were coming unglued.

"All right, YoYo. We'll not go anywhere."

A nova of daybreak yellow. A hammer of sound and shock punched the air from her lungs. Van Ark's CinemaScope window disintegrated into a swarm of razor-edged glass bees, flying before the burning storm-wind.

"I'm coming, I'm coming," said YoYo Mok.

The wreckage of the burning liftercraft was the epicenter of wider destruction. The facade of the Saint John Main Death House had collapsed into a scree slope of twisted aluminum framing and stressed concrete. Lagoons of blazing aviation fuel spread out from the hulk; the bodies of enforcers dark, charred desert islands in the sea of yellow flame, each surmounted with the single, frondless palm tree of a werewolf harpoon. Cars, pedicabs, public *foncabinas* burned; shocked, seared stallholders stood at a safe distance, watching their small livelihoods go up. A lone, dumb movie projector threw hellish, fragmentary images onto the billowing smoke: a lone pram rolling down the steps of Odessa.

Reloading their long, archaic weapons from shoulder quivers, a pha-
lanx of werewolves fanned out into the street, checking fields of fire.
Iago's flageskin suit tried to match the chaotic ungeometries of the burning wreck as he grimaced and rooted around in the open sewer.

"It's only a question of time before Tee-Tee notices it's down an
asesino squad," said Iago, fumbling and fondling in the litter with bare
hands. "Shit, where is it? Then they'll send out the toc-team, sure as
eggs is eggs. And this time they won't be aiming to miss. Come on you
bitch!" Iago grunted. Muscles strained like bridgecables in his neck;
veins throbbed on his shaven cranium. Millimeter by millimeter, Iago
heaved an elastic cone of golden liquid out of the blacktop like a man
pulling a volcano out by the roots. It came, millimeter by sweating millimeter, until it broke free from the embrace of the earth with a mandrake scream of ripping molecules. "Jesus Joseph Mary, there must have
been a porous layer down there. I just about got the handle I left on
top." The amorphous pool of amber liquid magically assumed form and
definition: the three-dimensional contour-image of a low, sleek car. The
surface tension stretched, puckered, creased, divided as the programmed
tectoplastic remembered what it was and reconfigured itself.

"Iago," said the pack-leader of the werewolves, "you right?"

"Yah, I'm right. And thanks *compadres.*" Flesh hand grasped wolfen
forepaw; wolfen claws closed gently on flesh forearm. Solidarity.
"Muerte y libertad."

" 'Give me liberty and give me death,' " said the pack-leader. A
closed fist raised; the wolfpack dissolved like liquid into the flamelit
night. YoYo could not rid herself of the nagging sensation that one of
them reminded her of *someone.* Perhaps Fred MacMurray in *Double Indemnity.*

"Los Lobos de la Luna," Iago panted. "Politics, they say, is the
mother of strange bedfellows, or something like that. What you have to
understand, YoYo, is that it's all part of a grander and wilder scheme
of things. The wolves, the Death House, the slamships up there, Tesler-
Thanos, even Van Ark's boot-girls: it's all choreographed. Even your
role in our little ballet of Industrial Espionage."

Clink clink clink. The pieces she had stored in the crannies and
pockets of her sensory skin came together, molecules bonding seam-
lessly, as under the hands of a miraculous pot healer. "There never was
a Codex 13, was there? If they can take away memories, they can fab-
ricate them too; what's memory but just another bunch of molecules
for the tectors to reprocess? It was all made up, all a game, all one big
maguffin."

Iago smiled and clapped his hands slowly. The broken varnished fingernails had not yet regenerated.

"I knew I hadn't made a mistake with you," he said. "Codex 13, the phony memory wipe, the prize of deathless immortality, Séora Semalang, or Fuentes, even you, YoYo, were set up by Tesler-Thanos to expose and erase Aristide-Tlaxcalpo's industrial espionage organization. Which it has done. Which is currently being liquidated by *compadres* of our unlamented friends back there." The fire had spread to the Death House; the lines of spectators drew back, their carnival costumes trashy and somehow menacing in fire light. "Of course, it doesn't stand up to too close scrutiny," Iago continued, "which is why I am kind of keen we should get into this car"—which had completed its transmogrifications and complexifyings and stood purring and pregnant with boulevard heat in the gutter out of which it had been summoned—"and get out of here before someone works out what happened."

The seats were upholstered in what felt like human skin, blood warm and tanned.

"How the hell do you do this?" asked YoYo, obeying the *fasten seatbelts* blinking, persistent reminder. "And where the hell did you get it from? I never paid you anything like this kind of money."

"Air-temperature superconductors. Replication and processing rates are up to five, ten percent light speed. Hypervelocity molecular processing. Decades ahead of anything Aristide-Tlaxcalpo or even Tesler-Thanos are working on." Iago eased into the driver's seat. In a grin of black tectoplastic, controls and steering column extended toward him. "The biggest nanoengineering laboratory in the world; the Death House." The car pulled away from the curb with a silent surge of gees.

"Where does that leave me, Séor Iago?" The woman YoYo knew as Martika Semalang spoke up from the back seat. "If you are to be believed, Tesler-Thanos is responsible not merely for erasing my memories, but for those very memories it erased. Did I work for it? Did I plan to betray it? How much of what I remember can I trust? How much of my life is mine? Am I what I remember I am?"

The low, oil-drop-sleek car pressed through crowds of pedestrians moving away from the conflagration.

"The substance of what you remember through the Linker woman reactivating your mnemochemicals is correct. We just changed the details. You were Madrilena Fuentes, you were working in Tesler-Thanos's R&D division on an important new application of nanotechnology, you were going to defect with the data to Aristide-Tlaxcalpo. Tesler-Thanos

Intelligence knew all about those clandestine tagalong calls, those surreptitious meetings with Roland Carver, those expenses-paid trips to
Nuevo Tenoch with a bottomless bag of chips. He didn't know what
you were offering: it was Tesler-Thanos made it into something he
couldn't possibly refuse. You're lucky, they just dumped you out the
window and spiced up a few memories to make you absolutely irresistible to Aristide-Tlaxcalpo. You could be dead, *querida*."

"I am dead, *querido*."

"Big Dead, *querida*."

If memory was a commodity to be erased and rerecorded, like the
one microdisc Ellis kept for baseball, where, YoYo wondered, did that
leave personality, identity, the idea of selfhood that stood upon the no-
longer-sure foundation that one knew what one knew? Where did that
leave the sensual world, perceived reality? Where—to be just a lawyer
once again, for that is all you are, and all you want to be, YoYo Mok—
does that leave laws of evidence founded upon the convention that a
witness saw what a witness saw? Feedstock to the ubiquitous, voracious
tectors.

In Van Ark's office, when she had felt herself thrown out of that
twenty-fifth-floor window, felt the thin, treacherous air slip through her
fingers as she clawed for a handhold, felt her life burst in a soft deto-
nation of bone and blood on the outflarings of the lower industrial levels,
felt herself *die*, she had not been able to imagine a more terrible thing
than to take life. Now she understood that a deeper violation had been
worked on the woman who was now Martika Semalang. To rip through
the memories of a life like two fat policemen searching a room, to finger
the intimate touches, the moments of love and caring, to masturbate
over the love makings and love takings, to project that life like a blue
movie at a stag night and then to take those beautiful moments and
make them ugly, to take those mornings of love and make them hateful,
humiliating, self-censoring, to dice and splice that remembering of a life
into something petty, grubby, venal, serving ignoble ends, was rape of
a depth and intimacy that those four small letters could not adequately
describe.

Dollars and deutsche marks. All it ever came down to in the end.

"You set the whole thing up, didn't you, Iago?" YoYo said. "You
worked for Tesler-Thanos, you arranged the deal with Aristide-
Tlaxcalpo. You set her up as the Maguffin, you got her running so
Aristide-Tlaxcalpo would prick up their ears. It was you sent the warn-
ing note in Tacorifico Superica's. You knew it would get tocked."
Cheerful diners, mellow on beer and *camarónes español*, look up. Hey,

what's that sound, isn't that lifter a bit low? "And the house too. They deliberately missed me. Like Trio, getting burned in the blowback, and that six million Rim; everything was there to be found. Everything was set up to make it look like Tesler-Thanos wanted to make sure their star turn was atomized just in case Aristide-Tlaxcalpo found a way around the memory blanking. Except it was just a running game to draw them out to grab her and then kill them.

"I was in it right from the start, wasn't I? Right from the first time I came to see you about the 'ware, you were thinking this, weren't you?"

"I needed a lawyer to make it believable," Iago said, peeling out of carnival traffic—pedicabs, dukduks, microbuses laden with *carnivalistos*, lumbering floats—veering across two lanes of oncoming traffic in a purr of power and vanishing down an alley so narrow, crash sensors lit up all over the control board.

"You built the fucking Carmen Miranda serafino," YoYo yelled. "You set that thing on me. You made me lose the Industries Gabonais case. You wanted me to lose Industries Gabonais, and get that contempt citation."

"I cannot tell a lie." Graffiti-sprayed walls blurred past. The headlights threw twin cones of light into the unrelieved dark. If anything came out of those lights, they were plasma.

"If you weren't already dead, I would kill you. I would take your very best razor, slit open your foreskin, and fold it out like a gutted fish. I would make two-centimeter-deep cuts all around the head of your dick. I would cut your balls down the middle and wrap your scrotum over your cock but not before I had pulled out your testicles and stuffed them up your ass. Then, over the period of nine, maybe ten, hours, I would slowly disembowel you while riding your mutilated cock."

"My type of girl, YoYo." The car leaped from the alley mouth onto a boulevard packed with placard-bearing demonstrators. Every palm tree was burning. "Funny. Never had you down for a necrophile."

"Iago, why did you take out the Tesler-Thanos *asesino* squad?" She answered her own rhetorical question. "Because you're working for someone else. Because you're a double agent. You faithless bastard."

Iago beamed a travesty of a smile at YoYo.

"Worked it all out in the end. I knew you were the right one from the moment you told me you wanted 'ware like no one else had, and none of your fucking adolescent air-brush chrome-nipple laser-visor mirror-finish cyberwarriorettes either. Yes, I am a double agent, yes, I am a worthless traitor. Which is why we are getting away with the goods to a safe place before Tesler-Thanos come to the conclusion that you've just reached and send their toc-team out with instructions not to miss this time.''

"If it's not Aristide-Tlaxcalpo, then who is it?" YoYo asked. "The goat! Mind the fucking goat!" The hurtling car minded the enormous papier-mâché fiesta goat by a film of paint.

"I should have thought that was obvious," Iago said, five millimeters of tongue extruded between glossed lips in concentration. "The Death House."

"But they're in Tee-Tee's tit pocket. Adam Tesler shits and the Death House licks him clean."

"Not anymore. Not ever. Where better to hide the focus of thirty years of Dead Liberation organization but under Tesler-Thanos's nose?"

"Hiding in plain sight," said Martika Semalang. "Like the purloined letter."

"The purloined what?" YoYo asked.

"Edgar Allan Poe," said Iago. "An early gumshoe story."

"I'm a Class Two functioning dyslexic," said YoYo proudly. "Neat though: Tee-Tee's own left hand conspires against it."

"With a little help from our friends."

"The Freedead, up there?"

"And my *compadres*, the *Lobos de la Luna*. Remember what I said about it all just being choreography? We've been rehearsing this for years. Decades."

On a fifteen-by-thirty screen mounted atop the El Cordobes Sportswear *Supér*, Scarlett drove a fiddle-dee-dee horse and cart across a back projection of the blazing Universal backlot.

The car shot lights; hurtled across a wall of oncoming traffic at eighty-five.

"Appearance and reality, YoYo. That's what it's all about. The Death House wouldn't show its hand for a lousy industrial espionage scam unless it had set up that scam with the express purpose of getting something with which it could nail Tesler-Thanos for conspiracy; hell, for an entire FBI-ful of conspiracies. I have the evidence, I have the victim, and—"

"You have the lawyer. Jesus fuck, Iago! That's why you wanted a lawyer. Not just to add a little verisimilitude to your game of chasies. To pitch your case to the Tesler-Thanos *corporada*. There's just one *problemita*, Iago."

"The Barantes Ruling," said Martika Semalang. "Like you told me in Tacorifico Superica's, YoYo. What doesn't legally exist can't throw itself onto the arms of the law. None of your evidence, Séor Iago, would be admissible. Not even I would be admissible. Jesus Joseph Mary: killed by Tesler-Thanos, killed by whoever took away my memories and gave me lies, killed by the law."

"Iago, no one has ever beaten the Barantes Ruling," YoYo said. "No way around it over it through it under. The Death House is strong, yes, the Death House reaches everywhere, yes, but it doesn't exist."

"There is a way." Multiple horns blared constantly. Iago peeled out and accelerated along the outside of a long line of stationary vehicles. "Dead evidence has no weight and is inadmissible. However, suspicion raised by that evidence may be grounds for further investigation. How many murder cases were reopened and solved on the strength of the victim's testimony? We don't want this ever to get near a court, YoYo. What we want is you to plea-bargain. Like some Drown Town Haka *Madre* haggling over a bucketload of squid. Go in there and tell them the Death House wants a binding agreement not to hurt one hair of yours, mine or your client's heads."

"Could have picked a more appropriate metaphor, Iago," YoYo said, stroking her head with her hand, enjoying the sensuous drag and prickle of day-old stubble. The first pale glimmerings of the dawn sky-sign lit the zenith. "Or?"

"Or copies of the Death House's files on this incident go to the Office of Corporate Affairs in VanColumbia who have been looking for an excuse to humble Tesler-Thanos since they achieved the monopoly on resurrection. *Corporada* wars; industrial espionage; assassinations; murder; violation of living rights: what more do they need? There is a vociferous minority on the Rim Council—with whom the Death House keeps regular and discreet contact—who blames Tesler-Thanos for the whole Freedead affair. They'll lose no sleep if Tee-Tee gets broken up and sold off."

Fifty kilometers above Necroville, the skysign spasmed and suddenly kindled. Curtains of yellow fire burned across the still-dark sky: curfew ended. This day's dawn migration might be the last.

It was a Faustian bargain Iago would have YoYo strike with Tesler-Thanos. The price of the Death House's silence—and independence, she supposed—was a stake through the naked heart of the Barantes Ruling. A deal was done with the dead, a bargain struck and maintained, conditions met and obeyed. The existence of the untouchables was stated and hallowed in contract. A precedent was set for others to follow, to widen and enlarge until someday, some virtual court recognized that there was a stage of existence beyond biological life and declared the dead human.

The golden shapeshifting car pulled in to the side of the road beneath the amber glow of the massive neon vee-slash that identified a Death House. Doors gull-winged open.

"Can't risk Tesler-Thanos getting a squint of it." Iago laid his hands on the curved tectoplastic roof. Hypervelocity tectors deconfigured: the car slumped into an amoebic mound of molten gold and dissolved into the street.

Wary of liftercraft, YoYo was watching the sky when it turned white. Dawn darkness became bright noontime. The translucent veils of the skysign were swept from the sky. Thin fingers of alto-cirrus threw sharp-edged, dense shadows across hills and valley. Birds took to the air in a scream and clatter of wings. YoYo cried out, blinded.

"War, baby," said Iago, peering into the fading nuclear glow as if expecting the smoking ion-trails of crashburning spacecraft to come falling out of the sky. "Mass microtok strike. The ships have engaged. We're committed now." He held YoYo's face between his hands. No dead had ever touched her like that before. "YoYo, it's going to keep on happening. You want that?"

"I can't do what you're asking me. What am I? Some twenty-centavo probationary lawyer from Sampan City who can't even get a full partnership and loses every case she gets to court. And you expect me to take on and beat the Tesler-Thanos *corporada*?"

"This is the compulsory courtroom drama poor-little-me self-pity scene?"

"I thought we were in gumshoe modality."

"Not anymore we aren't."

It was in courtroom drama that the attractive female lawyer got suckered by the sweet-talking rogue into taking the impossible case. In courtroom dramas they pulled off the brilliant legal twist and won. In the world beyond the final credits, the not-so-attractive female lawyer gets fried in her bodyglove by Tesler-Thanos webjocks, or flashed to ions by palm-size mass conversion warheads, or just plain hog-tied, gagged and hung up by her nipples by *corporada* grade legalwares. What's one less attorney?

Truth and consequence, YoYo. It gives you an itch, doesn't it, right under the bottom fly button on those so-street-credible shorts? It makes every last egg in your ovaries stand up, salute the flag and scream *yes, yes, do it, do it*. Why else fry your neurons with dexxies and Y-Dah-Wake on those all-night data searches long after everyone else in the faculty had gone to their or someone else's beds, but for the chance, one chance, one shot, at bringing down a Pacific Rim *corporada*? Blind dog's chance.

"Old Chinese grandfathers say, 'even a blind dog's chance is still a chance,' " said YoYo to Iago. "Let's give it a go."

The lift when the pretrial neural accelerators kicked in was what YoYo imagined very good sex must be like. The hot flush, the supersensitivity of the skin, the feeling that your body was squirming around inside your skin like a sackful of eels, the increasing sense of detachment from the material world as external and internal clocks began to diverge, the impression that your selfhood could no longer be contained by this gross parcel of meat, that with a flick of the mind it could be sent into a million different incarnations biological and cybernetic, an itching impatience-cum-anticipation both wonderful and fearful, like fundamentalist Christians awaiting the end of the world.

YoYo knew a lot about neurochemistry, and shit about very good sex.

The Death House employees that passed her in the corridor seemed to be moving very slowly. She was almost fast enough to mesh with the sixty-hertz strobe-flicker of the fluorescent deathsigns.

The door to Iago's Invisible Office—the unofficial center of his clandestine double-agent operations opened to his Kirlian field.

"Wooo," said YoYo Mok, and popped a final acetylcholine activator.

The room was a fired clay beehive five meters in diameter. The floor was ridged with tiny corrugations and around the wall ran a shallow bench seat that extended in three equidistant places into human-size slightly concave pallets. What drew an involuntary whistle from YoYo was the dome. Every centimeter of it was covered in terracotta statuettes of minor Aztec deities, hands held up before them, yellow ocherpainted mouths open in pain or surprise. Each was no longer than YoYo's hand, and arranged totem-pole fashion into long, curving ribs. Trapped inside a clay pipe-organ, she thought. The concentration drugs induced a non-specific polymania, anything and everything became compellingly fascinating. Hours could be lost in the contemplation of the white marks on the back of a single fingernail.

With his clever fingers Iago extruded a nanocircuitry filament out of each temple and let them fall to the floor. The clay floor rippled and accepted them. He stood feet slightly apart, arms relaxed at his sides, twin horns of tectoplastic curving back from his forehead.

"There are better things to do with blood-heat superconducting tectors than build liquid cars." He touched forefinger to third eye. "First they recruited me, then they rebuilt me. One of the universes's great ironies, that the ultimate information storage and processing system should be a couple of kilos of wet gray matter balanced on top of your spine. No machine can match its compactness, the miniaturization of its components. It's the original nanomachine, microprocessors the size of molecules. But slow, *querida*, so slow. Tied to lethargic chemical signals while its sedentary, idiot-savant silicon children whirred away at the speed of electrons. If our Freedead *hermosos* can adapt themselves to live in vacuum, why could the Death House researchers not reconfigure the brain into the ultimate portable computer system? Lightspeed transmission rates, zero memory failures, four terrabytes of storage and processing space. Onboard intelligence, five fine-tuned sensory inputs and, interfacing with the bodyglove, access to the entire web. *Querida*, I can run down and beat any mainframe on either edge of the Rim. We're working on the second generation superconducting tectors. Storage volumes multiplied by a factor of ten. In time, every human will be capable of storing and accessing a considerable portion of recorded knowledge. And time, *mi corazón*, is what we humans have most."

"My legalware," YoYo began, hyperacute senses picking on words, lawyer instincts thinking *human, he said "human," as if we living are an incomplete, adolescent stage, like an axolotl that has not yet become a salamander, and only the dead are fully human.*

Again, fingertip touched pineal gland. "Conceived, programmed, stored in here. I was quite amused when you asked me if I could load up the Stairway to Heaven program. *Guapa*, I literally couldn't have forgotten it even if I'd wanted to. YoYo, I am linked into the Death House satellite system. Through me you can access the web, the Tesler-Thanos legal heirarchy. I have all the evidence, every bit of it, stored in my memory." Thou recording Angel.

"No fucking wonder I never beat you at volleyball," said YoYo, carefully removing her clothes. She had never found a convincing reason why she had to enter virtuality clad only in sensory skin; there was no need for it, the bodyglove would function as efficiently clothed as naked. Superstitions. And sexuality. She looked around for a hook to hang her gear on. Finding none, she set it, neatly folded, on the dusty clay floor with some distaste. She walked into Iago's open arms.

She gasped as her bodyglove met and merged with Iago's and true skin pressed against true skin. Then the interfacers linked in and she experienced the familiar synesthetic shocks as the system checked itself. The color of heat as the optical interfacers grafted onto the backs of her retinas. The sound of blue as tectors tweaked her hammer and anvil and banged her eardrum. The smell of E flat pentatonic as sensory pads leaked molecules into her olfactory centers. The unique flavor of five-day-decomposed napalmed baby as nanoprobes tested her salt/sour/sweet/bitter receptors. And a strange full-body nausea she had never experienced before as tendrils from Iago's body twined past her inner ear into the hemispheres. One sinfully pleasurable moment of sensory shutdown, and out on to the Powell and Pressburger stairway.

She had forgotten the pure joy of monochrome. The marble beneath her feet was reassuringly solid and white. Far below, light gray clouds drifted across a dark gray heaven. To her left, ten steps beneath her, a jet-black Hammurabi glared out across the limitless virtual space. A similar number of steps upstairs on her right, Moses and his burning bush. And YoYo, dressed in her elegant, businesslike Calvinist black with just enough silver to look successful but not ostentatious, reveled in the solitude and listened to the wind that drew great shuddering harmonics out of the endless staircase but did not stir one silver bell on her earring. The pure white sun rose, a dazzling atom. The simulation was seamless, whether rezzed up on her old virtualizer or in the reconfigured neurons of Iago's brain.

The moment you start thinking that virtual is actual and actual is virtual, you are finished as a lawyer; they had taught her that on the first day in the Faculty. As a lawyer, and as a human being.

She summoned an Event Window. Beyond it spun the galaxy of the TVMA web, the 'wares of the big *corporadas* blazing out like quasars.

"The Tesler-Thanos *corporada*," she said in a loud, clear voice. Unseen diligent subroutines had accessed web codes and passes: a single blue-white super-giant detached itself from the main sequence and swelled to fill the Event Window. *Flash bastards.* The star burst; suit circuitbreakers cut in, filters reduced the sensory overload to acceptable levels. *YoYo Mok is not fazed by your pyrotechnic virtuosity.* She blinked down the optical filters and there was a twenty-meter golden samurai in full armor standing ten steps up from her. With battle pennons fluttering from its back in her private virtual wind. And drawn sword.

"I am *Procurador* Martina Martinez of the Tesler-Thanos *corporada* legal division," the samurai thundered down at her. Only the biggest combines could afford to keep full-time human fronts to their legal-wares.

"I am *Abogado* YoYo Mok of Allison-Ismail-Castardi," she declared loudly, looking the monstrous thing square in the face-mask. If there still was an Allison-Ismail-Castardi. "I represent my client Martika Semalang, formerly Madrilena Fuentes, erstwhile employee of Tesler-Thanos's research and development division."

Attorney Martinez placed her sword point down on the stair and rested gauntleted hands the size of small trucks on the pommel. The adamant marble cracked and split beneath the swordtip. The implication was clear and brutal. *We have the power to shatter you and your gimcrack private world.*

"Madrilena Fuentes is dead and not entitled to legal representation or consideration."

"Not so!" YoYo shouted, but the giant golden samurai had vanished, closing the Event Window behind it. Fresh Event Windows were summoned out of Iago's hindbrain; tracer programs bought direct access codes to the Tesler-Thanos legal system with Death House dark money. The windows opened.

Through the round window: the golden samurai, standing astride Hoover Boulevard, one foot in Necroville, one foot in the land of the living, swords upraised in *Men*, the middle attitude, the horizontal cut that was perfect for decapitations. She remembered an old Second Twentieth Century War poster of just such a samurai standing over Pearl Harbor, sword raised while old *Estados Unidos* wet-ships fired futile broadsides.

Through the square window: the armillary sphere of Tesler-Thanos's legalwares; a solar system of nested Dyson spheres, dark and lightless, slowly turning.

Through the arched window: a glowing bolide of information, the essence of the Semalang Case, her blackmail proposition.

She picked up the ball of data, tossed it, and served it through the square Event Window. It struck the outermost orbit, the legal Oort cloud, and passed clean through. Any *abogado* worth her boatload of marzipan could make it past the *recepçionista's* desk. The Event Window followed it in, through a dimension of attenuated, elongated images: steam trains, weeping women, frozen fireworks, mighty-thewed blond barbarians. Failed petitions; ghosts held in limbo while lower orders sought clearances from higher. The program fell toward the infinite gray curve of the second level.

The sound was exactly what the end of part of the world should be like: a combination of guillotine chunk! and clash of cymbals. Something—no, not something, a *nothing*, a plane of absolute black—had cut her monochrome universe in half. Top to bottom. Side to side. Another terminal crash and the black nothing advanced another step toward her. A cloud passed into it and was annihilated. The black neatly bisected a statue of Judge Roy Bean. One more step and the judge was utterly engulfed. The black nothing advanced steadily toward her.

"Iago!"

In a flicker, he was there. Black tapered pants with a velveteen stripe, knife-edge creases; white bolero jacket, a sombrero slung across his back. Given a small, hand-size chihuahua and a baton, he could have been the leader of an old cha-cha-cha dance ensemble.

"You look like shit," said YoYo Mok as her blackmail program shattered the second ring of legal defenses and fell on through the ghosts and litigations toward the third.

Iago did not deign witticisms. "I seem to be under attack from a highly sophisticated anti-AI viral system designed to identify, infiltrate and oust personality simulation 'ware from its memory space."

The clank of the advancing blackness was a constant rumble, like an approaching heavy armored division. YoYo backed away from it, up the stairs, pushing her Event Windows before her.

"Meaning?"

"I am being pushed out of my own head." He sounded frightened. Iago Diosdado sounded frightened. "I've tried dumping memories into redundant volumes, but the fucking things are pushing me out of there." The darkness was now advancing at walking pace. YoYo withdrew, up, up, up the staircase. "YoYo, to save myself, I'm having to utilize space that this program is running on."

"That blackness is you?"

"In a sense. To you, it's just occupied bytes. YoYo, you're running out of space."

She glanced at the square window. The third circle, the fourth circle. The orbits were opening up before the flying deposition; word of its contents had passed from outer levels to the coreware and the command had returned: *let it past*. But would it reach the core before the Stairway to Heaven and all YoYo's legalware ran out of operating space and crashed?

"Can't you stop it?"

"Yes, but . . ."

"But you would need the space I'm occupying to engineer antibody programs. Jesus Joseph Mary!" The blackness was sweeping up the stairs at a slow, relentless jog. "Iago, if you can't do anything, then get the hell off my staircase. You're just so many pixels that could be put to better use."

The sixth circle, the seventh circle. Behind her, steps, statues and pale gray stratus were consumed as the black leaped after her.

"Iago, stop pushing me out!" she shouted, knowing that he had no other option. Life for her was death for him. Life for him was her left crashed, naked, helpless before the lightning Tesler-Thanos's webjocks would summon, punch into her legalware and incinerate her in her velvet bodyglove.

The eighth circle. The ninth and final circle. The innermost sphere peeled apart and the sun burst in her eyes. The core. Streaming tails and trails of interrogatives and crosschecks as the lawcore took it apart, the cometary package approached perihelion. Fifty steps forty steps thirty steps. The dark thing gained on her. Iago was losing, driven from his own skull by viruses that liked the heat of human souls.

The realization was like a baseball bat swinging out of the Saturday night shadows straight for your eyes. The things were designed to attack artificial intelligences. YoYo put her fingers in her mouth, and whistled.

Fifty steps up, a travertine St. Benedict grew colors, contours, fruit, lipgloss, cork wedges and a frock to die for and stepped off its plinth onto the staircase.

"Hiya YoYo. Oh, but you look like you're having a bit of trouble. Can I help?" sang the Carmen Miranda *serafino*.

The nothing was like an endless black monolith, toppling on YoYo Mok.

"Stop it!" she screamed at the Carmen Miranda. "Just stop the fucking thing!"

"Oh, now, YoYo; language. 'You really shouldn't oughter say it; 'cause when you do, God gets iray-it.' I should know, I use a lot of redundant space in Old Catholic prayerware."

YoYo crawled away from the falling blackness.

"Because I like you, I'll overlook the little f-thing. This time."

Like a fruit-flavored rainbow, the Carmen Miranda liquified, threw itself at the blackness and splashed. The black nothing dripped grape, orange, fuzzy-peach, lemon-yellow and strawberry crush.

The black nothing stopped. For a hundred virtual heartbeats, nothing happened to the nothing. And for another hundred, and another. And at the end of those, the nothing retreated one step. And then another, and another, and the black nothing was retreating down the steps like an angel flying as the anti-AI viruses caught the spoor of the game for which they were made and gave chase. Through the Death House communication links the virus would hunt the Carmen Miranda *serafino*, through the mazes and labyrinths of the Necroville computer hierarchy and beyond, over a border that could never be sealed against angels and viruses, into the glittering galaxy of TVMA web, through the Old Catholic and Reform Buddhist and Ucurombé Fé prayernets and spiritwheels, through the multiverses of the *corporada* and Rim Administration 'wares. " 'And round perdition's flames!' " rejoined YoYo Mok, who as a functioning dyslexic had never read *Moby-Dick* but enjoyed the movie and never forgot a euphonious phrase. Like battlecars slugging it out fender to fender on the freeways of the night, the carnage the angel and the virus would leave in their wakes was incalculable. Entire sections could be cut out of the web; valuable 'wares and databases garbaged, choked with rotting virus. Civil suit damages and reparations could run to billions, Rim, if YoYo Mok were to point the finger.

Another one I have over you, my enemy.

She pointed.

The flame-wreathed Louis XIV sun of the Tesler-Thanos law core expanded and swallowed her up.

The virtuality was so clean, so sharp, she felt she could have circumcised herself with it. The slow-moving rings of the planispheres and stellar planes arched kilometers above her head, the stately motions of the constellations and their attendants—women with starry headdresses, men with moon faces, children with comets' tails for hair—around her, the fleshy behemoths of the four winds, elements and humors that upheld the central disc of patinated copper, the etchings of the known world and its oceans, that, on her virtual scale, were small, sharply edged ditches; the slow, inevitable, exactly calculated turnings of the wheels within wheels: the precision and scale of the simulation was staggering.

Be honest YoYo. Terrifying.

She guessed that few others had trodden this armillary disc before her. She was no longer patched into the 'ware stored in Iago's brain. Her bodyglove, her fragile flesh, were in direct contact with the Tesler-Thanos computers.

At the center of the orrery burned a golden sun-face so bright she had to stop down her opticals to able to look at it.

"The Tesler-Thanos legalware has referred your deposition to the central core," said the voice of the sun. "Your proposition has been considered, your alleged evidence analyzed. Our incorporation of it into our models indicates that if we refuse to accept your proposal, the probability that the Tesler-Thanos *corporada* will no longer exist in its current form in five years is eighty-three percent, an unacceptably high percentage. On this basis we are prepared to offer the following settlement to you."

Only the whisper of steel over air molecules, the instinctive step back from a falling shadow, saved YoYo from being cut in two by the sword blow. Sparks showered, metal rang. The tip of the blade had wedged in the soft copper ecliptic. The giant golden samurai wrenched its sword free and swung for YoYo's head. She ducked beneath the blade. The edge bit deep into the Mars planisphere: stars and constellations rang like a gong.

"You lied!" YoYo shouted at the sun-face. "You bastards!"

"I very much regret to inform you that our advice has been overruled at the highest executive authority," said the solar orb in the cybernetic analogue of consternation. "This is quite against reason and the best interests of the *corporada*."

"The *presidente*, he says no deal," said the golden samurai, striding after YoYo, armor creaking. "No blackmail. No compromise. No contract. Responsibility for the Fuentes/Semalang case has passed directly to the human lawyers."

"Don't be a dumb fuck Martinez," YoYo shouted, entering window codes. "You can't go against the legalwares. When this gets out, you're finished. Disbarred. You won't even be able to get a job as a twenty-dollar virtual hooker."

"If this gets out, Mok," said the golden samurai. The sword tip missed her breastbone by a kiss. Secret 'ware that could punch through a bodyglove's feedback buffers and turn it against its wearer. They'd done it to Trio, and burned away seventy-three percent of her skin surface.

"Stop her!" YoYo yelled to the moribund lawcore. In reply the golden samurai raised the sword two-handed above her head. YoYo caught the rim of the Event Window to swing herself through on to her stairway to heaven. And stopped.

Framed in it was a mockup of a liftercraft approaching low, hard, fast through the dawn's early light, looking as if it knew exactly where it was going. Death by matter-conversion firestorm or a thousand cuts. Death on either hand: if the lawyers could not take her, then the tocteam would make sure of the job.

No one had ever adequately explained to her where your spirit went if your body died while you were in virtuality.

Play the blind dog's card, and pray to your ancestors it's the ace of trumps. "Iago," she shouted into the Event Window, "do it. Send it. The *Monopolistos*. Send it." She looked up into the glaring golden mask. "You're fucked," she said.

The tip of the sword described a glowing arc in the air. She kept staring at the golden mask as the sword came whistling down.

Like the Cheshire cat in that other old movie, the brass grimace of the giant samurai was the last thing to vanish, hanging in space as the massive planes and angles of the body dissolved into the wheeling constellations and divinities. For a whole ten heartbeats she did not dare look behind her into the Event Window. Brave it. Dare it. Do it. She saw the liftercraft spin one hundred and eighty degrees on its jets and recede into a jumble of navigation lights. "Iago!" Perry Mason never screamed. Fuck Perry Mason. "Hold everything. Everything!"

The voice of the sun spoke again.

"There appears to have been a presidential coup within the *corporada*." Like announcing that it's raining, or the pizza's here. "The old president is no longer in executive authority. The new president has rescinded his predecessor's order bypassing his legal department. All operations against the person of *Abogado* YoYo Mok and her client have been suspended. *Procurador* Martinez is no longer entitled to represent the board and chairperson of Tesler-Thanos; human advocacy has been suspended. Therefore, the offer the computer legal systems were about to close with you still stands.

"If Tesler-Thanos accept your proposal, our simulations indicate a seventy-three percent probability, which is within our judgment parameters. However, the probability that the Barantes Ruling, and thus the current system of *contratada*, will survive unchanged is only thirty-one percent. Best-possible-case simulations, involving compromise between your client and the Tesler-Thanos *corporada*, yield figures of eighty-two percent and thirty-five percent respectively. On this basis, we are advising the directors and new president to accept your proposition on condition of a standard-form Gagging Clause contract."

"My client gets to keep the money already paid to her by Tesler-Thanos. There will be no attempts on my, my client's, or Iago Diosdado's lives. Including"—the fire-faced sun had rippled, a prelude to a statement—"attack by cybernetic and informational weapons of any kind."

"Provided you indemnify Tesler-Thanos and its subcontractees and agents against personal damage in this matter."

"I'm not greedy. You've got it. I'll not say who did it. I can't speak for any damaged parties who may trace the virus back to you independently."

"We could not expect you to. Claims from other injured parties will be settled in the usual manner."

"Anything more?"

"That concludes our conditions."

"Give me the contract and I'll sign it."

"The agreement is prepared. Please indicate your acceptance in the usual manner."

YoYo reached her left hand into the heart of the sun. It did not burn her. Law burns with a cold flame. In the heart of the sun she placed her identifying colophon, the white lotus on the black triangle, and her lawyer number. Signed. Sealed. Secure.

"Any further business?" asked the sun-kings.

She could not quite bring herself to ask the Tesler-Thanos legal system *what the hell is going on?*

"Actually," YoYo said, "I'd think I'd quite like to just get the fuck out of here."

There was once a man who lived in a high castle. All power was his; at his word the dead rose and walked, but there was one thing alone that was beyond his might, and that was the love of his only son.

Night after night, the man sat in his high tower and wondered why this should be so. He was not a cruel man, or temperamental; he had never struck his son, or behaved in a way that would make him ashamed to own him as father. His behavior had always been reasonable, accepting, even loving: he had set quality time aside for playing with him, for listening to the boy's stories. He had encouraged every childhood interest and not pressed the point when they had eventually ceased to interest, he had suffered silently through the excruciations and rejections of adolescence, he had refrained from judging friends and lovers, he had refused to condemn experiments social sexual chemical. He had done everything one human could to make another love him, but never had he heard his son tell him he loved him.

He could not recognize that this was the essence of his failing: that love was not a thing that could be made to happen. Love, even between father and son, was not an inevitable. It did not have to happen; it was not a physical law, like gravity, or the weak nuclear force. He could not see that his desperation was obvious in every act of kindness and understanding and trust and affection. They were offers of trade. They were contracts; promissory notes that were never redeemed.

The man in the dark tower knew rejection, and despaired.

He had met the woman who would bear his child long before he built his empire of the dead and sent vaults and spires thrusting out of the bedrock of Hoover Boulevard; grain by grain, molecule by molecule. In so doing he made the common mistake of the ambitious, that posterity is an adequate substitute for presence. He never knew of the lovers his wife took to the floform those long nights while he created his jerry-built New Jerusalem until the day she came to him in his spiretop throneroom, the marble floors still bonding and tacky underfoot to demand he divorce her before she sullied his high name with her shopping list of adulteries.

"And," she said, "I want the boy."

They fought then. They fought in the courtwares and the media nets and the gossip channels and the society rumor rings. They fought with accusation and insinuation and slur and slander and spies; they fought with the unrestrained hatred of those whose love turns to lies. In the end, the man in the high tower won his son by proving with videos and stills and audios that for the past three years his wife had been regularly fucking her dead houseboy—in those early days, an unspeakable sin—and as a necrophiliac, was no fit mother.

The man in the tower learned the fear of rejection and with it, the determination that he would never be rejected again. The more determined you are that a thing will not happen, the more certain it becomes that it will.

It was inevitable that the boy leave the tower to seek his fortune in the world. He left only a note, he took only the clothes he stood up in and an all-currencies cashcard. He was a romantic but he was not a fool. He traveled among the poor, seeking their wisdom, hoping to find in their society a meaning and community he had never known in the three towers. He lived with the dead in their ever-expanding dead towns and necrovilles to see in the reflection of their alienness his own humanity. He went to the ends of the earth to visit mystics and spiritual communities to prove to him that there was more to man than the molecular materialism of his father's philosophy. He rose with the dawn to worship the great trees, he tended fish beneath the multifaceted glass roofs of the Closed Order Biospherists, he drugged himself into the ecstasytrance of the Ucurombé fetishists who lived in the roots of the decaying *arcosanti* that was Miami, he cut his flesh and shared blood with the brothers of the plains, he swam out with the Milapa seal-people along the sunset path to the place where the great whales sang.

For ten years he wandered the globe, and on the first day of the eleventh year, he came back to his father's tower. His father was older, darker, thinner; by his side was a woman, much younger; his new wife. She had a look to her that the son knew too well: not today, not tomorrow, but someday, she would leave her husband.

"Hi," the son said. "I'm back."

"Promise me one thing," the father said. "Promise me you'll never leave me again."

"I promise," the son said. The man in the tower set about the job of king making.

The father did not believe in unearned merit, so his son served apprenticeships in all the divisions and departments that would one day come under his control. He learned quickly, he learned tirelessly, he learned catholically, he learned well. His time apart had deepened him, toughened him, made him quick and wise. His father made ready legal documents that would pass executive control of half the *corporada* to him.

Then, early one September morning, Jody-Lynn Kapeckni lost control of her car on the southbound express lane of the Pasadena freeway. It hit the central barrier at one hundred and fifty, flipped across the northbound highway and exploded on the Intersection 12 approach lane. Five vehicles were caught in the fireball: twelve people died in flames. Among them was Quebec Tesler, heir apparent and actual to Tesler-Thanos S.A.; the most powerful *corporada* on earth.

Nine months he lay in the tomb while the world mourned the death of a great prince, and, on the first day of the tenth month, was resurrected by his father's power. He stepped from the waters of resurrection not to the golden light that filled the high towers of his birth, but to the wan yellow bioluminescence of the Death House, not to the embrace of his friends and parents, but to the dark welcome of dead women dressed in mourning white. "Where is my kingdom?" he asked. "Where are my staff, my secretariat, my friends? Where is my father?"

He learned how mightily he had fallen. Half the world had been promised him, now he was nothing, no one, nowhere, nonperson, nonexistent. His inheritance had been half an empire, now his estate was fifty streets by fifty of crowded, stinking, noisy shanties. He had been the firstborn son of Adam Tesler, now he was dead.

The new family who guided him into the mysteries of the afterlife warned him: it is best to let go of those you have left. He went anyway, to the golden gate at the foot of the castle and ordered it to let him in. He got as far as the lower shopping mall before the warriors arrested him.

They took him to his father's throne room, where his father, with his fantailed peacock to his right and his green and gold tectosaur to his left, told him that however greatly he might personally wish it were otherwise, his hands were tied by the law that said that the dead did not exist.

Even his own son?

Even his own son.

He could see from his father's face that it was more than law and legalism. It was the final rejection of his hope and love. "You said you would never leave me," his father said. "You lied."

"You were right," the son told his guides and mentors. "I should not have gone back."

"It will fade," they told him. "It will seem to you like a long and involved dream from which you are slowly awakening."

As he had immersed himself in preparation to rule, and before that, in study of the wilder world, the dispossessed son now threw himself into working for the liberation of the dead. His dead friends had advised him half true; the life before did fade, but the memory of the wrong that had been done him lived on, immortal, growing in strength with every misdeed and injustice he saw in his new world until it became more than righteous indignation. It became anger.

The codes, his father had told him, were as much part of him as his skin; the identifiers bonded to his DNA. He came by night to the tower. On silent wings he dropped onto the ninety-ninth-level balcony. The alarms surrendered to him. The doors opened before him. He moved through the darkened rooms, opening closets, finding them empty but for his father's few, severely cut, old-fashioned clothes. As he had always suspected she would, his second wife had left him. Meat was fickle, meat was frail. Meat was vain and temporal. He paused at the door of his father's room to look in at the sleeping figure. The death would have been a simple matter, the simple cracking of a few fragile vertebrae. He closed the door and passed over, drawn to a glow and the faint sound of a voice from a half-open door at the end of the hall. Concealed by shadows, he looked in through the gap. A young woman sat with her back to him, playing with a three-year-old boy on the floor. After a time she stood and lifted up the child, put him to bed and poked a dangling mobile into motion. The exiled son fled the nursery, fled the penthouse, fled the high castle with the dawn skysign brightening in the air high above, he went to the Death House and asked them for a contract that would take him as far from the house of Adam Tesler as possible, a NightFreight contract, to the uttermost ends of the solar system.

"You should have killed him." Some emotions go too deep for outward signs. Numbness. Toussaint felt only numbness. "You should have broken the bastard's neck while he slept. How you must hate me."

"Why do you say that?" Quebec asked.

"To do this to me. To tell me this. It's not my fault, I didn't ask to be born, let alone be born what I am; I rejected him too, I walked away, like you, I don't want what he has to offer me. I am not your enemy."

"Quebec," said Huen/Texeria. Quebec raised a hand. *Later.*

"I know. I did not seek you out to make you my enemy. I don't hate you. Toussaint, we are brothers in more senses than the familial."

"You sought me out because I could get you what you wanted, where you wanted."

"I would be a liar to deny that. Yet I also hoped that the enemy of my enemy might be my ally."

"Twenty-seven years," Toussaint said. "Twenty-seven years, out there . . . You should kill him. It would be a mercy to kill him. Putting a sick, sad thing out of its misery."

"Quebec." Again, the interruption. Again, the raised hand.

"Brother, brother, haven't I told you? Our purpose here is not to kill him, but to change him. Anyway, I'm not feeling that merciful. What is it, Texeira?"

"Big buzz down among the drones, Quebec. Somehow some ten-centavo street lawyer is drawing heavy fire from Tesler-Thanos's legal department, meat and virtual. Whiteware, blackware; there're more viruses flying around than a pox doctor's waiting room."

"Evaluation?" Quebec asked.

"The Death House is behind her with a lot of heavy-duty processing 'ware—the brothers are nailing their colors to the mast—but a contract just went out to a freelance *asesino* squad. Whatever she has, Tesler-Thanos want it bodybagged."

Quebec looked up, seeing beyond the ceiling screens to the heart of his father's domain.

"Dawn. Perigee. Everything comes together. We'll never be readier than now."

"My brother's right," Toussaint said. "It will never be more ready than now."

His DNA unlocked the bronze double doors to the residential levels and they ascended the curve of black marble steps to Adam Tesler's suite.

The yellow light of the skysign poured through the glass walls onto the mica-flecked granite floor as they approached the small, dark figure behind the sweep of polished livewood. The preening, vain peacock, the jeweled tectosaur wrapped around its perch, the net of shadows cast by the window panels: the six years since Toussaint had last stood in this place might not have existed. Was it the same for Quebec? Were decades and billions of kilometers abolished by the unchangingness of their father's sanctum? Sons fail, sons flee, sons die, but glass and granite and livewood go on forever.

Adam Tesler rose a little stiffly and bowed to his visitors.

"Good morning." He lifted a small cast iron teapot from a tray on top of the desk. There were five cups. Toussaint saw that the whole horseshoe desk was lit up with flatscreens. Inverted images: earth, sea, sky, fire. "I've been expecting you. Would anyone care for tea? Very refreshing, very stimulating after a long and tiring night. No? Please excuse me if I do. The teapot is two centuries old, Japanese. Hand-cast in sand by one of the last of the living treasures. I like the idea that a human being can be as much a part of a nation's heritage as a piece of art or architecture." Toussaint compared his last memory with actual image. Not one hair, not one line, not one detail of appearance or manner was different.

"So. In the end you came back." Adam Tesler looked at Shipley. "Even thou, faithful Porfirio."

"He's with us, aren't you, Shipley?" Quebec said.

"You wouldn't understand," Shipley said.

"I understand better than you imagine," Adam Tesler said. Tea bowl cupped in hand, he crossed to the eastern window. Morning light moved slowly down the spires, dazzling from hundreds of windows. Shadow still engulfed the city beneath. "We never thought there would be so many; we had no conception of the scale of the work out there in the asteroids. You deserve to win. You have proved your fitness in the harshest of ecological niches. You are the new humanity you claim to be. You are my rightful heir after all." Adam Tesler inclined the rim of his porcelain tea bowl toward Toussaint—"Do you know? Has he told you what he is?"

"I know everything," Toussaint said.

"I'm not so sure."

Huen/Texeira had moved to the other side of the presidential desk and was calling up grainy, overexposed eyesat shots from the war in space. Ribbons of shredded insulation foil and cable, rippling in the solar wind through a glittering nebula of vaporized steel teardrops. Vacced bodies spiraling down on long, lonely funeral orbits. Hard-pressure environment spheres like diseased eyeballs half gnawed away into bubbling slag by tector strikes. The long spine of a slamship, snapped neatly in two, each half tumbling end for end away from the other. "Better than it looks. Much better." Huen/Texeira interpreted the images. "The gunline absorbed most of the strike, no hits on main body of the fleet. Eighty-six percent destruction of first wave decoys, remotes and warheads. Main fleet casualties to date: they've debugged *Susie Q*, but *Haile Selassie* and *Michael Collins* are dead, and *Malcolm X* is crippled and uncontrolled. The information I'm getting is patchy, there may be more casualties. Orbital Command is switching to automated defenses to cover its retreat. Main fleet is three hundred and twenty seconds from the picket lines. *Marcus Garvey* sends:—she's still with us! *No serious resistance anticipated. Second wave class three and smaller units engaging automated systems. Docking sequence initiated, whole fleet rendezvous with manufacturing complex in forty-eight hundred seconds.*"

"Why aren't you cheering?" Adam Tesler asked contemplating the rising day of the dead. "You've won a great victory."

"Why don't you surrender?" Quebec returned. "Recognize the fleet. Lose with grace."

"A 'let-my-people-go' scene? You know me better than that, Quebec. Toussaint." He remembered, *joder* him, he remembered. The right name. Always, the thing that went clean to the heart. "That Drown Town gold digger lawyer friend of yours turned out rather better than I'd imagined. She's trying to broker a protection deal for her client, an erstwhile employee of mine. Seems an industrial espionage episode I thought everyone had forgotten about has come home to roost, with the help of my own Death House, which has turned against me. Incredibly, my expert systems are advising me that I do what you are asking, surrender, recognize the usurpers, let the people go. But I am not going to do that. I am going to fight your friend, Toussaint, and I am going to defeat her and kill her."

The porcelain tea bowl shattered suddenly, shockingly, in Adam Tesler's grip.

"You're a fool," Shipley said in simple disgust. "An egomaniac fool."

"No," said Toussaint. "My father is not a fool. Lonely, frightened, afraid of being abandoned, but never a fool. If it pleases you to be called God, then I'll call you God; you're the closest any human has ever come in terms of life, death and creation. You've made your holy people, your New Jerusalem of the resurrected, but you're afraid that, like Adam and Eve in the Garden, they will turn away from you. You won't trust them to love you, so you'll make them worship you. You're a more jealous God than ever Yahweh Sabaoth was, but not even you can keep your children children forever."

"Such neat, glib answers." Toussaint's father's voice was brittle with anger. Twenty-one years beneath these roofs, and never one emitted photon of anger. Until now. "I am not to be dissected by your home-spun gung-ho *aguila* psychologies. If you must make me your enemy, understand me first, then be my enemy or my ally. You think I am the oppressor of the dead. I am not. The irony is that no one could be more in favor of the freedom of the dead than I am. True freedom. Valuable freedom. Not the cheap freedom of political slogans or nationalism or cultural identity, but personal freedom, individual freedom, freedom that is valued because it has been bought with a price." He turned full to the window, a man-shaped black hole in the dusty rays of sunlight. "Down there is what we are proud to call the freest society in history. Twenty-two million people live in these three valleys, and how do they celebrate their freedoms? They shop. They surf. They fuck. They take uppers and downers and someplace-elsers and lose themselves for weeks on end in virtuality channels. They drink too much. They get fat. They drive their cars badly. They abuse their children. They get into debt. I would not stop them: that is their choice, their right. Most of those twenty-two million never pause to think of the freedoms they have. They take them for granted. They forget them. They become slaves— of routine, of habit, of sensuality, sexuality, materialism: whatever.

"True freedom is terrifying. You are truly free only when there are no limits; in time, space, energy. The dead are the only truly free people. I applaud the Freedead because they are using their freedom to push at the limits of space and time. They are living like free creatures; they have earned, and constantly appreciate their freedom. Most earthbound dead are indistinguishable from their meat counterparts."

"Because you tie up that freedom in the *contratada* system," said Shipley.

"Because I make freedom something to be attained." Adam Tesler turned on the dead woman in his *teniente*'s body. "Something to be worked for, so that, when that freedom comes they will be able to say,

I have bought this with a price, it is worth something to me. I can choose to stuff my head full of pills and spend eternity hooked into the virtual soap channels, or I can colonize Alpha Centauri, but the choice is mine. I have bought the right to make it. Contratada is freedom. The Barantes Ruling is freedom, and the Death House with its legal power play is trading that for some abstraction called 'rights.' Rights apply only to those who, if their rights are removed, are diminished in some way, made less human. You cannot die, you can survive in hard vacuum, sunlight is your sustenance, you can change shape, form, steal another's body: what possible protection could a 'right' afford you that you do not already possess?''

"A seductively specious argument, that we need purgatory to properly appreciate heaven," said Quebec. "Whether you let them go or not, whether they're ready to go or not, we're taking the people. The Death House's legal challenge is a small part of a large strategy. The slamship fleet currently investing your orbital factories and launchers, even that is only a tiny part of it. The big part of it is the part that's most easily overlooked. There's a second wave of ships out there, behind the big slamships; mostly old, slow, homebrew lightpushers and cargo bodies. They're carrying tectors, father. Tesler-process DNA-transcribing resurrection tectors, but without the Tesler codes that lock the Death House, and thus the entire dead nation, into master and servant, owner and owned, God and subjects."

" 'Thou hast conquered and won, O Pale Galilean,' " Adam Tesler quoted. "My children have superseded me: I am redundant, genetically and evolutionarily obsolete."

"Come to me," Quebec said. His hands were open, his arms spread. Though the invitation was not made to him, Toussaint felt vaguely threatened. A tightening of the scrotum. A lift in the base of the stomach. *Something is going to happen.* "I know it's too much to expect the Great Satan to repent; but an honorable surrender is possible. Speak to the fleet. Recognize it has won. Call off your lawyers."

" 'Dethrone of God, deceit of Satan'?" Adam Tesler took five steps toward his son. Light filled up the huge room; the drowsing tectosaur woke on its roost, blinked its liquid amber eyes, frilled its ruff. "Son, grant me the right to one final act of defiance."

"You leave me no choice."

"You never had any other choice." Adam Tesler smiled. The two men embraced.

And he knew. Toussaint knew.

Quebec held his father's head between his fingers. He looked down into the smaller man's face. His own features contorted, melted, flowed. Vomited outward in a spurt of liquid steel. For long seconds Adam Tesler seemed to be wearing a flowing metal death-mask. Then incredibly, Quebec was reeling backward against the livewood desk, clutching his face as if it had been pressed into a dish of acid. Adam Tesler rose unsteadily from the floor to which he had fallen. He brushed imaginary dust from his long, elegant coat.

"After all, Satan is just another angel," he said.

"Will someone tell me what's happening?" asked Toussaint. Shipley and Huen/Texeira's expression echoed his question.

"He's dead, don't you see?" Quebec laughed. "Dead dead dead. Dead to begin with. Dead as a dodo. Dead as a doornail. Dead meat. I couldn't get my fingers into his soul. Neruro's engineers built me to reconfigure living protoplasm. They never imagined I would meet my match against dead tectoplasm."

Toussaint felt he was going insane.

"How?" he asked. "How long? Why?"

"Why does anyone? They die," his father answered. Knowledge imparted sinister resonances to his soft voice. "I died. Four years ago, I died. Correction, I allowed myself to die. I had been dying for a long time, since before you left for Lodoga, Xavier. I instructed my doctors to inject a little dignity and free will into the process."

"Brain cancer," Quebec said. "I tasted it."

"An elegant assassin," Adam Tesler continued. "Most symptoms are purely cerebral: paranoiac tendencies, irritability, a certain monomania in details and trivia, in my case, dress and etiquette. Up until the very last stages, one is outwardly presentable. One is dignified. You can imagine how important that was to me. Dignity. Presentability. Grace."

"Oh Jesus," Toussaint began, a burning ball of bilious guilt working its way up from the pit of his belly, choking him. His father shook his head slowly.

"You have no cause for recrimination. I would not have had you stay with me out of guilt, or duty, while your soul was off flying with the Lodoga eagles."

"Easily said."

"You don't pity your brother, any of these dead here. Why pity me? To answer your last question: 'how?' " He turned a slow circle, implying the monumental bulk of the *arcosanti*. "If a man isn't master of his own house, what is he master of? The technology is simple; security was the difficulty. The president of the Rim's—maybe the planet's—most powerful *corporada* dead? Resurrected? A legal nonperson, without status, property, authority? It had to be kept quiet from even my closest advisers. You, whatever your name is, the one in poor Porfirio's body: I presume you have access to his memories: this is a complete surprise to you. All those years, and you never suspected, isn't that right?"

"Yes," Shipley croaked.

"Only five members of my research and development division know. Two performed the actual resurrection, the others were responsible for certain, ah, design improvements over the standard model."

"Like no deathsign," Huen/Texeira said. "And being resurrected at your death-age. And simulated gradual aging. They did a fine job. I regret them having been rewarded so shabbily."

Big Death: at knifepoint or bullet-end or monomolecular loop or complex chemicals in a glass of whiskey, and the treacherous resurrectable flesh incinerated or burned away by acid or buried deep in the consuming earth. By their very utilitarian callousness these five seedy, unmarked deaths seemed the most monstrous of Tesler-Thanos's crimes.

"The succession was not secured," Adam Tesler continued. "The codes were all in place, the genetic identifiers and authorizations waiting for your return, Xavier, Toussaint, whatever you want to call yourself. Now you have returned, my kingdom is yours, and I can cease this charade, have my death gracefully announced, and move to my luxurious penthouse apartment in Necroville, from which I shall take a keen and paternal interest—non-proprietorial, of course, in the future of the glorious future of this *corporada*."

"You hypocrite," Toussaint said and the words became a shout, an accusation: "You fucking hypocrite!" He leaped for his father. Shipley and Huen/Texeira caught him, held him. "Kill him!" Toussaint shouted to his brother. "Just kill the fucker."

"Always a mistake to underestimate your enemy, father," said Quebec. His voice was deadly calm. "I always found it ironic that the one weapon that can kill the dead is named after the man who gave them new life. And us so carefully armed for the wrong final showdown. But what is a tesler charge but tectors: what am I but more tectors? Let's pit them: tectors against tectors, your flesh against my flesh, and see which is stronger; the scientists you killed, or the Neruro technicians who designed me to be a living tesler." Quebec seized the old man in a bone-cracking hug, lifted him. Adam Tesler struggled but he could not overcome Quebec's deathgrip. Centimeters separated their faces. The old man fought like a demon, like a clinging, aged, dead thing from legends of the Golden Age of Hollywood. Quebec held him. And slowly, molecule by molecule, Quebec began to change. His clothes bubbled and ran into long drips of molten plastic. His facial features softened and flowed like thick lava. The air seethed with flying tectors, Quebec's fingers dissolved holes through Adam Tesler's beautifully tailored, old-fashioned clothes.

"Xavier!" Adam Tesler cried out. "Toussaint! Take it, for the love of God. It's yours now; save it, keep it, for me."

The old man shrieked as burning fingertips seared flesh, cried louder as the skin of his son's chest fused with his own. Molecule by molecule, Quebec's outer self began to melt as his component tectors reprogramed themselves to feed on his father's synthetic flesh.

"Shipley." Quebec's voice was a semi-coherent bubble of syllables; the words dissolved in his throat. "Toussaint. Take him. We can't run the risk of him not recognizing the fleet. Take him. Make sure of it." The voice dissolved into a hiss of boiling tectors.

There was no escaping Shipley's speed and strength, even clothed in the flesh of an old man. She held him with the almighty ease of a parent a child.

"I'm sorry, *compañero*, but you know what they say about things being fair in love and war."

She bent over Toussaint in an obscene parody of a kiss. Her face gathered into a fist of silver tectoplasm.

There was a sudden soft explosion. A spray of boiling liquid. A stench of burned flesh. Fingers lost their grip on Toussaint's head. The alien face, contorted in terminal agony, fell away from him.

Something had punched a twenty-centimeter steaming crater of bone, muscle, blood and spiked-rubber jacket into the small of Shipley's back.

Huen/Texeira slid the tunker into the folds of the best silk jacket.

"Hi Toussaint. I presume that's what you want me to call you. It's me. I'm back."

Alive. Toussaint wiped a thin film of blood and vaporized flesh from his face.

"I couldn't let Shipley do it. I'm sorry it had to be her, she wasn't a bad one. She'll be back sometime, I expect."

"Huen?"

"That's me."

His numb expression asked all his questions for him.

"Texeira staged a coup de tête, I staged a countercoup. I tired him out. As soon as I realized I was a passenger in my own body, I started working on ways of getting my ass back in the wing. I've got all his memories, so I knew how long it had been since he'd last gotten a night's sleep. I'd wait until he dozed off, and then while he was out of my frontal lobes, I'd slip back in. I helped him a little along the way. I nagged him. I bored him. I talked to him, nonstop, every second he was in my head. Recite poems, make up haiku—at least I can get the right number of syllables—count to ten thousand in twos, threes, fours and fives, make up endless Navidad lists, reel off chunks of the Koran and the Upanishads; anything to keep him off balance. Toussaint, I bored him literally out of his skull. My skull. And just at the dramatic moment: ¡Olé! That's a wicked little gun, that.''

"He's gone.''

"He's still in there. I can feel him. I think I can hold him; they rely on shock to lower your defenses so they can get in, but I know the furniture better than he does. I'll work on how to get rid of him later. Right now you have more important things to do.''

The conflagration had consumed one end of the desk and was advancing at a slow but inexorable rate. The father and son locked in internecine combat were all but invisible behind the blur of hypercharged tectors. Half the screen icons were down; half of those that remained spewed informational gibberish.

"Xavier!'' A voice cried out. Toussaint could not say whose it was.

The King is dead, long live the King. Your people await you: the world listens. A drop-out chill-out haiku-spouting *aguila* sky-bum quasi-philosopher who has just taken the skull-topped scepter of the Lord of the Dead. What have you to say to them?

The power is in the DNA, he had said.

All around, display icons imploded soundlessly into the depths of the desk. *Structural alert: unidentified tectronic infestation in executive levels*, half a dozen screens flashed furiously at Toussaint.

Touch the screen.

"This is Xavier Tesler. Give me the legal department.''

He pressed his hand to the featureless smartwood.

Identification validated, said the screen. The legal system colophon of a nested orrery rezzed up on screen. Worlds within worlds, turning.

"Do you know who I am?'' Toussaint asked.

"You are Xavier Tesler,'' the 'ware replied.

"Do you recognize my authority?''

"You have full executive authority, which we are programmed to recognize.''

Toussaint took a deep breath.

"By that authority, I am ordering you to suspend any and all legal actions currently in progress against Advocate YoYo Mok."

"Are you countermanding your father's override instructions?"

"I am."

There was a pause that felt far longer than the few seconds of real time it occupied.

"It's done," said the 'ware. "Legal virtuality and direct actions have been suspended. Prior to Séor Tesler's override, we advised conditional acceptance of Advocate Mok's proposition. Do you wish us to resume negotiations with Advocate Mok?"

"Do it. Make it. Sign it," Toussaint said.

"It's done," said the legalware.

Huen pulled him away mere seconds before the roof pillar dripped tears of liquid stone onto the desk.

The servants of Seu Guacondo were waiting in the back alley. Three in number, poured into bicolor skinsuits, right hand yellow, left hand black, they were faceless; heads featureless curves of black skin. Yet when Trinidad stared at them, they turned their heads toward her and the ovals of skin where eyes should have been were prickled with goose-flesh.

Two long, thin parallel tracheotomy lesions fluttered to their exhalations.

Jens Aarp swirled his bush coat melodramatically. The faceless guides unpeeled themselves from the shadows and moved with supernatural surety and fluidity along the alley. The company followed.

The explosion of light and Rosalba's cry were almost simultaneous. Voices Babeled: *What happened? They've hit the city oh Jesus they've started on civilian targets no, it was a space attack, believe me, if it had been a ground burst, we'd have known about it, do you think they got a slamship? Could be, or they got one of our close-orbit manufactures I can't be sure, I'm querying databases but the tagalong channels are out, all hell is breaking loose in the TVMA web.*

"Brothers, sisters." Jens Aarp was the silken voice of seduction. "What does this matter to us?"

Though they betrayed no outward signs, Trinidad sensed their guides were smiling.

At the western end of Willoughby, palm trees were burning. A distant wild music drifted east on the wind. All the cinema walls were blank silver faces. To the east, the horizon lightened. The zenith gleamed with the first golden threads of the dawn skysign.

The faceless guides led them to a tawdry district of off-boulevard high-density tenements. *Cuadra* banners hand-painted on taped-together plastic sheets hung limply from the washing lines: *¡Andale! Los Leons'A'Judah*. Lions by name, lions by nature, some, both male and female, sported bodmod manes and muzzles and liquid gold eyes.

The basilica of Seu Guacondo was once a *parada* church: Orthodox Catholicism's final evangelical push that had expressed itself in shopping mall masses and services in municipal bus shelters. What the Radical Fathers and Liberation Theologians failed to realize was that the masses did not want a religion of the people, meeting them in the places they commerced, speaking to them in *favela* Angeleno. The sacred heart of the church has always been mystery, and a mystery devoid of grandeur, ritual, elaboration, pomp, circumstance, shiny tinsel, gorgeous frocks and Cecil B. De Mille stage sets with full supporting cast of saints and angels is precious close to no mystery at all. Therefore the faithful took their simple bus-stop chapels, adorned them with icons, statues, candles, altars and built them into jerryrigged Saint Peters. Most, after the Great Apostasy, became Ucurombé shrines. A few became way stations in the Via Dolorosa of the Zoo Cults.

Seu Guacondo's followers had exceeded even the *parada* builders' eclecticism. The small chapel was a hymn to comparative religious plunder: pale-cheeked plaster saints and Marian blue Madonnas committed frottage with Aztec sun gods and corn lords; seraphim and cherubim looped-the-loop with quetzalcoatls and thunderbirds; Boddhisatvas cavorted with four-armed Vishnu avatars and micro-Ganeshs; luminous Orthodox icons were festooned with exquisite garlands of Koranic Suras. Masks, fetishes, ritual objects from the animist religions of four continents hung from the roof beams and rattled in the breeze. In a corner Vladimir Ilich Lenin and Elvis Aaron Presley smoked some joss together; Chinese prayer tickets heaped at their feet in the final tickertape parade. Holographic images of the Ucumrobé saints glowed in dried mud niches; in a side-chapel an old flat-screen television replayed excerpts from the flesh-tone-and-red-leather bible of Johannes Ulfa, the early twenty-first-century Swedish promulgator of sadomasochism as spirituality.

"Are there any religions that aren't represented here?" Salamanca whispered.

At the center, where once-celibate priests had celebrated the death of a god who thought it better to burn out than rust, Seu Guacondo waited.

He was a pillar of twisted black tectronics taller than a man, like a tree all dripping roots in which, as in an ancient fantasy, a man has been imprisoned for offending the gods. Black hands on arms abruptly truncated at the elbow reached out of the dark pillar, fingers rigidly outspread. Above them, a head was embedded in the matrix. If an old, gentle, innocent priest had been dipped in liquid hell by a vicious god wishing to make an example to an apostate, his face might have worn the same expression of agony, betrayal and disillusionment as Seu Guacondo's. The tiny thalidomide arms, the head half buried in a tangle of roots and ribbing, might have been unintentionally comic; the face challenged you to smile.

Glossy with candlelight, he rotated on his powered dais to face his supplicants. The black lips moved. Seu Guacondo spoke.

"Hang out the flags! A new world order has been born! Only appropriate that on this Day of the Dead the old Earth dies screaming. Titans and Olympians slug it out in the orbital approaches; and still you come to stake your lives, your hopes of deathless immortality, on the toss of a coin.

"Well, you are not the first, nor shall you be the last, but perhaps you are the most timely. Whatever, I extend to you the same *caveat* as to all who have gone before and all who will come after: before you take my hand, ask yourself, is the game worth the candle; is the prize worth the stake?"

Seu Guacondo's voice was deeply beautiful, rich with the intonations and cadences of Old Spain. Of course, Trinidad thought. Lords of eternal life and death should have good dialogue coaches.

"Come on, roll up, roll up, see the show. You came through death, destruction, fire and war to find me, and now the ride's too fast for you, the Ferris wheel's too high? If you have only fifty centavos to spend at the fair, why waste it on mere merry-go-rounds and coconut shies? Spend it wisely, spend it well, spend it on something you will remember for the rest of your life. Step right up, ladies and gentlemen, for the ride of your life. Who's first?"

"Since someone must, it may as well be me," said Jens Aarp. "Age before beauty, and all that." He stepped up to the dais. A tall man, even he had to look up into the face of the *mediomuerte*. The tails of his long coat fluttered in a wind from nowhere.

"Who are you, soul, who has come unto me?" Seu Guacondo asked. "Tell me your name, your nature, your heart's deepest desire."

Ten thousand candle flames flickered.

"My name is Jens Aarp. I, sir, am a gambler. It is no more than truth to call myself the greatest gambler of my age. I have pitted myself against games of luck and skill and have never yet been beaten. I present myself before you because there is nothing for me anymore in these games of chance and probability, I seek a higher game, with the highest stakes. A game worthy of the candle, as you put it."

The silent guides inclined their featureless heads toward each other. Trinidad imagined hot, intimate telepathic communions: head inside head.

"I warn you man, this is no five card stud," spoke Seu Guacondo. "Here, you cannot throw the hand to win the night. There is one and one only turn of the cards."

"Please, you offend my professionalism," said Jens Aarp with deadly pride. "I have staked fortunes on the turn of a single card, or the toss of a coin."

"But never, methinks, a stake as high as this," mused Seu Guacondo on his candle-lit dais. "If I were to explain the rules, would that also offend your professional sensibilities? Understand this: I am a creature of chaos. The forces of life and death flow unpredictably through me: even I cannot say in which hand they reside from one second to the next. I have no power over it. The choice is yours, and yours alone. *Suerte*, or *Muerte*."

Aircraft passed low over the roof in a deafening blast of engines.

Jens Aarp hesitated but a moment before firmly seizing Seu Guacondo's right hand. He looked up into the half-living creature's eyes. His pupils dilated. He saw something in the reflecting blackness that Trinidad could not. The gambler turned to his comrades, smiling, radiant.

"Look! Look! See, there's nothing to it!"

He held up the hand that had touched Seu Guacondo Lord of Life and Death.

He stared at the hand.

His smile turned to a rictus of horror.

Before his eyes, his right hand blistered and blackened. Fingers shriveled to stumps; the palm creased, bubbled and erupted a long, curving claw of black tectoplastic.

Jens Aarp seized his right wrist in his left hand to tear the betraying black hook away from his wrist. As well spit on a forest fire. In one wave of transformation the tectors changed his right arm into a chitinous pincer. His scream was hideous as the nanoagents swept down across his body. Ribs burst through his clothing in obscene scrabbling fingers of black horn, legs melted into a pool of gnarled roots and reforged flesh; spine ripped open in a long tear of splintering bone, uncoiling tendrils and feathery antennae. The long scream abruptly terminated as his face outward on a long, glistening spine of black nanoflesh, neatly severing the trachea, sealing in a knobbed ridge of bone.

The Aarp thing clinked and creaked as it cooled from flesh heat to harden in death.

I shall not scream, I shall not vomit Trinidad told herself *because even in a world where dead movie stars walk and buildings grow and machines shapeshift and clothes change texture and color I cannot believe that men can be turned to stone.*

Pressed close against Salamanca, she felt his hand move inside the soft rubber of his jacket.

"No," she whispered. "Not yet."

Seu Guacondo turned left, right, left, right on his dais. The motor whined petulantly.

"Alas, Jens Aarp. So many times I have borne witness to this tragedy, yet so many times have I seen with my own eyes the tectors sweep down like refining fire; purifying, perfecting, giving life. The gift is the same, the odds are unchanged.

"Because one man has paid dear, that is no reason why the next should not succeed. If this were a horse race, who would not stake on odds of fifty/fifty? And the prize I offer is richer by far than any Mutuel. Who'll take those odds? Perhaps, you Madam?"

Seu Guacondo halted in front of Montserrat Mastriani and the visibly shaken Rosalba. The exoskeleton's hummings and pumpings were preternaturally loud.

"I know what it is to be imprisoned by one's own body; to be dependent on outside agencies to meet one's needs. The irony of it is that I cannot use my own power on myself: you, at least, would have the chance to be whole, sound, fit in mind and limb; healthy."

The hands reached out toward the two women. The exoskeleton whirred as it took Montserrat back one step, two steps, three steps, four.

"No. No. I won't do it. I can't do it," she stammered. "I thought it was a game, just a game . . . But it's not playing. It's real. It's forever. I never thought of what happened to those who gambled and lost, never grasped that it could be me. Oh Rosalba!" Montserrat cried out in the blind terror of an old woman seeing the face of death in the winter constellations.

"I'm here, *abuela*, I'm here, it's all right."

"What am I doing here Rosalba? What did I think I could find here?"

Their departing footsteps echoed from the nooks and crevices of the church. Seu Guacondo inclined his head: one of his dark guides materialized from the shadows to lead the old woman and her granddaughter back to the meat world. Trinidad felt terribly alone.

"My brethren," the *mediomuerte* said, "please take this thing away. The sight of death offends me." The two remaining black-and-gold-skinned acolytes disappeared into the recesses of the chapel to fetch implements.

"Now," whispered Trinidad, squeezing Salamanca's arm. *"Now."*

"And so our company is now two," said Seu Guacondo, rotating to face Salamanca and Trinidad. "Have you courage to face your greatest wants, your greatest fears, and take them by the hand? Will you turn and run into the night, or stay to embrace the dawn of true life?"

Salamanca stepped down into the area before Seu Guacondo and looked up into the adamantine features.

"I'll do it."

"Brave lad," whispered Seu Guacondo. "There is courage yet in this callow generation. What are you, where do you come from, what is your name?"

In one beautiful liquid movement the tesler was drawn and aimed, two-handed, square at Seu Guacondo's pineal gland.

"You can call me Nemesis, you long-winded death-loving bastard."

"Well well." Seu Guacondo smiled twistedly. "I praised your courage, never thinking it was the mask of a fool."

"Playing it right up to the end," said Salamanca. "Sorry I can't applaud. This is for Leon."

He leveled the tesler, sighted along the barrel. Targeting diodes winked like yellow eyes: *ready ready ready*. He pressed the firing stud.

The tesler clicked spastically.

Salamanca fired again, again, again, emptied the entire magazine of five remaining MIST 27s at Seu Guacondo.

Nothing happened.

"One does not live forever in this world of corporate mistrust and armed contempt without a trump or two hidden away." Smiling like a disease, Seu Guacondo held up his left hand. Gold glittered at the base of the third finger: a ring.

"Small, but highly effective. The jamming field extends to fill all this church, and, so the manufacturers say, is good against all mass-market anti-thanatic weapons. For once the product has lived up to the hype."

The faceless guards were on Trinidad before she could move. Hard hands gripped her upper arms and propelled her toward the dais. She shouted and swore and looked for somewhere to kick, hard, beneath the glossy skinsuits but the leverages were all wrong. Fingers bit into her coup scars as she was lifted up before Seu Guacondo. The vile undead thing looked into her eyes. Fingers hooked into claws ready to tear a soul out by its roots, the hand halted five centimeters from her face.

"Not everybody gets a second chance," Seu Guacondo directed at Salamanca. "But Seu Guacondo is merciful and generous. Set down your weapon and come to me again and make your choice." Salamanca shifted aim from Seu Guacondo to the guides holding Trinidad and back again. Whatever way he pointed the thing, he was impotent. "The odds will always be fifty-fifty, but dare you force them on your girlfriend here?"

"And what choice is that?" Salamanca said. "Whatever hand I chose will be *Muerte*. But that's always been the secret game, hasn't it? No one has ever chosen the right hand, no one will ever choose the right hand. There is no right hand, is there? There is no eternal life."

Seu Guacondo beckoned Salamanca nearer, nearer, to the embrace of the hands.

"If I will not guarantee eternal life, neither will I guarantee eternal death. You think that I will disclose myself to such as you. I am the enigma, I am the quantum paradox personified: the thing half-living, half-dead. I am unknowable, undecidable, uncertain until the moment your free will collapses the event space. If it has always been the death-hand until now, that is not to say that this one time it will not be eternal life. I will not say. I cannot say."

"Trinidad goes free," Salamanca demanded.

"If she wishes," Seu Guacondo concurred. At an unseen signal, the faceless creatures released Trinidad. Salamanca stepped between Seu Guacondo's outstretched hands.

Trinidad watched Salamanca lift up his right hand. Her own hands fell helpless, useless, to her sides. She felt something, in her nightbag, a silver flask, three-quarters full of Nuestra Dona de los Jaguares 120-proof mescal. Eyes closed, Salamanca's fingers closed around Seu Guacondo's.

"Salamanca! No! No!"

He turned, saw, dropped beneath Seu Guacondo's sudden lunge in the split second it took Trinidad to uncap her flask of mescal and fling it at the avatar's face and hands. The creature bellowed. A blind guard moved. Salamanca swept his elbow upward in a smashing blow to the point of the chin. Trinidad heard neck snap as she took the ceremonial candle in its sconce and thrust it at Seu Guacondo. The hands went up in a yellow blossom of flame. Seu Guacondo screamed, a hideous insane jibber of torment as he tried to clap out the flames. Drips of blazing tectoplastic fell to the floor, some black. Some, gold.

"Salamanca!" Trinidad pointed at the blazing pools of synthetic flesh. "The ring! The jammer!"

"Trinidad!" She whirled. A black empty face loomed over her. And the tesler bolt blew a ten-centimeter hole in the middle of it. The guide somersaulted backward as the tector pellets reduced him to a smear of viscous tar leaking from the neck hands and feet of a crumpled black-and-gold skinsuit.

Panting, Salamanca slowly leveled the tesler at the blazing, shrieking Seu Guacondo.

"You're fucked."

The eclectic bus-stop chapel rang to a volley of short, fast tesler bolts.

The allosaur's foot came down two meters from Santiago's head. From the eye slit in the *metropolitano* vent he could see encrustations of street dirt where claw met gold-green synthetic flesh.

Santiago did not move. Santiago did not speak. Santiago did not breathe until the foot lifted and he felt the tremor as it came down out of his field of vision.

The Pale Rider had loomed over Daft Eddie's translucent plastic roof. Miclantecutli had said *run*. Santiago had run and not stopped. Had looked back only once, on an avenue lined with burning palm trees when he heard the roar so loud, so close that he had felt the street shudder beneath the allosaur's tread. He had turned, paralyzed by the dazzle of the headlights, and a mighty grip had pulled him out of the death trance, over a low concrete wall and gone half scrambling half tumbling down a steep culvert into a shallow stream of sewage. The allosaur had snapped at his heels as he followed Miclantecutli up a rusting metal ladder and through a maintenance hatch too small for anyone less desperate than he. The roof over his head had shuddered to the steady pace of the Pale Rider's mount as Miclantecutli led him through a warren of crawlways and inspection tunnels to this vent shaft for the failed underground rapid transit system into which they fitted like segments of an orange into its skin.

Miclantecutli waited a thousand heartbeats before pushing up the inspection hatch and clambering out onto the wet street. She crouched there against the lightening sky, one hand thrust down to haul Santiago up.

"I don't want to come up."

"You want to hide like a rat in a hole."

"Yes. I'm safe down here. I'm happy to be a live rat and not a dead lion. And when the sun comes up and the Pale Riders go back to their coffins or turn to dust or stone, then this rat will creep out onto his mean streets and be happier than you can ever imagine, Miclantecutli."

She leaned over the lip of the hatch and looked straight down into his upturned face.

"When was it ever anything else, Santiago? When was it ever anything but hide like a rat in a hole of your own exquisite designing and let the world walk on by over your head? Your drugs, your virtualities, your parties up in the canyons, what were they but exquisite insulation against having to feel, care, be hurt? Be human? Even your fine friends: when they became something more than mere social wallpaper, when the joys and hurts and wants of their lives began to press through your skin into your so-holy flesh and demand something of you, you destroyed them. Too close. Too real. I have died, Santiago; not one but a hundred deaths, and I am more human than you. I am more human than you because what I feel is real. The knife that turns in my guts is real, the blade that gently severs my jugular: real, the impaling spike that drives my lungs out of my back: real. Real. Real pain. Real death. Real sensation. Real emotion. This is not seeming; this is being. This is the physical world: it stinks and tastes and sounds and feels; it pleases, it hurts, it and only it can kill you. No *escape* buttons in this unvirtuality, Santiago.

"And that scares the piss out of you, doesn't it? While you were a spectator in the Biggest Game, you could handle it, but now it's you up there in the spotlight and it's all too big, too bright, and who are all those people out there? For the first time in your life, it's outside your control, Santiago. It can do whatever it likes to you, *compadre*. For the first time you don't make the rules, the rules make you."

Miclantecutli looked up as once again tectosaurs sounded; voices raised together now in a hunting cadre.

"They're coming, the hounds of God. And we will play it to its finish out on the streets, we two, Santiago. We will live or we will die, and it will be real; the first real thing you have done in your piss-poor life." She reached down into the pit and grabbed a fistful of Santiago's shirt. "And you will come with me, Santiago Columbar, or I will surely kill you like the trapped rat you are." With a bestial strength Santiago had never suspected, she dragged him out of the inspection pit and set him on the cold earth.

The rain had ended, the street was wet and greasy. Carnival litter filled the gutters. On the wall screens Steve McQueen jumped his motorbike across the wire into immortality, Robert Donat and Madeleine Carroll fled handcuff in handcuff across bonnie Scotland, Jimmy Cagney made it to the top of the world, ma.

Top of the world, ma. Frightened, yes; exhausted, yes; humiliated, yes; doomed, almost certainly; yet through all these burned a deep exhilaration at merely being alive. Santiago recalled those instants of pure being he had felt running with Anansi and Miclantecutli over the rooftops of Necroville. Beyond the moment, beyond the laser-tight focus of all you felt, all you hoped, all you were onto the cutting edge of reality, nothing had existed. Beneath these icons of escape and flight he understood the paradox and ecstasy of the hunted, that lives without thought, or foresight, or self-consciousness, that burns with pure existence to the very edge of death. Top of the world, ma. *¡Salud!* Séor Jimmy on your silver screen.

Down on the avenue streetcars stopped dead in their tracks, buses and bicycles pulled over to the side of the road, *contratistos* stopped on the sidewalks to look up and marvel. The Pale Riders were coming. The Pale Riders were here: proud, alien, noble at the controls of their mounts. The Pale Riders paused, and passed on. Their prey had long since fled.

By the time they came to the burning, Santiago and Miclantecutli had passed into the satori of the hunt. For many long seconds they stared at the collapsed building, the blackened wreckage in its pool of fire without comprehending what they were seeing.

"It looks like a liftercraft hit the Death House," said Santiago, awed by the magnitude of the destruction. "And the bodies . . . What are those things?"

"Harpoons," said Miclantecutli. "The Wolves of the Moon have been here. Some of those bodies are meat."

Santiago looked her a question. Her expression told him no explanation would be forthcoming. He bent to relieve one of the killed of its tesler. The kick sent the cruel little weapon spinning away into the fire. Santiago rubbed his wrist, feeling for broken bones, reading Miclantecutli's message. That was not how it would be played.

Behind them, the hunters howled to drive down the rising sun.

Long before they had paid the dead town flesh engineers to sculpt them for life as Milapa Swimmers, Santiago's parents had taken their one, their only child with them to an alternative life-styles summer camp up in the BeeCee Rockies. The one, the only Santiago had been eight. The joys of Zenshu drumming; mask making; totemic counseling; Christian contemplation; symbolic burial and rebirth, had been lost on him. His one, his only clear memory had been of the night he had sat outside the teepee with his father to watch the stars and a very large rat had sat on the grass in front of them, punctiliously cleaned its face and calmly sauntered off into the night as if the humans and all their works had not existed. In fact, Santiago's father explained, they had not.

"Rat space and human space are two separate but overlapping universes. We see a universe of names: meanings, purposes. A tent is something more than just a pile of synthetic moose hides; a human is more than just a shape that sometimes moves and makes noises. Not so to a rat. The rat lives in a universe of food, threat and reproduction. Those are its dimensions: everything to a rat is judged as to whether it is edible, *joder*able or threatening. A teepee has no meaning to it, save as a place where food may or may not be found, that may be safe or threatening. And what is threatening to it may be trivial to us, what is threatening to us may be beyond its comprehension. It has no names, it goes about the world seeing only what it needs to see, understanding only what it needs to understand. The universe it perceives is quite different from the one we perceive. Yet, at certain moments, in certain places, human space and rat space overlap, touch, and there is communication and communion."

Communion with a rat? thought Santiago Columbar age eight.

Rat space. Hunter space. Hunted space. Meat space. Dead space. Ten million universes in the naked city, each the size of the human head, divided from each other by gulfs of incommunicability. You need look no further for parallel universes than the person next to you; in your bed, in your car, at your desk, in the checkout line, than the woman running at your side with the unselfconscious grace and freedom of an animal.

Unique in Necroville, there are no silver screens in Century City. No silent shadows of movie gods conjured from shutter-flicker and dancing fans of light. Century City is the spirit of place incarnate. The town it invokes has always been more a state of mind than a geographical location. Century City is the ghost of a place that never really existed: Old Hollywood. Its gaudy corpse. Its jeweled shroud. Its Baby Jane.

Century City is a place all facades. Without substance; the thickness of a sheet of ply, a film of paint, a chip of celluloid. It is constructed entirely from the lost and lonely movie sets of the Golden Age of Hollywood. Look, there is the very gutter through which Gene Kelly splashed, and there the tenements from *Dead End*. Is that the glitter of Jimmy Stewart's telephoto lens as he looks down from his rear window, and listen, oh listen! Can you hear Sam playin' it for the lady behind the neon of Rick's Café Americain? Who could resist looking in through the door to see if maybe, maybe it is all true, but you find behind them nothing but timber props, key grips' chalk marks, and more sets. Faces. Fronts. Facades.

Memories. Santiago snatched his hand from the door handle of the mansion from Peyton Place as if burned. The briefest of contacts, yet in that instant he had been another person in another time: a little girl in a yellow sundress, a balloon caught in a tree, children running across a striped lawn from the debris of a birthday party. He touched it again. The suddenness of the transition shocked him: the children were around him now, he was crying, the balloon was floating away into the sky.

This was holy ground. They stood in a small square: Peyton Place faced them; behind them, the Tattooine cantina; to the right, Blanche Dubois's apartment in the Quartier; to the left, the gates of the Emerald City. The ghosts of Shirley Temple and Mickey Rooney haunted Santiago's peripheral vision; faded giggling into the dissolve whenever he tried to look at them. He was not certain he could find his way back to the land of the dead, let alone the land of the living.

"The Tinsel Town of Memory," Miclantecutli said. "The Greeks came up with the idea but it was the Renaissance Italians who elevated it to an art.

"The Theater of Memory was a method of constructing an entire architecture of mnemonics, say, a house, where each room was a specific area you needed to remember: its layout, decor, furnishing, its statues and ornaments—we're talking memory mansions here, not architectonic project housing—were chosen and placed for their specific associations. An entire wing could house your investment portfolio: that suit of samurai armor could be your stock in Home Island Munitions; that gilded sunburst on the wall your two-percent option in Sudoeste Solar; that stuffed bear with an orange in its paw a reminder never to get involved with juice-crop futures again. Medieval virtual reality: What are 'ware icons but mental images charged with memorized material? Some theaters of memory grew so dense with mnemonics piled on mnemonics that their managers had to offload memories from inner space onto outer space. Real buildings, actual places, became storage spaces for information; a walk through the piazza to the Duomo was the equivalent of reviewing and updating the files on your houseware. A thing of great sophistication and baroque beauty that was rendered totally obsolete by the Rolodex and the personal computer."

"All this is an immense real time Theater of Memory?" Santiago asked. Roads led from the small square into deepest memoryland; to his right Doris Day By-the-Light-of-the-Silvery-Moon Smalltown America, to his left the red-painted town of hell where the Stranger with No Name settled scores.

"This is to the classical Theater of Memory as the Theater of Memory is to Every Good Boy Deserves Fucking, or Richard of York Gave Battle in Vain," said Miclantecutli. "You've touched it, you've felt it. Living memory; the memory of our people, our pasts, our lives invested and kept safe so that in a thousand, ten thousand, a million years, when we have lived through just so fucking *much* that our brains cannot hold it all, we can come back here and let the symbols we have imprinted onto these cardboard streets lead us back to our forgotten pasts."

Santiago laid the palm of his right hand on the clay wall of the alien cantina. *Blue pearl earth-mother hangs above your head; beneath your feet spread solar wings of a scramjet orbiter emblazoned with the stars and stripes of a vanished civilization.*

"How?"

"A nanoprocessor is basically a machine for storing and reproducing information. The Tesler process is the reading and recording of chemical information from our cell DNA and transcribing into a tectoplastic rather than a protein matrix. What else is human memory but agglomerations of chemicals in the brain; chemicals that can be stored and processed by tectors, like any other? You need me to tell Santiago Columbar that the human spirit is nothing more than a shaken-not-stirred neurochemical cocktail?"

"These stage sets are sheets of memory storage tectors," said Santiago, calculating the information density of one square centimeter, multiplying by its walls, buildings, streets, cities.

He crossed the small square and touched the doorknocker of the Emerald City. *Blue sky, green sea, one small boat and I; an eye on the bobbing glass spheres of the neutrino detectors, like the net floats of Japanese fishermen across the far Pacific: in such magnificent solitude, with such attunement to the quantum universe, the mind elevates toward the condition of Zen.* Next, the pillar of the French Quarter balcony. *No, God, no, the darkness, the struggle for breath, the heart unbeating in the breast, the brain cells burning out one by one, consciousness fading, failing, falling into darkness, the darkness, the light, the light!* He tore his hand away.

"Too raw, too real for you, *muchacho*? This isn't kiss-and-tell for amateur voyeurs. These are people's lives. What bit you?"

"A woman . . . died. I felt her. I was her. The intensity, Miclan, the light . . ."

"The ultimate high, Santiago? The big trip? The way out? What's death to you is birth to us. Unlike meat birth, we remember our births, our deaths. We remember the light, the heat, the intensity of it, and when we come out of the tank or the clay, something of it stays with us always. Meat can't understand how death changes us. Outwardly we wear human form; within, we are changelings, aliens."

The dying echoed within Santiago: the fear, the anger, the fight to cling to a life that slipped away. And then the light; the utter serenity of the surrender as consciousness evaporated into *ur*-light. And beyond: the darkness that was brighter than any light. The Cloud of Unknowing. The house of Yahweh. Nirvana. Atman. The spirit paths. All religions knew this land where consciousness could not go, the domain of pure being, the kingdom he had sought all his adult life.

Miclantecutli was right, no one could comprehend who had not passed through it, but mere meat could appreciate how that taste of annihilation, that brief immersion in the destroying light, that moment of nothing-and-everything, might draw them back time and again until it hooked its barbs and arrows through their hearts. Addicted to death.

He had been horrified when they had run the Pale Rider woman hard up against the wire and Miclantecutli had kissed her before slitting her throat. Tiger-stripes of indigo cloud were visible on the brightening sky; beyond, the writhings of the skysign. Sunrise could be only minutes beneath the horizon. In the morning light he understood the two-sided nature of the Judas kiss.

"Each loves the thing he kills, each kills the thing he loves," he said. He had touched the mystery. "Miclan, I understand."

"Santiago, *muchacho*," Miclantecutli whispered, intimate as a lover placing a breakfast order, "I'm glad for you, truly, but don't you know it's never over till it's over?"

Three of them waited halfway down the Doris Day street: two men, one woman. Their allosaurs shifted from foot to foot, impatient. Skylight kindled the heads of the outrider's lances to golden flame: the central rider touched the head of his spear to his forehead before dipping it to the ground; the salute of a warrior to a worthy foe. Miclantecutli returned the salutation with a shallow bow.

And Santiago went blind. A hand took his and dragged him, stumbling, sightless after it. The sky was burning. Burning. He was blind. Blind. His eyes were twin tears of melted jelly running from scorched sockets.

"Get your fucking ass moving!" Miclan's voice. Her brutal rasp was oddly comforting.

"What? How?" he gasped, running for his life through looming shoals of afterimages.

"Some big bang up in space; those fleets, I don't know. But like I said, it's never over till it's over, so run and pray. Miclantecutli is not going to let the Pale Riders whitewash her first *caza* out of the trap. I want to be able to hold my head up at the *fiesta*."

Eastwood country led to a district of Wild West sets: saloons, livery stables, banks, sheriff's offices, whorehouses. The grand Theater of Memory jolted into higher resolution with every running step. Do not forsake me, oh my darling. They rounded the General Store and found themselves in Main Street Tombstone Arizona, facing the open gate of the OK Corral in classic gunfighter's pose.

"You party with the people who have hunted you?"

"What better way to resolve your differences with someone who's killed you than kiss and make up? That flageskin is kind of cute."

Light poured through the wooden gates of the OK Corral. The light of the rising sun. A hair-thin cord of solar disc silhouetted the hilltop wind rotors. Shadows moved within the light, figures riding monstrous anachronistic, bipedal mounts. The Pale Riders stepped out of the light: the allosaurs cleared the tumbledown rails in a single stride.

"They're behind us too," Santiago said. "I felt them."

"So did I, *corazón*." She drew a line on the concrete with the toe of her boot. "*Joder* if I let them run me down like a jackrabbit on a highway. If I have to die, I want to see the eyes of my killer." She took off her rubber jacket of many faces and threw it to the ground. "Face me like an enemy!" she shouted. "I've given you the best fucking run you've had in years. I demand better than to be skewered like a pig on Corpus Christi!" All at once the allosaurs lowered themselves to the ground. The Pale Riders dismounted by steps cunningly carved into the shoulderbones and encircled them, pikes and lances raised. Their flageskins were a hazy shade of sunrise.

The sun stood one third above the encircling hills.

Miclantecutli turned to Santiago.

"When it came down to it, I couldn't do it. Throw you to the dogs of war, Columbar." She took a shot on the sun. "Cocker-spaniel morality is one hell of a way to run your life. If you make it to Daft Eddie's, I'll get Anansi to buy you a drink." For the last time she held out her gloved hand. Santiago reached to take it. He saw instead the ridged sole of Miclantecutli's boot. It took him hard in the chest, sent him sprawling and retching across Main Street Tombstone.

"Sorry, *corazón*, but a girl's gotta do," Miclantecutli said, and ran.

She made it all the way to the door of the marshal's office. And Santiago saw her stagger and her gloved hands go up and clutch for the air and the sun-red/bloodred head of a spear thrust through meat and skin and stretch mesh into the light. She went down on the boardwalk, fingers scrabbling at the shaft.

"Oh Jesus Jesus Jesus," she whispered.

"Miclan!" Santiago howled. And without thought, without intention, in pure animal awareness, he was at her side. He reached for her.

Something moved.

The pain was a white blast of shock and ecstasy. The javelin had been flung with a master's precision. His left hand was pinned through the ball of the third and fourth fingers to the boardwalk by a meter of polished, flighted steel. He tore, tore, tore at the impaling shaft with the mindless gnawing need to be free of a gin-trapped animal. Barbed steel grated on tarsal bone. Blood, his own precious, sacred blood poured across the weathered wood.

The Pale Riders closed in. Half the sun had risen above the horizon.

Miclantecutli gibbered on her spike, delirious with pain. A Pale Rider woman stood over her. The last time Santiago had seen her, she had been a sad huddle of darkening flageskin in a lake of her own blood. She knelt beside Miclantecutli; the tips of her long hair were streaked red with gore. The two women kissed. Then the Pale Rider stood, took a long, thin spear and thrust it through Miclantecutli's throat.

The Pale Rider waited for Miclantecutli to stop moving, and then some, before wrenching free the javelin. Smiling savagely, the huntress wove patterns with the spearpoint in the air before his eyes. Blood dripping from the tip scribbled ideograms on Santiago's chest. Santiago tried to scramble away from it: the javelin through his hand was an immovable axis that pinned him to the surface of the earth. The bloody spearpoint mesmerized him.

"Please," he begged, fetched up hard against the lathe-and-canvas illusions of Old Hollywood. "Please." He could think of no other plea. The Pale Riders laughed. The woman drew one bloody line across his forehead and crossed it with a second, down his nose, across his lips and chin and throat. The spearpoint came to rest in the hollow of his thorax above his breastbone. He could feel barbs catch and tear the soft skin as the woman jostled the weapon. A spreading patch of warmth and wetness: his bladder had let go. He was beyond dignity, beyond reason, beyond language, beyond humanity, beyond everything but the desire not to die.

"No!" he howled. Tears streamed unheeded down his face. At some point he had shat himself. "No! Let me live, please, I want to live. I want to live! I want to live!"

day

november 2

There was no shame now. No pride. No self-consciousness. No cool. Only the desire to continue to be.

"I want to live." He knew his words were nothing now but a slobber of fear and tears and pain. Pure. Mindless. Everything he had hunted down all the years and he would have traded every milligram of it for just another second of fetid, fleshy meatlife. "I want to live."

Time. Time was a pattern tattooed in the fabric of space by the bloody point of a spear. Planck time: each quantal chronon a jab of scarlet steel.

"I want to live."

And the spear was gone from his throat as if it had never been. The Pale Riders stood back, weapons sloped, a siege of silhouettes. Between their bodies he saw the face of his savior. He saw the thin cord of clear sky between the lower limb of the sun and the mountaintops.

Again the Pale Rider woman bent over him. She was smiling. Santiago could not understand her smile. Santiago understood nothing but the direct reportage of his senses. The light of the sun, the cool of the dawn air, the smell of woodsmoke, the sound of distant traffic.

The monstrous, terrible, wonderful blast of pain as the Pale Rider woman, still smiling, laid a forefinger to his lips and with her free hand wrenched the barbed javelin from his hand.

The beautiful, bloody, engulfing blackness of unconsciousness.

Their kindness staggered him. They had staunched the bleeding, sterilized the infection, dressed the wound, anesthetized the pain with adhesive analgesic dots.

The strange mercy of the hunter that tends and heals the very thing it kills.

The two irreparably maimed fingers they had neatly amputated. No pain. No nothing. But for those missing fifteen centimeters of himself, the Night of the Dead might have been a bad virtuality trip.

Perhaps that was their reason: there would always be something left behind to remind him. Reality hurts. Reality kills.

Miclantecutli. Anansi. Angel. Asunçión. Duarte. Only I am left to tell. The street where the Pale Riders had left him was still busy with the last of the morning traffic. Staggering, still high and a little crazy, Santiago pushed against the flow, inward against its outward. Salmon swimming upstream. He knew where he was. He knew where he must go before he could turn and run with the flow, away from the heart of Necroville.

Down along the boulevard every palm tree was a headless smoking stalk, curled and carbonized like a burned-out match. Up on the rooftops, the big movie screens were folding up on themselves, silver buds of nightblooming flowers, closing in the harsher light of day. The beautiful bodies of the dead arranged themselves in strategic positions on balconies and verandas; basking, soaking up the sun, photosynthesizing the light of day for the excitements of the night.

Santiago continued inward.

There was a street party outside Daft Eddie's. Most of a *cuadra* were drumming and dancing and passing around three-liter plastic flagons of homebrew rice beer.

"What's going on?" Santiago asked a tall Chinese woman with a red, gold and green hip-slung drum.

"We've won, we're free, we've won!" she shouted. Dancers decked in eclectic snatches of other people's costumes cheered and sprayed rice beer over each other. Liftercraft dopplered low overhead. Numb with null-shock and analgesia, Santiago slipped between the parked trailers into Daft Eddie's. The tables had been cleared away: on the still-damp concrete, bodies moved to the music from the impromptu band outside. The Pale Riders were all there. Santiago recognized the woman he had seen killed, who had run her spear through Miclantecutli's throat: the woman who had spared him as the sun rose. They smiled, they laughed, they drank spirits from bottles which Daft Eddie constantly replenished, they passed joints to each other and their friends.

Santiago knew the friends. There was Duarte, and the *desconfigurado* Asunción. There was the ectomorphic Angel, more ghostly than ever in the light of day. There was Anansi, mystical disciple of pain; oddly cute and vulnerable in her leathers.

There was Miclantecutli.

He saw Miclantecutli and the Pale Rider woman laugh without inhibition, play and pour Daft Eddie's rough, raw spirit over each other. He saw Miclantecutli slip off her rubber jacket with the spirit faces on it. Her breasts were naked beneath the jacket. He saw hunter and hunted embrace and kiss.

He saw Miclantecutli lying on a porch in the memory of Tombstone, her throat a lacerated mess of blood and pipe and gristle.

He looked at his half a hand. He looked at the memory of fingers. He saw Miclantecutli pull the Pale Rider to her with naked delight. He turned and walked away, toward the brightening hills.

For one so well built, there was very little weight in Camaguey's body. Nute's natural strength was enough to lift and carry him across the warm grass to the cool of the cloister where the women in white waited. She talked to him. She joked with him. She laughed, she smiled. She was happy for him: flesh's frailties and failings were behind him. True life began here. She was not mourning a death, she was celebrating a birth.

The Death House women smiled, understanding her happiness as they led her to the resurrection hall.

"It's a good day to die," said the tall black woman as her assistants stripped the body. Nute folded the clothes, stroking the soft mesh and warm leather against her cheek, striving to catch that faint, fading scent of *Camagueyness*.

Nute lifted him to place him in the tank. The black needles pricked her flesh. Ugly things. Vile things. The Jesus tank would wash them away. Wash them away, wash away all the sickness and wrongness and rebuild him as he could be, as he should be. Perfect. Whole. Well. She kissed him.

Falling in love with the johns, Nute?

She held his hand until the descending lid forced her to let go.

Iago's arms were strong around her, his chest broad, solid, beneath her head, gently rising and falling as he breathed, his shaved skin smooth, soft, like fabric against her cheek, with just that sensual nap of stubble dragging across her nerve endings. She squirmed herself around his contours, warm, comfortable, pressed her parted lips to his flank.

And then she remembered where she was.

And then she realized what she was doing.

And then she discovered that she was as naked as he, bodygloves peeled back into a soft oval of gel lining the terracotta nest in which they lay.

And it was good. So damn good, with the rows of open-mouthed, ocher-faced terracotta gods looking down at her lying with the dead man with no hair.

While space fleets clashed and *corporadas* fell and unjust laws unraveled and old kings died and new kindgoms were born and new princes enthroned and ambassadors from alien nations were welcomed and the necrovilles rose and the palm trees burned and the Day of the Dead broke over the hills of Old Hollywood.

YoYo rolled onto her side.

"Iago," she whispered into his pectoral muscle, "I can't stay." She knew he would not be asleep, for the dead never slept, but he was a long time replying. Waking dreams, Iago, of that life before that they say is only a dream to the dead?

She slapped his rump. "Pre-Law 202: Practice and Professional Ethics. The lawyer shall at all times give primary consideration to the welfare of his client and exercise his best efforts to those ends. It's not over till it's over."

YoYo slipped into shirt shorts boots, adjusted cap to the correct degree of *streetness*. Disentangling her bodyglove from Iago's could wait. Strange, this unfamiliar sense of nakedness beneath her clothes. Touching air. Uncomfortable.

The 'ware in the Death House lobby accepted her lawyer number and colophon specifications and then asked her to wait. All calls to the Tesler-Thanos *arcosanti* were being triaged by the reception 'ware and subject to delays of up to twelve minutes real time. No Sunset Boulevard *abogado*, however *street* the tilt of her hat, could inflict that level of damage on a full *corporada*. However, kudos counted for something; the unit chimed her back immediately and extruded the hardcopy contract. YoYo recognized the Tesler-Thanos corporate ident and her own triangle-lotus seal. The rest was chicken's feet. She showed it to Martika Semalang, sipping strong *café negro* in an unused office, waiting. Jury's in. All rise.

"You're free."

She peered at the paper, reading the words. Cool, handsome, tall, and literate. Pre-Law 202: Practice and Professional Ethics does not permit you to envy your clients. And six million Rim—spare a pocketful of change and so—richer.

"They'll hold to this?"

"Computers can be relied on to follow the letter of the law. It's the frail meat who follow the spirit. They'll hold to it."

Iago appeared in the doorway; the Iago she knew who wore sneakers, baggy basketball shorts, sleeveless T-shirt; not the strange and varied selves of the night. He threw her a soft volleyball of barely solid tectoplastic: her bodyglove.

"Word is up, *compañeros*. We've been invaded. Those ships, up there, they're building something; I don't know what; the city web is still shot to hell with that Tee-Tee cogno-virus chasing my little Carmencita, but they seem to be taking apart the abandoned orbital manufactories and spinning them into construction beams. Looks like busy times ahead for Iago Diosdado."

"Tesler-Thanos?" Martika Semalang asked.

"Tesler-Thanos is fucked, *corazón*. Palace revolution, a change of the guards. Corporate heads rolling. Don't ask me, I've been trying to run my fingers through their 'ware but all I get back is official P.R. stuff that trading is suspended pending an announcement from *el presidente*."

"Iago," said YoYo suddenly, terribly, utterly, crushingly, *tired*. Suddenly realizing she had been up all night. Had been running all night. Had almost died a dozen times this past night. Had pulled off the legal coup of her career before breakfast. "This is all very interesting, but I think I'd like to go home. Now."

The summit of the San Miguel spire was failing, dripping like a kilometer-tall paschal candle.

"There must be some limit point," Toussaint said. "They can't transform an entire *arcosanti*." He and Huen had sought temporary refuge in the communications center.

"Can't they?" Huen glanced upward. "Their buddy-boys are doing just that to the moon."

"These are human beings."

"Not anymore they aren't. It's not your father, Toussaint, or your brother, if they ever were in this incarnation. Just bundles of guilt and hatred, remembered and rebuilt by the tectors until that became all they were. They have each other now; they have what each of them wanted."

The ceiling screens showed Toussaint the news from space. The world watched the skies, pointing and gasping at the occasional bursts of orbital pyrotechnics as the fleet cleared up the remaining automated defenses. On the sunward half of the planet the night's violence had ebbed. People there too watched, waited, rebuilt their neighborhoods and lives.

Toussaint let the floform chair settle itself around him and linked in the audiovisualizer. Subtexts explained the effect—the slamships had sent out camera remotes to aid maneuvering—but could not dispel the magic. Toussaint saw with the eyes of God. The cloud-mottled blue plane of the Pacific was bisected by the curve of the terminator. Clusters of lights emerged from nightside into the light of day, slamships, dozens of them, more than he had ever imagined there could be, and behind them, the second wave of freighters and processors, folding up their light sails hundreds of kilometers across like Japanese fans. Maneuvering thrusters were hard white diamonds against the clouded blue of ocean.

The point of view shifted to another remote, this one station-keeping some dozen or so kilometers above the massdriver ejection head of a slamship. An ungainly collection of spheres, booms and solar panels hung off the port bow; the assemblage turned into the sun and Toussaint read the legend: Ewart/Western Australia Minerals. Slowly, very slowly, ponderously, the slamship matched velocities with the orbital factory. A second ship slid up across the field of vision, maneuvering jets firing in a Gatling-rattle of bursts: the huge, ungainly thing seemed to be trying to turn sideways.

The point of view shifted again to the high orbit camera. The superimposed schematics were unnecessary; the grand plan was instantly apparent and breathtaking in its ambition. The thirty-four surviving slamships of the Freedead fleet had formed into a colossal grid, five kilometers on a side, bracketing the abandoned space factories. Thrusters flickered and went dark. Toussaint—the whole watching world— held breath.

And the ships blossomed.

Spirals of cable went wheeling out across vacuum, linking ship to ship. Tector packages detonated softly against manufactory hulks and began to disassemble them. The heart of each ship opened and released the plantations of vacuum trees they had nurtured and kept safe there. A million leaves glittered green in the sunlight. Where there had been a fleet of invading ships was now an orbital city.

A patterning of autumn leaves
evergreen forests
upon blue sea

"Toussaint." Huen's voice. "It's *Marcus Garvey*."

The control blister was unoccupied now, the freefall computer clusters unmanned, the combat stations stood down.

"To whom am I speaking?" asked the dead commander, Marie-Claire. Impossibly limber figures scrambled up the outside of the transparent dome. The fractal-edged green sphere of a freefall tree drifted past, steered by *quadros* equipped with warping lines.

"My name is Toussaint Xavier Tesler." He had thought of the name in an instant, now that he knew it was what he would be for the rest of his life. "I am president pro tem of the Tesler-Thanos *corporada*. Please listen to what I have to say. The Teslet-Thanos *corporada* is not your enemy. I am not your enemy. Please tell me how I may help your mission and I will be glad to oblige."

"Where is Ellen Shipley? Where is Quebec?"

"Things did not go exactly as planned." ("That's saying some," Huen commented via closed circuit.) "I don't think you will be able to speak with them. However, please be assured that the objectives of their mission have been achieved. I am now in sole executive authority for the *corporada*."

"Adam Tesler?"

"My father is dead." No word of a lie. The dead woman held silence for longer than was justified by the ground-to-orbit relativity lag.

"The construction process that you are witnessing is the establishment of a new Clade," she said, deciding to trust. "It is the near-earth-orbital Heaven's Gate Clade. Its purpose is to act as an interface between the planet and the space-dwelling Freedead, and also in the other direction as the gateway by which the dead of earth can move off planet into the solar system and the wider universe."

A humanity no longer bound to a cocoon of flesh, a twist of chemicals, a ball of iron and silicates orbiting the sun; that had always been the endgame. Transhumanity. Toussaint pictured chapters of them, nations of them, flying like angels, like *aguilas*, away from the sun, borne on the solar wind, outward.

"Please believe me, we want to help you in any way we can. Tesler-Thanos is your ally in this, not your enemy."

"Forgive me, Séor Tesler, if I find that a little hard to accept."

"Perhaps a token of good faith might convince you that my intentions are true."

"Such as?"

Wonderful, the illusion of omnipotence when a *corporada* is at the fingertips of your manipulator glove. Seductive, the sense of mastery as the mega giga beva terra bytes flock to your command.

"Media links established," whispered the spirit voices in his cochlear bud. "You're through to all the Rim newswebs; PanEuropean, African and Central Asian systems copying."

Simple, the decisions that can be made when they have to. What's in a name? Everything, it seems.

"The Tesler-Thanos *corporada* recognizes the Heaven's Gate Clade and its embassy to Earth."

Apocalypse on earth always being a surer bet on bang-for-the-buck than apocalypse in heaven, the Lions of Judah turned out to watch the Church of Seu Guacondo burn.

As any good iconoclast will tell you, churches are especially combustible. All that wood and incense.

"Should have brought marshmallows," Salamanca said.

Jerk, Trinidad thought. They had fled from the collapsing building, and she had made an important discovery. She did not like Salamanca. She had never liked him. He had come into her life, deciding she needed to be rescued, helped, assisted, making all kinds of assumptions about her that if not true then—and she doubted they had ever been true—were certainly not true now.

"Look at it," he yelled triumphantly. "Look at it! Isn't it magnificent! How does it make you feel, YoYo?"

I feel like any sane, sensitive, thinking feeling person should. I feel appalled, I feel elated that I am free and alive, I feel nauseated, I feel shocked, I feel exhausted, so exhausted that I cannot believe that everything has not been a long and involved dream. All this she felt. Before, she would have given some ritual man-pleasing answer of the *I feel free, I feel alive, I feel so safe when I'm with you*. No more, Trinidad.

"You want to know? I feel sick, Salamanca. I feel used and pushed and shoved about in your game of heroes and villains, but mostly, sick." He was a bastard. They had all been bastards. Stupid vain egotistical bastards. But none so stupid vain egotistical as Trinidad for believing so long she needed them. She started to walk away.

"Hey, wait a moment Trinidad, until this burns down and I'll come with you," Salamanca said.

"Salamanca," Trinidad said in that aspect of her voice she knew never failed to command men's attention. "I don't want you to come with me. I don't need you to look after me. I'm going on my own."

"But Trinidad, the streets . . ."

"Salamanca, we have just faced out and exterminated Seu Guacondo and his Zoo Cult." And possibly the world's sole hope of deathless immortality. Right here, right now, she felt more sympathy for Seu Guacondo in his long hell of quantum indeterminacy than for Salamanca the Dragon Slayer. "I'm hardly going to be terrified to walk a few blocks through Saint John in broad daylight. I'm going. I don't need you. In fact, I don't like you. I can think offhand of fifty more fun ways to have spent one night in Necroville. So don't assume that circumstances have given us some kind of special relationship. Don't assume that we will be lifelong *amigos*. We won't. Don't call me, don't try and see me, don't ask about me, because I won't call or try and see or ask about you. And when you come to tell the story, remember who was the hero when it came to it. Any fool can point a gun and pull a trigger."

The lion-faced residents parted before her as she walked away from Salamanca and his silly, spent gun. The Church of Seu Guacondo collapsed in a heap of glowing coals.

As she reached the street entrance, the heel that had been threatening to break all evening finally betrayed her. She went over, hard. She saw a smile cross Salamanca's face. Without taking her eyes off him, she removed her intact boot, lifted it up in front of her face and with one clean jerk, snapped off the heel.

A great cheer went up all around her.

In the strangely deserted street, Iago paused to pull his car out of the blacktop.

"You don't have to," he said as the tectors reconfigured.

"Oh, I have to, Iago. This is not my place. You are not my people."

"Anywhere you want to go," said Iago, sliding into the driver's seat. The control panel oozed blackly toward him.

Suddenly ravenous. Suddenly thirsty. Suddenly needing the company of the living. Coming down from the neur-acc high. Remembering old friends, and the place to which they returned after their adventures on the Night of the Dead.

"The Terminal Café." She owed Santiago an apology. "If it's still there."

"Terminal Café it is." The golden car slid silently away from the sidewalk. "One thing, YoYo."

"Iago."

"Can I shave your head sometime?"

"You can shave my head anytime, Iago." They sped unhindered along the boulevards. Above them, the heads of the palm trees, long burned out, leaked smoke into the sky. Pickups and electric mopeds dodged discarded postcarnival *tristesse*. Behind the windows of the *panaderías*, diners and all-night bars that had never closed, patrons crowded the tables, intent on tagalong screens.

"Somehow," Iago said, "I don't think the world's going to end today."

And then she saw him. Wandering like a damned Vandervecken, empty drink cartons and snack containers blowing unheeded about his feet, though his attention was focused on the oil-stained sidewalk. As the car whispered past, she saw him lift his head to the morning sun that poured between the smoldering palms.

"Santiago!"

She irised open the window, leaned out.

"Iago, stop the car."

He pulled in beneath a monster movie screen from which the strengthening sun was banishing *Friendly Persuasion*. Celluloid ghosts. All they had ever been. And was it truly Santiago, lost and wandering on the dawn of the dead, or another ghost of Old Hollywood?

"Maybe we can shoot a few serves sometime?" Iago called from the open door. YoYo waved to him. She did not hear the car pull off and turn in the street, for she was walking toward him, trotting toward him, running toward him, the bodyglove tucked under her arm like a running back heading for touchdown.

"Santiago!" she shouted. "Santiago!"

He looked up.

He had expected three, maybe four seconds before the blast. The stunned silence lasted a full ten seconds—a geological epoch in web nanotime—before the 'wares came clamoring back *who what why how when tell us explain to us.* His own lower managerial echelons were asking for advice, policy statements, requesting urgent meetings real and virtual; his brother and sister *corporadas*, emerging from stun into a jabber of memoranda and interrogatives, governments, nations lofty and nations lesser requiring clarifications, the oceanic, monotheistic boom of the Rim Council; all demanding explanations. His legalware was advising of a dozen imminent court actions questioning Tesler-Thanos's authority to recognize what the law said did not exist. A cabal of his own section managers was mounting a challenge to his claim to presidential authority.

He had nothing more to say to any of them than what he had already done. The Great Satan had repented and joined the angels. Where he had led, others would follow. The bravest, the smallest first, those few with nothing to lose, but little by little the flow would grow until the rush became inexorable.

He pushed up the virtualizer hood.

"Is there some word for the way that time and circumstance turns us into the things we despise most?" he asked. "For most of my life I wanted to destroy this place; tear it apart molecule by molecule. Now I can do anything I like with it, and I don't want to. I can't. It sounds like blasphemy, but there is a kind of beauty in it. Not just the sheer architectural scale of the arcology, but its dirty, inelegant industrial core, its inner organization and hierarchies, its invisible spirit of capital investment and return; a beautiful crystalline symmetry; inhuman, but strangely attractive. Like the hourglass marking on the belly of a black widow spider."

"Honor your father by honoring his creations?" Huen asked. "Your bourgeois values are showing. If you want to trash this place in one big party, you do it. You don't owe him anything, Toussaint. He was mad and bad, Toussaint. He was insane, man, and wanted the whole world to reflect his insanity."

"He was a sick, sad man."

Huen sucked in her lower lip. "Funny thing: I know who were the good guys, who was the bad guy, but somehow, it doesn't feel like that. In this western, all hats are gray.

"So, *Séor Presidente*, what now?"

"Go and talk to people, I suppose." Presidential authority overrode the door locks. As they headed to the elevators, Toussaint added, "Huen, I could use a good assistant, you know."

Huen looked at him as if he had suggested some improbable and illegal act of sexual congress.

"The only thing you can do for me is next time you're talking to those Heaven's Gaters, could you ask them if they'd like their agent back? Look at that sky. Better things to do, *hermoso*."

He looked at that sky. He could feel the night's storm front as a distant pressure on his spinal ridge. Gone east, out across the desert, bringer of thunder and rain. The air behind was still, calm, clear. On such a morning, with such a sky, you could see all the way to the edge of space. There, at the limits of vision, those glints and hints of light: could an eye adapted to look into the sun make out the vast, delicate lattice of Heaven's Gate? No; the flecks of mica embedded in the cerulean blue were *aguilas*, catching the early thermals as they formed, rising up above the great ugly dirty busy noisy smelly city. Good flying sky. The best flying sky.

He summoned an executive elevator: keyed the codes. The glass cage started downward.

Heaven, Earth, cities of life and death
In an eagle's eye
Suspended!

Heelless, Trinidad cruised along the avenues of the dead. Heelless, heedless.

Not afraid. Not needing. Not depending on the permission of others. To be able to tell herself that Trinidad Malcopuelo was all right. Better than all right. Was fine. Mighty fine. Mighty fine indeed.

Broken glass littered the intersection on which the Terminal Café stood. Not the residue of violence, rather the detritus of the living; weary, bleary, hung over on a dozen crashes from as many different highs, drained. Bottles, glasses, old-fashioned hypodermics for the mutilation freaks. Some of the survivors were still in costume, some masked, some dressed in improbable hybrids from half a dozen clothes-swapping encounters. Scorning bourgeois affectations like *chairs*, they lined the curbs and walls; spread themselves beneath the branches of the dusty almond trees, sprawled prone on the scrubby grass.

Sometime between sunset and sunrise, some bastard had ripped her car out by its roots and stolen it.

A quantum of movement; something, in the shadows of a back-of-boulevard alley where the rising sun had yet to penetrate. A glitter, a scratching, as if of claws on concrete.

The something, Trinidad felt, had advertised its presence only because of her.

"Hello?"

Scritch scratch. And there was a figure, half in darkness, half in light, too tall, too thin, too loosely jointed to be human. Golden eyes caught the light: a werewolf, a *Lobo de la Luna*, leaning casually alert on the barrel of what looked like an outsize spearfishing gun. It was not naked, as those wolves she had seen from the café mezzanine had been; it wore a small athletic pouch decorated with the symbol of a Man-in-the-Moon with a bullet in his eye.

She knew, though she did not know how she knew, that it was the same Wolf of the Moon that had confronted them in the warren by the *Posada* and chosen to let them pass. And she knew that now, as then, it knew who she was.

A certain familiarity; the eyes, the loose-limbed slouch, the curl of the lupine lip.

"Peres?" she asked. The werewolf bared canines in a smile. Shadows flurried about it. "Peres! Peres!" The sun rose above the rooftops around the Terminal Café, pouring light into the deserted alley. She entered the alley, poked through the broken glass and cardboard. There was not the slightest evidence that anyone but herself had been there.

The night's few surviving glasses were racked up behind the bar in the Terminal Café, cleaned, dried, ready. Floors cleaned, tables wiped, chairs upturned. A few late-or-earlies drank among forests of chair legs. Breakfast smells: pig meat, hot fat, coffee from a leviathan espressometer with a leering chromium deathshead on its steaming belly. She went up the steps to the mezzanine level.

The old familiar places. He might never have moved.

"Santiago?"

His hand. What happened to his hand? And with him:

"YoYo?"

"Trini? Trini? Oh Jesus, woman. Oh Jesus, it's you."

They embraced. Old lovers friends sisters.

"Still the leather gear?"

YoYo shrugged coyly. "You know what it is with me and clothes that do things."

"Trinidad." Santiago's voice was a famished whisper pushed through a miasma of drugs. "Trinidad. You came back. I did it, Trini. I've been there, and I've come back."

"He's out of his head," YoYo said. "I've been trying to bring him down by stuffing him full of coffee but I still can't get any sense out of him. I don't know where he's been or what he's done but at some time someone has neatly amputated the last two fingers of his left hand, sealed and cauterized the wound, dressed it and rammed him full of nullshock and painkillers."

"Trini," Santiago said. "I've been there. I came back, Trini."

"I know where he's been, YoYo." Trinidad poured herself a coffee from YoYo's industrial-size cafetière. "I met him here twelve hours ago and he told me. He's been a place from which few come back. He's been with the Night Hunt."

"Jesus Joseph Mary."

"I wanted to find the place beyond," Santiago whispered. He rolled his head back against the wrought iron seatback. He grimaced in pain: the caffeine was beginning to work on the opiates. "You know what I mean, YoYo. You always knew, you, of all of them, you know what it is to be always searching for the elusive key, the way out, the way through. I went with Miclantecutli: she's the goddess of death, all those years, it was right in front of my face, and I didn't understand it. I went with her hunt; I would either find it or I would die in the search: I didn't care, YoYo. It didn't do it anymore. I would find something that did it, or I would die because there was nothing left to live for. Trini knows this, I told her, I told you, didn't I, Trini?"

"Santiago," YoYo said gently.

A smile became a grin of pain.

"They took my fingers to let me touch. I can touch, Trini, YoYo, I can touch, I can be touched. Look." He held up his maimed hand. "Half a hand. You can't hold too tight with half a hand. You can't seize and grasp and grip and own. Possess. You take hold of things lightly, you hold on to things loosely. You live by grace, not by possession. I can touch, but I can't grasp."

"Excuse me?" None of them had heard the woman approach the table. She was small, powerfully built, dressed in a stretch lace one-piece and a beautiful gold-and-green fitted brocade coat. Her manner was uncomfortable, slightly apologetic though she was clearly a woman at ease in both body and world; the manner of one interrupting strangers. "You don't know me, but are you the friends of Camaguey Quintana?"

All the way over in the dukduk the driver had treated her to his interpretation of the interesting times into which everyone had suddenly been forced to live.

"Why the hell are they still going off to work?" he had complained, gesturing emphatically at the mass of pedestrians and public service vehicles as he tried to ease his little bubble of vehicle against the flow. "Don't they know that now that the Death House has gone independent, it's no more *contratado*?"

"Drive the thing," Nute said. "I want political analysis, I know half a dozen minor prophets. Beer and gasohol are still going to cost money, *contratado* or no *contratado*."

They lurched forward. Sun poured into the streets: the temperature curve in the dukduk's passenger bubble was going asymptotic.

"Half the necrovilles on the planet have risen up," the driver shouted to his fare. "They can't ignore that."

"They've been ignoring it for forty years, *compadre*. A few peons burning their hovels isn't going to change their minds."

"It's a new world order," the driver shouted, hooting furiously at a dray drawn by six dogs as he threw his machine into "this real good shortcut I know."

"So what are you going to be doing tomorrow that you aren't today?"

"The colonization of space, lady. That's what it's about. The future of the species. Those Freedead up there, they live in space, can you believe it? Walk around the asteroid belts like we walk around the *cuadra* to the *panadería* down here."

"When you set up a taxi rank on Jupiter, I'll be your first fare, *corazón*. Now, if it's not too much trouble, maybe you can get me to the Terminal Café before these meats I'm to see decide to go and do something more interesting?"

The real good shortcut, of course, was an even better dead end. The dukduk driver argued spectacularly with the driver of a *dulces* delivery pickup that was blocking the way but Nute had been around too many *cuadras* not to know that the more spectacular the argument, the less the likelihood that it will produce any results.

"Maybe you should just back up?"

"They recognized the fleet!" The driver pressed the radio dangling from his rearview to his ear, beckoned for the *dulcisto* to come, hear and corroborate. "Sweet suffering fuck, Tesler-Thanos has recognized the fleet. Adam fucking Tesler him fucking self."

"Give me that." The *dulcisto* snatched the little radio away, held the furiously grasping driver at arm's length. "They're calling it Heaven's Gate. It's an embassy, a Freedead embassy to Earth. It's five kilometers on a side, can you imagine that? Wait, wait, there's more. There's a new president of Tesler-Thanos. Something's happened to the old bastard. It's the son, his name's Toosant, something like. Seems it's him recognized Heaven's Gate."

"Listen," Nute said. "This is all mighty epochal stuff, but as it isn't getting me any nearer my destination, I'll just step out here."

"Hey, my fare!"

Nute treated the *cochero* to her oldest, vilest, most obscene gesture. Ultimately every good whore goes alone, on her own two feet.

Because Camaguey had told her where she would find them, she did not bother searching the sad meat faces lined up in the street outside. Neither would she find them in the main bar, he had said—though the coffee smelled mighty fine this morning—but on the mezzanine. At the old familiar table, by the window overlooking Terminal Boulevard.

Exactly as you said it would be, Camaguey. The good-looking black *cerrista* with the expense account is Trinidad; the big one with the strange aura: so, that's the famous Santiago Columbar. What the hell did he do to his fingers? That *chino* in the clever leather would be the *abogado* YoYo. No sign of the fourth one, the white boy *aguila*. Something deep going on here. Deep, dark. Deeper, darker things to tell, Nute.

"Excuse me? You don't know me, but are you the friends of Camaguey Quintana? I have something he has asked me to tell you."